DJINN CITY

Saad Z. Hossain

The Unnamed Press
Los Angeles, CA

The Unnamed Press
P.O. Box 411272
Los Angeles, CA 90041

Published in North America by The Unnamed Press.

1 3 5 7 9 10 8 6 4 2

Copyright © 2017 by Saad Z. Hossain

ISBN: 9781944700065

Library of Congress Control Number: 2017955593

This book is distributed by Publishers Group West

Cover design & typeset by Jaya Nicely
Cover Artwork by Brendan Monroe

Praise for Saad Z. Hossain's *Escape from Baghdad!*:

"An engrossing cross between *Zero Dark Thirty* and *Raiders of the Lost Ark* that takes a sobering look at America's troubled legacy in Iraq."

— *Bookslut*

"Set in the aftermath of the US invasion of Iraq, Bangladeshi author Saad Hossain's debut novel is a riot of mordant humour and gonzo storytelling… The Gulf war may just have found its *Catch-22*."

— *Financial Times*

"It's a marvelous mix of genres, blending the visceral atmosphere of a war movie with the casual nihilism of *Catch-22* or the original *M.A.S.H.* complete with an Indiana Jones–style treasure quest… A gonzo adventure novel that shreds the conventional wisdom that pulp can be pigeonholed."

— *Kirkus Reviews*

"Hossain daringly shows us that war isn't just hell but absolutely insane."

— *Library Journal*

"Saad Hossain has given us a hilarious and searing indictment of the project we euphemistically call 'nation-building.' With nods to *Catch-22*, *Frankenstein*, *The Island of Doctor Moreau* and the Golem myth, *Escape from Baghdad!* weaves fantasy, absurdity and adventure into a moving counter-narrative to the myth of the just war."

— *NPR*

"Hossain's perplexingly weird debut novel, *Escape From Baghdad!*, captures the pure insanity of the Iraq War. At the same time, it's not a war novel. Instead, it's a skillfully constructed literary IED that brings together the sharpest aspects from multiple genres. It's a Tarantino-esque *Heart of Darkness* set in war-torn Iraq, filled with absurdism and dark humor, a mash-up of satirical Joseph Heller-style comedy and sci-fi fantasy with a gratuitous mixture of good old-fashioned ultra-violence."

— *VICE*

TABLE OF CONTENTS

KHAN RAHMAN FAMILY CLAN: MAIN PLAYERS

Kaikobad: Emissary, drunkard, polymath

Indelbed: His son, a little boy of no particular importance

Butloo: Their butler

Grand-Uncle Sikkim: Patriarch of the Khan Rahmans

Vulubir Khan Rahman, the Ambassador: Kaikobad's cousin, one of the stalwarts of the Khan Rahmans

Juny: Badass wife of the Ambassador, loan shark to the djinn

Rais: Their son, a wastrel

Uncle Pappo: An eminent doctor and Khan Rahman by marriage

Barrister Asif: Well-respected legal counsel for the family

Barabas: Patron djinn of the Khan Rahman clan*

*For more on the djinn players, please see the glossary (page 399), which includes complete lists of djinn types and djinns relevant to this story; also see the appendices, which include the charming djinn nursery rhyme "The Charnel Road," as well as an excerpt from the *Register of Kings*, by His Excellency, the Grand Ifrit Mohandas, the Most Efficacious, Lord of the Frozen Waters and the Lands Therein, Holder of One Hundred Patents.

DJINN CITY

CHAPTER 1
A Full Account

The first persistent conviction of Indelbed's life was that he was poor. This was not in itself a surprising observation, for he was surrounded by the poor in a country notorious for being poor. It would have been a statistical aberration had he *not* been poor. The problem was that Indelbed could see certain signs of incongruity in his family's particular brand of poverty, minute and widely prevalent indicators that: a) they had fallen from grace in some way, and b) his father had been responsible for this calamitous disaster not too far back, for which many members of the extended family still shunned him.

They lived in Wari, in a rambling building whose original outer shape was no longer visible. It had been covered by outgrowths: add-ons, lean-tos, television towers, dish cables, animal shelters, and other superstructures of such fantastical nature that no sane human could discern their purpose. Surrounding buildings had encroached on its airspace. The entire thing was a decrepit, jagged fire trap, one fatuous giant's stomp away from collapse.

For as long as Indelbed could remember, his family had assured him that Wari had at one point been a very fashionable area. Most of these people lived in the *actual* fashionable areas of Gulshan, Banani, or Baridhara. Some of them lived in the semi-fashionable area of Dhanmondi, which was still much better than Wari.

The gate of the house was an immense work of ironmongery, gently settling to rust. It opened into what had once been a driveway and then a garage, evidence that they—or some progenitor—had at some point owned more than one motor vehicle. The approach to the house must have been spacious too, matching the ambitious width of the gate, but steady encroachment by shops, habitations, and boundary walls had narrowed the street into a choke point only several feet wide, capable of allowing, at most, the egress of the pernicious three-wheeler baby taxis. No car could ever squeeze through the gate now. When Indelbed visited relatives in other parts of town and they deigned to drop him off, their cars had to park at the mouth of the alley and let him down on foot, right next to an open drain.

This was humiliating enough, although in hindsight it was perhaps a blessing that his cousins did not have to approach the house and perhaps meet his father by accident. Indelbed's dad was a perfect adornment to the house: an eccentric drunkard so incoherent with rage that he was often bereft of speech altogether. In moments of lucidity he expounded on the misfortunes plaguing his life, one of which was Indelbed, although to be fair most times he was classified only as a minor irritant.

There seemed to be some implacable, invisible doom stalking Indelbed's father. He had started life with all the trappings of wealth and success, and in a few short decades he had squandered everything. This too had a story. The house in Wari had once been the principal residence of some important ancestor. This gentleman, apparently anticipating the arrival of Indelbed's father, had left his property entailed to the male line in a complicated legal maneuver, which meant that it could never be sold, leased, mortgaged, developed, or gambled; in short, it was absolutely useless to them in any form other than in its primary function, as a roof with four walls.

Even though it was Wari, the house and grounds together constituted such a large square footage that they could easily have repaired their fortunes had they been able to sell it. Often his father lamented this very point. If only. Instead, they were stuck with the care of this humiliating pile, with walls salt-encrusted from damp, the roof seeping water, the floors a treacherous mosaic, and all the woodwork so rotten that even the termites had decamped. It was, however, his home, and in the solitary games of his imagination, each nook and crevice contained a world filled with adventure, each room a castle, each hallway a jungle trail.

Indelbed's father was one Dr. Kaikobad. In the bewildering tradition of his family, his father also had another and completely unrelated name, which was Dr. B. C. Khan Rahman. The custom was to have a Muslim name and then an eccentric one, and this accounted for Indelbed's own current misfortune, for his father, completely hammered on the eve of his birth, had simply named him Indelbed, entirely forgetting to give him a proper name.

Possibly the larger misfortune was that Indelbed's mother had died in childbirth. Indelbed sometimes fantasized that she had instead taken the opportunity of childbirth to escape, perhaps by the back door. "Death by Indelbed." This was the official cause written on the death certificate, scrawled in Dr. Kaikobad's own hand.

In any case, it wasn't easy going around without a proper name. By the time the Doctor had sobered up, the birth certificate had already been issued. Kaikobad refused to rectify the error, apparently overcome with grief. He had subsequently proceeded to combat this grief with bottles of dubious vintage for the next decade.

Thus this branch of the Khan Rahman family remained at two. The Doctor never married again, perhaps from fear of being saddled with a second Indelbed. Indelbed had tried to procure siblings through purchase, yet had failed, not the least because he had very little money. The two children he had managed to entice as far as the living room were scared off by the Doctor, whose charming habits included roaming the halls in his dressing gown with a full-length British cavalry saber in his hand.

Indelbed's great-grandfather had apparently killed a British cavalry officer in Calcutta during the Great Mutiny, taking both his head as well as his sword. The sword was still in good condition. The head had been pickled in a jar, and although it was still resident among the family heirlooms and given pride of place on a center table, it was not possible to verify now whether it was in fact a British cavalry officer's skull or just an ordinary local makeweight.

Indelbed, for this and many other reasons, did not receive visitors at home.

His father had, once upon a time, been very well educated. The doctorate was real. He was a physician as well as a PhD in mathematics, with a near-genius IQ. However, the drink prevented him from practicing medicine, and higher mathematics had fled his mind upon the death of his wife. Indelbed's uncles always said that the Doctor was living life in reverse. He had started out with everything and gradually lost it all. Whiskey had been helpful in this regard, and in line with his reversal of fortune. His first drink had apparently been a priceless single malt stolen from a cache hidden by his father, who had been a well-respected judge. He had meandered through Johnnie Walker Black Label, then Red Label, and finally just anything foreign. Of late, the Doctor was lucky to drink something that contained ethanol. Quantity, in fact, had replaced any sense of taste he had previously been burdened with.

The Doctor had his first drink at twelve P.M., as a sort of hair of the dog. Lunch was a fluid affair depending on finances, but some kind of meal was served any time between one and three by the ancient butler. This gentleman claimed to be a butler (he pronounced the word *but-loo*) but had in fact been the old driver's son, from that ancestral time when there had been cars in the driveway. Butloo had vague ideas about the dignity of his station, dimly remembered from back when his father had served in a more prosperous home.

After serving lunch, Butloo would proudly bring out a silver tray with glass and water. The tray was one of those heirloom pieces that, inexplicably, the Doctor had never sold. Possibly because it was *his* drinks tray and made whatever slop he happened to be ingesting more palatable. More likely, it was because Butloo jealously guarded this prized possession, the sole remnant of a more romantic age and his badge of identity, without which his claims of being a gentleman's gentleman would be scorned out of hand by the other domestics.

Regardless of its undoubted psychological value, no one in the house knew how to polish silver (not that there was any money to buy polish). So the tray was tarnished black, yet still managed to gleam in a reproachful way whenever it was brought out.

After the post-lunch drink, the Doctor often dozed off for a while or retired to his "study," a roomful of rotting, barely legible books, the good ones having been sold off long ago. After his nap it was time for the evening drink, which coincided with the depressing dusk of Wari, which coincided with Butloo using *dhup* throughout the house to drive out mosquitoes. *Dhup* was a treatment of coconut fiber, which could be burned with coal to create a fume noxious to both humans and mosquitoes. The theory was that humans could withstand the poisoning longer than mosquitoes and thus emerge victorious.

After this, the drinking resumed at a rapid pace and continued until the bottles were finished or the Doctor passed out. Dinner again was a fluid affair in the middle of the drinking, served anywhere between eight and eleven P.M., or not at all, depending on the vagaries of the kitchen.

Butloo was accompanied by a half-mad, enormously fat maid, who served as both housekeeper-chambermaid and cook. She contrived to feed the four of them plus the guard at the gate with whatever pittance the Doctor gave her every week for grocery shopping. Food at the Khan Rahman household was a taboo subject. Each of the dishes had a grandiose name according to ancient family recipes—another clue to their august past. Indelbed had made discreet inquiries and found that none of his neighbors had any fancy ancestral recipes. What they *did* have in more abundance was actual food.

Indelbed frequently thought that the availability of food ought actually to be the most important part of the whole dining experience, but to voice any traitorous thoughts toward anything of ancestral value was to go deeply against the family, many of whom already seemed to hate him. The recipes called for the flinging around of many expensive ingredients, such as ghee, saffron, and gold leaf. In fact they also called for semi-expensive ingredients, such as meat and fish, which were also a problem. The cook had been forced to replace or drop so many parts from each vaunted recipe that the dishes no longer resembled anything edible at all.

Take the *ghono dal*, for example: ancestrally, a mixture of lentils thick enough to stand up straight on a plate, adorned with all manner of fried onions, molten ghee, and candied ginger; the Doctor's version resembled muddy water with three-day-old beans, which coated the rice with a tired slime. Thus they maintained a mythical bill of fare for dinner each night, where Butloo was obliged to recite a spurious number of items being served, which the Doctor would decline to eat before they got down to their rice and dal.

Indelbed didn't mind this so much, since he wasn't a big eater anyway. Nor was he upset about his father's refusal to buy him clothes, since he inevitably received all the hand-me-downs from the vast horde of second and third cousins of the clan. Taking pity on Indelbed was a sort of favorite pastime, and although it chafed a bit, he had to admit that most of the clothes were of good quality, on the higher end of the comparative scale of sartorial brilliance in his part of Wari. He was skinny so the clothes never fit right, and he had actually never had the experience of walking into a store to buy something just for himself, but he had seen it done plenty of times when following around various older cousins. Not being blessed with vanity, he couldn't really see what the fuss was about.

The one real thing he hated about his father was his obdurate views on schooling. At the age of six, Indelbed had realized that all the neighborhood kids were going someplace in neat blue-and-white uniforms. When charged, his father had no adequate response other than declaring that he was not about to throw away a parcel of money trying to educate a six-year-old.

As time went by, however, Indelbed became increasingly anxious. Although all his neighborhood friends proclaimed him enormously lucky for somehow avoiding the traumatic experience of school, he was smart enough to realize that this was going to be a major problem.

"I wish I could go," he said sadly one day to Butloo, his confidant and advisor. "What do you think they do there all day?"

"I never went to school, Choto Sahib."

"What did you do then?" Indelbed asked, momentarily distracted.

"I came from the village straight over here when I was a little older than you. My father worked here then. I used to run errands for your grandfather. Judge Sahib, they called him. Everyone in the neighborhood knew him. They used to come all hours of the day to get his opinion on things."

"Must have been nice," Indelbed said. "But I'm sure the Judge went to school!"

"Don't worry. Those dullards at the school don't know half as much as your father," Butloo said. "You're better off without them. God knows what upside-down things they are teaching over there."

"You think my father knows anything?" Indelbed asked dubiously.

"Dr. Sahib was the best student!" Butloo said. "Didn't he win awards when he was young? Didn't he go to the best universities abroad? He was the youngest doctor in the city. Judge Sahib was so proud of him."

Two years rolled by. His father, under increasing pressure from Indelbed, declared that he was going to homeschool him. This entailed sitting down at some unspecified hour during the day and receiving very garbled lessons from the Doctor, who himself had attended schools in Dhaka, Karachi, and finally England. To be fair, Indelbed could see that his father was trying to help. Under the fugue of cheap alcohol there remained some semblance of intellect, enough, actually, to impart a very creditable amount of math, history, philosophy, and physics. He was taught to read the old-fashioned way, by the twin pillars of memorization and the rod. Any mistakes were punished with a whack across the shoulders.

This shameful secret of non-schooling continued for a few years, until it dawned on the family that ten-year-old Indelbed was not attending any kind of institution at all. It was his cousin Rais who first brought this to light, and it is here the saga of Indelbed really begins.

CHAPTER 2
The Wrath of Sikkim

Rais was the son of his father's elder cousin. This branch of the family had gone into the diplomatic service. Rais's father was an ambassador; they had lived in Cairo, Moscow, and Bhutan during the last three postings. Rais was ten years older, but of a bookish, kindly disposition. He had never bullied Indelbed as a child, and in the past few years he had treated him with regular, albeit flaky, consideration.

Indelbed himself made a point of trying to attend most family gatherings for a number of reasons. One, his presence always created an awkwardness among the elders, particularly as he came alone most of the time, and he enjoyed their consternation and various deliberations on what terrible future awaited him, how his life was being wasted, and, more immediately, who exactly was going to take him home. Two, the food was always good, and any change from home fare was welcome. Three, he often netted a monetary reward from some uncle or other, which he correctly labeled as guilt money.

On this occasion, they were celebrating the Ambassador and his wife's wedding anniversary. Rais, back from some foreign university, casually confirmed that Indelbed was already ten, a fact not easily discernible given his slight stature, before asking, just as casually, about school. Indelbed, caught by surprise, blurted out the truth. He did not expect this to create any great effect. Rais, however, grew incensed. He started waving his hands and feet around, shouting loudly for his father. Soon they were surrounded by family. There was a heated argument, with wild accusations being fired off by Rais, who, it seemed, was some sort of champion for education, while also holding alarming, revolutionary ideas about overthrowing the family hierarchy.

Indelbed was getting scared. In his experience, garnering too much no-tice was a sure way of inviting trouble. Finally, the Ambassador took him aside and extracted the details about his daily schedule. It was too late to lie. The case was referred to the patriarchal chief of the Khan Rahman clan, the august Grand-Uncle Sikkim.

Nobody knew why GU Sikkim was named after an Indian state. In fact no one knew why he was so powerful either; the dynamics of the Khan Rahman clan were convoluted. He was a retired businessman who had accumulated a quantity of wealth, tied up mostly in real estate, and with the astonishing rise in land prices, he was making more money in retirement than he ever had in active life. His various alliances tentacled throughout the clan and across the city; he had a keen eye for human faults, possessed an inherent bossiness, and had at his disposal acres of free time.

"Uncle, it is not right that this boy is ten years old and not yet a day in school," Rais's father, the Ambassador, said grudgingly, all the while glaring at Rais.

In principle everyone agreed that this was wrong, and the Ambassador was assigned to take the Doctor to task. This was done immediately by telephone, putting the party on hold. Indelbed, quite terrified now, could hear one side of the conversation and easily imagine the rest:

"Kaiko, really, the boy needs to go to school," said the Ambassador.

I'm better educated than ninety-nine percent of the teachers in this damn country. Whash more, I've got no money to throw away on school fees.

"Kaiko, it's not that much."

Tell the boy to work for it, if he's so keen...

The phone call was inconclusive, and the family sat down to properly dissect the situation.

"This school business is well and good, but who is going to pay for it all?" GU Sikkim, with his usual perspicacity, got to the root of the matter. Indelbed took this as a clue as to why the family tolerated the bossiness of GU. He had the ability to save a lot of time during family powwows by cutting straight to the money. His great age shielded him from accusations of crassness or insensitivity.

The Ambassador looked around uncomfortably and murmured some-thing about low government wages. His younger brother, a barrister, said that elementary school was okay, but what about high school and college? That was going to be a hefty bill. With all the consummate skill of his profession, he also simultaneously managed to imply that *he* certainly was not going to pay.

GU Sikkim took a poll of the thirty-odd "mature heads" present, men and women who carried weight and might make a contribution. Everyone had kids, worthless in-laws, bad loans, unlikely dependents. Most of them lobbed insults at Indelbed, accusing him and his father of wasting an incredible legacy. Astonishment too that all that money had been drunk or gambled away, without a single morsel being kept for a rainy day.

The family storm was now reaching frightening proportions. Indelbed, seated firmly in the middle of the drawing room, held in place by GU Sikkim's cane, was barely able to keep his tears in check. Tears of shame, mostly, and not a little bit of fear, for he had seen his father in black rages before, when the senile amiability leeched away from his face and something demonic and violent peeped out. In his more lucid moments, the Doctor held his family in contempt equal to what they bore for him, and he would not take kindly to this intrusion.

Who would pay? Even if the money were found, who would take the awful responsibility of finding a school, etc.? What about books, uniforms, all the extra crap schools extorted out of you? The money couldn't be given to the Doctor; he would surely drink it away.

"And look at this whelp." GU Sikkim prodded Indelbed. "He's undernourished. Has iodine deficiency, I think. Probably a stutterer. It's a disgrace. I say we send him to the village."

Terror struck Indelbed. He knew about the village. It was where the family sent people who were retarded, mad, or terminally ill. Funnily, there was a fair quantity of these. Madness ran in the genes from multiple sides, apparently.

The Ambassador leaned forward and whispered something in GU Sikkim's ear.

"What?!" GU exclaimed. "That nonsense again? Are you sure?"

The Ambassador nodded gravely.

"We must keep it secret at all costs! Will Kaikobad bring no end of trouble to us?"

This lamentation had enough genuine merit to elicit a general wail of agreement. Various people remembered anew how the Doctor had embarrassed or inconvenienced them in the past. Indelbed, attuned to public opinion, could feel something sinister at work, however. What had the Ambassador said that needed to be whispered? What new horror was in store for him? He couldn't imagine anything worse than the village, yet it seemed like the clan had even more hideous repositories for the graceless.

GU dragged him into one of the bedrooms and the Ambassador followed, clearly in discomfort. The door clicked shut. Indelbed stood in the corner, tears flowing freely now. Even his nose was blubbering.

"Stand straight," GU said, rather meanly.

"Indelbed, *beta*, has your father ever said anything about why you don't go to school?" the Ambassador asked.

"No, of course not," Indelbed said, thinking, *Isn't it obvious? He's a raving lunatic.*

"Does he ever pray or chant things at you?"

"Ye-es," Indelbed said. "Every night he comes to my room, stands at the doorway, and mumbles things. I pretend to be asleep. He's drunk all the time, you know that, right?"

"Indelbed, do you have any brands or tattoos or anything?"

"No!" Indelbed knew where this was going, and he certainly was not going to admit to anything.

"Oh, the boy is lying!" GU glared at the Ambassador. "Any fool can see that."

"Uncle, please."

Indelbed was terrified now. He stared at the Ambassador, who seemed to be the most likely adult to help him. The Ambassador looked grim. Tears spurted from Indelbed's eyes. He had never felt so alone.

"All right, fine," the Ambassador said to GU Sikkim. "It's late. I'll take him home."

"Have a word with Kaikobad while you're at it," GU Sikkim said.

"At this hour?" the Ambassador scoffed. "I'll drop in tomorrow afternoon."

"Make sure about the other thing. We don't want to have any more of that kind of trouble," GU Sikkim said. He glared at Indelbed and lowered his voice to a menacing whisper. "I have my eye on you, you sterile, mongoloid freak. You've got tainted blood. Any more trouble and I'll personally lock you up forever."

CHAPTER 3
Sleeping Beauty

As the Ambassador's car made the long trek to Wari, Indelbed sat in the back with Rais and listened politely to Aunty Juny's stony silence. Rais squeezed his arm once in quiet sympathy, and it made Indelbed feel a little bit better about the whole evening.

Finally, when she couldn't hold it in any longer, Aunty Juny started venting: "Why are we in charge of him? Kaikobad is such a weird drunk. I hate going to that house, it smells funny. Oh god, the car won't even fit in that road. Why do *we* have to drop him off?"

The Ambassador, himself in a foul mood, said, "It's your precious son's fault. He brought up the whole thing."

Whereupon Aunty Juny clamped her pale lipsticked mouth shut and glared at Indelbed through the side-view mirror. He was terrified of Aunty Juny. She was younger than the Ambassador by almost ten years, haughty and fashionable. Her perfectly coiffed skull protected a brain like a rabid German U-boat loose in the Atlantic. No nuance of character or action escaped her, and everything was turned to advantage with the rapidity and precision of an active field marshal. It was said in hushed corners of the clan that if *she* had been the Ambassador instead of, well, *the Ambassador,* then the Khan Rahmans would once again have had one of their number sitting as the foreign minister.

As it were, Aunty Juny's genius was parked firmly in the corner of the Ambassador, propelling him from posting to lucrative posting, deftly side-stepping the wiles of lecherous junior wives, guiding him inexorably into the favor of powerful men while stamping down on the pretensions of lesser aspirants. Most intimidating to Indelbed, however, was that she was one of the few members of that generation of aunties who wasn't fat, frumpy, or maternal. Oh no. With her glossy leather purses and polished nails, her dangerously high heels, her thin, rangy body, and her razor-sharp tongue—she was like a very pretty raptor. She filled his mind with excitement and dread at the same time. He was normally unflappable with adults, but she always reduced him into a stammering, uncouth wreck.

Rais, with the easy confidence of a university student, glanced at his parents contemptuously and ruffled Indelbed's head in support.

"I think I'll stay over for the night," he said, leaning toward the front seat.

"What?" Aunty Juny's voice, normally a kind of low growl, always jumped an octave whenever her son provoked her with some foolhardy plan. "Whatever for? You've only been back a few days. I've hardly seen you..."

"It's been a week, beloved Mummy dearest," Rais said. He delighted in calling his mother outlandish, mocking names. People said Rais was smart, but Indelbed could see in him only an insane kind of bravado that was the fair opposite of smart.

"What are you up to, boy?" the Ambassador asked.

"Just want to help out my cousin," Rais said. "Indelbed could use some company, right? I can talk to him about schools."

"Are you some kind of communist?" the Ambassador asked suspiciously. He could not keep track of all the youthful fads. In the past year he had seen the various scions of the extended family imitating Goth rock stars, Mohawked red Indians, and, incredibly, some kind of wimpy floppy-haired vampire. Rais didn't have earrings or tattoos or dyed purple hair. It figured that his son's debaucheries must be mental in nature. Rais had a distressing habit of reading everything *except* for what he was supposed to study. It was very likely he was infected by some aberrant philosophy.

"No, sir."

"Are you experimenting with boys?" the Ambassador asked.

"Vulu!" Aunty Juny glared in shock and anger.

"No, guys, I'm not gay," Rais said, laughing. "I have a girlfriend in school."

"What?" Aunty Juny screamed, apparently finding this worse.

"Hehe, good for you," the Ambassador said. "I remember when I was in—"

"I don't think the boy needs to hear about your conquests, Vulu," Aunty Juny said. Her tone made it quite clear that there were no such conquests to speak of, and had she not deigned to take him on, he would be withering away to a lonely death.

"Quite right, quite right." The Ambassador gave Indelbed a glance through his mirror. "Still, let Rais stay with the boy. I'll have to come here in the morning anyway to talk to Kaiko."

Aunty Juny declined to argue further. When the car could go no more, they let the boys out and drove off. The alleyway was still crowded even this late at night. On either side of the lane were hole-in-the-wall shops hosting food vendors grilling kebabs, tailors sitting on mattresses, ISD phone operators, rice wholesalers, and even an enterprising gentleman who sold stolen signboards. The smell of cigarettes and food was undercut by the rich, bubbling broth from the open drains. This was a far cry from what Rais was no doubt used to in his posh Baridhara apartment, but he wasn't complaining, so Indelbed shrugged off his nascent embarrassment.

Normally he would have cringed a bit, walking his cousin through this maze, but right now he was too worried about his father's temper. By the time they had reached the front door and negotiated entrance, he was in fact quite relieved that Rais had so magnanimously offered to help him. They were met in the hallway by Butloo, who informed him that the master was in a rare rage. Indelbed turned to Rais to confer, just in time to see the back of his traitorous cousin as he slinked off toward the stairwell, cell phone in his left hand and a rolled-up joint clamped between the long fingers of his right. Rais winked back at him.

"I really needed to get away from them, man. I'm going to your room for a smoke. Same place, right?"

Indelbed nodded.

"I'll see you later then."

"Thanks," Indelbed replied, trying to inject as much awful sarcasm as possible into his voice. It came out sounding sulky and immature instead.

Indelbed went to the study, bracing himself for a torrent of abuse. Automatically he checked for the saber and saw that it was hanging from its usual hook on the wall. While his father had never actually stabbed him with it, he had felt the flat of the blade more than once. (The Khan Rahman family was very much in favor of corporal punishment for young children, and the Doctor was one of the preeminent champions of this philosophy. The saber was the worst, but the belt wasn't too nice either, and the Doctor's hands, long and bony, were also deadly weapons of retribution.) The Doctor was sprawled in his armchair, muttering incoherently. He was for once dressed decently, in a white kurta. It even looked fairly clean. He must have unearthed it in some remote closet. His whiskey bottle was rolling on the floor, his glass cradled protectively against his bony chest. The man's head lolled sideways, and a thin line of drool connected his chin to his shoulder.

Indelbed tidied his father up a little bit, taking care not to wake him and trying not to let his relief get the best of him. The armchair and footstool, joined together, could form a sort of couch-bed, which was not an unusual place for the Doctor to sleep on drunken nights. Tomorrow the hangover would be terrible, and the punishments might be further enhanced by this. It wasn't an ideal situation, but like any little boy, Indelbed was an optimist at heart, and on the whole preferred a delayed punishment to an immediate one.

He reflected on the hints made by the Ambassador and GU Sikkim, and tried to imagine this wretched creature—this whiskey-pickled flop—harboring some dangerous secret. It made no sense to him. He tried to dismiss this as hearsay, but could not conceive why such lofty members of the clan would bother playing a prank on him.

He stood in front of the mirror and pulled up his T-shirt. It wasn't a tattoo so much as a brand, a rough circle of raised flesh between his shoulder blades, with hardly any details. He didn't remember getting it. He had always thought the Doctor had injured him by accident somehow. *Why were they asking about it? How did they know?*

Fired up somewhat by curiosity—imagining for a moment that he was the secret prince to some underground kingdom—he poked around his father's books. They were a sorry lot, most of them water damaged. The drawers held plenty of notebooks, handwritten both in English and Bangla, and even some in Arabic script, which was probably Urdu. He knew that some of the older members of the family spoke Urdu, but only behind closed doors, because after the war it had become unfashionable to do so.

He tried to read a few of them, but he didn't know most of the words, and the slanted handwriting confused him. There were diagrams of the human body and various medical notations, including pages and pages of recurring letters: *ATCG*. Then there were solid pages of math, numbers and letters jumbled together in bewildering formulas. Indelbed couldn't be sure if this was genuine work the Doctor had been doing or simply the gibberish of a deranged mind. These notebooks covered a number of fairly recent years, the cheap paper undamaged yet by age, the handwriting steadily deteriorating as the drink wrecked the Doctor's nerves. He resolved to ask Butloo about it tomorrow. The man didn't know how to read, but he knew the mind of the Doctor, and if there was some horrible secret, he was sure to have a clue. Feeling slightly let down, he left his sleeping father and went upstairs to his room, only to find that Rais had appropriated his bed and was now lounging on it—with his shoes on, no less—smoking cigarettes and yapping away on his cell.

"I'm going to be a while, buddy," Rais said, looking up. "You better grab the guest room."

"That's just great."

"Sorry, dude." Rais at least had the grace to look remorseful. "Girl I've been seeing here. Trying to dump her gently. I hate this part. This might be a long night. Don't want to keep you up."

Indelbed grabbed his stuff from the bathroom and stalked out, glaring at his cousin. He wasn't sure what "this part" or "dump" meant, but he was sure the girl was better off. The guest rooms were not habitable, of course, having neither bedding nor, for that matter, working beds. Plus they were full of mosquitoes, since the windows did not close properly, and if anyone thought mosquitoes were not a big deal, they'd never spent all night fending off bloodsuckers the size of sparrows.

He sat at the foot of his bed and waited, arms crossed.

"Sorry," Rais said, finally hanging up after twenty minutes. He didn't look the least bit sorry. "You talk to your father?"

"He was asleep," Indelbed said. *Fat good you were, though.*

"Find out anything mysterious? I had my ear to the door, back at the party. Heard pretty much everything GU Sikkim said. His voice really carries."

"I'll be sure to warn him next time," Indelbed said.

"So you actually got a tattoo or what?" Rais asked. "Why'd they keep hassling you about it?"

Indelbed shrugged.

"I've always wanted one," Rais said. "My mom would kill me, though. Plus they hurt a lot I bet."

Indelbed wordlessly lifted his shirt and showed the mark on his back.

"Whoa! You do have one! It looks a bit like a snake swallowing its tail," Rais said. "If you squint. Pretty cool."

That made him feel better. He hadn't really ever felt cool before. Rais had a way of making everything seem easy.

"I was going to ask Father about it, but he hasn't even woken up yet," Indelbed said.

"It's the drink," Rais said knowledgeably.

"Rais *bhai*," Indelbed ventured, "what is a mongoloid?"

"It's like a baby with an extra chromosome," Rais said. He looked at Indelbed. "I don't think you're one; they always have stretched-out heads."

"What's wrong with them?"

"Their brains don't work properly. Yours is fine. I'm pretty sure."

"Thanks. And what's 'sterile'?"

"You know how kids are made, right?" Rais made a halfhearted poking gesture with his hands.

Indelbed shrugged. He didn't really, but it didn't seem like particularly *secret* knowledge. After all, the world was full of kids.

"Why do you ask?"

"GU Sikkim called me mongoloid and sterile."

"I'm sure that can't be right," Rais said. He frowned. "You look perfectly normal to me."

"Well, you're not studying to be a doctor anymore, are you?"

"History major for now. I did the premed stuff, but I definitely don't want to be a doctor."

"You probably wouldn't know anything about it then," Indelbed said. He sniffed.

"No point sitting around," Rais said, giving him a pat on the head. "Let's look for clues to this awful secret."

His enthusiasm was genuine and infectious, shaking Indelbed out of despondency, and soon they were rifling through the Doctor's private notebooks, expounding outlandish theories. Rais seemed to have no compunction about going through the Doctor's private stuff.

"It's about DNA, I think," he said finally, after poring through the pages. "See the squiggly lines? Looks like chromosomes to me."

"Looks boring to me," Indelbed said.

"Maybe he was charting the family tree or something," Rais said. "Hey, how come there's none of your mother's stuff around? I don't even know what she looked like."

"I don't either," Indelbed said, surprised. He hardly ever thought of her, and his father never spoke of her, other than reassuring him that she was dead. He realized that there was not a single picture or reference to his mother in the house. No favored artifact. No portrait. No sepia photograph of the happy couple. Not even an article of clothing. Had she been some kind of hideous monster?

"I bet that's it, she's a monster," Rais said, showing colossal insensitivity, Indelbed thought. He had always hoped that his mother was secretly alive and would one day come to reclaim him. He wasn't quite ready to let go of that yet.

They asked Butloo about it, but that worthy creature clamped his lips shut and said that Dr. Sahib had forbidden him to ever speak of her. The other staff had all joined after her demise and knew nothing except far-fetched rumors. They claimed she had been a memsahib, a witch, a rare beauty possessed by djinn.

"It's got to be something weird about your mother," Rais said.

"Maybe she was mad?" The village of the insane always weighed on Indelbed's mind. "That's it, and I'm probably going to go mad too, which is why he never bothered sending me to school." He tried to take his fate philosophically, but the little quaver in the end gave him away.

"It's like *Jane Eyre*; maybe your mother went mad, and she's locked up somewhere in the house!" Rais said.

Indelbed shot him a dirty look, but then another thought took hold: "You don't think she got sent to the village, in secret?"

Rais leaned back, wondering for a moment, and then shook it off as impossible. "Let's just go to sleep. We can look some more in the morning, and my dad'll be here."

When the Ambassador finally arrived the next afternoon, it was past four o'clock and Indelbed was quite sick with worry. The problem was that the Doctor wasn't actually showing any signs of distress. His temperature was okay: he wasn't sweating or shivering, and he hadn't even vomited once. Indelbed, the veteran of two separate cases of alcohol poisoning, and numerous cases of very bad binge-drinking hangovers, just could not see how this was drink related.

"What's more," Rais said, after they had told the whole affair to the Ambassador, "the bottle is only half empty. Surely Uncle wasn't a half-bottle man..."

"No, it would definitely take more than half a bottle to put him down," the Ambassador said ruefully. "Still, let's call a doctor, eh?"

The neighborhood doctor, by dint of Butloo's penchant for gossip, had already heard about the peculiar ailment of his colleague and had been sitting with his medical bag on his lap for the past three hours, waiting for the summons. Everything that happened in the big house was a source of constant entertainment to the neighborhood, and he expected to live off this incident for many weeks.

To his chagrin, he could reach no diagnosis. After checking all the vital signs, the best he could offer was a saline drip and plenty of rest.

"There's nothing wrong with Dr. Kaikobad," the physician said. "He just seems to be asleep. Probably he'll wake up. Perhaps he was very tired?"

The Ambassador, not the least bit impressed, ushered him out with great haughtiness. They ate a take-out dinner in silence, and then Indelbed was quite relieved when the Ambassador announced that he and Rais would be staying over.

"If he doesn't get up by morning, boy, we'll have to have a rethink," the Ambassador said.

Indelbed desperately wanted to ask what this was about, but he didn't dare.

"It's probably the madness coming on," Rais said. For an adult, even a young one, he had a peculiarly ineffective method of cheering people up.

Indelbed spent the night next to his father, trying desperately to stay awake. In the dark his father's still form seemed monstrous. When he finally succumbed, he dreamed of ghosts with doglike faces hounding him. Several times in the dark he imagined his father reaching for him. At dawn, the sound of the muezzin woke him, and he wandered outside, bleary-eyed. He felt a miasma of unknown dread pressing down on him. The familiar objects in the house failed to comfort him. Everywhere he saw evidence of insanity and loss, years of neglect. For the first time he contemplated the awful certainty that he might soon become an orphan. He would have to leave the house. They'd probably send him to the village (where perhaps he'd be reunited with his supposedly dead mother).

In the morning, the Ambassador and Rais rejoined him, only to learn that nothing had changed with respect to his father. The Doctor remained asleep and undisturbed. If anything he seemed even more restful than before; yet there was no movement of any sort, no response to shakes, or slaps, or pinches, or any other minor physical torture.

The Ambassador was a methodical, sound thinking man and, in the absence of his wife, well able to handle most situations. He made some phone calls, and within the hour two more doctors came, one a relative by marriage to the Khan Rahmans and the other a promising youngster cousin of thirty years. Both of them were highly placed in the Apollo Hospital, which was the medical facility endorsed by the clan elders. Neither of them looked pleased to be out here, but they had answered the summons, and extremely promptly. Not for the first time, Indelbed marveled at the push and pull of the extended family. He had seen it in action before, but never for his benefit.

"Well?" the Ambassador asked, after they had consulted.

"I can't say, Vulu," Dr. Pappo, the uncle by marriage, said. He was a heart specialist at Apollo, a recognized expert in cardiac distress. "There is nothing wrong with him. I've told him many times about the drinking, but that would lead to stroke or liver failure. Nothing like this. He seems to be asleep. I can admit him if you'd like, but then what? He doesn't even need a respirator or anything."

The junior doctor had the good sense to keep his mouth shut.

"A man doesn't sleep for two days if there's nothing wrong with him," the Ambassador pointed out.

"For god's sake, he doesn't even have a fever," Dr. Pappo said. "It's probably the other thing..."

"Ahem, what?"

"You know," Dr. Pappo said. He shrugged apologetically. "We've all heard the rumors, eh?"

What rumors? What rumors? Indelbed wanted to shout. *Does everyone know except for me?*

"Thanks very much," the Ambassador said, ushering the doctors out. "And let's keep this quiet, eh, Pappo?"

They went through the study again with the Ambassador, looking for clues. But of course there was nothing to be found, Rais and Indelbed having already ransacked the place. The Ambassador examined the floor and discovered something, however, bending down and tasting it with one finger.

"Salt," he said. "Circles of salt everywhere."

Gathering up some courage, Indelbed confronted his uncle. "Can you please tell me what's going on? So what if there's salt on the floor? He's a drunkard. He does weird things all the time."

"You see, Indelbed, your father was a bit of an important man in some ways," the Ambassador said, clearly uncomfortable. "I mean, you don't want to know, we've always discouraged him—well, there was no talking to him, even before the drink. Look, let's just focus on waking him up, and then we can let *him* explain everything."

"Didn't Father tell you anything else when you called him?" Indelbed asked. "I know he said something. Your face changed."

"Hmm, he was agitated, said *you* were under some kind of threat," the Ambassador said. "Difficult to tell with Kaiko, how coherently he was thinking. He said he was taking some steps to protect you."

Threat? Me? Indelbed was flabbergasted. He pictured the police coming after him, or perhaps the black-sunglass'd RAB guys—the rapid action battalion, a sort of SWAT team known for killing criminals in cross fires—with their big guns. He couldn't imagine what he had done. Did they come after you for not going to school?

"Er, neither of you geniuses checked his cell phone," Rais said, holding up the phone in question.

"What?"

"Cell phone," Rais said. "Uncle Kaiko made like ten calls to this one guy, before he croaked."

Rais was already hitting the redial. After some rings, a man answered. Indelbed heard his voice come across the line quite clearly: "Hello, Kaikobad?"

"It's his nephew," Rais said.

"Give it here, son."

"Where is Kaikobad?"

"Hello, this is the Ambassador speaking."

"Who?"

"Sorry, I mean this is Vulubir Khan Rahman," the Ambassador said. "I'm Kaikobad's cousin. You might have seen me on television; I'm on all the talk shows..."

"Er, no."

"Sorry, hmm, this is a bit awkward. Are you a bootlegger of some sort?"

"Bootlegger?"

"Well, Kaikobad called you a number of times two nights ago, and then he went to sleep."

"Sounds perfectly normal."

"Well, he hasn't woken up since."

"Oh dear."

"So the thing is, do you know anything about this? Might I ask your name?" Not for nothing was the Ambassador considered the politest man in the Foreign Service.

"Certainly," the man said with a flourish that somehow carried through the phone. "I am Siyer Dargo Dargoman, emissary, consultant of the occult, and barrister of contract law in the Celestial Court. You must have heard of me—I argued the case for the inheritance of Harun al-Rashid's fifth concubine's enchanted bedsheet."

"Sorry, haven't, must have missed it..."

"Oh."

"Are you human, then?"

"Human? I am Afghani!"

Indelbed looked at his cousin, stricken. What else could the man be but human? The Ambassador pressed on: "Well, could you help us?"

"Yes, of course, Kaikobad has already employed me in this matter," Siyer said. "I am more than three-quarters of the way to Dhaka. You say he's in some sort of coma?"

"Yes, something like that."

"That could be a problem." Siyer sounded pissed off. "I normally take an advance, see, but as it was Kaikobad, I agreed to fly out at my own cost and everything..."

"Well, don't worry, man, I'm sure we can scrape together your lawyer's fees," the Ambassador said in his haughty way.

"Really?" Siyer said. "If Kaikobad is asleep, then you can't use his dignatas. Have you got emeralds? Or some of Solomon's artifacts?"

"What? What the hell is dignatas?"

"Look, never mind, I've already left. I'll reach out tomorrow," Siyer said. "You bunch of jokers better figure out how to pay me."

The Ambassador put the phone down, highly discomfited.

"Well?" Rais asked.

"It's an Afghan lawyer whom Kaikobad hired," the Ambassador said. "He's coming here tomorrow. He wants to be paid. Not in money. In some dignatas and jewels and Solomons."

"What?"

"I think, Rais, that we better call your mother."

CHAPTER 4
The Mother of All Mothers

Aunty Juny took one look at Indelbed and sniffed. Then she grabbed him by the ear and marched him to the bathroom, where she made him strip and get into the shower. From the other side of the curtain, she spent a mortifying half hour taking him step by step through the bathing process. It was quite possibly the worst day of Indelbed's life. Nearly dead from embarrassment, he came out to see her going through his closet with a look of utter disgust.

"Is this your actual wardrobe?" she asked.

Indelbed nodded. She unerringly spotted his best clothes and made him put them on, and then she made him sit on his bed and began to comb his hair with tight, rough strokes.

"So you have never set foot in a school?"

"No. Father teaches me at home."

"Wretched man. Can you read and write?"

"Yes." He hoped she wouldn't make him take a test.

"And these are your clothes? Hand-me-downs from the family I presume?"

"Butloo gets the tailors to fix them when he can."

"I see."

"They're good clothes," Indelbed said. "The buttons never come off, and there are no holes in them either."

"This Butloo, is he in charge of your food?"

"The cook and Butloo."

"And what do you eat every day?"

"Rice and dal."

Aunty Juny frowned. "Milk? Eggs?"

"Sure, every day," Indelbed said. In reality it was whenever Butloo could scrounge some up, which wasn't that often. He suspected the man used his own wages to buy them, but he wasn't sure.

"You are pathetically small for your age," Juny said. "I had no idea things were so bad over here. It is shameful. I am glad I do not have any more children."

"Sorry. Aunty Juny?"

"Yes."

"Can I ask you some questions?"

"Must you?"

"Please?"

"All right."

"Is my father going to die?"

"No."

"Did you know my mother?"

"No."

"Do you think she might still be alive?"

"She died when you were born."

"Were you there?"

"I heard from the hospital. And, of course, we visited as soon as we could."

"So there's no chance she got away?"

"No."

"Like totally sure?"

"I'm sure." She looked at him. "I'm sorry, Indelbed."

She did not sound that sorry, but it made him cry a little bit anyway.

"No one ever talks about her. Will you tell me some things?"

"All right." She sighed. "Ask."

"What did she look like?"

Aunty Juny frowned. "You have never seen a picture of her?"

"No. There aren't any in the house. Butloo said my father burned all of them when I was born."

"She was very beautiful," Juny said.

"Like you?"

"I only met her three times," Juny said, her eyes far away. "The first time in London, when Kaikobad brought her out, then again at their wedding, and one final time when she was pregnant with you."

"Were you friends?"

"No, I don't think she had any friends. She did not need any."

"Was Father always like this?"

"No, Indelbed, this happened mostly after she died."

"She wasn't mad then? Rais said she was mad."

"She was not mad," Juny said. "She loved to paint. I remember seeing some of her work before—it was fantastic. She gave me a small sketch once, about twelve years ago."

"I've never seen any art by her."

"I will find the sketch and give it to you. You should have one thing of hers at least."

"Is it very valuable?" Indelbed asked, knowing never to expect anything for free.

"It is to me," Juny said.

"I can't give you anything for it." He wanted to be clear beforehand.

"I will loan it to you then," Juny said. "And you may repay me when you are grown up."

"What if it breaks?"

"You will be very careful with it," Juny said.

"Thank you."

"What else... She made superb biriyani. I remember she told me she loved it more than anything else."

"So she must have been fat then, like Aunty Sikkim." Indelbed loved biriyani, especially the kind served at weddings, which was cooked in a giant sealed pot, the flavors of the rice, lamb, and potatoes infused together over a wood fire.

Aunty Juny smiled. "No, she wasn't fat at all. She was as tall as your dad, thin, and had black hair. She liked to read. I think she married your father for his books. There was a huge library in this house, before Kaikobad sold it off. Your grandfather had thousands of books collected over three generations, and before Kaikobad became ill, he also added to it every year. When she got married to him, your mother brought hundreds of books of her own with her. I remember they had to put in extra shelves and convert one of the sitting rooms into a second library."

Indelbed couldn't imagine such scenes of grandeur.

"I wish Father hadn't sold everything," he said.

"One day, I hope you will buy it all back," Juny said.

"Aunty Juny, was she... was she normal?"

"She was, in all the ways that count," Juny said. "Now enough questions. You look barely human. Come with me."

She dragged him to the top of the stairs and shouted, "Vulu!"

"Yes, dear," the Ambassador said.

"For god's sake, go and get the boy some clothes that fit," she said. "Take him to Gulshan. And take Rais too. And ask Rais about his girlfriend."

"What are you going to do? Uncle Sikkim will be coming soon."

"Let him come. I'm going to clean this disgusting dump," Aunty Juny said, leading them down into the formal living room. It was, indeed, a disgusting dump. "I don't know how you expect to be taken seriously in this house..."

"Dear, what about Kaikobad?"

"What about him?" Aunty Juny bullied them to the front door. "If he recovers, at least he'll wake up to a clean house."

CHAPTER 5

Bahadur Siyer Dargo Dargoman

The Afghan knocked on their door at the stroke of five, just when Butloo was fumigating. He thus walked into the house wreathed in smoke, his black shoes striking the floor, and for a moment Indelbed thought it was the devil—but at least they were receiving him in good form, thanks to Aunty Juny. She had thrown back the clock on the long abandoned living room. She had marshaled Butloo and the guard, as well as the cook and her daughter. Somehow, she had injected a fresh fervor into their nonexistent work ethic. The threadbare, rotten carpet had been removed. The floors had been scrubbed with powdered soap, revealing a tolerable geometric mosaic. The walls and ceilings had been swept, several tons of webs and an indigent clan of spiders removed. The walls had then been scrubbed with a dry brush, knocking loose all the peeling paint and dirt. The few pieces of furniture had been polished and arranged strategically. The room now looked stark, austere, elegant, in a ruin-porn sort of way. By this time, GU Sikkim had also arrived, sulkily ensconced in the best armchair, muttering about the undesirability of inviting strangers into family affairs, and it was the five of them who received the Afghan.

"Hello, family of Kaikobad." Siyer bowed at the waist. "I am Bahadur Siyer Dargo Dargoman."

Siyer was quite simply the best-dressed man Indelbed had ever seen. Even to his untutored eye, the cut of the man's charcoal-gray suit was exceedingly fine, making him appear tall and slim. The fabric was a mixture of wool and silk so sleek that it seemed to eat the light. Siyer was a handsome man of middle age, with the striking, craggy features of his race, short hair graying nicely, and light eyes. His shoes were soft black loafers with waxed laces most perfectly aligned. All his other accoutrements spoke of wealth: his wafer-thin gold watch, the dull emerald on his finger, the wink of diamonds on his bone-white cuffs. On his arm was a cane with a leather grip, which Indelbed took to be some kind of weapon, since he had no evidence of a limp. He took them all in and then smiled at Aunty Juny in a particularly smarmy way.

"You are welcome, sir," the Ambassador said, coming forward and making introductions. If he was surprised by the quality of their visitor, his diplomatic training was sufficient to cover it. "We are most concerned with Kaikobad."

"Let us see him immediately," said Dargoman. "I must examine his body."

They trooped over to the bedroom, where the Afghan made a careful examination of his client. He took out a horn-handled magnifying glass and looked deep into Kaikobad's eyeballs. He studied his fingernails, his chest, and then turned him over to look at his back. Indelbed was shocked to see a faded snake tattoo on his father's shoulder blade, a small mark like a sideways 8, an etching of thin lines depicting the world serpent devouring its own tail. In shape it was similar to the hideous mark between his own shoulders, except Kaikobad's was finely wrought and his was a mangled cattle brand.

Dargoman left Kaikobad alone and went on to minutely examine the salt circles in the study, sometimes sniffing the air like a dog.

"Yes, he's in an occultocephalus coma," Siyer said finally. "I have seen this before. It is decidedly an attack."

"He was attacked?" The Ambassador looked around, alarmed. "By who?"

"You mean you don't know?" The Afghan looked genuinely baffled.

"Pooh-pooh, what attack?" GU Sikkim said. "He is just in a drunken stupor. Much ado about nothing..."

"You are mistaken, sir," Siyer said. "See the salt circles, drawn for protection? He must have put warding spells everywhere too. An experienced man like Kaikobad would not be taken without a struggle. Yet you see nothing was wrecked. This was no physical attack. We must perforce jump then to the obvious conclusion. He is a victim of the occult!"

Spells? Occult? "Er, he was drunk," Indelbed said, but his heart was beginning to beat faster. Hadn't his father mentioned something about Indelbed himself being in danger too? Was he going to end up in a coma as well?

"What nonsense," GU Sikkim said harshly. "You are mad, sir!"

"Well, who attacked him? Do you have any idea?" Aunty Juny asked. "Surely he must have discussed it with you."

"It is undoubtedly a djinn, a most powerful Ifrit!" Siyer declared, and the room itself seemed to gasp. Everyone stared at him, flabbergasted.

"What is an Ifrit?" Juny asked finally.

"They are a most numerous and powerful type of djinn—"

"I forbid you to say that word!" GU Sikkim shrieked. "You liar! Take it back!"

Siyer squared off against GU Sikkim, his nostrils quivering. "And by what means do you intend to compel me, *sir*?"

"Let's all relax," Rais said, stepping between them. "Are you seriously saying Uncle Kaikobad was attacked by a djinn?"

Siyer looked astonished. "But of course. Surely you are aware that your uncle is a magician."

"A what?" Indelbed blurted out.

"A purveyor of magic and a well-known adept of the occult," Siyer said.

"No, we were not aware of this," Aunty Juny said, looking hard at her husband.

The Ambassador exchanged a sheepish look with GU Sikkim.

"Is that why you were asking me all those weird questions the other day?" Indelbed ventured.

"Out with it, Vulu," Juny ordered.

The Ambassador sighed. "Indelbed, there are some things you need to know."

It never boded well when you needed to know something. In Indelbed's limited experience, these words always presaged some fresh disaster.

"Indelbed, son, it's a bit of a shameful secret," the Ambassador said. "Only a few of us know. We begged him not to go down this path, of course. But Kaiko never listened to anyone. He went into magic; he's a magician."

"And you guys all believe in magic? Like Harry Potter–type magic?" Rais, with his usual insouciance, was pursuing his own line of inquiry.

"Look at the university boy, knowing everything about the world," the Ambassador snapped. "Yes, yes, we know all about the magic. Any fool villager will tell you it's real."

"I see," Aunty Juny said. Her displeasure was extremely clear, and even Siyer recoiled from it. "And what of his attacker. This djinn, you said?"

"There are no djinns! There are no djinns! Go away all of you!" GU Sikkim was fairly frothing at the mouth.

"My dear lady, it is perfectly natural for the djinn to attack him," Siyer said. He had apparently come to the conclusion that Aunty Juny was the person to deal with here.

"It might be natural to you, but we are as yet in the dark," Aunty Juny said. "At least I am." She glanced coolly at GU Sikkim before addressing Dargoman again: "I understand you spoke to him before he was attacked?"

"Well, yes, Kaikobad felt he could take care of himself. He called me to assist in a separate matter," Siyer said. He pointed one theatrical finger at Indelbed. "It's the boy. He's the one really in danger."

"Really?" Aunty Juny just about kept her skepticism under wraps. "And pray, what has he done to earn their wrath?"

"As you know, dear lady," Siyer said, "it's his mother. When she married his father, it was something of a scandal. When she had a child, there was a furor! The conservative party of the djinn did not like it at all. The boy has been targeted ever since."

"Don't bring her up, damn you!" GU Sikkim waved his stick at Siyer. "Bloody lawyer. I forbid anyone to mention her name!"

"What about my mother?" Indelbed's heart was pounding in his chest.

"Why, has no one told you?" Siyer asked. "She's a djinn, of course. You're a half-breed, the first live one I've ever seen."

"My mother, a djinn?" Indelbed's eyes went big.

The Ambassador sighed. "I suppose it is time we told him. I had hoped Kaikobad would do it..."

"What more can you expect from that scoundrel!" GU Sikkim said bitterly.

"Grand-Uncle, please tell me!" Indelbed said.

"It's in the family," GU half whispered. "We have the blood. My grandfather had it. We had to lock him up in the village in the end. Clearly mad. And his own uncle, my great-great-grandfather—they say he was arrested by the British for witchcraft. They executed him. Burned our house down in Kolkata, even the family mausoleum. Necromancy, they said."

It occurred to Indelbed that perhaps GU, Siyer, and the Ambassador all might be drunk. They didn't smell like it, but you could never underestimate the cunning of a dedicated drunk.

"Are you saying our family is possessed or something?" Indelbed, always one for clarity, wanted it on the record that this alleged problem was not a phenomenon isolated to *himself*.

"Possessed?" GU shook his head dismissively. "They weren't possessed, you idiot. It's in the blood. Magic. We've carried that tainted blood for ten generations! Two hundred years ago, Amir Khan Rahman married a djinn. Two hundred years of drooling half-wits and sterile mutants, and it still hasn't washed out. What is the one thing we learned over two hundred years? Don't fornicate with djinn! And what did your father do? He did just that, and then he *married* her. Do you get it now?"

"Uncle, please," the Ambassador said. "He's just a boy."

"We should have strangled him at birth," GU Sikkim said, sitting down, clutching his chest. "I'm going to have a heart attack because of this, Vulu."

"Did you know?" Indelbed spun toward his aunt, momentarily forgetting himself. "You knew!"

"I did not know," Aunty Juny said. "I had heard rumors. I dismissed them as village slander. In this country they accuse every beautiful woman of being possessed."

"Look, Siyer, how serious is this?" the Ambassador asked. "Let us speak plainly. What are we dealing with here?"

"Half-breeds are rare. Under some circumstances, that places little Indelbed here under the jurisdiction of djinn laws," Siyer said. "Or so certain djinns are lobbying. I have made some preliminary inquiries. A minor hunt has been declared on him."

"A minor hunt?"

"Djinns have an ancient tradition of hunting minors," Siyer said. "Before it was mostly a kind of intrafamily affair. But sometimes a formal hunt would be declared, where anyone could participate, the winner getting a prize, et cetera. There hasn't been one in quite a while now. This is very bad for us, of course. It means any number of djinns are probably looking for Indelbed. To kill him."

"Random djinns want to kill my nephew?" Aunty Juny seemed offended by this. "For what reason? Are they all idiots?"

"Not sure about the reason," Siyer said. "I haven't formally taken the case, so I can only make limited inquiries. I think it might have something to do with his mother's inheritance."

"What inheritance?" Aunty Juny asked. "Kaikobad spent everything. He is penniless."

"I am not certain. There are rumors that she was from some bastard royal line. It is possible that she might have posthumously inherited something. The thing is, Indelbed is a minor, so they don't really need much more than an excuse to kill him. It's archaic, but you see in Djinn Lore, only mature adults are protected by law. There were hunts every few seasons to target the youth—they were a big part of a year's social calendar. I think it was a practice to weed out misshapen children in the old days. There was always a prejudice against half-breeds, you see... It has fallen out of practice the past few centuries, but djinns love reviving traditions."

"How charming," Aunty Juny said. "Now I take it you can stop this hunt from taking place?"

"Such was the gist of my conversation with Kaikobad."

"And how do you intend to do so?"

Siyer went over to the comatose emissary and jabbed his cane at the tattoo on Kaikobad's shoulder blade. "That marking—allow me to inform you, madame, that I have a similar one on my person." He duly proceeded to roll up his sleeve and show them all a very distinguished tattoo on his forearm, the snake twisting over itself, scales and fangs clearly visible.

"Since time immemorial, the djinn have avoided humanity," Siyer said. "I have been informed by an old colleague that they find us noisy, brutish, and boring. To limit their interaction with our species, they only condescend to recognize a few of us at any one time. These are known as the emissary families. We are, of course, the true nobility of humanity. I trace my ancestors to the fifth century of Christ, to the kings of the Pashtuns. The Medicis were an emissary family for a time. So was the house of Saud. So too the line of Solomon and the great Moghuls. It is said that the great Buddha was an emissary, as was Ashoka. Napoleon was not, which is why he lost the only battle that really counted."

"And you mean to tell me that Kaikobad is an *ambassador*?" The Ambassador looked slightly put out.

"Certainly. Your family is known in our circles as old emissary blood. Your ancestor Emir Khan Rahman was a notable emissary who fought in a great magical battle and ennobled himself. And of course Kaikobad himself has spent much time among djinns," Siyer said.

"And this mark is a badge of honor from the djinns?" Aunty Juny asked.

"Well, yes and no," Siyer said. "The djinns sometimes have trouble telling humans apart. The mark of Bahamut indicates we are emissaries—that we are authorized to be in djinn space and protected by the djinn Bahamut. It stops them from harming us for no reason."

"The boy has this mark." Aunty Juny pulled up Indelbed's shirt roughly.

Siyer bent down to have a close look and frowned. "Well, it might be the mark of Bahamut—just barely. Kaikobad must have done it himself. In the dark. With his left hand."

"I don't remember getting it," Indelbed said.

"No doubt he hoped it would protect you," Siyer said. "But an experienced man such as Kaikobad should have known that just marking the boy would do him scant favors. Only full emissaries are permitted to bear the mark of their patron djinn. I'm afraid it is no protection against a formal hunt."

"What are the terms of this hunt?" Aunty Juny asked.

"I have to check the notice. As I said, there hasn't been one for many years. Normally they last for a month or so and are open to the public. Proof is taken in the form of a body part. Perhaps the head."

"They want to cut my head off?" Indelbed asked, getting scared now.

"Well, you won't feel it—they'll kill you before," Siyer said. "Sometimes there are added clauses, for fun. Like you have to kill the victim left-handed, or using the form of a dog, or something like that."

"And does anyone survive?" Aunty Juny asked.

"Mostly not," Siyer said. "It's a bit of an honor, being targeted for a hunt. If Indelbed survives, he'll have a lot of dignatas."

"And what exactly is this dignatas thing?" Aunty Juny asked.

"It is, quite simply, the essence of the djinn. It is the personal worth of a character, the force of will, the influence, the charisma, the wit, the sheer handsomeness. It is a deeply personal thing, the full measure of a person. And most importantly, it determines the auctoritas of an individual," Siyer said.

"Wait a minute, I remember this stuff from Roman history class," Rais said.

"The Romans, young man, stole the idea from the djinns," Siyer said.

"And this auctoritas business? What is that good for?" Aunty Juny asked.

"It is, madame, the currency we use in the djinn world," Siyer said. "It is the authority of a man to command goods and services from others, to shape policy, to influence the direction of the polity. It measures his rank in the social hierarchy, even the safety of his person. A djinn without auctoritas is nothing, an ignored, wretched creature, a veritable beggar."

"And you work for auctoritas, I take it?" Aunty Juny said.

"Yes, madame." Siyer drew himself up proudly. "An emissary without auctoritas is a useless fool. When you ask for something, auctoritas determines whether the answer is yes or no. Auctoritas itself is determined by dignatas. Asking favors reduces dignatas, whereas granting favors increases dignatas, among other things."

"And we ordinary mortals have none, I suppose?" Aunty Juny said.

"None at all," Siyer said.

"Then how do you expect us to pay you, for god's sake?" the Ambassador asked irritably.

Siyer stood up. "That, sir, is your issue. I have come out of respect for Kaikobad. As he is no longer lucid, I see no further reason to stay here."

"Good, good, get out of here," GU Sikkim said.

"Wait a minute," Aunty Juny said. She glared at Sikkim, and he ceased his grumbling. "We are unaware of occult customs. Please bear with us. I understand that you would be willing to work with Kaikobad?"

"Certainly," Siyer said. "He was a man with considerable auctoritas. Aiding him would put him in my debt, thereby decreasing some of his dignatas and increasing mine."

"Well, why can't you use his auctoritas now? Just take all of it, for god's sake."

"Madame, he is in a coma," Siyer said. "Auctoritas cannot be transferred or inherited. You cannot negotiate on his behalf, nor spend his auctoritas."

"He asked you to help his son, didn't he?" Aunty Juny asked.

"He merely asked me to pay him a visit to discuss these matters," Siyer said. "No formal contract was struck."

"Well, who has to know that? You can be sure that Kaikobad, if he ever wakes up, will never contradict you. Why not just help yourself to some of that great auctoritas and help out this poor emissary child at the same time?" Aunty Juny asked.

Siyer Dargoman looked thoughtful. A cunning look descended across his face, momentarily transforming the noble mien into something vulturish.

"Yes, well, my prior conversation with Kaikobad was rather detailed," Siyer said. "I suppose I can proceed on that premise. I accept the contract. I will observe him for tonight. If he wakes up, we'll see." His expression said that he carried scant hope of that ever happening.

They went back to the living room for tea and samosas. Indelbed, who had been avidly studying the emissary, was left with the lingering suspicion that his future was being settled with undue haste.

CHAPTER 6
Traitors

"This is all happening very hastily," GU Sikkim said, as he pulled on his hookah. Some of the younger children of the family had banded together and bought it for him. They called it *shisha*, like the damn Arabs. And they had the cheek to give him some awful apple-flavored stuff instead of real, manly tobacco.

His guest was the djinn Matteras, who affected the human form of a stocky, bald psychopath. His teeth, when he smiled, were two rows of needle fangs. GU Sikkim thought that this pretty much summed up his entire personality.

They were sitting on the roof of GU Sikkim's Baridhara duplex. He owned this part of the roof outright and had girded it with latticed walls and various plants to maintain privacy. It felt like a garden. The open air was good for him. It was also easier to entertain guests like Matteras. The space around the djinn glittered, as if agitated somehow. Each djinn had a distortion field around him, a sort of spherical area of influence where quantum distortions occurred.

Matteras had an exceptionally powerful distortion field. He could flatten a building a hundred yards away. Right now, out of consideration for his host, he had compacted his field into a ball a few yards in diameter. Sitting inside the djinn's distortion field made GU Sikkim sick. He got vertigo and heard noises. His teeth hurt. His heart felt like flopping out of his chest. On a good day, more than a minute would make him puke. Thus, Matteras sat at the opposite end of the roof, keeping a polite distance. This was a sign of extraordinary consideration on the part of the djinn, who, like most of his race, was overbearingly arrogant.

"Sikkim, times are changing," Matteras said. "You were told to control the emissary Kaikobad and his son. In this you failed."

"Control that madman?" GU Sikkim shuddered. "I kept him pickled in alcohol."

"It was not enough," Matteras said. "He put the mark of Bahamut on the boy, and then he applied for permission to enter him as an apprentice. This created many ripples, I can tell you."

"He's a runty half-wit, that boy," GU Sikkim said. "And Kaikobad is in a coma. Can't we just leave it at that?"

"It has become political," Matteras said. To djinn this was a catchall phrase for matters far too complex for humans to understand. Djinn politics was notoriously convoluted. Nor were the rewards tangible or, often enough, even predictable. Huge amounts of auctoritas were used on ridiculous gambles with obscure payoffs. Alliances between individuals shifted like sand. No djinn trusted another. It was the Great Game. "I know about Kaikobad. Forget him, he's never waking up. The boy concerns me. You will deal with him."

"You want me to help you kill my own grand-nephew?" GU Sikkim asked. He should have felt more outrage at the thought, but in reality, he was just irritated that the unwelcome whelp was still causing him trouble.

"I shall not kill him, I'm not barbaric," Matteras said. "He must be removed from the board nonetheless. You should have kept him in obscurity, as I asked. You always knew this day would come." He waved his hand around the rooftop garden. "You have certainly enjoyed the fruits of my favor. Do not act squeamish now."

"Obscurity? I kept the boy damn near locked in his house for the past ten years. He didn't even know his mother was a djinn."

"Regardless, it is now open news that my sister had a son," Matteras said. "There is no saving him now. It is his very blood that is the problem. My enemies would love to parade him around like a dog on a leash. My position is untenable. Forget the boy. You had better concentrate on preserving the rest of your clan... and all your wealth."

GU Sikkim had, in the past, entered into a bargain with Matteras. Over two decades ago, at the supposed peak of his business career, he had in fact lost a lot of money. Led astray by an old friend, he had sunk his capital into a factory devoted to making skin-whitening products for men. Due to some faulty advertising and unfortunate chemical reactions, they were deluged with lawsuits from irate customers suffering severe disfigurement. The whitening product, far from creating a milky complexion, had turned certain victims a deep orange. More than two dozen prospective grooms had used this product, only to find their faces literally sloughing off on the eve of their weddings. The hoopla was enormous, with media coverage, court cases, and mob action outside the factory.

His partner ran away to Nairobi, leaving him with a mountain of trade debt and bank loans for which he was jointly and severally liable. The Standard & Bartered Bank had his personal guarantee, which meant all of his properties, including the Baridhara duplex, were up for grabs. Worst of all, the government initiated an investigation against him, with alarming talk of criminal charges.

None of his banker friends came forward to help him. His lawyers advised him to let the cases hang in court for the next fifty years and then charged him outrageous fees. His friend, the editor of the *Daily Star*, informed him with mock sadness that he just hadn't been able to stop his rabid journalists from covering the story. The family offered gratuitous advice with ill-hidden glee. They would have stopped him from going to jail, but he would have lost everything! He would have been a shirttail relative like Kaikobad, living in squalor. Intolerable!

And then, like Faustus's demon, Matteras arrived. He offered immediate relief. The chief victim was defenestrated. Others rescinded. The defaced orange bridegrooms were married off. Opposing lawyers withdrew their cases. The bank directors, so snooty only days ago, suddenly became sweet, offering extensions and reschedulements. His local branch once again started sending him diaries and calendars and wishing him happy birthday.

Funds appeared in Sikkim's accounts, wired in from the Caymans. Best of all, the Directorate General of Drug Administration, hitherto investigating him with unnecessary zeal, was suddenly blessed with a dream from the angel Gabriel, who expressly declared Sikkim innocent of any malpractice. He closed the investigation the very next day and sent Sikkim a handsome letter of apology along with a box of iffy sweets. The related files subsequently disappeared from the archives, leaving no trace of the initial findings.

All in all, Matteras had delivered. In return GU Sikkim signed a 743-page contract; the djinn being an extremely litigious race, their contracts were so intricate that not even Sikkim's handpicked team of five barristers had been able to make heads or tails of it. His main man, Barrister Asif, had finally shrugged and advised him to just sign. What difference would it really make? (Barrister Asif had then charged him a hefty fee for this extremely cogent legal opinion.) In the end he had signed what Matteras had assured him was a simple client contract, making Matteras his legal patron.

In djinn culture the patronage system was a long-cherished tradition where patrons offered the weight of their auctoritas as protection and guidance to their clients, who in turn supported their patron in myriad capacities. It was a binding legal obligation, going both ways. In reality, as far as Sikkim could determine, it meant that he had to do whatever Matteras said, on pain of falling foul of djinn law. On top of that, Matteras looked like he could literally bite a man's head off, and it was simply out of the question to disobey him.

"Now, because of some overreaching political debates between various djinn societies—mainly my own faction and that of Bahamut—this has become a sensitive issue. I do not want a huge hue and cry about this," Matteras said.

"Well, you shouldn't have called the hunt on him then," GU Sikkim said.

"I did no such thing," Matteras said. "The minor hunt was called by my enemies to draw attention to him. They wished to embarrass me. Then the Evolutionist faction latched on to it, trying to claim djinn status for the boy. The minor hunt has been declared legal, but it is tied up in protests, injunctions, and countersuits. It has reached a point where it might even incur negative dignatas on the one who completes the hunt. A most piquant situation."

"What do you want from me then?" GU Sikkim waved his hand irritably.

"I want to apprehend the boy quietly," Matteras said. "I want him to disappear, not paraded in front of the courts as some trophy of a hunt. And I want everyone involved to forget about it. Who do you have with him now?"

"I've sent the Ambassador," GU Sikkim said. "He's mostly up to speed on things. He'll deliver the boy to you, no problem."

"I can tell from your fatuous expression that there *is* a problem."

"Kaikobad contacted an emissary colleague for help," GU Sikkim said. "I tried to stall him, but he's actually here now, in Wari, living at the house. Some creature called Siyer Dargo Dargoman."

Matteras uttered a string of djinn curse words. The air shimmered around him with flits of locust lights. GU Sikkim fell back in alarm. It was all too easy to forget the lethal force these ancient creatures commanded, especially while drinking tea on the roof garden.

"I couldn't stop it," GU Sikkim said feebly.

"You are utterly useless," Matteras said. "The emissary knows djinns, you fool. He can publicize this thing. I will have to neutralize him."

"Kill him?" GU Sikkim was starting to get a sick feeling about this.

"Emissaries cannot be killed so easily," Matteras said. "Not even an Ifrit of great nobility and tremendous dignatas such as myself can flout the Lore. You infantile humans naturally cannot understand concepts such as the Lore, but suffice it to say that it is the full sum of djinn wisdom and tradition; for a djinn to be caught transgressing would cause a great deal of censure. I would lose dignatas."

"Yes, patron," GU Sikkim said.

"I cannot deal with the boy in Wari. His house is well known to djinns interested in the hunt. It is protected by ancient runes, moreover. You must get the boy and Siyer away to a secluded spot. When they are alone I will deal with them both."

"I will tell the Ambassador to get them out of there," GU Sikkim said. "I cannot control where Siyer will go, however—"

"Do you still have that little apartment in Mirpur, where you kept your mistress?" Matteras asked, without blinking.

"Er, yes."

"I trust the mistress is gone?"

"Yes, I mean that was just a one-time thing..."

"Spare me, you cretin," Matteras said. "Is it empty now?"

"Yes."

"Good, then send Siyer and the boy over there. Make up whatever story you like."

"And then what?"

"Once I have the boy, it will all be over. Forget about it."

CHAPTER 7
Last Day on Earth

Everything was moving really fast. Hardly a day had passed, and they had regathered at the Wari house. There was no change in his father's state; the coma appeared permanent. The Ambassador had already progressed to the idea of packing him off with Siyer Dargoman, who, despite his natty attire, still seemed fairly shady. Surprisingly, Aunty Juny, who had hitherto always shown a propensity toward wanting him gone, was putting up a degree of resistance to this idea, backed up ably by Rais.

"We don't know this man," she hissed finally, within his earshot.

"I don't want to do anything rash, dear," the Ambassador said. He was showing an unusual degree of backbone, Indelbed noted. "But whatever got Kaikobad is bound to come back here. It simply isn't safe to be in this house a minute longer than necessary. Uncle Sikkim has an apartment in Mirpur, very private, no one knows of it. It is the ideal place to hide them. I insist, dear, everything has been arranged."

And that was it. The Ambassador hustled Indelbed upstairs without giving anyone a chance to voice a dissenting opinion. He was left alone and told to pack. Indelbed had actually never packed before. His first instinct was to gather his meager supply of toys: his precious cricket bat and ball, the stuffed dinosaur that had been Kaikobad's own, the three old Hulk comics someone had given him. He stacked these on the bed and then realized that he had no bag.

Luggage, however, was not something in short supply in the Wari house. Kaikobad's bedroom had an attached dressing room that was never used. Presumably in some distant past it had contained the clothes and artifacts of his wife. Upon her death, Kaikobad must have destroyed all of her things. Now it was filled with luggage of varied origin.

Indelbed had spent many hours playing in this room, rooting through trunks and suitcases for hidden treasure. He had once unearthed a hat box with a proper top hat that could be snapped flat. Here were the myriad traces of his family's former prosperity. There was a huge wood-and-leather trunk with intricate compartments inside, including silver-handled combs and brushes, now tarnished black. This had been one of Indelbed's favorite pieces of luggage. He had stuffed many secret things in here. There was a time when he had even fit himself into the main compartment.

He considered pulling it out, but then thought that Siyer was unlikely to appreciate baggage this cumbersome. It occurred to him that he would probably have to carry his own bags, previous experience making him suspect that grown-ups were unlikely to help him carry his stuff; in fact, he thought darkly, it would most likely be the opposite, and he'd end up lugging *Siyer's* bags.

After rummaging through various hard and soft suitcases, he found what he was looking for. It was a small leather case with little brass wheels at the bottom and a leather strap for pulling. A small brass label on the top said BALZAC—ARGENTINA. This had been another favorite of his. It pulled smoothly, and the wheels swiveled in their little brass sockets. The zipper ends were heavy steel balls that clinked together. The leather was veined and nicked with age, but it was still smooth to the touch and supple, like a thick, cool blanket. There was a shoulder strap too. He hefted it a few times and decided that it would do.

Going to his room, he began to pack, but of course he had no idea what he should be taking. The bat and ball seemed childish somehow. He worried about food. Should he load up on bread and butter, perhaps? Clothes? He added his toothbrush, toothpaste, and soap. The bag had a little compartment that fit these things.

He pulled out his sleeping suit, which was a Disney hand-me-down from some distant cousin. He added his small face towel and some underwear and socks. His favorite pants and the best of his T-shirts followed, along with the new stuff the Ambassador had bought him. Already the bag was full. He slid the Hulk comics on top and then sat on the bed, next to the bag. A wave of self-pity brought a lump to his throat, and he almost started crying.

Luckily, Rais entered just then. He sat next to Indelbed and wordlessly went through the bag.

"You might want a coat," he said.

Indelbed, who had no coat—who needed a coat in Dhaka?—shrugged it off. Rais, who was riffling through the closet, seemed to realize his mistake.

"Or a blanket maybe," he said. "Or this sweater?"

The sweater was less bulky than the long quilt he used as a blanket. He compressed it into the bag and pulled the zipper.

"I think I'm ready," he said.

"Take this." Rais pulled out his Nokia cell phone and a black charger. He pushed them into Indelbed's hands. "Look, I've entered my number under Rais and my mother's number under Juny. She said you should send us a text every day. Just to keep in contact. And you can call either of us if you need anything, even in the middle of the night. She'll come get you."

"She said that?" Indelbed looked dubious. Aunty Juny had previously shown a positive aversion to receiving calls from him.

"Look, I'm not sure I like sending you away with someone we don't know," Rais said. "And mother doesn't like it either. It's important you send a text every night. Give us a progress report. Don't worry about the phone bill, I'll be paying it."

"Okay," Indelbed said.

"Do you want to say good-bye to your father?"

"No," Indelbed said. "I already saw him, when I was getting the bag."

Rais gave him a long hug and helped him down. There was nothing much else to do. The Ambassador patted his shoulder and gave him a five-hundred-taka note. He added some vague instructions. Aunty Juny just glared at all of them and said nothing. She seemed angry, at whom he could not decipher.

Butloo had managed to find a yellow cab, which was parked on the main road. He carried Indelbed's luggage up to the car and seemed a bit teary-eyed. Indelbed had never particularly thought about the man, but he considered that it might be said that Butloo had, for all intents and purposes, pretty much raised him until now. Certainly he had been a more reliable figure than Kaikobad. On impulse, he shook Butloo by the hand and pressed the five-hundred-taka note into his palm. Butloo gave him a deep salaam and a sad smile.

The driver honked once. Siyer was getting impatient. Away from the others, he had dropped some of the theatrics in his manner. His movements were brusque now, his face cold and tired. Indelbed got into the backseat beside him, and they drove off.

The apartment in Mirpur was next to the zoo. Indelbed had never been to the zoo, so he craned his head around to see if he could catch a glimpse of anything interesting. Siyer was sleeping, his face scrunched up against the dirty side window. He looked considerably less impressive now. The taxi battled its way to the pavement, stopping abruptly. An irate *rikshawala* was tipped to the ground. Indelbed woke up Siyer, got out of the cab with his luggage, and waited on the pavement. For a moment the Afghan glared at him, and then he grudgingly paid off the driver.

The apartment building was an old redbrick affair with grilled balconies hung with washing. Some of the windows had air conditioners hanging out, staining the walls with the discharged water. The man at the gate looked at them suspiciously, but Siyer's grandiose manner had returned somewhat, and after some key waving and broken Bangla, they were allowed in. There was a dirty, decrepit lift, the floor blackened with the grime of countless sandals and bits of rotten food.

GU Sikkim's apartment was shabby and small, with two cramped bedrooms, a kitchen, a drawing room, and a dining room all set along a central corridor. Indelbed could see down the length of the entire apartment from the front door. It had a musty, unpleasant odor. Siyer stood at the door, the very picture of disgruntlement. He seemed unwilling to go in. He was clearly used to finer things. Indelbed looked back and saw the Afghan's expression change suddenly from disdain to fear.

A heavy fist grabbed Indelbed by the neck, literally swinging him around. He looked into the face of a bald, glitter-skinned man, squat and powerful, somehow toad-like. His mouth glinted with something unpleasant. In his gut, with the absolute certainty of a child, Indelbed knew that this was, at last, the promised djinn.

"Come in, emissary," the djinn said. "I'm sure you recognize me."

"Matteras..." Siyer closed the door mechanically. He seemed to be in shock.

"You will appreciate that this situation is quite serious," Matteras said. "I am willing to make accommodations with you, emissary."

Siyer said nothing. The grip tightened inexorably around Indelbed's neck, making his blood pound in his ears. Up close, he noted with horror the needlelike rows of teeth crowding the djinn's mouth. The hot gust of his breath smelled of kerosene and something burned. For a terrifying moment he thought the djinn was going to bite him. It seemed inconceivable that he would survive this. His lingering hope that Siyer would do something useful was dashed when the emissary meekly put his bags down and stood still.

"You, boy, are coming with me," Matteras said.

Those demon fingers tightened even more; Indelbed squawked in pain and then mercifully passed out of all consciousness.

CHAPTER 8
Kaikobad

Kaikobad woke up in the dark. It wasn't really waking up, more of a gradual erosion of unconsciousness, a brick-by-brick accumulation of thoughts until a tenuous gathering of self was achieved. It wasn't terribly different from waking up from a bender. His first instinct was to reach for the bottle, a habit ingrained for ten years or more, an immediate hair of the dog to stave off the crushing hangover. He then realized that he had no bottle and no hand, that he was, in fact, disembodied entirely. His second realization was that he was sober, all the way—crystal-clarity sobriety, like a TV signal suddenly becoming good—not confused or hungover or buzzed, but actually god-awful sober, and bodiless, he did not even feel the craving, felt nothing physical, just a cold certainty that he was sharp, his mind whirring at speeds unknown any time the past ten years.

This brought its own problems, of course. He had cause to drink. There was nothing wrong with his memory of the hospital bed in the crappy clinic—the only place safe for a djinn birth—and the gynecologist, an ignorant fool, a homeopathic quack but easily bullied. He himself had brought his wife there, racked with pain, and watched her bleed out in front of his eyes, his frantic calls for help unheeded. And who could help? Who knew at all that djinn were vulnerable during birthing, that half-breeds could kill coming out, that the nascent field of the newborn negated the mother's, making her temporarily mortal, an Achilles' heel that no one had written about.

The grief and regret crashed on him in waves, as raw now as it was then, and he craved the obliteration of alcohol, almost wept for it. She had warned him, had tried to steer him away from the normal human urge to replicate. Djinn lived for centuries; they had no overarching drive for offspring, for their immortality was stitched into their own sinew. He had wanted a son, a daughter, something to remember their union by, for his years would be short and hers indescribably long, and over the course of her djinn life stretching into infinity, he would have become a road bump, a brief dalliance, one mortal husband among many, half forgotten over centuries of ennui. Perhaps subconsciously he had struck against that immortality, had secretly wanted to bring her low for a time, make her step fully into the messiness of human life, the business of bleeding and pushing and bone-crushing pain. Ironically he had succeeded far too well, had stamped out her djinnness, left an indelible mark on her life by ending it abruptly. Death by Indelbed. Had she guessed, perhaps, his secret desire, but acquiesced anyway? Djinn were maudlin like that, prone to gestures of deep sentimentality.

He had not been prepared. Not to be alone, not to raise a child.

"Indelbed!" The cry came out involuntarily, but he had no voice, so it just reverberated in his own head.

His more immediate memory ended with a phone call from his cousin, some farrago about schooling, and then a blank. He had gone to sleep and woken up strange. Had he passed out? Where was Indelbed? He couldn't see. There was nothing to see actually. How did one tell the difference? Being blind and inhabiting a place with absolutely no light amounted to the same thing. So he moved, untethered as he was to the physical world.

Whatever had happened to him had fixed his brain. Concern for Indelbed now overrode his grief. He had marked Indelbed. He had woven spells around the house, had begged and borrowed favors from powerful djinn for protection. Yet something had happened to him. Disembodiment was not normal. He was not delirious. This was something else. He had not left the house—that last memory confirmed it. He remembered cradling the phone to his chest, one hand curled around his glass. Had something broken in? If so, then Indelbed was alone and vulnerable, the house no longer ironclad. Was it Matteras, come to exact vengeance for a myriad transgressions? It must have been. Who else could break wards like water?

Hesitantly, he drew on the field, trying properly for the first time in ten years, and the power came cleanly, without the hint of madness, like a cold drink of water. Whoever had broken him had unwittingly given him a fair exchange. More than fair, for he had traded his husk of a body and his alcohol addiction for perfect clarity of mind and an abrupt return to his full magical potency. The field twitched around him, responding to his will, hinting at malleability. Disembodied, he could move fast, although there were no markers, just a sense of the field shifting, like he was floating in dark waves, in a vast, directionless black ocean. Movement was just a flicker of the imagination, an instinct.

Still, there were flavors here, and far away he felt a hardened point, a point of distortion, something else here, perhaps something similar to him. If he was in the field he was not dead. He did not worry about his body, did not worry whether he was dead, or severed, or in some in-between form. Djinn orthodoxy claimed paradise for all djinn, the superior race, a special heaven just for them, and it was left at that. Others had speculated that the field itself might store information, perhaps even the souls of the dead; might be a layer of reality laid atop the physical world, entwined in it, and physical law was like an onion. He had once been interested in these things, before love and death and alcohol had proved much more powerful than the dry lure of intellect.

And now, a deep-rooted longing, an almost physical need to hold his son, came over him. It was Indelbed he looked for, desperately, trying to conjure up the essence of him, counting the ways he could have survived whatever had attacked the house. There was nothing but that faraway node, so he made for it, and the arrival was almost instantaneous, or time was piled up on top of itself; either way, he found himself in front of a structure. It was a giant door. This was not a physical thing. In this place, there was no matter as such, only energy. Still, he could discern this was a gate. The sheer size of the distortion was what had drawn him. It was a choke point, like fine muslin drawn through a ring.

It was locked, but not against him. He went in of course—what else could he do?

It was a paper shredder. The thing elongated his mind, or whatever information matrix he consisted of, in the field, and then crushed him to a singular point, and then let him pass, rendering him safe and jumbled up, a ball of alphabet soup. It took a long time to reconstitute. But on this side there was no progression of time; time was compressed on top of itself without thought to causation and all things happened in disorder, so it turned out that, in the end, he had all the time in the world.

When he regained consciousness for the second time, he was still in the field, but beyond the gate. This place had structures, other information matrices he could discern. It was like trying to read a machine language. There was an internal logic to it, clearly, but he did not have a Rosetta stone, nothing to start code breaking, not even a single point of reference. He floated toward them, through them, touching structures that could not be altered.

Inert. They perhaps represented nonliving things. They did not respond to him in any way. Size was misleading here. He had inflated himself to his maximum ability, but could not gauge yet the relative dimensions of anything, what these things were, how big they stretched. Perhaps he was like a fly, not yet worthy of swatting.

He went back to the gate and compressed himself, looking small, trying a different tack, and the darkness shifted to a more focused, detailed surface of the field, behind which loomed the gigantic bulk of the ring gate. He enjoyed, for a moment, a sense of wonder at this place, the ease with which the field responded. It was like flying after a lifetime of trudging through sand. *I should have given up my body a long time ago,* he thought.

He found a small monument by the gate. It seemed statuesque, upright, in his mind, like the sphinx, or one of the big statues at Luxor. It was not dead or, rather, was not completely inert. He speared his thoughts toward it, hoping there was a method of communication here as easy as telepathy.

"Hello," he said. "I am the emissary Kaikobad. Kaikobad. Magician of Bengal. What are you? Who are you? Are you alive? Am I alive?"

There was a pause, and the creature regarded him. It was most definitely alive.

"I am Thoth. Of Gangaridai. I am the Captain of the Road."

"Thank god," Kaikobad said. "What road? Do you mean that ring gate?"

"I don't know," Thoth said. "I don't know if that is the road. The road I was meant to guard was the Bone Road, the Charnel Road. I have not moved, but the road has moved away. I cannot find it."

"Something happened to me too," Kaikobad said. "I lost my body. I woke up here after a drink. I think this is the field. Are you djinn? Or man? Or something else?"

"I am djinn," Thoth said. "Djinn of Gangaridai. I guard the road. You say you lost your body?"

"I was attacked, I think," Kaikobad said. "Destroyed by my enemy. Or partially destroyed, anyway. I don't think this is where the dead come, for we appear to be alone here."

"Perhaps I too was attacked. I have forgotten many things. I think I am damaged. No one has come this way for a long time. Or a short time. I cannot tell, because time is nonlinear here. Do you think I was attacked, and the road taken from me, much like your body?"

"It could be, friend," Kaikobad said. "I am looking for my son. Or I'm actually hoping that he is still alive, still in the real world, and I can help him somehow."

"I am looking for my road," Thoth said.

"Yes, but my problem is more immediate," Kaikobad said. "My son might be attacked and killed any second. Can you help me? I will then help you find the road, if I am able."

"And if you find it, you must help me guard it," Thoth said, with a degree of cunning. "Our enemies might come up the road, and we will stop them."

"Fine, I agree," Kaikobad said. *What road, you insane creature?*

"That is a good bargain, friend Kaikobad," Thoth said. "If your son is in danger, I will certainly help you. It is the right thing to do."

"The question is how. What manner of place is this?"

"I do not know all the laws of this place," Thoth said. "It reflects the real world. It is perhaps a parallel in the field of the physical world. The gate is the key—the gate that you entered. What was on the other side? I have never been able to cross over. Is the real world on the other side? It is so close."

"No, friend," Kaikobad said sadly. "Outside was worse. There were no structures, no boundaries, nothing. It was like a black sea, featureless. To swim there is to drown."

"I thought perhaps this was the afterlife," Thoth said. "Although there is no one else here, no one else conscious at least. Or perhaps this place is so vast that we—"

"What about the gate?" Kaikobad interrupted. "You said there was a key?"

"If you step inside the well of the gate, you get visions," Thoth said. "Memory shards of the world, or futures, or alternate possibilities, I cannot judge. If we search, we may find your son."

"So we are going to look at random memories? Whose memories?"

"The memories come in streams, like rivers of connected events, and we must latch on when we spot something familiar."

"How long is this going to take?" Kaikobad asked, aghast. "We might be literally looking through the memories of every djinn who ever lived."

"What does it matter, how long?" Thoth said. "We have nothing but time. If you look long enough, you will find your son—if you are strong enough, if you can stay inside long enough. Are you ready?"

"I guess."

"Be prepared. It is a deluge."

CHAPTER 9
Underground Parties

Indelbed woke up in pitch-blackness. It was not the shadowy darkness of night, but an actual, absolute absence of light. His head ached fiercely, and pain lanced up and down his spine as well as in all his extremities. It hurt to breathe. Bruises in his back throbbed fiercely. Something sharp pounded in the base of his neck.

Indelbed was no stranger to physical pain, but he realized now that all his previous experiences had been childish. This was serious *adult* pain. It occurred to him that he had been dropped into some pit by the djinn and left for dead. He moved his fingers and toes, instinctively testing for paralysis. He tried to raise his head, but all sorts of alarms went off.

He dozed off again and woke thirsty, nauseated, and still in approximately the same amount of discomfort. This time he rolled over onto his hands and knees. The headache, at least, had subsided to a gray wash of dull background static. He was on rough clayey ground. Everything was wet and clammy. He found his bag next to him and hugged it tightly. The soft leather was extremely comforting. He unzipped it and found the cell phone. There were no bars of service, but at least it switched on.

The dull glow of the screen revealed a dismal sight. He was somewhere deep underground, at the bottom of a well, it seemed. A dull dark cylinder of air rose above him. Matteras must have thrown him down the shaft. There was not even a sliver of light above. The walls were stone or possibly concrete. Indelbed knew nothing about wells, but he had never heard of stone being used for anything in Bangladesh.

He felt slightly disappointed. Death by djinn should have been entirely more spectacular than this. He looked and decided that this was not, in fact, a well, at least not a functioning one. First of all, there was no water. The ground was slimy, but more from some kind of underground moss.

Second, as he swiveled the phone around, he found a four-foot-high vaguely roundish passage gouged into the wall, sloping down. It was narrow and Indelbed had to get on his hands and knees to fit comfortably.

The tunnel went on for some time, sloping down, perhaps switching back even; it was impossible to tell because the cell phone light faded after a few feet. The air smelled funny. There were no sounds, but he did not for a second doubt that there was something unpleasant awaiting him.

After some dithering, Indelbed decided to continue on. The crawling was slow and quickly became painful. In addition to the aches and pains, the wheels of the bag kept clipping his toes. He started shivering. Hunger and exhaustion threatened to drop him. He wished he'd put on the sweater. He thought of Rais and tears welled up.

The minutes dragged into hours, and he became a mechanical beast, following the downward curve. He could no longer tell directions. His mind had long ago shut down; he felt no fear, no panic, nothing other than the marathon runner's simple compulsion to keep stepping on. The claustrophobia no longer bothered him, nor the darkness. He had turned off the phone long ago. It was a trance state of putting one hand in front of the other, of crawling on. Stopping meant dying, quite literally, since he assumed that if he lay down he probably wouldn't get up again.

Eventually, he fell again, this time down a steep curve. It was a series of small falls from ledge to ledge, rather than any kind of slide. It took him down much deeper underground. His body flopped around, bruising like discarded fruit, but nothing fatal happened. Jacked up on adrenaline, he got to his feet after the last bounce with something approaching a grin. By the light of the indestructible Nokia, he saw he was in a low cavern.

It wasn't very large because he could almost see the entirety of it, but it was considerably roomier than the well shaft he had first woken up in. There was a pool of black water ten feet from him, still and profoundly deep. The raging thirst welled up in him and he dove at the water, dunking his head, drinking long draughts. The water was clean and cold. He imagined that this is what the water bottlers had in mind, when they advertised deep spring mineral water.

The adrenaline had given him a second wind. He walked around the pool and saw numerous tunnel offshoots at different heights. These shapes were clearly not human-made and filled him with dread. He could not imagine what manner of creature lived here. He could hear nothing, but the silence struck him as ominous.

He was halfway around the pool when he noticed that one of the tunnels was glowing with some kind of light. He blinked several times and turned off the cell phone. It was very faint. He could not be sure. Shadows seemed to be moving against the wall, dark on dark. He stood still for a long moment, willing the light to sharpen. Then there was a flicker, and he felt like cheering. *Light*. Perhaps someone was there.

He moved toward it, unheeding. He managed only two steps before his ankle turned on something round and he collapsed facefirst. His nose hit something hard. Instinctively he turned on his cell phone and screamed. He was face-to-face with a skull: roughly humanoid, with elongated eyeholes stretched at the top and a grinning, leering mouth darkly empty, where scraps of flesh still hung like ragged curtains. There was something birdlike here, a crested ridge along the top of the head like a bone Mohawk, and Indelbed was so close he could see the little circular teeth marks all along the ceramic blue, the crosshatched scoring of calcium on calcium, where some grinding circle-mouthed predator had repeatedly raked the surface for flesh.

He swiveled his head and saw that the rest of the skeleton was all around him, far too many bones for one person. There was something akin to an arm, finger bones stretched elegantly on the floor, the index finger pointing at him with mild accusation. Another part of the body curled around, and it was an impossibly long spine, the rib cage tapering into a series of smaller, fitted bones, leaving a snake's tail coiling around the dark, bits of cartilage still stuck in the hinges. It was an obscene creature melded from disparate animals.

It was too much. Something in his body switched off. He grew lightheaded, either from fright or exhaustion, and sank to the floor. He closed his eyes to try to still his heart. Within seconds he was fast asleep.

He was woken up by a cripple. The first things he saw were two stumpy legs ending at the knee bone, bound by dirty rags. It did not faze him. There had been a beggar of similar proportions who had occupied the drain outside their gate in Wari. Indelbed had often given him food and scraps of clothing. The man had been remarkably philosophical. His legs had been broken by choice, as a sort of professional investiture. He had once confessed to Indelbed that he actually earned quite a bit of money and even had a retirement fund in the bank.

"Ah, you're awake," the cripple said.

"Water," Indelbed said. His mouth was almost gummed shut. "Light." This was more of an observation. There was a small light hovering near the cripple's head, an amorphous blob of dirty yellow that floated above his hunched shoulder like a particularly seedy angel.

The cripple poured water into Indelbed's mouth. The cup was a piece of hollowed-out bone, heavy and irregular. Indelbed saw that they were in a kind of circular nest that would have been cozy under different circumstances. The cripple must have dragged him from the main chamber. He wondered briefly whether he was about to be eaten. There were tools here, of bone and rock, which spoke of some long period of domestic effort.

"Water is plentiful," the cripple said, proving somewhat omniscient. "Food, on the other hand, is a bit more problematic. Not to worry, boy, I still have a bit left over from dinner. We will hunt when you are recovered."

"What are you?" Indelbed asked.

"I am the Ifrit Givaras." The legless djinn tried to draw himself up. "Philanthropist, historian, anthropologist, *biologist*, at your service."

"Are you thinking of eating me?" Indelbed thought it best to get this out of the way.

The djinn pretended to examine him minutely. Up close, Indelbed saw that he had a gaunt, mostly human face, marred only by two stubby horns sprouting from the top of his head, nothing sharp or threatening, just two studs worn with age into a deep rich color.

"Hmm, not much to you, is there?" Givaras said. "I suppose I will have to pass. You won't taste very good, I can tell. Stringy."

"Where are we?" Indelbed asked. He had a list of questions he wanted answered and was determined to waste no time. Givaras looked like a nice guy, but his experience with adults had shown him that they were mercurial and prone to getting irritated when pressed for vital information.

"We are in a murder pit, dear boy," Givaras said. "Somewhere underground in Sylhet, if I'm not mistaken."

"Murder pit?"

"We djinn are very civilized," Givaras said. "We don't like to kill each other in public. Massive loss of auctoritas and all that. Goes against the Lore, the Mos Maiorum, as the Romans coined it. They were great copiers, the Romans. This murder pit is our little game."

"So someone put you in here?"

"Matteras," Givaras said. "An ingenious pit, this one. I will congratulate him on it, if I ever get the chance. Yes, Matteras. He and I had a difference of opinion. I should be flattered, really, that he bothered, given the vast height of auctoritas separating us..."

"Well, did he put me in here?"

"He must have," Givaras said. "This is, after all, his murder pit."

"Why?"

"We will try to figure that out presently."

"What was the snake thing outside?"

"Ah, the skeleton that so frightened you. That was the noted Ifrit historian Risal," Givaras said. "You screamed, you know. I came to you as fast as I could." He pointed at his stumps. "That scream saved your life."

"The head looked eaten," Indelbed said. "I saw little tooth marks."

"Rock wyrms," Givaras said. He looked glum. "Beauty of this murder pit, really. The rock wyrm is the larva of the earth serpent, or earth dragon, as they are sometimes known. Of course the dragons are so rare that they are almost mythical. The rock larvae are rare in themselves. They are the ones who have dug these tunnels in the rock. They are omnivorous—they eat each other at the drop of a hat. They are attracted to our distortion fields. Stronger the field, greater the attraction. Cunning plan, eh? The stronger the Ifrit Matteras stuffs in here, the quicker the rock wyrms will swarm."

"These wyrms ate your friend?" Indelbed asked. "But why was she like a snake?"

"She was trying to change," Givaras said. "We can do that, you know, although shifting shape takes a long time and a lot of effort. She was very powerful. I warned her, but she thought she could withstand the wyrms long enough to shift form. Was trying for a wyrm shape herself. In the end she only got halfway there. As I said, the rock wyrms eat distortion fields."

"Why are you still alive then?" Indelbed asked suspiciously.

"I am exceptionally weak for an Ifrit," Givaras said. "I couldn't even begin to shift into a rock wyrm, even if I wanted to. The best I could do were these horns. They are useful too; I can sense the vibrations in the ground with them." He pointed at the smudge of light hovering over his shoulder. "This is my real discovery, however. The light, see? The wyrms hate it. They have eyes that are not fully functional yet. This wavelength of light really burns them. This is why your arrival is so fortuitous, actually."

"What do you mean?" Indelbed had visions of Givaras trying to make a lamp out of him. The djinn did not look particularly threatening, but then, he didn't look particularly sane either. If it weren't for the dead snake thing outside, Indelbed wouldn't have found any of this story credible.

"Survival is not really a one-man job here." Givaras pointed at his legs. "The light has to be on all the time. Every time I fall asleep, the rock wyrms keep coming. I've lost both my legs to that..."

"They ate your legs?"

"It is rather tedious," the djinn said. "It hurt a lot, and I was ever so weak afterward. I can probably grow them back, but I'm afraid that much distortion will call down a whole swarm of them."

"I'm not a djinn," Indelbed blurted out.

"Hmm?" Givaras looked puzzled. "You're wrong, you know. Matteras wouldn't make a mistake like this. No use throwing humans into a murder pit. Why bother? Mos Maiorum doesn't forbid killing humans."

"They said my mother was a djinn," Indelbed said. "I never met her. She died giving birth. But I've always been human." He said this last part to clarify any doubts this Ifrit might have. He didn't seem to be the sharpest of djinns, despite his ingenious get-your-legs-bitten-off survival strategy. "I didn't even believe in djinns till now."

"You're not fully human, you know, whatever you are. The air in here, not really suitable for your sort. You should be dead by now. Asphyxiation," Givaras said. "Rather odd that Matteras stuffed you in here. A bit insulting to me, really."

"They said my father was an emissary."

Givaras tapped his head significantly. "Ah, politics then. Who was your father?"

"Kaikobad."

"I don't recall. What family is it?"

"Khan Rahmans," Indelbed said. "We're not the rich ones, however." He always liked to clarify that at the onset, to avoid disappointing people.

"And your mother?"

"I don't know her name. Father forbade any mention of her. I don't even know what she looks like. I just found out she was a djinn two days ago."

"I see."

"I don't see," Indelbed said. "They said this djinn called a minor hunt on me. And then this emissary friend of my father's came to help me, except he took me right to a place where the bad djinn was waiting. The bad djinn tried to eat me and I woke up in here."

"Hmm, there are clues in your story, you know," Givaras said. "Now I've been locked up here for a long time, so I'm not up to date with the exact politics. But I can deduce. The minor hunt is the first big clue. You see, djinn family units are not nuclear, like you humans. We are tied more along clan lines, or lines of patronage. Parents, siblings, et cetera, do not have any excessive feelings for one another. The minor hunt—a sort of culling of the younger members of a clan—was originally a practice used to remove the misshapen or aberrant djinn from the bloodlines. Djinn are long lived, you see, and even the hideously deformed ones can survive to pollute the gene pool.

"Since you're a half-breed," Givaras said, "your status is undecided. Whoever called the minor hunt on you was effectively making a statement about you—was in fact according you djinn status. It is possible they were trying to help you..."

"By calling on adult djinns to kill me?"

"It's political. There have long been two lines of thought among the djinn. An argument of creationism versus evolution is one way to look at it. The exact nature of human-djinn offspring has long been a point of contention," Givaras said. "I believe things are coming to a nodal point—a cycle of rapid change, if you will. We djinn have seen that societies tend to undergo rapid, *exponential* change in certain cycles. I myself have long wondered why Matteras dropped me in this splendid murder pit. His choice of other victims has confirmed certain suspicions. Your own arrival leads me to a theory that I will share with you—"

"Wait a minute," Indelbed said. An awful thought had occurred to him. "How many others have been dropped here?"

"Not counting ourselves, there have been three victims," Givaras said. "I shall take you to study their remains when you are better. I have saved their bones for a rainy day."

"And they were all eaten by the wyrms?" He was still a bit scared that Givaras was a cannibal.

"Yes, they did not adopt the light trick," Givaras said.

"How long have you been here, exactly?"

"Well, seventy years at least, by my count." Givaras smiled. "I lost a bit of time in the middle, when I went mad. It was the endless chattering, you see. I'm so glad you're here..."

CHAPTER 10
Mastery of Light

"The mastery of light is the only pertinent lesson in life," Givaras said.

Indelbed had woken in the same nest, with the djinn hovering around him. He was shivering. The djinn seemed to be impervious to the chill leaching through the stones. Indelbed put on his sweater and changed his socks. He felt the urge to brush his teeth, then realized that he would most probably never have to do it again. The thought was not as cheering as he would have liked.

"Breakfast?" Givaras asked.

Indelbed was starving. He would have fallen on a bed of broccoli and torn it apart with his teeth. He would have slurped up fish head curry and eaten the fish heads too. But the wyrm larva meat Givaras offered him was on a whole other level of disgusting. The carapace was hard and segmented, with crazy patterns made by the constant scoring of rock on chitin. Givaras had used a sharp stone chisel to break into the joints of each segment to get into the soft flesh inside. This had the putrid smell of a carnivore's back teeth; it was a grayish mass of vein-encrusted meat that the djinn ate raw, chewing methodically through every bite.

"It's actually very good stuff. Lots of protein, lots of vitamins," Givaras said. "And god knows what other benefits we might accrue. You must remember that these are the larvae of creatures that might well become some kind of dragon in the far future."

Indelbed sat dully staring at the djinn. A segment of carapace sat on his lap, upturned like a plate, the meat quivering like a small hill of Jell-O. He had once had Jell-O at a family gathering; it had been marvelous. Later, he and Butloo had tried to re-create the Jell-O from a packet, but they had managed only a watery mess. Possibly their oft-repaired fridge was not capable of freezing it properly.

Givaras took some pity on him. "Look, what if I cooked it a bit, eh?"

He clamped his hand on the larva plate. Indelbed choked back a scream as the plate suddenly got too hot to hold. The djinn's hand glowed red, as if a flashlight were pressing into his palm, and for a second Indelbed could *see* the distortion field at work, and this brought home the insanity of his situation more than anything.

Givaras returned the carapace to him with a flourish. This time the meat was charred along the outside and smelled faintly of overripe bananas. He was so hungry that he didn't hesitate anymore. Givaras let him eat in peace, holding off on any discourse with obvious impatience. Indelbed reflected that conversation was possibly what the djinn hungered for most after his long solitary confinement.

He napped after eating, and then woke up and ate again, feeling slightly better. Givaras had spent this time making a kind of bed for him, using loose dirt and a ring of rounded stones from the water. It was a small thing, but it brought tears to Indelbed's eyes.

Fully recovered now, he took the guided tour. Their sleeping chamber was the largest niche, a collapsed tunnel shaped carefully by the djinn. It tapered off into an alcove, where Givaras stored all of his extra carapace segments, dried strips of cartilage, and chipped mouth parts.

Back across the cavern, a deep-pitted niche served as a latrine and compost. Givaras had ringed this space with plates from wyrm carapace, the edges fused together with heat to prevent leakage and contamination of the water source. He used the compost to grow wild mushrooms along the banks of the pond, a crop of various edible fungi that augmented the meals of wyrm meat. Mushrooms fried in wyrm oil was a firm favorite on the menu.

Beside the farm there was a largish nook for a workshop, a makeshift larder with a shallow reservoir of water, and a number of other fancifully titled niches, including a library of Givaras's own works etched on shell and a map room. Everything was made of wyrm parts or bones: knives cunningly fused from teeth; rope from dried tendons plied together; chisels, shovels, hammers, and picks from a variety of bones; and even a set of slightly creepy duvets made of inner membranes pressed together. Indelbed was most impressed. The djinn had clearly not been idle.

"You have djinn blood, you are djinn," Givaras said, when they returned to the nest. "You can see the distortion field when I use it, correct?"

"Yes," Indelbed admitted.

"That is an indication," Givaras said. "This vision is not granted to humans. You have sensory apparatus in your brain that is not normal."

"I heard djinn are made of fire and humans from mud," Indelbed said, remembering some garbled religious lessons from Butloo.

"That, my dear boy, is literature. What I am interested in is science! Evolution, dear boy, is at the root of our existential crisis," Givaras said. He seemed to have no notion of Indelbed's age and treated him exactly as he would a slightly dim-witted contemporary.

Indelbed found this refreshing. When the elder djinn's musings became incomprehensible, he just let them wash over him like a soothing lullaby. Givaras was a kindly conversationalist, however. He never failed to repeat himself.

"Evolution. It is the bane of our existence."

"Existential crisis?"

They would spend long hours doing random things, and when the silence became oppressive, old conversations would be restoked like promising coals.

"Us djinns," Givaras said. "By and large, we believe in divinity. The Great Creator. One God. One of our greatest schisms is the old divide: Are we unique or are we, like man, the product of evolution? That is the root of our existential crisis: the very key to our racial pride, our entire attitude to the physical world."

"Evolution says men came from monkeys, right?" Indelbed had seen something of this on television. Also, Rais had taught him the rudiments of Darwinism in one of his rants. "And those giant turtles on some island, right?" He knew turtles were involved somehow. The whole thing intrigued him.

"All physical life on this world share the same genetic markers, the same genetic chemistry," Givaras said. "That alone is irrefutable proof that all life is related. The Creationists among the djinn maintain that we are superior creatures not of this earth. The Evolutionists, such as myself, believe that we too are an unlikely manifestation of the usual collisions and mutations of the messy thing that is life."

"And the turtles?"

"Wonderful pets, turtles," Givaras said. "I myself had one for a time. A giant brute. I used to ride him around in the water. He tried to eat me several times. Come. Let us look once again at Risal and reflect on the valuable lessons of survival."

Looking at Risal was a ritual they indulged in with some regularity. Their day was boring enough, and the tunnel end, while providing some degree of safety, grew cramped and fetid after some time. The open cavern with the black pond was a pleasant, if risky, spot to promenade.

"Look at Risal, swarmed in the full glory of her power," Givaras said, as they stood over the skeleton. "How many conclusions can we reach from her pitiful condition?"

"Don't do magic in a nest of worms?" Indelbed did not like going into the technical details of the distortion field. It sounded like magic to him.

"Hehe, yes," Givaras said. "That is, of course, the primary lesson. Risal died because she was too powerful. I survived because I am weak. When I realized this, I became weaker still. That is what we must achieve with you."

"Me?"

"The light," Givaras said. "You must learn to make the light." He pointed at the stumps of his legs. "Remember, the light is the only thing keeping the worms away. If the light fails, we are finished."

"You think I can do magic?" Indelbed had some doubts about this part of the plan.

"My dear boy, I am almost certain of it," Givaras said. He seemed supremely excited by the prospect. "And what's more, once I teach you, it will further prove my hypothesis."

"Which is?"

"A theory of everything: physics, evolution, our own place in this universe," Givaras said. "Topics the djinn do not wish to explore."

"Was she your friend?" Indelbed pointed at Risal. It bothered him somewhat that they were using her bones as plates and glasses, among other things.

"Risal? She was, in some ways," Givaras said. "We were part of the same club. We shared the same interests. As I said, she was a lot stronger than me. That gave her far greater dignatas. Come, let us look at the bodies of the others. They too died in various states of change. The wyrms get agitated by strength, as you know. I will relate my theories to you."

Indelbed rolled his eyes. Givaras was big on theories. "When will you start teaching me magic?"

The magic did not come easily. It was weeks before Indelbed could even understand what Givaras was saying. At first he had to master the basic tasks of gathering food and water. The threat of the wyrms kept them on edge. Givaras's method of hunting was extremely risky too, and food was necessarily scarce. He would select a tunnel and turn off the light. Then he would send out a beat of magic, a kind of siren signal in a mathematical pattern. Wyrms would come, larvae of different stages. Even the smallest ones were dangerous.

They made a kind of grinding, shuffling noise. It was one of the most terrifying things in the dark. At this stage, it was a matter of simple luck. Givaras would turn the light back on suddenly. The wyrms would all freeze. The idea was to seize the smallest one and kill it, the smaller ones having breaks in their carapace. Givaras had a tool made from Risal's ulna, a bone sword. Most of these hunts were unsuccessful. Some of them had resulted in serious injuries for Givaras.

The light destroyed the wyrms' delicate eyes. If they ever grew to sufficient size, they would enter a different level of development and the light would cease to be a deterrent. Eventually, they could become dragons. If any of these things happened, it would wreck the fragile eco system in this underground cavern. It would certainly result in both Givaras's and Indelbed's deaths. To the best of Givaras's knowledge, no new dragon had been born on this planet for at least twenty thousand years. It was indeed highly speculative whether these wyrms were actually dragon larvae at all or just some other species altogether.

It was Indelbed's job now to wield the bone sword. He was much weaker than the djinn, but with two intact legs, he was a sight more agile. It was riskier for Givaras. The wyrms did not use vision to hunt. They were drawn to the brilliance of the distortion field. Only the djinn lit up on their sensory apparatus. Givaras was the bait, and it was on Indelbed to make a kill as quickly as possible, before any of the wyrms actually reached the djinn. It was a gruesome, dangerous job. Indelbed took to it with a certain glee. It occurred to him that he might be eaten, but this seemed such a bizarre thing that he found his courage buoyed by an unexpected recklessness.

The hunting of rock wyrms was ideally a two-man job, and once Indelbed got the hang of it, their food supply improved drastically. The magic took a lot longer. For weeks they would practice hours at a stretch. Indelbed imagined the distortion field as a lattice of molecules around him. He could put up a few points like tent pegs, but his concentration inevitably failed and the whole thing collapsed in sparks. (It reminded him of his dad teaching him algebra at age six, the sheer impossibility of it, the unexpected patience Kaikobad had shown, and this made him feel weepy and miss the Doctor, and wonder, as he always did, whether he had ever woken up from his coma, whether he remembered he had a son and was out looking for him somewhere. It was always a comforting fiction, that someone outside still loved him.)

"Keep it up, don't worry." Givaras was always cheerful. "You're over-thinking it. It should come naturally. I think I might have to hypnotize you."

Indelbed, who had no intention of allowing any of this, hastily assured him that he was on the verge of a breakthrough.

"Not to rush you, dear boy," Givaras said, "but it's getting to be a bit of work keeping the light on for both of us."

He finally got it during an almost trance state brought about by extreme tiredness. It was like a mental click, a moment of perfect balance, when some organ in his brain suddenly started working properly. The distortion field blinked on like a nest of fairy lights, cocooning him in every direction. A feeling of warm bliss came over him, an airiness akin to floating in water in the center of a still pond.

These wonderful feelings didn't last long. Givaras cuffed him hard on the head, making him spill over. He was about to shout when the look of panic on the djinn's face made him pause.

"Congratulations, congratulations," Givaras babbled. "Really must turn that off, though. It's like Eid for the wyrms…"

"Did you see that?" Indelbed asked. "It was beautiful!"

"You did it, very nice distortion field," Givaras said. "I remember my first one, I spent the whole day knocking things over with it. You've got to be careful now, though. No time to be childish. You must learn to make the light, and *never* use the distortion field for anything else. Remember, if the wyrms come, the light is your only defense."

The light took even longer to master. The urge to float around in the distortion field was almost overpowering. Givaras was onto him, however, and kept a vigilant eye. It took months to get the light right, to adjust the various strands of the distortion field just *so*, and then to understand how to tweak wavelengths and colors and densities. The things a djinn did instinctively had to be learned step by conscious step.

"First time in sixty years," Givaras said, when Indelbed finally got the light floating above his left shoulder. "First time I'm turning this off. Keep yours on, mind you."

He had a look of pride on his face that made Indelbed's eyes water. The light promptly went off, of course, but Indelbed's skill was hard-won: once he knew how to do a thing, he knew it forever.

"My aunts really hated me." Indelbed liked to reminisce, not least because it gave him respite from Givaras's incessant lessons. "Most of the uncles were pretty nice. I wondered why the aunts didn't like me, but then Butloo once explained that maybe they were scared they'd be asked to take me in or something. I told you about Butloo, right?"

"Ah, yes, your butler. A very grand life you must have had up there," Givaras said.

"Yeah, not really. I mean I guess the Ambassador and GU Sikkim and Uncle Pappo and all the others had a pretty grand life. I never saw much of it. Plus I never got to go to the real fancy parties, you know? Butloo told me you had to have a car to go to those, and of course, they wouldn't want a rickshaw pulling up to the gate in front of their friends. I wouldn't have minded going around the back or eating in the kitchen; it's the food that I missed. Butloo said when my grandfather the judge was alive, they used to have big parties at home and everyone used to drink champagne and dance. I think Butloo made that up. He only heard it from his father, so it's not like he saw it either."

"Well, dear boy, there will be no dancing here, I'm afraid," Givaras said, indicating his lack of legs.

"Haha, of course. Do djinns dance, though?"

"Oh yes, we invented all the best dances. We can dance weeks on end."

"Like those swirling guys in skirts?"

"Whirling dervishes," Givaras said. "Yes, they're copying us when they do that."

"I've never seen any dancing," Indelbed said. "I think Aunty Juny knows how to dance. They lived all over the world, because the Ambassador was an ambassador, you see. Rais told me that. Aunty Sikkim is really fat, I don't think she can even walk much. The other ones are kind of fat too. Aunty Juny used to hate me, I thought. She was mean all the time, but then I watched her, and she was mean to everyone, so it wasn't just me."

"She sounds like an interesting lady."

"Rais gave me her phone number." The Nokia was his prized possession here, the battery long dead, but otherwise in pristine condition. "She didn't want me to go, I think. Rais told me that. She never said anything. No good-byes or anything. But she looked angry. I think maybe she looks angry when she means sad, like her face is mixed up."

"Humes are complicated," Givaras said wisely.

"I wish..." Indelbed said. "I wish she had tried harder."

"My theory is this," Givaras said. Not having to keep the light on had removed a visible quantity of stress from the old djinn. Indelbed powered the light now all the time, except when he slept. The strain and effort had faded with months of long practice. It was second nature now.

"Mind you, don't go quoting my theories to the public. I'm something of a heretic. You might get your head cut off, haha."

"Well, we'll probably die here anyway."

"Quite right, quite right," Givaras said. "Well, my theory is that matter in this part of the universe exists in different forms, some of which interacts with each other and some of which doesn't. Human physicists have theorized the same thing, clever boys; it is what they call dark matter and dark energy. Of course those names are catchalls for some very distinctive types of particles, but they will suffice for now. You with me so far?"

Indelbed, who had heard more scientific claptrap over the past year than he ever had a desire to think about, could only nod wearily. It was not until they got into the higher mathematics of Givaras's "work" that the urge to sleep always became too strong to resist.

"Imagine that these different kinds of matter exist in the same space but do not affect each other. So when you move your hand through what you think is empty space, you are in effect going through some sort of 'dark' or 'other' matter, except neither you nor it can feel each other. I imagine they are particles or quanta of energy that do not interact at all with regular matter, unless under special circumstances." Givaras backed this up with vigorous hand motions. "This, of course, is how the distortion field works. It is a manipulation of dark matter. A djinn, in my opinion, is simply a creature who can manipulate two radically different kinds of matter."

"Right," Indelbed said. "So it looks like magic, but really I've got a dark matter hand that is going around knocking things over."

"Well, it's not really a hand . . ."

"Of course it's not a *literal hand*." Indelbed tried to head off another fruitless tangent.

"But how, you might ask, did the djinn evolve such a useful and unlikely ability? Which dread organ allows this 'magic'? Which terrible forge was this... er, forged in?"

"I might ask," Indelbed said, suppressing a groan. There were times of extreme boredom when he was half tempted to let loose the distortion field and have the swarm eat him, if only to enjoy a bit of peace.

"It is obvious that the djinn physically exist in two different planes of existence," Givaras said. "The djinn are, in fact, made up of two different kinds of matter: the physical matter of this world and the dark matter of some other. The dark universe, I surmise, is one of more energy and less physical matter. Thus my body, and even your own, has some organs that are *made of dark energy!* Now isn't that exciting?"

"Er, is it?" Indelbed let his creativity roam. "Do you think I have a dark penis? I mean another one?"

"You utter philistine," Givaras mourned. "Of all the punishments Matteras has inflicted upon me, you, undoubtedly, are the worst!" He said this, however, with an affectionate cast to his eyes, which never failed to make Indelbed slightly teary. "I was thinking of our eyes. We can see constructs made out of the field. At the same time, we can see the visible light spectrum of humans. How remarkable that the same sensory apparatus can interact with both types of particles. It leads me to believe that when we manipulate the dark matter energy particles, our distortion fields somehow alter their fundamental nature, allowing them to interact with the physical matter of this universe. We are a gateway between two fundamentally different planes of existence!

"Now how, you might ask, did we receive this beneficence? Why are we djinn so exalted as to exist on two different planes, whereas the rest of the world drudges along in the physical world? Is it a sure sign of the Almighty?"

"God?"

"Not at all!" Givaras said. "As I wrote in my thirty-fourth treatise on this subject, it is, in fact, evolution! We are not at all unique. We are merely rare. There are other animals, other forms of life that are similar to us, that carry components of both kinds of matter. Indeed, there might be more than two kinds of matter, who knows? What if there is a third, a fourth, a fifth type of matter, all of them occupying the same space, none of them interacting with one another? Could it be that when we are alone, we are in fact walking through an infinite crowd? Needless to say, the djinn do not like to explore this idea, since it might blow up their natural sense of superiority."

"So you've got like djinn turtles?" Indelbed was still sure that turtles came into this somehow.

"And irony of ironies! Matteras himself has proven me right," Givaras said. "For what do you think these rock wyrms are?"

"They can see the distortion field," Indelbed said. They had had this conversation before.

"Precisely!" Givaras said. "They are like us! They too exist on different planes. In some distant past, whatever mechanism created the first protein molecules also created molecules of two different types of matter joined together. Binary molecules, I call them. When unitary life formed, so too did binary. Imagine little binary cells manipulating dark energy to protect themselves. Imagine protozoa made of binary cells with tiny distortion fields! Imagine—"

"Is that a rock wyrm over there?"

CHAPTER 11
Kaikobad

Kaikobad stood on a tall tower, at the very lip, looking down until vertigo seized him. He could have fallen unhurt, for he was merely a ghostly observer in this place, but he stepped back. It was unpleasant to fall or burn or be damaged in the hundreds of different ways he had endured since the visions had started. The mind did not easily accept disembodiment.

A crystal city glittered beneath: domes and towers lit up by the setting sun, balconies suspended in air, wide streets paved with marble, delicate bridges arching over running water, merchants floating on carpets, carrying fruits and wine, winding through the branches of a great tree in the very center. Humans and djinns cohabited in plain sight—bargaining in the market square, smoking on street corners—peaceful, unhurried.

In front of him, two of the flying carpets collided, a fender bender of sorts, one of the irate passengers nearly falling off, and a crowd gathered—djinn floating up in their fields, a magician swooping down on the back of a seagull—to watch the threats of lawsuits, attempts at mediation, and testimonies of eye witnesses, all jumbled up in a great Babel of conversation.

It was a mawkish dream of a city, sanitized wishful thinking that made his lip curl. Where was all the shit, the sewers, the beggars; where was the grimy crystal underbelly of gamblers and whores; where were the perverts and drunkards?

"It is the First City," Thoth said, beside him. "Is it not wondrous?"

"I want to see my son," Kaikobad said. "Not this shit."

They were in the field, and the field carried memories, or copies, or perhaps the actual thing itself, the Platonic ideal of the thing that projected onto the real world—it was impossible to tell. Thoth had shown him how to see it, to read the particle script, but the guardian himself knew nothing more, could not choose what they saw.

"Patience," Thoth said. "The stories carry their own logic."

Kaikobad blinked, and the scene changed. He was on a field of snow, at the edge of a frozen lake. An armored djinn rode past, close enough to touch. His breastplate was bone white, like enamel, perhaps carved from ivory, invested with rings of power, leveling up with the rising sun. He carried a spear the height of a man, the haft corded with human hair, an oversize crescent blade made of dull metal weighing down the end. The djinn rode across the lake, heedless of the cracking ice, the hooves of his destrier beating divots into the surface. He was chasing something, and Kaikobad followed him unseen, easily keeping pace, a pale ghost for a pale rider. The djinn caught his prey at the far edge of the lake, a ragged woman wearing simple hide clothes stained with dirt, her hair braided with elk bones, and as Kaikobad looked closer, he found a bulge tied to her back, a newborn baby tightly bound with rawhide, the head bobbing between her shoulder blades.

With sickening slowness, the rider caught them, and the great spear casually ran her through, piercing both child and mother in a single thrust. Dark red blood arced across the snow, and Kaikobad could hear the snap of bones breaking, as the warhorse trampled over the bodies. The djinn did not stop.

"Kuriken!" Thoth said, catching up. "He prefers solitude. The Elk tribe strayed into his demesne, so he killed them. This woman was the last."

"He is a murderer," Kaikobad said. "He was then, and he is now."

"He was our best warrior. They used to say that Gangaridai would never fall as long as he held the gate."

"What happened then?"

"He stopped holding the gate," Thoth spat.

"I am sick of this. I can't take too much more."

"You are tired," Thoth said. "We have scryed for days."

"Days? Who can tell? There is no time here," Kaikobad said with a laugh. "My son could already be dead."

"You love him dearly," Thoth said. "I am envious."

"You never loved anyone?"

"Djinn do not love like that, I think," Thoth said. "Or perhaps it is just me. I did my duty. I took pride in that. When it was time to guard the road, I stood up, I swore to stand there forever, and I did, I think."

"Until you landed up here," Kaikobad said. "Wherever the hell here is."

"Perhaps it *is* hell," Thoth said. "And we are the only two denizens."

Kaikobad stared at him. "You have a very strange sense of humor."

"The gate shows you what you want to see," Thoth said. "Perhaps it is Gangaridai you truly search for."

Kaikobad fell silent as the awful truth of this crashed through his mind. He railed at the gate, throwing himself at it, pushing against the waves of feedback come from it, willing himself to swim through it, to reach the core. It was like fighting the tide. He returned to the shore no matter how far he went. *NO. No. Indelbed, where are you? I want to see you. I love you, my poor son, I have always loved you. Haven't I? I didn't leave you, did I? I can't remember your face anymore. How old are you now? I can't remember, you were a baby yesterday, a little silent thing, never crying, never hungry, watching me with djinn eyes. The gate is wrong. I searched for the city, yes, the City of Peace, the City of Death, where else would I find my wife? But not at this price. Never for your life. I would give a hundred Gangaridais for your life, Indelbed, I swear.*

"Come, friend," Thoth said afterward, when his weeping had subsided. "Let us try again. Perhaps this next vision will be peaceful and ease your heart."

They were now inside the First City again, in one of the glittering chambers high above the ground; windows lined with crystal reflected the sun in wondrous ways, channeling the light into the far depths of the tower. These djinns of old were profligate with their power, for there were signs of magic everywhere in the city. From the windows they could see fountains spewing water into the air, sculpting shapes that held for brief minutes, before crashing back down. Great trees rivaled the towers in each neighborhood, their canopies spreading shade and color across the sky. The city itself was threaded with cool sea air, a breeze that ran perpetually through the streets, chasing its own tail, calming tempers on even the hottest days.

"This is the court of the High King," Thoth said. "See him there upon the throne."

The High King wore a scarlet mask, and the rest of him was swathed in so much power that he appeared formless, indistinct, as if he existed in many different states at the same time. This chamber was stark, unfurnished. There was no need for embellishment in the face of the High King's awful puissance.

"He passes judgment," Thoth said. "I myself have stood in this chamber many times. I once served as his advisor, before the war came."

"The djinn in my time hate kings," Kaikobad said. "They are unruly. They do not accept authority at all."

"Anarchists!" Thoth said. "I am thankful I am not from your world."

A gargantuan djinn squeezed through the archway, bending almost double to fit. He was armored in gold plate so bright that it hurt Kaikobad's eyes to look at him. His beard was ringed in gold, and gold lay upon his brow, a thin circlet. He carried a great sword inked with blood, flecked with the remnants of recent use. He bowed before the king, a slight genuflection that showed more contempt than respect.

"Memmion," the High King said.

"I have come," Memmion said. "As you asked."

"Once again you break the peace. You murder in cold blood. This is not what I wanted," said the High King, his voice atonal behind the mask.

"I dueled to the death, as is my right."

"This is the City of Peace. Your barbarity cannot continue."

"I cannot change my nature," Memmion said. "And I cannot bend the knee."

"Cannot or will not, it is all the same," the High King said. "Why do you continue to defy me? What is it you want, Memmion? They say that you love gold. I will give you minefuls. I will give you a mountain of jewels from Lanka, all the incense in Babylon. Just alter this course of destruction you have put us on."

"I want to rend djinn from bone to sinew!" Memmion said. "I want to crush Nephilim joints between my hind teeth! I want to eat the meat off your ribs. I want to tear the towers down and let the jungle grow over the bricks. Give me this, and I will be happy"—he bowed mockingly—"High King."

"We are finished then," the High King said. "You must leave. Exile."

"You keep your fine city," Memmion said. "The wilderness is mine. I take the rest of the world. I exile *you*. You and your effete lords. Come outside at your own peril."

"Your sword cannot hurt me, Memmion," the High King said. "Go now."

"I am not alone," Memmion spat in parting. "Others rise. Horus is with me."

The doors closed, and Kaikobad was alone with the High King.

"Horus," he said from behind his mask. He sounded troubled.

CHAPTER 12
Wyrming Out

Givaras loved theorizing, lecturing, and generally pontificating, but he was oddly reticent about his own life. Indelbed thought the djinn had probably been lonely, without friends or family. He spoke incessantly about politics, however, trying to teach Indelbed the various nuances. Indelbed didn't have the heart to tell him that he was seventy years out of date and probably all those things had changed. Or perhaps it hadn't. Djinn seemed to spend a lot of time sleeping or just loafing around.

"You see, very early on we had the imperials versus the republicans, which is to say the argument of empire versus anarchy, order versus chaos," Givaras said. "Now republicanism started more as a voluntary association, a loose gathering of like-minded djinn who joined forces to achieve some single project and then disbanded. What it means now is very different in human terms, because, as usual, humans have corrupted everything. But in the pure form, we were really arguing about rule versus nonrule, and lucky to say, nonrule won, because otherwise you'd be living in a very different kind of world."

"Well, we're both stuck in an underground prison," Indelbed pointed out. "Can it get much worse?"

Givaras pooh-poohed this suggestion out of hand. "Then over time, we started getting a conservative party who valued the Lore, sometimes to a literal extent, and was very eager to 'return to the way things were,' which is funny, because possibly most of them have no idea how things actually were and would not like it at all if they went back to it. In any case, what they really mean is that they are antihuman and wish to limit the growth of our coinhabitants on this planet. Intersecting with them are the Isolationists, who wish to avoid all contact with humans in order to better conserve 'djinndom.' These are the people particularly bent out of shape with human currency. They feel dignatas is being diluted. Again, how they intend to avoid humans altogether is beyond me. Then a further subset of the conservative movement are the Creationists, who follow the most rabid doctrines and are my avowed enemies. They believe that djinns were created perfect, that the world was in fact created as a gift for djinndom, and that all other life on it is simply put there for our amusement by God. This is backed up by a bunch of pseudoscience and a lot of ranting."

"It seems like all djinns like ranting," Indelbed observed.

"Humph. Instead of being a smart-ass, I'd pay attention if I were you," Givaras said. "Now that you are djinn, you will need to know all of this. A young djinn your age would be drinking in politics with his mother's milk. Of course, you never had a mother."

"Well, you've got no legs."

"I suppose we are a fine pair."

"I don't miss learning djinn politics at all," Indelbed said. "And I didn't like milk. Not even the chocolate kind, which Butloo got me once. I don't remember my mother, so I guess I don't miss her either. I definitely don't miss my father. I miss the trees. I wish I could sit on my roof and watch it rain. Have you ever seen that? Our street was full of trees. They'd be all dusty during the day, but when it rained, the leaves would get clean, and everything would be shiny, and it would smell great. And rain hitting your skin? It's like a shower, only a hundred times better. You never worry about trees, you know, until you're stuck without them."

"You are a good boy, to be worrying about trees."

"Well, I didn't have too many friends, because of not going to school, I reckon," Indelbed said. "But I miss Ali, from next door. We used to play marbles. He mostly won, so by the end he would have all of them and I would have none, but then he always gave mine back. I think he felt bad because he had a lot of marbles to begin with. His mother made really good korma. That's like chicken curry but much better. She'd give me some whenever I went over. I didn't go over that much, though, because whenever Ali came over we only gave him rice and dal. He didn't like eating it. If I had money I used to buy biscuits for him. Then Butloo could give tea and biscuits to us. I like the toast biscuits with jam. Or condensed milk. That was pretty good too. You ever had condensed milk? It's like a thick concentrated milk and it's so sweet that your teeth hurt."

"I have not eaten any of these things," Givaras said. "But your words are making me hungry, and we are low on provisions. On to the hunt!"

The hunt always cheered Indelbed up. It was now a much-anticipated part of their routine, and it was during a hunt that they made their break-through. It wasn't Indelbed who thought of a way to escape, but he claimed a little of the credit, as the idea resulted directly from some of his foolhardiness. In an attempt to enliven the now rather boring mechanisms of the hunt, Indelbed had taken to trying various tricks and embellishments, one of which involved him jumping on the back of a wyrm and trying to ride it like a bronco.

After doing this maneuver several times, they realized that the wyrms, having never encountered this problem before, could not easily get a rider off, nor did they have a clue as to what to do in that situation. Indelbed, tucking his knees behind the flaring ridges of the segmented carapace, could easily avoid the useless gnashing of mouth and general thrashing around.

This was not, of course, particularly useful, although it was quite fun. The wyrms eventually just retreated into their holes, at which point he had to jump off or get *scraped* off. Givaras in particular was a chief proponent of this sport; while his legless condition made him unable to participate, he was always keen to offer suggestions on form and scoring.

Indelbed was at first surprised by Givaras's ready acceptance of an obviously reckless and unnecessary pursuit, until he realized from various anecdotes let drop by his mentor that djinns in general were a thrill-seeking and foolhardy race, quick to accept bets and challenges of all sorts, and seemingly given over wholly to pursuing pleasure. They could also regrow most limbs, which took the sting out of possible injuries, not withstanding the massive loss of dignatas that normally ensued.

"You are gaining dignatas, you see," Givaras said. The djinn having explained this invisible currency to him, Indelbed was happy to pile up the kudos. "If only there were others here to see your skill! It would spark off a new craze! A veritable new fashion in sports, I don't doubt it."

"Djinns play a lot of sports?" It seemed rather frivolous of these dread creatures.

"Oh, we love sports," Givaras said. "Whale surfing, giraffe racing, ostrich baiting—why back in the day they used to ride pterodactyls. Dragons! Some of the old-timers are always going on about riding dragons, although many say that's pure nonsense..."

A look of such cunning suddenly came over Givaras's face that Indelbed was taken aback and let his light go off, which momentarily plunged them into darkness and presaged the distant rumble of a predatory wyrm. Restoring order, he found the djinn bent over several discarded carapace shells, touching them thoughtfully.

"How are you enjoying your time here?" he asked absently.

"Er, fine?" Indelbed answered. *Aside from the boredom, the murderous wyrms, the constant threat of cave-ins, the gnawing irritation of keeping the distortion field leashed in, the awful food, the stench of rotting meat, the mad conversations...*

"I mean how would you feel about going outside?" Givaras asked.

"Escape?"

"Yes!"

"Are you mad? Of course I want to escape! Why haven't you said anything before?" The awful thought occurred to him that perhaps Givaras *liked* being here...

"It has just occurred to me," Givaras said. "A flash of brilliance! A plan of such outrageous dignatas that we will be positively showered with adulation once we are outside. An intellectual coup of such audacity that—"

"Well, what is it?"

"I have noticed, in the midst of your antics, that the rock wyrms possess individual markings along their carapace joints, much like the unique patterns shown by the Derigoz birds, alas extinct—"

"The plan please, Givaras!"

"And that unconsciously, you have been favoring this character." Givaras held up a bit of shell that had been scraped off earlier. "This gold-and-brown God's-eye pattern. You've been favoring him as your steed, probably because he's the biggest and slowest, therefore presenting the least threat. Also, I've been noticing that lately your runs have gotten easier, because he is not thrashing about as much. What does that tell you?"

"He's learning?"

"Precisely!" Givaras looked pleased. "Somewhere in his wyrm brain he's realized that you're not a threat so much as a nuisance, and the fantastic expenditure of energy required to throw you off is not warranted. Moreover, he's realized that all he has to do is retreat into a tunnel, and you'll be forced off anyways. All this gives us two vital pieces of information: a) these wyrms are individuals—we can differentiate between them, and b) they are capable of rudimentary learning and have some degree of functional memory."

"Very fascinating," Indelbed said, slightly dejected. It seemed as if the escape plan was in reality a cunningly disguised lecture on wyrms.

"Now what do you think these wyrms eat?"

"Other wyrms?"

"Well, yes, among rock and sand and other things," Givaras said. "They are omnivorous at this stage. Now I suspect that these wyrms are earth dragon larvae, as mentioned in our histories. They should, given unlimited food, grow to their full potential. And what happens then, I ask you?"

"They get really big?" Indelbed said. His eyes got bigger. "They become something else?"

"Yes!" Givaras said. "Like the caterpillar, these rock wyrms will move from larval stage to adolescence. They will leave the incubation of the earth and seek the balmy comfort of water: riverbeds, my dear, riverbeds, estuaries, ocean mouths. That is the next step. For that, they must burrow; they must make a passage up to the surface."

"And we could follow them!"

"Yes," Givaras said. "The problem, I suspect, is that these wyrms never leave the larval stage. Evolution has caught them out. Some imbalance in their food source has resulted in their physical stunting. Thus, they live and die as worms in truth, never fulfilling their glorious future."

"So they're hungry," Indelbed said. He began to see the light. "And we keep one, like a pet, and feed it! The brown-and-gold one, who's bigger already, who can remember stuff! We kill the others and keep feeding him until he becomes a dragon!"

"Right!" Givaras rubbed his hands with glee. "I told you it was stupendous. Well, he won't be a dragon yet, he'll probably be some kind of river wyrm. Yet even those are unheard of these days. Can you imagine the entrance we'll make?"

"We're going to escape on the back of a dragon!" Visions of glory flooded his mind. Naturally suspicion took over. "Wait a minute. How long will this take?"

"We have to feed him enough to metamorphose." Givaras smiled. "Can't be much longer than ten more years?"

CHAPTER 13
Surface Tension

In London, Rais lived above a sweet shop in Brick Lane. He liked the sweets. The Sylhetis housed and fed him for cheap, in return for minimum rent and help in maintaining their accounts, basic stuff that he remembered from his two-semester stint at Northwestern. His parents hadn't been impressed with that particular decision. Dropping out of expensive business schools was a thing that stretched even the Ambassador's bonhomie. They'd cut him off for a few months in despair. Familial love had been somewhat restored when he had transferred to SOAS, to try his hand at a new city, a new continent. By this point, they just wanted him to finish something, *anything*. Anthropology, archaeology, Japanese boatbuilding—anything that ended in a degree.

Looking for a place to live, he found the Sylhetis online. They thought he was an immigrant and, touchingly, were very proud that he went to SOAS, often bragging about him to their friends. They were also interested in marrying him off, considering him almost a default Sylheti, and kept shoving pictures and bios of eligible girls at him. They were well-meaning, good company, the younger ones hilarious (sophisticated and cynical at the same time). It was the sheer number of them that defeated him sometimes.

On Friday, he ate ramen alone in his room, as he typically did. He ate in silence, reading a book and fanning himself in the heat. If the Sylhetis detected him, they would force him down to join in their three-hour-long family meal. He finished all the forkable bits in his Cup Noodles and then drank the soup. When it was all gone, he stood up reluctantly. Then he threw away his cutlery and unplugged the microwave, wiping the inside. There were a few objects on his desk, things he had picked up on his trips: a stone from the temples in Karnak, where he had spent weeks one winter trying to read the hieroglyphs; a small round-bellied fertility statue from

Angkor Wat; beads from the Mundeshwari Devi Temple in Bihar; a little rock from the Feroz Shah Fort in Delhi, where people gathered to write letters to the djinn. He touched them a few times, mementos of failure, for he had never found any of those creatures, seen nothing but charlatans and madmen. He swept it all into the trash and emptied his little can into a garbage bag. He did a final sweep through the room, dumping papers, an errant sock, an old toothbrush, an empty cologne bottle, his collection of half-finished soaps and shampoos. There was a pile of pennies in one corner, and he stacked them nicely on the table. Finally he stripped his sheets and pillowcases, balled them into the clothes hamper. The room now looked exactly as he had found it.

His suitcase was a battered Mandarina Duck his mother had given him a few years ago. It was already packed. He sat on his chair and wrote a short note, mentioning his address in Dhaka and the promise of future visits.

His ride to the airport was covered on Uber. He had cash in his pocket for the rest of the night, enough to close the tab at the bar and then one last splurge in town. He put his ear to the door and listened to the cadence of the footsteps outside. He could tell from the creaks on the narrow stairs who was coming and going. When he was sure the path was clear, he sneaked out for the last time. He felt a brief pang leaving like this, but had they been preinformed, they would have insisted on feasts and farewell speeches and quite possibly a shotgun wedding to Mina, the very pretty third daughter of the house he had secretly hooked up with. It was just easier. He left them all little notes, and a much longer one for Mina.

He took the tube to the Bernard Street station and then walked through Russell Square, saying good-bye to the SOAS buildings he had come to love. He lingered in various spots, exchanged words with passing acquaintances, and eventually wound his way to the bar. The stage upstairs was giving off strange noises, some ethnic band gearing up to play. Soon the place would be thick with people, the smokers spilling out on the streets, hugging the stairs, and the bar below would be swamped. Mercifully it was still half empty.

He smoked half a Marlboro outside and went in, hoping Achike was tending bar. She was alone, propped up with a book. She waved at him, and he sat in front of her, as he had done a hundred times, and ordered a beer. She was half Nigerian, half something else, typical of SOAS, where you could find almost any mongrel mixture if you looked hard enough. It was her accent he had loved at first, that sarcastic lilt that made every joke funnier, every drunken pronouncement a scathing indictment of the world. Achike was fiddling with her tap, but she paid attention to him eventually, frowning.

"What?"

"What?" Rais raised his eyebrows.

"You look sad, man. I thought you passed everything."

"Yeah, couldn't drag it out any longer. I thought Easton would fail me, but the fucker refused. I didn't turn in the last two papers, for god's sake."

"Easton wouldn't fail a lobotomized hamster. Well, congrats. Drinks on me."

"Thanks."

"You seem depressed."

"I've been doing postgraduate studies for six years in three different universities."

Achike shook her head. "Your parents are angels. Fucking angels."

"I ran out on the Sylhetis. Not a word. Not one good-bye."

"You're an absolute dick." Achike knew about the Sylhetis. He'd taken her to tour Brick Lane once. "Wait, what do you mean you ran out?"

Rais took out his ticket, slid it across the bar.

She stared at it. "You're leaving."

"For real."

"You didn't say anything."

"I thought about it."

"That's the kind of asshole you are."

"Achike, you know I love you, right?"

"Yeah, yeah, I've got tits and I'm a bartender, believe me, I've heard it—"

"No, I mean I've spent the last three months wishing I had the courage to ask you out. Properly. Never had the nerve."

"I knew that," she said quietly.

"So quit your shift. Come on, let's go drink somewhere good, let's go dancing, let's eat random food in the middle of the night."

She pushed his ticket toward him, touching the back of his hand. She took his drink and finished it. "Okay."

It was a great night, a proper good-bye. She took him home in the end, when neither was anywhere near sober. In the morning, he kissed her head, burrowed inside the duvet, and felt like crying. When there was no more time left, he wrote a letter on the back of her favorite book and left. He was finally going home.

When he landed Dhaka hit him with the smell of fresh rain, of wind and thunder on the balcony; with shiny leaves; with pluviophiles jumping in puddles and drinking tea on rooftops. He wondered why he had spent so long away. Then he went inside the airport and remembered some of the reasons. The main concourse was a microcosm of the country: a utilitarian building with little pretension, creaking under the weight of thousands and thousands of passengers, just trying to process everyone in a reasonable amount of time without anyone losing their temper. It was a cowboy sort of place where errant smokers might light up anywhere, the lines snaked for miles, and people regarded signs and instructions with blatant contempt.

The immigration lines were packed, the officers gruff with their own citizens, stolidly courteous to the foreigners. The laborers from the Gulf flights, collectively responsible for earning a healthy dollar reserve for the country by working abroad, were often incapable of filling out forms. They clogged up the lines and were repeatedly sent back for mistakes, shameful-ly harassed in their own airport. Rais helped them fill out their forms while he waited, as he always did, and marveled at the far-flung villages people came from, the sheer courage it must take to go to a strange desert land where you were hated and abused, treated like animals by so-called Mus-lim brethren. They were grateful for his help, though a little bit surprised that he bothered to wait in line instead of cutting ahead, but he had never really mastered the pure dickishness required to cut queues, so he just end-ed up spending the extra half hour chatting with his neighbors. When it was over he waited again for his battered suitcase and then strolled through the green channel, where customs waved him on, keeping their eyes peeled for more lucrative prey.

Rais was too old for anyone to receive him at the airport anymore, but his mother had sent her old driver, who sat rheumy-eyed in the parking lot, confident that Rais would find him. Rais wanted to have a smoke in the car, craving that morning hit of nicotine, but the driver wouldn't let him, so he ended up holding the cigarette in his fingers and sniffing it periodically.

He found his parents at the breakfast table. They made a show of keep-ing everything casual, as if he had just wandered in after a night out. They were scared he would spook and disappear once again, if they made a big deal about finally settling down. His father put down the paper, smiled, and offered him tea. His mother gave him an omelet. It was not their way, to be demonstrative. There was a pat on the back, slight fussing over his luggage, and he was back in the old pattern, eating the food put in front of him, stealing the sports page from the Ambassador, having a halfhearted conversation with each parent.

"Good to have you back," the Ambassador said, once they had lingered enough. "I have to go now, I've got some meetings. I'll see you for dinner. Uncle Ahmed was asking after you. He wanted some help in his office. I said you'd drop in."

"Yes, of course," Rais said. This was his father's way of getting him a job. There was never anything crass like an actual interview process or an application. The post would probably be extremely cushy, and Uncle Ahmed would treat him like a treasured asset. "I'll go tomorrow, if he's free." He had plenty of experience tanking "interviews."

"Vulu, let him get over the jet lag at least," Juny said.

"It's okay," Rais said. "Baba, I wanted to ask you about Uncle Kaikobad. Is he still in a coma?"

"Oh." The Ambassador looked surprised and then slightly embarrassed. "I haven't thought of him in years. Yes, I suppose he is. Pappo put him in a clinic. I think the trust picks up the bill every month. I'll have to ask Uncle Sikkim. They would have told us if anything had changed. Why do you ask?"

"I guess it was the last big thing that happened before I left. It kind of stuck with me," Rais said. "Any news of Indelbed?"

"No, no, of course not," the Ambassador said. "Look, just put him out of your mind. No use stirring up bad memories. The poor boy. He's long dead, though we never found the body. One shudders to think what this city is coming to. Look, Rais, I'll see you tonight."

"He does not like to talk about it," Juny said, when her husband had left.

"It seems like everyone has forgotten Indy," Rais said.

"I have not," Juny replied. "I still pay the phone bill."

"What?"

"The phone you gave him. I have paid the bill in advance for the next twenty years. I believe one day he will call."

Rais stared at his mother. "I didn't think you liked him."

"That's beside the point. Little boys do not disappear from the face of the earth. Not from *my* care."

"We should have done more to keep him," Rais said.

"They didn't search for him, you know. Sikkim wouldn't let me file a police report. I made them hire a private detective, but when he couldn't find either Indelbed or the Afghan, they stopped paying for him after a month. You were still in America then. I hired my own people. They combed the hospitals, the lakes, the borders, every place a child could be trafficked. Sikkim ordered me to stop. Ordered *me*, as if I were one of his simpering daughters."

"What did you do?" Rais asked, laughing.

"I gave him the look," Juny said. "And I told him that while I certainly appreciated his sentiment, actually obeying him was absolutely out of the question. It would physically kill me to lift even one finger at his command."

"You actually said that to his face?"

Juny gave *him* the look. "I see no reason to pander to his wishes anymore."

"Do you think Indelbed's dead?" Rais asked.

"I had RAB and CID investigate the Mirpur apartment three times," Juny said. "They found no trace of blood, no trace of violence. Yet there is evidence that both of them at least reached the apartment alive, however briefly they stayed there."

"You made RAB and CID investigate the case?" Rais asked in admiration. CID was the central intelligence department, a high-powered organ of the state. Juny's inroads into these organizations were quite impressive.

"They reported to me personally, off the record," Juny said. "Many people owe me favors."

"So what do you think happened?"

"I think the djinn kidnapped the boy," Juny said. "And I think the Afghan betrayed our trust. There are only three options: the djinn kidnapped Dargoman, killed him, or let him go. There was no reason to kidnap him. They did not kill him or we would have found the body. If they let him go, that can only mean he was on their side to begin with."

"If Dargoman is from an emissary family, can we not find his clan?"

"I have tried," Juny said. "The fact that he comes from Afghanistan makes communication difficult. There is some mention of the Dargoman clan, but no one has admitted to seeing or hearing from him. You have to understand that emissaries are extremely secretive."

"You have been busy," Rais said.

"So have you, son," Juny said. "You've traveled a lot."

Rais shrugged. "Normal tourist stuff before I settle down. Pyramids, temples, whatever."

"You also went to Palmyra, to Jerusalem and Petra, then to Pakistan, to see the ruins of Mohenjo Daro."

Rais raised an eyebrow.

"I keep track."

"I can see that."

"What have you been looking for, Rais?"

Rais shrugged. "You wouldn't care for it, I think."

"Try me. Perhaps we have been looking for the same things."

"Djinns," Rais said. "I've been looking for djinns."

"Is this why you can never finish anything or hold down a job?"

"Well, yes," Rais said. "I mean, how can you spend your life being an accountant or a lawyer or something, knowing that there are djinns walking around out there?"

"I wish you had told me," Juny said. "We have wasted a lot of time."

Juny led him by the hand to her study and unlocked the door. It was a small converted bedroom crammed floor to ceiling with shelves, the window closed off by a whiteboard, which she had covered on every available inch with names and diagrams. Other than lamps, the only furniture was a single round table in the middle of the room and one chair. Whatever she was doing was apparently a solitary pursuit. Rais dragged in a dining room chair. His mother locked the door after him.

"So secretive," he said, sitting down.

"I don't want the staff to think I'm crazy," Juny said. "They think I'm writing a book."

"What are you actually doing?"

"Look closely," Juny said. "I'm investigating djinns, just like you."

The books on the walls were occult histories, from crackpot fiction to studies by respected anthropologists. There were rare volumes in there, even books in different languages. She had Kaikobad's notebooks and the remainder of his entire library neatly cataloged, plus charts listing missing pieces as well as her own observations.

"He sold off so much," Juny said. "I've been trying to get it all back."

"Mother, this is incredible," Rais said. He was studying the whiteboard. It was an organizational chart of emissaries and djinn, their links, details of sightings, known associates, habits, aliases, even the most outrageous rumors.

"When I couldn't find Dargoman, I expanded my investigation to *all* of djinnkind. See, it's easy when you know for real that they exist. Once the curtain falls, it's possible to see their spoor everywhere," Juny said.

"Indelbed's mother," Rais said. "I can't believe my own aunt was a real live djinn."

"That's the tricky thing with djinn," Juny said. "They've lived among us for thousands of years. It's hard to find them unless they want you to." She took out a dossier. "Nevertheless, this is what I have gathered about her. She has a brother, called Matteras, who is a very prominent djinn, one of the leaders of the arch-conservative faction. I have tried to get in touch with him many times, hoping he would interest himself in his nephew, but to no avail. He is apparently antihuman."

"What about our own emissary position? Can we investigate Uncle Kaikobad's past for clues?"

"I have identified several djinn whom Kaikobad mentions by name in his notes. Deciphering those took two years, by the way; his handwriting was a marvelous example of cryptography," Juny said. "I have been writing to them, asking for information, begging for meetings, even bartering Kaikobad's auctoritas. So far I have received a couple of messages, but nothing significant. No meetings have been granted to me."

"That's it?" Rais looked disappointed. He waved his arm around the room. "What's all of this then?"

"I extended the search to emissary families. There, I have been much more successful. Emissaries still live in the human world, and they require real currency and physical assets. I have been able to identify and contact eight living emissaries in Asia. Five responded, and one of them writes to me regularly, in return for favors."

"Favors?"

"I got him out of jail in Singapore. He got drunk one night, broke into a mall, and fell asleep in a Starbucks. Naturally they took him to jail in the morning. The Singaporean consul here is a friend of mine. His brother-in-law happens to be a police officer in the Tanglin Division. Long story short, they let him off with a stern warning and a very big fine. Which I took care of, naturally," Juny said. "Much of what I've learned—names, relationships, et cetera—is from him."

"What about GU Sikkim? Doesn't he know anything about Uncle's past?"

"Your father and GU Sikkim have not been... helpful," Juny said. "They are the only ones who know everything. I believe they might be involved somehow. I am conducting this investigation in secret, which has slowed me down. If you join me, you must be clear that this is dangerous and might pit you against your own family."

"Mother, I have dreamed of djinns ever since that day," Rais said. "I can think of nothing else. I've wandered the earth looking for them. I can't go back to the regular world, get a nine-to-five job. I'm ready to do this. It seems like I've been waiting my whole life for it."

"You wish to become an emissary?"

"More than anything," Rais said.

"Are you absolutely sure? There will be no going back from this, Rais."

"I know."

"And your cousin? Do you want power or do you want justice?" Juny asked. "Let me be clear, my son. I believe a crime has been done, and it was done under my nose, it was perpetrated in my name, and this I cannot condone. He is our family. If he is still alive, I will bring him back. If he is dead, I'll make damn sure someone regrets it."

"Mother, do you want this because of what happened to Indelbed or because you hate being crossed?"

"It's the same thing."

"Mother, I swear that I will not rest until we find out what happened to Indelbed," Rais said. "I swear to God."

"Then let this be our cover," Juny said. "You will let your father know of your ambition to take the place of the comatose Kaikobad. I know something about the workings of emissaries. The rank is usually passed on within the same family, but it must be ratified by the djinn."

"So I can inherit Kaikobad's post?"

"That is the argument we can make."

"Is there an apprenticeship?"

"It is Kaikobad's job to train his own replacement," Juny said, "which he cannot do, obviously. He is also supposed to introduce you to a patron djinn, his own or some other sympathetic creature. Finally, you must go to Bahamut, who is one of the chief djinns of this region, a Marid of great dignatas. He will formally ratify you as an emissary by giving you his mark, the tattoo that Kaikobad has on his back."

"So we are stuck again," Rais said.

"GU Sikkim knows a lot more about djinns than he is letting on," Juny said. "You will start by pestering him day and night. I readily acknowledge that my understanding of Kaikobad was imperfect. His family portrayed him as an insane drunk. He was certainly that, but he was also a man of some genius. He was immensely well respected in some circles. You must impress upon Grand-Uncle Sikkim that our family would suffer a great loss of dignatas should we lose our emissary status. At the same time you must convince him that you are wholly his creature, willing to do and say whatever he wants. Remember, he loves money above everything. Let him know that you will share everything you get."

"You want me to play him! Mom!" Rais said. "You're a shark!"

"He's a pompous gasbag," Juny said. "He could never control Kaiko-bad. You saw yourself the contempt Kaikobad had for him. It will be very tempting for him to replace Kaikobad with yourself, a callow boy whom he can rule."

"Will he trust me?" Rais asked. "Will he trust *you*?"

"I will throw myself into your career. I will make it known that I am only interested in making you a grand success in the emissary world," Juny said. "They will think that having abandoned hope in your father's career, I am now focusing my effort on yours. You will lead Sikkim to believe that I have been training you to become an emissary ever since that day. I have a reputation for ruthlessness in our family. Hopefully he will dismiss my interest in djinn as vulgar ambition."

"Ammi-jaan, you are quite terrifying."

"Then remember never to cross me."

CHAPTER 14
The New Man in Town

It took several months for Rais to worm his way into GU Sikkim's trust.
The old man was wilier than he had expected, and on the subject of djinn, he seemed almost paranoid. At first, he would not even acknowledge the existence of djinn, even though it was now known that Kaikobad's own wife had been one. All manner of arguments failed. Rais was repeatedly told to drop this bullshit and join the real world. Even his father went so far as to forbid him any further discussion on this topic.

Rais, however, did not give up. He had a claim on the emissary post, however tenuous, and it was just enough to acknowledge a response from the secret world. He had his mother in his corner, and her active assistance was more than enough to combat any early disappointments. He kept chipping away at GU Sikkim, showing him the fruits of his research. Juny had opened lines of communication with other emissaries, friends of Kaikobad's, who were willing to speak to Rais. There were promises of help, introductions, even vague recommendations. Bit by bit, Rais pieced together the mosaic of Kaikobad's hidden life and his current status in djinndom.

Kaikobad was not dead. Yet he was not fulfilling his emissary role, on account of being in a coma. This was exactly the kind of legal kerfuffle that the djinn adored. All manner of solutions were being expounded from interested parties. One extreme group was even advocating that Kaikobad's body should be possessed by a minor spirit and brought back to animation to fulfill his role, until such time as his mind regained liveliness.

Rais's letters started doing the rounds. Juny had finally decided that the best course for them was a moderate one. To push for full emissary rights at this juncture would undoubtedly be rebuffed. Their carefully worded suggestion was that while Kaikobad was temporarily incapacitated, his duties could be taken up by his nephew, whom he had trained somewhat (a gross exaggeration) and who was very respectfully desirous of following his esteemed uncle's footsteps. The laws of primogeniture being subverted due to the mysterious loss of Kaikobad's son, Rais was, in fact, the closest living relative of the emissary. It was further argued (in subtle hints) that as Indelbed was himself half djinn, he could not be an emissary, and therefore this post was de facto Rais's in any case.

Rais's proposal had numerous merits. First, it was a temporary appointment, which allowed the continuance of the delicious legal drama occasioned by Kaikobad and his son. To the various djinn factions lovingly wrangling over this issue, it was imperative that no permanent solution be hastily enforced. A good legal battle was hard to find these days, after all, and this one had all the promise of lasting several hundred years.

Second, Rais being part of an emissary family, there was some precedence in the Lore for his stepping into his uncle's shoes. It also fulfilled the inherent djinn bias toward preserving bloodlines and ancient privileges. The long-lived race had a horror for all things transient and greatly valued keeping emissary families intact, so that they would not have to bother to learn the names and faces of yet another set of wretched humans.

Third, some parties were arguing that Kaikobad's dignatas, now dormant, could in part be "borrowed" by his nephew. This was a novel situation, and more than one djinn was taking credit for the idea. Hardly a day went by without some codicils to the law being proposed, new precedence being set, and heavy lobbying done behind the scenes to get ownership of any particular amendment. There was, of course, massive dignatas to be gained in adding an amendment to the law or, even more ambitious, contributing to the Lore itself.

Slowly, other emissaries started replying to Rais's queries. Djinns loved letters, and as Rais took care to flood the mail with fat sheets of creamy linen paper, djinns began to take note of him. His proposal was openly discussed in certain lower courts, his name dropped in salons and bars where djinn gathered.

The clincher came when he finally received a letter from the djinn Barabas himself, who had lately been Kaikobad's direct patron. This august personage invited Rais to meet for a discussion on various issues relating to the affairs of Kaikobad and possibilities therein. This was so close to a direct espousal of his cause that Rais howled in jubilation when he spied the cipher and seal.

At last, the world he yearned for was opening up. It was hard proof that the djinn really existed, that he and Juny had not been so far the victims of some cruel hoax perpetrated by unknown persons. It was direct confirmation that the hours they had spent had not been in vain. The seal of Barabas was a glyph made of blue fire that burned ceaselessly on the parchment and left the receiver in no doubt as to the authenticity of the communication. It also made the letter hard to read, and Rais had some difficulties, which included singed eyebrows and a badly damaged finger. Barabas apparently was of the mind that his words were sufficiently valuable to risk severe facial damage on the part of his correspondent.

The letter made a great impression on GU Sikkim. He knew at once its provenance, for he had seen before some communications between Kaikobad and his patron. He could no longer deny the progress Rais was making. It filled him with dread. He called for Matteras incessantly, fearing the response of the djinn who had so forcefully commanded him to scotch the entire Kaikobad affair. Matteras, however, had gone up in life since those days. It was beneath him to meet directly with humans, and this was a link he could not afford to expose. The end result was a tersely worded note to GU Sikkim, instructing him to "shut the brat up and make sure he stops meddling." At the same time Matteras threatened him with dire repercussions, including loss of property and life, should Barabas and his ilk get wind of any irregularities regarding Kaikobad and his dead son.

GU Sikkim, foreseeing the end of the Khan Rahman clan, at last acquiesced to Rais's new profession, provided he kept him appraised of everything and did precisely as he was instructed. It was made explicitly clear that henceforth, Rais would report directly to him.

It ended, or began, depending on perspective, with a grand party, as most such things did in the Khan Rahman clan. Birthdays, weddings, commemorations, religious festivals, promotions, funerals, and even divorces in the family were inevitably greeted with copious feasting and the consumption of staggering amounts of bootleg alcohol.

The party for Rais was a combined graduation *cum* first job celebration. It was held in Dhanmondi, in the lakeside house of Rais's aunt, the Ambassador's half sister. This lady, Aunty Amina, was a childless widow who had by dint of the complicated rules of inheritance come by a third of an acre of land in the middle of a most heavily populated and expensive residential area. The house was a small one-story building with a vast garden in the back. Garden was a misnomer, for it more closely resembled a wilderness.

It was the Khan Rahman custom to descend upon Amina's house for particularly big parties, all the luminaries of the same mind that if this prime piece of land *had* to be wasted on the nutcase Amina, the least she could do was host everyone. The Khan Rahmans in general were fond of overeating and dressing up. When they began to pile out of their cars in their rather opulent finery, passersby quite reasonably assumed it was a wedding. Rais, identified as the groom, was mobbed by the street people for money and only allowed to leave when a friendly traffic cop beat them back for a suitable bribe.

When Rais finally got inside, he was whisked away by the upper echelon of the clan into a private sitting room where Amina kept her late husband's personal effects. These included dozens of books on Marxism, a black-and-white TV, an arcane-looking radio, a gold-tipped cane, some different kinds of hats, and a peculiar stuffed ferret. Everything was coated with a thick layer of dust, as Amina felt no need to clean this mausoleum.

"We had to make a cover identity for you, my boy," GU Sikkim said with no preamble. "Same as we did for Kaikobad, of course, before he went a bit funny."

"Nothing glamorous, I'm afraid," the Ambassador said. There was a slight wistfulness in his voice. He had despaired of ever getting any useful work out of his son, and this new career, despite filling him with dread, was at least something tangible. "You're going to join an import-export business in Dubai. It will explain why you might be gone for periods of time and also your irregular workdays."

"And no one cares about import-export," GU Sikkim said. "It's so boring that no one will ever think twice after asking you what you do."

"This is real now, son," the Ambassador said. "Once it begins, you cannot turn back. You must be very careful. You will face strange and wonderful things, and perhaps terrible danger. What happened to your uncle and cousin should be warning enough for you. Tomorrow is the day you meet Barabas. Remember that you represent the entire family, the entirety of Bengal, even. The djinn will think nothing of annihilating us if you offend them."

"Even worse, they can ruin us all financially!" GU Sikkim could not help interjecting. "They own a lot of banking resources. Some of them are very money minded, dignatas be damned. You can gain great riches for us if you play things correctly. Kaikobad never understood this, and look what happened to him. Remember that your first duty is to bring glory and wealth to the family."

"Glory and wealth!" Everyone in the room spontaneously raised his glass to this toast, momentarily dazzled by future prospects. Then each gave Rais a present: a Calatrava watch from his father, which had belonged to his grandfather; a gold chain and jeweled *ayatul kursi* from his younger uncle, the Koranic verse written on a topaz instead of the typical gold coin; a gilded Koran from his father's cousin, who was a pious man engaged in the manpower trade to Libya; a beautiful Italian suit from his maternal uncle, who was an aged retired general and still remembered the times when all the officers were gentlemen and would have drinks at six at the cantonment bar. Uncle Pappo gave him a nice little painting from Kalidas, easily worth several thousand dollars. GU Sikkim, his mentor and confidant, came with a solid offering: the keys to the flat in Mirpur.

"You will need privacy now, boy," GU said fondly. "Can't have djinns traipsing around your father's house at odd times. It's not much, and the area is not what you're used to... I don't suggest you live there. I doubt a namby-pamby like you could ever survive outside Gulshan. Still, keep it for meetings and such, whenever you need to work. There is anonymity in Mirpur. No one will notice you there. The old caretaker is a loyal man. He will be your personal servant."

Rais, instilled with Juny's lively suspicions, thought that it was a very useful way for Sikkim to spy on his every move.

"Remember, son, everyone here has sworn to help you in any way possible," the Ambassador said in closing. "Always consult with us, so we may guide you."

The association of the djinn then all solemnly swore to keep everything secret and to aid Rais in whatever capacity they could. In return he salaamed each of them by touching their feet in ritual obeisance and further swore to uphold the honor of the family by placing his hand on his new gilded Koran. Rais had carefully worded his promise. The honor of the family also demanded an explanation of how a helpless little boy had disappeared from their midst so many years ago.

They all dispersed then, grinning like a sackful of monkeys, each anticipating glory and wealth, a manifold return on their investments tonight. If Kaikobad had disappointed them, it was certain that Rais would make good. After all, wasn't his mother the most practical and ambitious of women, and was not his father a good and rational man? It was all about breeding. Any son of the viper Juny, they thought, could not help but be successful.

CHAPTER 15
Coffee with Barabas

Coffee with Barabas was slightly anticlimactic. They met at the newly opened Gloria Jeans café in Gulshan 1, which was routinely packed to the gills. Rais drove his father's car and had to spend half an hour looking for parking. Shaking with nerves, he ended up grazing a rickshaw and spending another ten minutes placating the passengers. By the time he got inside, he was in a terrible panic.

Pushing his way through the crowd, he realized, absurdly, that he had no idea what Barabas looked like. He had assumed the djinn would be enlivened with blue fire or something—hardly possible, now that he saw the café was filled with perfectly normal-looking people. Feeling stupid, he nodded to the manager at the door and was about to ask him if he had seen a djinn, when a large hairy fist grabbed his shoulder.

He spun around to face a giant mullah in sandals and a sweat-stained shalwar, beard and hair dyed red, and fingers full of multicolored rings.

He grinned, and his teeth were orange and repulsive. "Good, eh?"

"Barabas?" Rais blurted out.

"Yes, little envoy," Barabas said. "Let's get some coffee. I like the sweet icy ones. And some pastries. You're buying." He looked around craftily.

In a slight daze, Rais paid the exorbitant prices and waited in line, while Barabas appropriated seats. People were giving him funny looks, the upper-class clientele of Gulshan clearly uncertain about whether mullahs needed to drink coffee. Barabas kept flashing his hideous grin at everyone. Pretty soon there was a wide, empty space around him.

"So, thanks for meeting me," Rais said, after the pastry plate had been thoroughly ransacked. "Er, what should I call you? Master?"

"Certainly not!" Barabas said. "We djinns don't believe in that kind of hierarchical nomenclature. I was a friend of your father's, you know, god rest his soul."

"He's my uncle, and he's not dead yet," Rais said.

"Right, right, young Kaikobad. I remember many nights of fun I had with him," Barabas said, tugging at his beard in reminiscence. "He used to take me drinking, you know. Most unlikely places. The man had a genius nose. You may call me Uncle Barabas."

"Thank you, Uncle."

"So times are bad for us," Barabas said. "Politics. Know anything about it?"

"Nothing much," Rais said. "I've just started."

"Well, you'd think Kaikobad would have trained you up before croaking." Barabas looked put out.

"My mother told me something about conservatives running amok."

"Smart lady," Barabas said. "Well, the conservatives have got Matteras, who is the top dog now, *and* Kuriken. The younger djinn follow Matteras, and the older ones sort of follow Kuriken. It started because the Isolationists suddenly woke up—all those right-wing, it-was-so-much-better-twenty-thousand-years-ago nutjobs. They think they're better off without humans. Their leader is Hazard, who's a famous duelist. You definitely don't want to run into him at night. They've joined together with the Creationists and made a voting bloc. Creationists are the real crazies. They translate the Lore literally. They've got their own leaders, but Matteras has sort of brought all the pieces of them together under the banner of the conservative party. You probably don't know this, but after Matteras put down the Broken seventy, eighty years ago, his dignatas has really gone through the roof. So suddenly all these nutcases get together and start making noise about creationism and turning back the clock on living space, racial purity, and instead of everyone having a laugh, a lot of djinn are quietly nodding along."

"What side are we?"

"We're kind of middle of the road. Live and let live. Most of the big clubs follow centrist policies. Memmion is the bigwig at the Royal Aeronautics Society, or RAS. He and Bahamut go way back. The Royal Anglers' Club are sort of with us, plus the bunch over at Giza, as well as the Old Hag Davala in Baghdad, although she said she's busy and can't help. Basically most of the sensible djinn want things ticking along, no fuss. Unfortunately everyone else seems to have gone crazy."

"So where do we stand right now?"

"We're lucky if we *get* any standing room," Barabas said, suddenly gloomy. "I can't command a porter in a train station these days, it's gotten so bad. Absolutely plummeting auctoritas! Even Bahamut is feeling the pinch."

"Er, do djinns have trains then?"

"What?"

"In the sky perhaps?" Rais felt a glow of anticipation. "Or underwater?"

"Don't be silly, we use *your* trains," Barabas said. "Trains in the sky? What nonsense! How on earth would we get them up there? Well, that's not to say that we don't have terribly advanced technology, because we do, I can assure you. Why, we could flatten all of you in a second, if we wanted to. Well, a few days at the most. Really, you people are incorrigible breeders. I took a nap once in 1033 and woke up to find the entire delta crawling with humans."

"Sorry," Rais said.

"Well, don't worry. Truth is we've gotten quite used to you people making roads, trains, ships, and whatnot. Do you know in the old days it was such a bother to get around? Oh, and air-conditioning. We love air-conditioning! Of course, we are the ones who taught you all this stuff to begin with."

"Really?"

"Everyone knows djinns invented everything. We're great inventors, we are. You humans have always been stealing our ideas. There are 322 million running cases at our patent court. When some of those reach a decision, you guys will be in big trouble. That Apple fellow will be bankrupt, I tell you; we've been using those touchy-thingys for hundreds of years..."

"I didn't know. I thought djinns were not really into tech—"

"Oh, we're very much up to date on technology!" Barabas said. "High tech is the real fashion nowadays. Of course we djinns are the most fashionable race around. We've *invented* most of your fashion. That backward cap thing? Invented by a djinn. Fact. It was old Hoodiveras who did that first. You humans started copying him right away. And did he get any credit for it? Not a bit. He was very hurt, was Hoodi. Put him right off humans."

"Wow, I always thought djinns were all about magic and stuff," Rais said, a bit nonplussed. "You know, dark powers. But of course, you guys appear very fashionable."

"Yes, about that," Barabas said with a slight trace of embarrassment, "people are giving us some strange looks. Is it possible that you're not quite up to date with fashion?"

Rais regarded his clothes. He was wearing an old pair of Diesels, worn through and finally comfortable (the first three years had been horribly tight around the crotch), and a very soft white Muji shirt. Nothing exciting, but hardly deficient for coffee.

"I think maybe *you're* getting the looks," he said finally.

"Oh?"

The place suddenly got very frosty. Little icicles formed around the corners of the table.

"You're, well, dressed like a fundamentalist mullah," Rais said. "Not that there's anything wrong with that—plenty of people dress like you. It's just that this place is a bit upmarket, and they probably don't get too many customers like you..."

"What?"

"You know, most people drinking coffee here are a bit Westernized, you might say..."

"Really?" Barabas was aghast. "Kaiko told me this was all the rage. He said this was real upper-class stuff. He helped me pick out the rings..."

"He might have been, er, joking," Rais said.

"The devil," Barabas said. "That rotten bastard has been leading me on! Are you sure?"

"He always had an odd sense of humor."

"I can't believe it! People have been laughing at me!"

"That's Uncle Kaiko for you."

"Ohhh, I went to the Westin poolside dressed like this," Barabas said, holding his head in his hands. "No wonder those girls were sniggering..."

"I'm so sorry," Rais said.

Barabas slumped in his chair abruptly, crestfallen. "Can you imagine how much dignatas I've lost? Kaiko must have raked it in! Ohh, I could just die..."

"Look, I can take you shopping, get you really fitted out," Rais said. "I have friends with garment factories. We can get you some good stuff from their sample sections. I know a really good tailor in Malaysia, we could get you some suits made."

"You're a good boy," Barabas said, sniffling.

For the next few weeks Rais settled into a strange routine of essentially following Barabas around and correcting a whole host of misconceptions the djinn harbored. It quickly became apparent to both of them that Kaikobad had been an inveterate liar and prankster, trespassing horribly on Barabas's good nature.

Consequently, Barabas became pathetically insecure and often took to dropping in at odd hours. Rais started spending more and more time at the Mirpur apartment. As the bizarre minutiae of the djinn's life began to take over his existence, he felt the mundane world begin to slip away imperceptibly, until all of his old associations appeared to him hazy and uncertain. He began to realize in part the kind of madness that had afflicted Kaikobad.

The simple acts of eating and sleeping became erratic. He needed a caretaker, but some form of paranoia had set in, and he was unable to fix on a trustworthy servant. In the end, a flash of genius reminded him that Butloo was currently unoccupied, being the majordomo of that empty, wrecked property that was his cousin's birthright. Butloo, who must have shared in the adventures of Kaikobad, who must have a treasure trove of knowledge about djinn hidden behind his mild gaze, was the perfect candidate. Yet would the old man leave his domain?

The proposal was made and duly rejected. Rais then told his mother, with every expectation that Juny would solve the problem. Juny went over to the house in Wari and had a conversation with Butloo, fifteen minutes of which was sufficient to reduce the old man to tears. The very next day Rais found his flat being stringently organized by the stalwart, who threw away half the things and applied to Juny religiously for whatever he required, bypassing the *choto sahib* entirely. This suited Rais fine.

Rais's role being part adjunct, part advisor to Barabas anyway, he could relate to Butloo completely and even picked up some pointers from the old man. Barabas was going through a phase of intense curiosity about mankind and wanted to spend his days taking pictures of everything. Rather than sporting a sensible digital camera, he stubbornly continued to use his ancient manual-focus Contax RTS III, which was a bulky device with a lot of accoutrements, including cases of very heavy and expensive lenses. Rais had to carry all this stuff, which made him irritable. Furthermore, Barabas's pictures were not really very good, and he could spend half an hour trying to capture a single image unsuccessfully.

"Why on earth are you taking so many pictures?" he said one day, as they stopped in front of yet another random tree in Gulshan.

"Oh, you know, memories," Barabas said.

"Memories?"

"Oh yes, in case all of this goes."

"Goes? You mean trees?"

"Trees, ants, buildings, the city..." Barabas said absently.

"Barabas."

"Oh, didn't I tell you? I'm sure I told you..."

"Your eyebrow is twitching, like when you bluff at poker."

"Well, it's Matteras, isn't it?" Barabas said. He sat down heavily on the sidewalk. "The Iso-Creationists have gotten so strong now. Rumor has it he's building a murder pit for them."

"What's that?"

"It's a kind of a trap, a technicality. You cunningly create a situation that results in death, as opposed to directly killing people. Like if I somehow lured and trapped you inside a sinking ship and then you drowned, it's not my fault. A small distinction, you might say, but it holds up well in court, I can tell you," Barabas said.

"That's kind of fucked up."

"All part of the Lore. Matteras is an expert at them. World renowned. A nasty sort of mind, I can testify to that."

"Who is the murder pit for?"

"For this," Barabas said, spreading his hands out. "For all of you. See, he's going to turn the whole bay into a murder pit."

"You must be joking."

"Imagine the dignatas he's going to get."

"*Could* he do it? I mean how?"

"He might have made a mechanism that could cause earthquakes and tidal waves and stuff."

"That sounds like science fiction."

"He might have tested it on Indonesia a few years ago."

"Barabas, are you really serious? Why would he do this?!"

"Well, it's the isolationist bit of their philosophy, isn't it?" Barabas looked aggrieved. "Don't look at me, I'm not supporting his policies. I *like* having humans around."

"So this djinn is going to wipe everyone out?! And he's allowed to do this? What happened to the 'djinns don't kill anyone' rule?"

"Well, that's a bit more of a guideline than a strict rule," Barabas said. "Plus he keeps harking back to the days when this area was quite a bit—how do you say it—less *crowded*. It's playing very well with the nostalgic crowd. Quite a few sensible-type djinns have been nodding their heads. I'm telling you, Matteras's auctoritas has gone right through the roof."

"This is just crazy. Who's stopping him?"

"Well, we were hoping you might stop him."

"Me?"

"Strictly speaking, it's really the emissary's job to sort this out."

"Emissary? I'm just a trainee. Your courts haven't even granted me official trainee status. I'm not even confirmed as Kaikobad's heir."

"Shirking responsibilities won't get you anywhere," Barabas said huffily.

"Shirking? *Shirking?*"

"Look now, Kaikobad would have risen to the occasion, sure enough," Barabas said. "In fact I wouldn't be surprised if Matteras had him put away for just that reason. Then we thought Dargoman would step up, but he's just gone missing. I called the other emissary in India, but he said he's emigrating to America and doesn't want to get involved. In fact, none of the emissaries seem to be fighting back at all. Everything is always dumped on me! That fat-ass Memmion hasn't left the RAS hub in like three hundred years. I've tried to call the Old Hag in Baghdad a hundred times, but I don't think they even have phone service there anymore. Well, it sucks. If these right-wing crazies get their way we'll be set back for centuries, and no one seems to care. Poor old Bahamut. He lives in the bay, you know. Matteras will destroy his dignatas if he pulls this off. Literally knock his front door down."

"*You'll* be set back? *We'll* be wiped out, Barabas!"

"Calm down, calm down, it's not like he's wiping out all of humanity. Most of the inland people should be fine. Unless he starts renting out his earthquake machine."

"Are you saying this nutjob can just go around the world making earthquakes and tidal waves?!"

"Well, really, something ought to be done," Barabas said weakly. "I mean this is exactly why we have emissaries. Where are all of them, eh? I miss Kaikobad. He would have known what to do..."

"And what about Bahamut? Isn't he some kind of big-shot djinn? Surely he's not going to stand idly by?"

"Yes, he told me he was counting on you."

"Oh god. You're actually going to pass the buck to me."

"I'd hurry if I were you."

CHAPTER 16
Benedict Arnolds

GU Sikkim was in no hurry to meet Matteras, but when he got a short message to be ready at midnight, he had no choice but to comply. Fobbing his wife off with various excuses, he took his hookah to the rooftop and sat in fear, cursing Rais for putting him in danger. When the elevator door finally opened, it wasn't the djinn who stepped out, however, but the Afghan emissary holding a cane.

"You!" GU Sikkim snarled.

"At your service," Dargoman said, sitting down.

"You betrayed us!" GU Sikkim said. "How dare you come here? I will have you arrested! Kidnapper! Pederast! Where is my nephew?!"

"Oh, calm down, you old fake." Dargoman smirked. "I work for Matteras now, same as you. He told me all about your little deal."

"Nothing more pathetic than a man with two masters," GU Sikkim sneered.

"I had no choice," Dargoman said, "as you well know, since you sent me and that little boy to certain death. I remember that day very well. I have often been tempted to remind your family of what exactly happened."

"It was so long ago, who knows what happened?" GU Sikkim said. "Such a tragedy. Thankfully we have all recovered. All is forgotten."

"Indeed."

"So, are we expecting His Greatness? Or will it just be the two of us?"

"He is busy," Dargoman said. "He has given me the job of handling you and your problems. Be thankful, Sikkim. I am far gentler than our master."

"You appear to have landed on your feet," GU Sikkim said. "Matteras promised you the earth, eh? Let me tell you, he's not your regular type of patron. Be careful what you wish for. He'll take his pound of flesh before the end."

"I have become one of his most trusted servants," Dargoman said. "Unlike you, I have not failed every single task I've been given. One day soon I will become his emissary and wear his mark."

"Two marks, eh?" GU Sikkim said. "I'm sure you'll be very popular."

"You have none," Dargoman said, "and thus no status in our world. I could kill you now without any fear of retaliation."

"Oh please," GU Sikkim said. "I've been dealing with Matteras for years. Do you think a cockroach like you can frighten me? I'm a Khan Rahman. This is *my* country. As you said earlier, you're a servant just like me. The only difference is I like to keep my head down, whereas you seem to think you can lord it over everyone with emissary this and emissary that. Well, let me tell you, djinn don't give a shit. They don't care. They'll cut your head off the same way they'd pluck a flower from the ground."

"Enough, enough," Dargoman said. "You'll keep me here all night with your great wisdom. Tell me instead, how is it that this fresh nephew of yours is making so many waves, bandying Kaikobad's name around? Matteras is most displeased."

"He's nothing, a wastrel, a loser," GU Sikkim said. "Hasn't done a day's work in his life, never finished his studies, always drinking and chasing women. I know that his father paid through the nose sending him to university in three different countries. Is still paying. And he's failed every job interview he's ever taken."

"He's getting traction in the courts," Dargoman said. "His application has not been thrown out."

"That's his mother," GU Sikkim said. "She's an ambitious harpy. Still, can't make gold out of shit, is what I always say. Don't worry about the boy, he calls me every day and asks permission before taking a piss."

"He has made contact with Barabas nonetheless," Dargoman said.

"Between you and me, Barabas is a fool," GU Sikkim said, "a drunkard and a lecher."

"Matteras will tolerate it if he stays at this level," Dargoman said. "Make sure he does not go any further. Matteras wants the name of Kaikobad to be forgotten."

"Any chance he'll patronize my nephew?" GU Sikkim asked. "It would be nice to have an emissary in our ranks again. He'll be a lot easier for me to control if I can get him something official."

"Not a chance," Dargoman said. "Matteras does not want his name associated in any way with the Khan Rahmans. In fact, he has half a mind to make your entire clan disappear. I have assured him that will not be necessary."

GU Sikkim shuddered. "No, no, tell him I've got everything under control."

"Sleep well, Sikkim."

Indelbed wasn't sleeping well. Rock wyrm snoring, he had discovered, was much worse than any other species of snoring. The snore started at a subsonic level and then traversed irregularly throughout the pitch and tone of human hearing, meandering in an unpredictable and highly irritating way, before ending in some dark energy spectrum, which caused Indelbed's bones to twitch uncontrollably.

Givaras slept just fine. The wyrm, whom they had named God's Eye, was now double the length and girth of his brethren. His physiology had changed measurably. The head was more pronounced, with more distinct features emerging. The eyes now blinked with worrying intelligence. Communication was possible through gestures and words, which the proto-dragon understood, although his own responses were a series of snorts and grunts. The mouth itself was still a horrendous collection of grinding teeth, although this too was elongating into a more serpentlike snout. Givaras's speculation was that the dragons communicated telepathically, and anyway, they were such monstrous creatures—who would wish to talk to them in the first place?

Lately, God's Eye had taken to hanging out with them in their little grotto. He was too big to easily fit into the tunnel network that crisscrossed the bedrock; already, he had passed a critical threshold. Wyrm hunting had evolved. Givaras had designed newer forms of sport. He had taught Indelbed how to make an invisible shield using the distortion field. This was materially different from keeping the light on. Thousands of hours of practice, however, had made Indelbed strong. The idea was to force the distortion field into a tight, solid sphere around God's Eye, protecting him from any freak injuries. Givaras would then send out his frequency beam like a fisherman's lure, the djinn having worked out perfectly the pitch most palatable to the rock wyrms.

The wyrms, unable to resist the bait, would come rushing into their cave, only to be ground up in the waiting maw of God's Eye. God's Eye quickly adapted to the hunt. He would position himself slightly off-center from the target tunnel and then shoot his head forward like a snake, catching the prey in his jaws. The jaws themselves were bigger now, big enough to snap a runty rock wyrm in half. Givaras, who was infatuated with God's Eye, spent a lot of time studying his mouth and reported that the dragon was now developing different kinds of teeth, in anticipation of a different kind of prey, perhaps. Indelbed pointed out that the only other prey in this pit was the two of *them*.

Also there was a vastly exciting pair of stubs growing somewhere between the third and fourth carapace, which Givaras theorized might become the base of wings. Wings!

"Of course, such a creature could never hope to fly just on pure aerodynamics," Givaras said. "Consider birds: they have sacrificed every ounce of excess weight, including a functioning brain, just to stay afloat. No, the dragons of yore were heavy creatures capable of great force and fierce intelligence. Their wings were for steering, perhaps. The real power must have come from their duality. Even now, God's Eye might be preparing to grow those very same dark organs, which will one day allow him to take to the sky!"

"He's working on some dark smells, I can testify to that," Indelbed said.

"What was that?"

"He stinks. He farts nonstop, Givaras."

"Well, if you're going to be juvenile... you are, in fact, acting like a typical teenager."

"Speaking of juveniles, you think this is only phase two of growth, right?"

"Yes, of course, the hinge of the jawline is nowhere near what you should see in a mature—"

"Well, do you have any idea what will happen once he *does* mature?" Indelbed asked.

"What do you mean?"

"I mean at what point can we, er, abort him?"

"Abort him?"

"Er, Givaras, he might get rather large at some unspecified future—"

"You mean *kill* him?" Givaras was outraged. "*Hush*... He'll hear you..."

God's Eye indeed was staring balefully at Indelbed and sneering with his slightly elongated snout.

"Just something you might consider."

"Yes, well, if you're going to have homicidal thoughts about killing off priceless extinct creatures of absolute wonder, then perhaps you've got a bit too much time on your hands," Givaras said. "It is time we revisited your duties as my apprentice."

"Apprentice?"

"Well, I realize we've never formalized the relationship, but you have been serving as such on an ad hoc basis, and we appear to have solved the problem of being eaten by rock wyrms—"

"Other than God's Eye..."

"Other than God's Eye, who is extremely slothful and has shown zero aggression toward us," Givaras said. "In any case, I would formally like to anoint you as my client, and furthermore to upgrade such status to that of apprentice and master, with myself being the master of course—"

"Okay, I agree, what do I have to do? Clean your shoes? Haha."

"A joke in extremely bad taste," Givaras said. "I was thinking it's time we worked on your distortion skills a bit."

"I've kept the light on for like four years now."

"Yes, very good, but outside of this cave, keeping on the light for years at a time will be absolutely useless."

"Yes, probably you're right. Unless it's at night, and the electricity goes off. Then you fuckers will all be looking for me."

"I'm thinking that when we actually emerge from this murder pit, the person who engineered our demise might be none too happy."

"I thought he's not allowed to harm us directly?"

"*Kill* us directly. He can harm us, all right. And it's more of a guideline than a rule. If he's sufficiently desperate, who knows? Plus he might have one of his clients do it for him. God knows how high his dignatas is now, he might well afford to flout the Lore. I'm going to teach you combat."

"So you guys have some kind of karate?"

"Well, nothing that formal—djinns are notoriously hateful of discipline, you know. All that training and work and meditation isn't really for us."

"Yes, Master, I know." Indelbed had taken over all the menial work long ago.

"Anyway, we do have a bill of rules, which I must tell you was ripped off completely by the Marquess of Queensberry, that rotten plagiarist. Dueling with the field. It's a bit like fencing, I'm told. The idea is to push you around using my distortion field. Normally, we take turns attacking and defending."

"Sounds fun."

"Oh, djinn adolescents spend decades doing it. There are even tournaments and ladder matches," Givaras said. "Now, first you must make yourself a shield. That's easy, you just have to tighten your distortion field into a ball all around you and make it rigid."

"All right."

"Now see me pushing you? There are various attacks. I might try to spear through your field using a sharp pointy thrust. Or I could try to crush a part of you using brute pressure. Or I could even try rolling you back, which is possible if your shield is spherical. It's quite funny to see..."

Indelbed, who was indeed rolling back, found his head lodged against an outcropping of rock and, being upside down, had the ignominy of vomiting all over his own face.

"Amateur mistake, really," Givaras crowed. "Now if you were still able, it would be your turn to have a go at me."

"You take turns?"

"Yes, it's all very civilized. It's meant to show off offense and defense turn-wise, see? Plenty of fellows just practice their attack and then lose the coin toss, and there you go: upended and vomiting after the first hit..."

"And you're an expert at this?"

"Well, I have a remarkably weak distortion field, as I've informed you," Givaras said. "Consequently, during my checkered youth, I was forced to endure a lot of bullying in the form of countless duels. It should not surprise you to know that the strongest do not always win in combat."

"So basically you spent your childhood getting rolled around in a distortion ball."

"Yes, in a nutshell," Givaras said. "But I learned a valuable lesson, which I will impart to you if you are ready."

"Although I have a very good idea what this lesson will impart, and quite possibly I can anticipate your words, I still basically have no choice and therefore will listen."

"It's remarkable," Givaras said. "Just listen to you. Marvelous. My pedagogy has been wildly successful. You sound now like an educated young djinn with a litigious mind, whereas when you first entered this cave you could barely rub two words together."

"Thanks."

"In any case, back to the lesson. The first part of the wisdom is that patience is a key factor in duels. What I learned was that in most cases, when the assailant failed to damage me after his first few attempts, he quickly ran out of ideas as well as stamina, and essentially gave up trying to do any serious dismemberment, settling instead on some face-saving maneuver to achieve a points win."

"You still lost."

"Oh yes, my lack of offensive power ensured that, to this date, I have never won a competitive duel," Givaras said with irritating complacency. "A record that I still hold and, ironically, has conferred on me dignatas, which even top-tier duelists would be proud of. At one point I became quite a draw in the leagues. There was a subculture of dueling that focused on various contenders trying to puncture my shield to deliver a knockout blow."

"I don't get it. You want me to become a subculture punching bag?"

"You're missing the point," Givaras said. "You are not going to face league matches. Your attacker will be trying to end your life. Almost certainly you will be overmatched in experience as well as strength. Your first task will be to avoid immediate destruction."

"Oh, great."

"The learning of which I will now expedite by mercilessly attacking you!"

"Gah! Stop! Stop!"

"Mock me, do you?" Givaras said. "Then let's see how well you do upside down!"

Under the baleful gaze of God's Eye, they were able to put in a solid half hour of practice—excruciatingly painful for Indelbed—before the random blasts of power drew the rock wyrms in sufficiently high numbers to make it prudent to stop. The wyrms were deterred by God's Eye, but God's Eye himself was not driven into a mindless frenzy anymore. He simply watched them with a predatory gaze, much like a cat looking at a couple of hamsters, trying to decide which one to eat first.

Givaras had mathematically worked out that at fairly subdued power levels, they could practice dueling for forty-minute intervals at a time without risking a massive convergence. A rest period of at least three hours was required afterward, to allow the juvenile wyrms time to settle down. This was great news for Indelbed, since it allowed time to heal his bruises, and he adopted a delaying strategy to try to avoid these windows of opportunity to pursue a form of "education," which, for all intents and purposes, was simply a period of unmitigated pummeling at the hands of a laughing and sadistically bored djinn.

CHAPTER 17
Kaikobad

He stood again on a different tower, the abandoned home of Barkan, called Beltrex by his friends, the King of Mercury, who had left for parts unknown and never returned, yet another defection that rocked the city.

The gate was relentless. Despite his railing and pleading, his screams and tears, it showed him only the city and the countless stories of its butchers, cobblers, and artisans; of djinn smoking on balconies, perfumed air wafting into the canopy of great trees; of music coming from the towers where troubadours sang for lords and ladies and from the plays in the penny theater, the infamous *jatra*. But lately the mood had paled. The markets were empty, the birdsong stilled. He could smell smoke in the air, and there was a haze on the horizon, a smudging of the tree line, where Memmion camped with an army of humans, Nephilim, and djinn.

They said that Horus, known as Givaras the Maker, was behind him, his machinations the fuel for this vast rebellion. The High King sat closeted with the Society of Horologists, in their sealed catacomb beneath the King's Tower, where they tinkered with time so that no one aged within that building, no food spoiled, and the grains of sand in the great hourglass would not fall. His people called for him, but he did not come out.

It was unthinkable. Citizens stared in disbelief toward the fields, which were abandoned and now burning, farms destroyed, the rice paddies ruined. War had come to Gangaridai. Kaikobad stepped off the tower and flew to the gate, reorienting himself over the barbican. For the first time in a thousand years, the bronze doors were closed, the portcullis lowered. The air reeked of magic.

The High Lords stood on the wall watching, djinn and Nephilim in their regal armor, bearing invested weapons as yet unused, many of them never blooded, for the peace of Gangaridai had held for a generation. Across the field, Memmion led from the front, as was his wont. There was no hiding him in the battlefield: he was the golden giant, with such brutal strength that if he reached the gate it was possible he could wrench the doors open with his bare hands. His great sword was the height of a man and a half, capable of cleaving Nephilim in two. The opposing lines faced each other, separated by a bare arrow shot, a moment of promise, a strange pause, as if Memmion himself was questioning the finality of this move, this total sundering of the First Empire. Behind him, his armies stretched back in ten lines, djinn of different ranks reinforced with Nephilim sorcerers and human infantry far outnumbering the defenders, enough men to encircle the city thrice. And behind them, Horus perhaps lurked, with Davala, and Barkan and his kin Elkran, and even mighty Bahamut, the traitor kings betraying Gangaridai in its time of need.

Yet the city was far from defenseless. The horn sounded, and Kuriken rode out on a white horse, his banner streaming behind him. He raised his lance in challenge, and the sun overhead turned his white armor aflame. For djinn, it was always primacy of self, every battle a duel, with a disdain for fighting chaff and a sacred duty to headhunt champions. Memmion was crafty. He did not answer. It was well known that while the sun shone, Kuriken was unbeatable. His armor could not be punctured. He was the solar warrior; his power waxed at noon. Kuriken sounded his horn again and then again, this time in mockery, shaming the many djinn before him.

Finally, a young prince of Lhasa came forward, unable to stomach the derision. He rode a gray horse and his lance bore the pennants of all the champions he had slain. He did not wait for pleasantries, merely lowered his head and charged, the destrier snorting with eagerness. His field expanded outward in a near-solid surface, pearlescent, and as his charge gathered momentum, it seemed as if a great jewel were rolling upon the plain.

Kuriken sat atop his horse, toying with the horn, his spear slack in his hand. A hundred yards, then fifty, then thirty, and finally he moved, letting the enemy field hit him, and it shattered, disintegrating into shards. The Prince of Lhasa stumbled, shocked, and Kuriken darted forward, reaching over his horse, his spear piercing low. The prince clutched his thigh and fell, blood spurting. On his knees, he struck with everything, aggressive till the end, fire jetting out from his hands like dragon flame, hotter than the sun, but once again his power failed against Kuriken's bone-white armor, and the dull black spearhead, made of meteorite, caught the prince in the face, taking the top half of his head clean off. It was a stolid blow, a butcher's minimal effort to split bone.

The body of the djinn twitched on the ground, spurting ichor, and the invading army flinched back. Duels between champions took days, often ending inconclusively. It was not easy to kill djinn. Kuriken stripped the Lhasa armor, fine filigreed scale, and held it aloft. His war cry was jarring.

Memmion did not wait for any more challenges. He sounded his horn, and his army lurched forward, furious with shame. The war had begun. Kaikobad breathed in the copper taste of blood and let the chaos take him.

CHAPTER 18

Enter the Squid

"Really? This is where you live now?" Maria, his semi-girlfriend of the past year, was over at Rais's new place for the first time. It had taken a lot of effort to get her out of the tristate area. She was not impressed.

They had grown up together, on and off—family friends, then an abortive summer fling at fifteen; drinking wine filched from their parents, sneaking joints out on balconies—and he found somewhere along the way that she had grown up to be really hot.

"It's not that bad," Rais said. He couldn't quite put his heart into it. It really was pretty bad. The furniture was shabby. There was also a damp smell he couldn't get rid of. Even the wall fixtures gave off a dejected yellow light that, far from brightening the room, only seemed to highlight the deficiencies.

"Rais, baby, I think you should move back into your mom's house," Maria said. She was standing at the edge of the living room, not quite wanting to commit to a seat.

"I can't. Don't worry, it's only for a while," Rais said. Having treated her with a casual droit de seigneur the past few years, he was now shocked to find that he wasn't quite prepared to accept the look on her face.

"Look, you've obviously got a lot going on," Maria said. "So I'm just going to go, let you get organized."

"Wait, wait, just sit," Rais said. He felt like a fool. "Drink?"

"No, Rais, it's not even noon," Maria said.

"Joint?"

"No."

"Sorry I dragged you over then," Rais said, lighting one for himself, trying to fake his normal insouciance. He felt like a child talking to an adult.

"Rais, babe, I was going to do this over Facebook, but I'm probably going to keep running into you for the rest of my life, so I thought I'd come over."

"You're pregnant?" he joked, knowing where this was going.

"Ew, no," Maria said. "I'm moving to Chicago."

"What?"

"I'm getting married. He's an engineer. He lives there."

"Married?"

"His father is a friend of my dad's. They kept sending proposals," Maria said.

"And you accepted? You haven't even met the guy."

"Don't be silly, of course I've met him. He flew down to see us last month."

"You never said anything."

"You were busy," Maria said. She lit a cigarette, took a long drag. "It was just for fun, you and I, Rais. It wasn't ever going to go anywhere. I think we both knew that."

"I didn't know that," Rais said. "I guess I do now."

"Oh, Rais, don't act the victim, please," Maria said. "You of all people should let this go gracefully."

"Well, Maria love, it's not every day girls leave me for engineers," Rais said.

"I need to get my life started," Maria said. "And I don't think you're heading in the same direction. I've really got to go. Mom's waiting at home. See you around."

She bent over and gave him a quick peck on the cheek, before retreating into the little foyer and out to the elevator, trying not to touch anything, not sparing a further glance back. Rais, shell-shocked, could only finish his joint in silence.

There was to be a lot of silent pot smoking over the next fortnight.

Up until this point of his life, Rais had had things rather easy. He was conscious of it now. Hitherto his real greatest complaint had been boredom, an ineffable dissatisfaction with life and a sense that momentous or at least *interesting* things were passing him by. He had never been able to muster the passion for deal making, or scamming, or politicking, or even the simple grinding out of wealth that seemed to move most of his friends. His disengagement had come with a smug superiority, a faux sense of philosophical accomplishment and empty intellectualism, fueled by a kind of dabbling in various subjects without ever really committing. He was a writer who had never written a book, a historian with no papers to his name, a great traveler who had never really penetrated the secrets of the places he had scoured.

Now, faced with the gut-churning anxiety of real adversity, he was perilously close to breaking. Everything depressed him. The apartment was dank and lonely. He had filled it with the accumulated junk from the Khan Rahman family storage unit, where old furniture went to die, stained and nicked by previous users, forgotten even by their own descendants. This detritus of past lives reminded him keenly of how small and pathetic his accomplishments were to date. He imagined himself joining the ranks of the many hundreds of anonymous Khan Rahmans, colorless people who lived and died without a trace.

As a would-be emissary, he had expected a life of intrigue and high glamour, of ancient djinn courts and magic. None of this had materialized yet. The only djinn he had managed to meet was Barabas, who seemed to prefer a low, dirty sort of existence among the dregs of society. Far from gaining anything, Rais had actually squandered the last of his savings trying to settle the djinn's numerous bar tabs and prevent various strong men from beating them up. The sojourns into the seedy underbelly of illegal bars, brothels, and gambling dens had been entertaining in a ghastly way at first, but had eventually left him with a patina of psychic grime, a sense that he was becoming a *part* of this scene of desperate squalor, instead of a superior observer.

He missed his old Dhaka life, the constant stream of parties and dinners, the little excursions and entertainments. Everyone seemed to have forgotten him, even the family, once they realized that he had nothing to report and no djinn favors to offer. Pockets empty, he drew away from invitations where he might not be able to pay his share. Living abroad, nearly anonymous, he had been perfectly happy being skint. In his hometown, where everyone expected him to be rich, it was a different thing altogether. Maria's loss was like a sore tooth. He was half convinced he loved her now, his days spent imagining her with the engineer, cuddling on her couch, drinking champagne and laughing at him.

As he sat in front of the TV flipping channels and drinking gin, his mind polished each of these little gems of misfortune, and he came to the bitter realization that by far the worst thing to happen to him was Matteras. At first he had taken Barabas's statements with incredulity, but subsequent conversations had gradually convinced him that their doom, in fact, was inevitable. This abstract threat had become an awful black reality, choking all hope. Matteras was implacable, Matteras was all-powerful, Matteras hated humans for some reason. He wanted everyone to drown. The family would be wiped out, all of their wealth and culture and history buried under tons of silt and fish corpses. He was supposed to be the token resistance to all of this, the perfect fall guy, so unequal to the task that he might as well have gotten a head start and drowned himself in the tub. Which he would have done had his shitty bathroom been equipped with one.

He was all set to wait out the apocalypse in his shorts, but his mother came over eventually, and one look from her was enough to make him unburden all his woes.

"That girl is a bit of a gold digger," she said, after hearing him out. "Everyone but you, dear son, has become certain of it during the past two years. If you could only see the way she smarmed around your father and Sikkim, you would be thankful she has revised her intention of marrying you."

"Mother, you say that about every girl I've dated," Rais said. He remembered bleakly the short list of his previous girlfriends, brief relationships that had amounted to nothing. "And she's perfectly wealthy on her own."

"In any case, I don't blame her much for abandoning you, because even a gold digger has standards, and sad to say, you look as if you grew up in a *bosti*. Why on earth can't you clean up around here? And why have you stopped shaving?" A *bosti* was a slum, of which there were many in Dhaka. In his youth, Rais had actually visited many of them in pursuit of drugs.

"I'm tired, Mama," Rais said, slumping down farther on his broken couch.

"Tired of what, exactly?"

"This shitty apartment, having no money, no friends, *no life*," Rais said. "They're ashamed of me, you know."

"Who?"

"All the old crew. Maria. Moffat. All our friends. They think I've been cut off. They won't come to Mirpur, wouldn't be caught dead out of the tristate. I'm just an afterthought now. It's like I've stopped existing."

"I see."

"They all drive Beamers. I can barely afford the fuel for the '81 Corolla you gave me. I never cared about the money thing before, you know? But—"

"All your life you've been given everything on a plate and you've swanned around with high principles. And now you've been shoved out into the real world and you don't like it one bit. Is that what you're saying, child?"

"Well..." This sounded a bit too much like the truth to be entirely palatable.

"Listen, you foolish boy!" Juny's eyes pinned him down like a vulture contemplating a broken-winged pigeon. "You've been given a chance to enter a world of mystery and knowledge and incredible power, the *true* reality, and you're whining about cars? You pathetic boy, if you want something, then damn well *earn* it."

"That worked so well for Uncle Kaikobad, right?" Rais said. Kaikobad had seemingly lived in squalor for years until his coma. Rais's secret dread was that he was facing down the same barrel.

"Your uncle married a djinn princess. Never forget that, when you're pining after your gilded Maria."

"She was a princess?"

"So I believe. It is a pity she didn't survive childbirth."

"Hmm, I wish uncle was awake now. We could use his help."

"Why? What happened with Barabas? Did he rebuff you?"

"Barabas is the problem, but not how you think," Rais said. He then recounted the entire threat. "It's particularly galling that I'm probably going to meet the end in my boxers holding a dirty glass. I always pictured myself going out with a bit more style."

"Are you serious?" Juny asked. "Even Matteras cannot be so cavalier, surely. He will have to go to court to do this. Or at the very least have an Assembly. There are always formalities with the djinn. Stop mewling like a little girl. And if you want to go out in style, then for god's sake grow a pair of balls and put on a good suit."

"Barabas seems to think this is more or less a foregone conclusion," Rais said.

"Have you told your uncle?"

"No," Rais said. "I actually haven't left the house at all. Too busy mewling like a little girl."

"All right, let's keep it from him for now," Juny said. "Did Barabas ask you to do anything specific?"

"No," Rais said. "He said that as the next best thing to an active emissary, it was my job to sort this out. Oh, and he said that Kaikobad would have fixed this by now."

"Okay, that's good," Juny said, "because he has just unwittingly given you official status."

"What?"

"He has explicitly asked you to take an action befitting an emissary. Also he has implied you are Kaikobad's replacement and therefore his legal equivalent. This is good."

"How does this help us?"

"Did you study the patron-client relationship charts I made for you?"

"Er, a little bit. I've been busy—"

"Wallowing, yes," Juny said. "Barabas was Kaikobad's patron. In djinn practice, the patron-client relationship has a legal status with manifold rights and duties that go both ways. Now we can argue that by equivalating Kaikobad with you, he has implicitly granted you client status for this particular situation. As his client, you now have certain rights: one of which is the right to request an audience with *his* patron."

"Bahamut."

"Precisely," Juny said. "He has just given us access to Bahamut."

"Do you think Bahamut will agree to meet me?"

"Ordinarily, no," Juny said. "However, this situation involves us somehow, specifically Kaikobad and his son. I have found that these djinn are not as stupid as they look. Don't be surprised if Bahamut set this up as an unofficial channel for meeting you."

"I don't know about Bahamut, but Barabas is *definitely* as stupid as he looks," Rais said.

Barabas, in fact, went into a towering rage when Rais approached him. He bellowed and blustered, he shook his fists and turned purple. Rais was well prepared for this, however, having spent three days boning up on the Lore. While information on this was scant, Juny had compiled a formidable collection of all things djinn and had access to certain correspondents that baffled even Rais.

"Where on earth did you learn all this from?" Barabas said, finally defeated.

"My mother," Rais said.

"That—that horrible woman!" Barabas said bitterly. "She has been plaguing us ever since poor Kaikobad went to sleep."

"Are we going to go, then?"

"Not right now," Barabas snapped. "Do you think we can just drop in on Bahamut? He lives in the bottom of the ocean, for god's sake!"

"Can't you just... ?" Rais waved his hand in a vaguely magical gesture, which further enraged the djinn.

"No, I most certainly cannot. Do you have a submarine, hmm? Do you have a pressure suit? Do you know how to avoid the ninety-nine wards that protect Bahamut from intrusion? Hmm? I didn't think so."

"Do djinns use submarines?" Rais asked, curious.

"We invented submarines, ha!" Barabas said. "Come to think of it, you actually *might* have a submarine."

"I'm quite sure I don't."

"Your uncle did."

"He had a *submarine*?"

Barabas gave him a knowing glance. "I helped him build it myself. He was smarter than you Khan Rahmans gave him credit for. Plenty of djinns owed him favors too."

"Where is it?"

"It was moored in Kanchpur, along the Shitalakya River. Probably still is," Barabas said. "He had an understanding with one of the factory owners there. I'll see you on Friday. I have to explain to Bahamut why exactly I'm forced to bring a random Hume to visit him."

Barabas's capitulation quickly dispelled Rais's ennui. Here, at last, was the magical kingdom he had glimpsed the edges of. Once again the old excitement gripped him, and he spent a day riffling through the Wari house, looking for Kaikobad's secrets. He questioned Butloo minutely, but that worthy was not extremely helpful, either from a lifetime of paranoid secrecy or genuine ignorance. In the end, he found a collection of biblical texts: a translated copy of the ancient Masoretic Old Testament, another copy of the translated Greek Hebrew Bible, and a moth-eaten King James New Testament—some of the few books left in the house, the rest having long ago been ransacked by his mother. There were notes scribbled along the margins and empty spaces, but these were incomprehensible and faded.

Still, his spirits were much improved, and he entered the Two Brothers Jute Mill on Friday ready for anything. Juny had called ahead and spoken to the owner of the factory, who turned out to be a mutual acquaintance and pleased enough to entertain a scion of the Khan Rahman family. The manager met him at the gate and escorted him to a lavish lunch, where he found Barabas already availing himself.

They ate for a long time, Barabas apprising him of the fact that further food might be in short supply for an indefinite amount of time, Bahamut not being particularly known for hospitality. In fact, the djinn appeared to feel that there was a strong possibility that Rais would not return at all, depending on that great creature's displeasure, and was treating this in part as a farewell feast. This was not enough to dampen Rais's mood and he made an excellent lunch. Any action was better than just sitting and waiting for the end.

After dessert, they retired to the short concrete jetty for some tea, at which point the manager raised the slight issue of outstanding payments and moorage fees.

"Did Uncle Kaikobad actually ever pay you?" Rais asked with some skepticism.

"Not as such," the manager said. "As per our agreements, he actually owes us seventeen years of dues. He always signed for everything, though. Am I correct in assuming that you wish to take over this vehicle?"

"Er, yes," Rais said.

"And you'll sign for the entire liability?"

"Certainly," Rais said with great haughtiness, appreciating for the first time the way Kaikobad conducted business.

"Enough of this accountancy!" Barabas belched loudly. "We must be off. Be sure to take the packed leftovers, human."

The manager ushered them down some steps to a boat that was rocking gently. Laborers began hauling on thick, tar-blackened rope, which eventually went taut. As their muscles strained and beaded with sweat, a slight bulge appeared in the water, and then a smooth brass sphere broke the surface. The laborers started tying off the rope against the jetty.

"Quick, quick," the manager said, literally pushing them off. "Someone will see!"

"Thank you for lunch and everything," Rais said in parting. "And of course, give my best to Uncle Iqbal, in case I don't return..."

"Sir, you know that man is a djinn, right?" the manager asked, clutching his shirtsleeve convulsively.

"Yes, I am aware."

"Just checking," the manager said. He motioned to the ferryman to start rowing. "Good luck."

They rowed out to the brass bubble. Barabas spent a moment fiddling with it before he managed to release the catch, and the sphere slid open to reveal a thick glass top, which also had to be levered up. The aperture was barely wide enough for a medium-size man, and the djinn lost some skin as he slithered in feetfirst. Rais followed him into a cramped interior lit by a greenish glow, which revealed a mess of instrumentation surrounding two semi-reclining car seats of aged leather. This was the bulbous front of the machine. There was, additionally, large glass portholes directly in front, below their feet, and above their heads, giving them a roughly 180-degree view of the scummy river water. These were covered with a grille of brass rods and hinged from the inside.

This central cabin was roughly 130 square feet and so crowded with gear that they had to literally climb over each other to reach their seats. The cabin, and presumably the submarine itself, was shaped like a comma. The rear tapered off to a narrow oval door, beyond which lay the engine chamber. This housed a marine engine, very old but beautifully maintained.

As his eyes adjusted to the gloom, Rais realized that the entire machine had been lovingly built with extraordinary attention to detail. Each meter was mounted in a heavy brass case buffed to a gleam. The cables were aligned perfectly in their grooves, sheathed with a crosshatch of thin copper wire. Toggle switches were heavy and moved with audible clicks. Even the seats were trimmed in soft leather, the safety belts forming a cross harness across the chest.

"This is beautiful," Rais said, sitting down. "I can't believe Uncle Kaikobad built this. We always thought he was a drunk."

"He was," Barabas said. "But he was brilliant too. I helped him with some of it. You see how everything is polished and tip-top? That's me. Anti-rust spell. Slows down entropy in the cabin."

"What? Like you don't age if you stay in here?"

"Probably. Kaikobad always looked pretty young considering all the things he drank..."

"He was so poor," Rais said. "We always pitied him..."

"Yes, in your world he was poor," Barabas said. "But in ours he was wealthy. Don't you know that it is his dignatas you are using to see Bahamut? Now strap up, we have a long way to go."

The engine caught on the first try, and the rotors started spinning smoothly. The displacement chambers took in water, and the submarine slid deeper into the river like a predatory eel, until they were grazing the bottom. The water was murky, and very soon Rais was too disoriented to see how fast they were going or even in which direction. Soon they were entirely reliant on the gyroscopes for navigation. There was also a SONAR, which was mainly tracking the seafloor to avoid any collisions.

The ship continued to accelerate until Rais was pushed back into his seat and the brass fittings began to rattle. Still Barabas pushed the throttle. Rais's fillings began to hurt, and his eyeballs sank back into his skull in a funny way that presaged some kind of medical catastrophe.

"How fast are we going?!" he screamed. His lips started to peel back.

Barabas turned to him with a fierce grin. "We augmented the engine with some djinn-tech! This is the fastest submarine vehicle in the Bay of Bengal!"

"Slow down! Slow down!"

The djinn eased the throttle somewhat and the red glow tingeing Rais's vision began to fade.

"You humans are so fragile," Barabas complained.

They continued at a more modest pace. It had never occurred to Rais that he might become bored cruising the bay in a djinn submarine, but the view was an unchanging murky black, and after closely examining all the varied dials and levers, he really had nothing to do. Eventually, the drone of the machines and Barabas's arcane muttering over charts was enough to lull him into a nap.

He was woken several hours later by a violent commotion. Barabas was swearing fluently in two languages. The submarine was creaking in distress and various alarms were ringing. Gigantic tentacles armed with suckers slapped against the multiple portholes, scrabbling fiendishly, the vacuum cups trying to find purchase against the smooth outer finish. The front view was most alarming: a large beak-like mouth was trying its best to swallow the submarine whole!

"Bahamut!" Rais screamed incoherently. In his mind he had pictured the djinn as this very kind of Cthulhuian nightmare.

"It's not Bahamut, idiot," Barabas said. "It's his damn colossal squid!"

"What? Like a pet?"

A gigantic eye, as large as the entire frontal porthole, was now peering at them curiously.

"Sort of..." Barabas was wrestling with the controls. The submarine was now shaking with the whine of stressed metal and overheating engines. "Remember I told you Bahamut had wards? She's one of them."

"Why is she attacking us? Aren't you Bahamut's client?"

"Yes, well, Bahamut doesn't like visitors," Barabas said. "And if I recall it was your great idea to come here."

"We're going to be flattened in a minute," Rais said, looking around in a futile search for weapons. "Don't you have torpedoes or anything?"

"This isn't a war craft," Barabas said, scrambling out of his seat. "I'm shutting down the engines before the propellers get wrecked!"

"Wait!" Rais had found the switch for what appeared to be two powerful front-mounted headlights. He flicked the knob and prayed.

The lamps switched on, and djinn-powered light speared directly into the giant eye. With an eldritch shriek the squid threw the submarine aside, blinking rapidly and generally agitating her tentacles in pain. Rais jammed the throttle to maximum. With a great metallic rattle the engines kicked into an ultrasonic whine; water surged across the portholes in a dark curtain as they shot down toward the ocean floor, below the squid's grasping arms, the sudden kick throwing both of them violently forward.

"Keep us going down!" Barabas said, crawling toward the engine door. "Try to lose her!"

"She's chasing us! Oh god, she's fast..."

"The engines are smoking," Barabas called out. "I must say, I did an excellent job with them . . ."

"She's catching us, for god's sake—we're too slow!"

"Just keep the propeller between her mouth and us," Barabas said. "Zigzag a little bit. That's it."

"You're enjoying this," Rais said with some disbelief.

"Well, it's rare sport," Barabas said. "Not too many kraken to be found these days."

"Er, Barabas," Rais said. "There are two red glowing things up ahead moving around. What are they?"

"Sentient sea mines," Barabas said. "It's a Bahamut specialty. Try to avoid them."

"What do you mean 'avoid them'?!" Rais said, aggrieved. "They're moving right at us. And you're in the same boat."

"Well, I'd probably survive the explosion."

The glowing red spheres were now approaching them with menace. All of a sudden they swerved to the side. Something heavy hit the back of the vehicle. Rais could feel the propellers getting fouled. A suckered tentacle slapped across the top porthole and slowly slid off, leaving some kind of foul lubricating sucker gunk. The squid had caught up.

"Awesome!" Barabas shouted with idiotic excitement. "It's trying to eat us now! Turn on auxiliary power! The kraken has stuck her beak into the main propeller!"

"What the fuck is auxiliary power?" Rais screamed. "Barabas, for god's sake help me instead of being retarded!"

Barabas flipped a lever, and two auxiliary steering motors started spinning below the main rotor. The submarine, still attached to the kraken, started to limp forward. The mines, meanwhile, were quivering in distress.

"Look, they're confused," Barabas said. "I don't think they're allowed to blow up the kraken!"

"Well, that's great, because we're halfway down her gullet," Rais said.

"Just keep moving forward," Barabas said. "We're nearly there. Steer for that pillar."

"Pillar? We're in the bottom of the damned ocean."

There was, however, a pillar of sorts, a great crud-encrusted monolith that looked like a vaguely man-made finger. The kraken by now was apparently reconsidering her decision to swallow them, except the main propeller was stuck inside her beak, and thus they were truly melded together into a semi-organic floating device with retarded mobility, a peculiar machine-squid hybrid monster leering this way and that, escorted in agitated fashion by the glowing red mines.

"Ramming speed!" Barabas yelled, seizing the auxiliary throttle from Rais and jamming it forward.

The squid-submarine lurched up, threatening to approach a pace that would actually lend a modicum of weight to the concept of ramming.

"*Stop!* Stop at once!" A colossal shadow came over them, swallowing all sense of perspective. The voice was deep and heavy, a rolling timbre that rattled the teeth in Rais's mouth and slammed the instrumentation into a dizzying spin. The mines stood down, red dots dimming in contrition and general bashfulness; the squid was even worse, turning from ferocious beast to spineless, near-somnolent pet radiating a palpable air of injured innocence. The submarine too went slack, as if apologizing for even threatening to approach ramming speed. It rolled to a gentle stop, its snub nose just bumping the monolith. Rais wanted to flash the headlights at the gigantic shape above, but he didn't dare.

"You have hurt my *Mesonychoteuthis hamiltoni*," the voice said quietly.

"Meso what? Is he talking about the squid?" Barabas muttered.

"Hurt the squid? The thing damn near ate us," Rais said.

"Shh, he can hear you..." Barabas hissed.

"I CAN HEAR YOU! ARE YOU INSULTING THE *MESONY-CHOTEUTHIS HAMILTONI*?!"

"Er, sorry, Bahamut," Rais said, and then for good measure, "Sorry, squid."

"That's better," Bahamut said. "Barabas, I see you loitering there. I heard you trying to ram the pillar of Gangaridai."

"Sorry, Bahamut," Barabas said.

"You know that is my favorite pillar," Bahamut continued.

"Won't do it again, Bahamut."

"I think I see a crack." Rais was studying a part of the pillar scraped clean by their ramming and further illuminated by the great headlights. It was indeed man-made, for the newly revealed surface was covered with Sanskrit-looking writing and diagrams, etched deep into the stone and seemingly plated with gold. At the top was a great seal, a crudely drawn elliptical serpent eating its own tail.

"Will you shut up... ?" Barabas pinched his arm painfully.

"What? The pillar is cracked?! Impossible! The pillar of Gangaridai is indestructible!"

"Now look what you've done," Barabas hissed angrily.

"What did *I* do?" Rais asked. "It's a great big crack. Anyone can see it. The damned thing can fall on us any minute. I'm backing up."

"Will you SHUT UP?" Barabas said. "Stop agitating him, okay? I told you he's a bit sensitive about this Gangaridai stuff."

"What the hell is Gangaridai?" Rais lowered his voice into a barely audible murmur. "And what the hell is wrong with him? Is he brain damaged?"

"He's just old," Barabas said. "We have this thing. In djinndom, some individuals grow really old, well beyond the regular life span. They become a bit strange."

"We have that thing too, it's called senility..."

The shape of the great Marid above, which had been a huge indiscriminate shadow, was now coalescing into a form flecked with silver, an undulating dervish of scales catching the light, something bizarre and beautiful, a thousand eyes glinting out from the depths, focused all of a sudden with unnatural intelligence at Rais. Bahamut was not, in fact, a whale, as Rais had been imagining. He was a massive school of alien fish.

"Tell that human, Mr. Barabas, that I am *not* senile..."

"Er, yes, Bahamut," Barabas said. "Might I present to you this newest scion of the ancient emissary family, the eminent clan of the Khan Rahmans, the—"

"The nephew of Kaikobad, hmm?"

"Yeah."

"Sit up straight, Hume. Let me get a look at you."

Rais straightened up in his chair as best he could.

"Most unimpressive. Singularly unhandsome. I cannot believe the inconvenience Kaikobad is putting us through. So what is it you want?"

Rais was quickly discovering that senile or not, Bahamut's full regard carried with it a physical weight. The thousands of eyes were literally pinning him down with the force of magnified gravity, and he was beginning to feel nauseated. All the protocols drilled into him by his mother left his mind, and he found himself blurting out the truth.

"Barabas says that the djinn Matteras is going to blow up the Bay of Bengal with an earthquake, and it's my job to fix it."

"Hmm, is he now? I should not like that."

"So I was hoping you would stop him?"

"Do not worry, young Hume. I have been saving something for this very day."

"Oh, perfect," Rais said. "Like some kind of secret weapon?"

"Yes, I have a device of ancient and venerable lineage, old even to the ancient masters of Gangaridai, before the ending of the Ice Age."

"Right. Sounds fantastic. I can't believe I was so worried. Of course you've got it covered."

"It will disrupt the flow of time and remove us permanently from this linear progression."

"Er, what?"

"The ancients created many devices trying to penetrate the secrets of time."

"Ahem," said Barabas.

"I have just been dying to use it."

Barabas raised his hand to signal his desire to speak. "Bahamut, was this the fabled device that started off the last ice age and almost destroyed all of us?"

"Hmm, yes, well, fracturing time like that will have certain effects."

"But you've fixed it, right?" Rais was getting an all-too-familiar sick feeling in his gut, a churning dismay that seemed to go hand in hand with all djinn conversations.

"Not as such, young Hume," Bahamut said. "Not as such."

"Lord Bahamut, sir, er, could I confer with my, um, patron Barabas here for a second?"

"Certainly. I shall withdraw to tend to the *M. hamiltoni*."

"Barabas! He's a damned lunatic!"

"I told you..."

"Does he really have this fractal time bomb thing?"

"Who knows?" Barabas shrugged. "He's eccentric. He might have built it for the first Gangaridai for all I know."

"Don't you guys keep track of this kind of thing?"

"Us djinn are more free-spirited, antiestablishment types," Barabas said. "We don't go in for big government."

"His solution is worse than the problem!"

"That's Bahamut for you," Barabas said. "Got to admire his style. His dignatas is going to jump through the roof if he detonates that bomb."

"It's like the cure is worse than the disease."

"It always is, my young friend."

"I might as well start building an ark."

"Noah tried that once."

"I think that's just a myth."

"No, no, some of the old djinns have records apparently. He was a boating enthusiast. Antediluvian times. The good old days, for us..."

"Barabas, what the hell are we supposed to do?"

"You could always ask for a bit of time."

"Yeah, like seventy years or so. Let me die an old man before you destroy everything."

"That's the spirit."

"Barabas and Hume!" Bahamut returned, his myriad eyes shining accusingly at their brass vessel. "The *M. hamiltoni* has been telling me of your reckless and fickle harassment of it."

"Our sincere apologies, Bahamut," Rais said. "We mistakenly thought that the *hamiltoni* was trying to eat us."

"That is a ridiculous accusation. He is a dedicated vegetarian."

"Yes, I realize that now—he's obviously a very peaceful creature. We in fact mistook his affection for ravenous hunger."

"Quite so," Bahamut said coldly.

"Bahamut, as the acting trainee emissary substitute, could I ask that you hold off on your, ah, fractal time device until we have had a chance to try more conventional means?"

"Certainly, if you and Barabas wish to have some sport against Matteras, who am I to deny you your fun?"

"Then could you offer any insight into another method of stopping Matteras?"

"Well, he's stronger than you, cleverer than you, much more dignified, and blessed with a large following of djinn supporters, apparently, according to Twitter."

"You follow Twitter?"

"Follow? We're the ones who invented it! Djinns love brevity. It's a racial trait, I'm sure you've discerned."

"Not really, no."

"In any case, I should think that any frontal assault on Matteras would be completely useless."

"Well, can we negotiate with him?"

"Ah, yes, we djinn love negotiations! But do you have anything he wants?"

"I don't know."

"That, in a nutshell, is your problem I'd say." Bahamut seemed amused now. "Matteras, after ages of disdaining humanity, has once again delved his nose into the affairs of mortals. What exactly does he want? Is he an Iso-Creationist buffoon? Does he truly believe their crackpot theories? Or is there something else? Discover that, and you might well have something to negotiate with."

"I see. Is there any chance of you being more specific?"

"No. I am not up to date with current affairs."

"Well, Master, can I say something?" Barabas said. "Should this human filth, a lowly client of a client, somehow forestall Matteras, or even put up the shadow of a good fight, would that not result in a massive gain of dignatas for us, mostly you? Could you not, in fact, prance around saying that even your lowliest Hume servant is a match for Matteras?"

"Hmm, yes, the dignatas accrued would be astonishing. Although I'm quite sure that I never prance. That sounds vaguely insulting, Barabas. Let me offer further advice then, Hume. Look specifically into the history of Matteras's own bloodline, which is bound intricately with Gangaridai. The progeny of human and djinn are very rare. There was a time, however, when it was not so."

"Before the Great War," Barabas said.

"Yes, I would look into ancient history, things forgotten by modern djinn," Bahamut said. "There is a certain historian djinn who might have access to this and other curious information. A very erudite lady, although not known, perhaps, for clarity. Seek her out discreetly. She is the Marid Risal, who lives in the sky. I believe she has a reputation for collecting frivolous and obscure facts—a collection of seemingly useless knowledge that might in this very particular time cause embarrassment to the power of Matteras."

"Thank you, great Bahamut," Rais said.

"Do not take too long, Hume and Barabas. If the waves start getting big around here, I will be forced to retaliate."

CHAPTER 19
The Man with Two Tattoos

Matteras's cabal was moving out of Southeast Asia, and Siyer Dargo Dargoman was in charge of liquidation. It was a job that he enjoyed, for the most part. He was sitting in a cold, airless room on the fifth floor of a semifinished building, a defunct shell that some developer had managed to raise up to five stories before running out of funds. Now it was stuck in legal limbo and a perfect spot for a clandestine office. The cabal had at least two dozen of these dungeons spread throughout the city.

He tapped his cane against the dusty floor as he awaited his next appointment. The cane was white ivory, richly carved, something of an affectation, except when he pulled a sword out of it. During those times, the cane was deadly serious.

He was, in living memory, perhaps the only emissary with two tattoos. The stylized serpent of Bahamut lay coiled on one forearm, slightly forlorn and faded, whereas his entire right shoulder now bore an intricate mark whose placement Matteras had personally supervised.

More important, Matteras had given him entry into the cabal, a shadowy board of a human-djinn conglomerate that sprawled the world, ruling over private equity firms in Brazil and Sri Lanka, oil fields in Mongolia, coal mines in Indonesia, rubber plantations in Malaysia, a supermarket chain in Nigeria, property in London and New York City, half a casino in Macao, and the entirety of a very secretive Swiss bank that was more than six hundred years old. The cabal was also the largest landowner in Bengal and had been since the British Raj.

Matteras was the "High King," yet every ruler needed a cabinet, and the members carried out his will and their own. Siyer was rich now, powerful beyond his wildest dreams. In fact, after joining Matteras, he had been forced to concede that previously even his dreams had been tattered, poverty-stricken things.

Presently, a couple of men came in, looking like supplicants even though they carried suitcases of money. The lead man was Babur, a real estate mogul, one of the largest developers and land grabbers in the country, a venal hyena kept barely constrained by a skin of education and some distant claim to an effete lineage.

"Sit," Siyer said, using his cane to push out one of the cheap plastic chairs. He loved being rude to the very rich, to make them come slumming. "The money."

The suitcase was duly opened. A flunky riffled through the bundles, but Siyer could gauge money with his eyes alone. They would never think to cheat him. On top of that was a bank draft for the rest of the amount. Siyer pocketed that. The official amount was for tax purposes and would be deposited in the bank. The cash would be dispersed to various other cabal purposes.

"Take the deed on your way out," Siyer said. "I expect you to complete the rest of the sales by the end of the week."

"It's thirty-five properties!" Babur said. "Thirty-five! In a dull market..."

"Shut up about markets!" Siyer thrust his face forward, his long nose cleaving the air and almost touching the man's forehead. "Shut up! We have lifted you out of the gutter! We have allowed you to purchase these expensive ancestors! *We* know you're just a bastard from the Taanbazaar brothel, *literally a whoreson*. Do your job now without any more fucking excuses!"

"More ti—"

Siyer leaned forward and slapped him. It was a light, feathery tap, but the real estate man fell stumbling back in shock, the cheap plastic chair buckling, skittering across the floor. The second man, much younger, his son perhaps, moved forward a step, shouting, until Siyer's cane slammed into his knee, crumpling it. He fell to the floor and curled up, whimpering. These second-generation industrialists were so soft.

"I am not joking," Siyer said. His voice was bored and all the more menacing because of it. "We are on a timetable here. Obey me as if your life depends on it. Because let me assure you, it does."

"What?" the developer snarled. "What the fuck do you mean? Are you threatening me?"

Siyer sighed. These little demonstrations were getting more and more tiresome. He flexed the fingers of his right hand and uttered a short cantrip in djinni. The lights flared out as a mini distortion field snapped into existence like a rabid black hole, sucking the air out of the room and heaving the sprawled Babur into the air, spread-eagled, constricting streaks of dark power throttling him.

Siyer slashed his hand sideways, and the spell winked out. It was a minor construct, powered for only a few seconds. Coiled around his wrists were far more potent spells, purchased on the black market from indigent magicians. It was Siyer's constant regret that he did not have the talent, not one drop of that ennobling djinn blood, so he was reliant on the spells of others, the best that money and dignatas could buy. It was better than nothing.

Babur fell to the ground in a heap, vomiting, his body twitching as various nerves misfired. The distortion field had that effect on people.

"Listen to me, Babur," Siyer said. "Your survival is immaterial to me. There are plenty of men like you. If I crush your throat now, another will take your place before your body cools. The only reason I am sparing you is because I do not wish to train another monkey. Do you understand? A nod will suffice."

"Yes, yes." Babur struggled to his knees.

"Then get out. I have other people to see."

Later, when the stench of vomit and voided bowels had faded somewhat, and the day's business had progressed, Siyer took a moment to go to the roof and light a cigarette.

"Your preference for half-wrecked slums amazes me, Dargoman."

Siyer spun around. "Matteras!"

The djinn stalked him down, grabbed his wrists. "You have some new toys. Who made them? Imoris?"

"Yes," Siyer said. The grip tightened and he felt his wrists creak.

"Nasty little spells, these ones," Matteras said. "You ought to be careful. They could blow your wrists off." The grip tightened further.

Siyer felt a moment of panic. Matteras was insane.

"We are on schedule with the disinvestment, Lord," Siyer said, beginning to bend.

"Good, yes." Matteras released him. "You have a larger problem."

"What?"

"Barabas saw Bahamut recently. He took with him one of the cursed Khan Rahmans. Some nephew of Kaikobad's, I presume. Did I not ask you to keep track of this?"

"To Bahamut? Impossible. I have heard nothing from Sikkim. Nor is there any news of any new Khan Rahman being given emissary status."

"It has happened nonetheless."

"But the Lore! How could Barabas take a human to Bahamut just like that?"

"Fuck the Lore!" Matteras snarled. "These are end times. Find this boy and take care of him."

"Kill him?"

"If necessary. But I would prefer him to be simply deflected. I do not wish more undue attention falling on this stupid family."

"I'll handle it," Siyer said.

"I no longer trust that fat oaf Sikkim."

"I have other people watching him."

"Well, they failed miserably."

"The boy has a weakness, his girlfriend."

"What about her?"

"She just left him. I understand he's heartbroken."

Matteras snorted. "Not enough to stop him from riding to the ruins of Gangaridai. You had better put her to use."

"Don't worry, I've been saving her for a rainy day."

She was sitting at home watching TV in her pajamas when the doorbell rang. It was noon and her parents were both at work. The maid was busy cleaning, the cook was in the kitchen—all was right in the world. She opened the door, and Siyer strolled in.

"Miss Maria Kabir?" Siyer had his gray suit on, his cravat and his cane. He looked like a most distinguished gentleman.

Maria stared at him and felt a shiver of unreasoning fear, but it was daytime, the sun was streaming in, and he looked elderly and rather harmless, so she assumed he was one of her father's diplomat friends and ushered him into the formal drawing room.

"Papa's at work," she said casually, bored.

"Of course," Siyer said. "I'm an old friend. I just flew in from London. I thought I'd take a chance and see if the old fox had retired."

"Please, sit," Maria said, thawed somewhat by his aristocratic accent. "Some tea? Or cold lemon juice?"

"Tea would be perfect." Siyer took a turn smoothly, his cane clicking on the beige marble. He waved the manila envelope he was carrying. "I have a small present for him; perhaps I'll leave it with you."

They had tea, and Siyer proved to be such an urbane conversationalist that Maria soon began regaling him with her life story and quite lost track of the fact that she had never seen him before.

"And you're getting married, I heard," Siyer said.

"Well, it's supposed to be a secret." Maria frowned. "Nothing is final yet."

"Your father still writes to me, infrequently," Siyer said. "Tell me about the boy."

"He's American, lives in Chicago. He's a software engineer, very smart," Maria said, happy to dwell on this paragon. "He went to MIT. He's already a VP in his company."

"Sounds wonderful. And will you be moving there?"

"Yes, as soon as my papers get done," Maria said. "He rents an apartment in the city, but Papa is going to give us a down payment, and we're probably going to buy a house..."

"How lovely," Siyer said. "And does he have a lot of siblings?"

"Not really, only an older sister, and she lives in Toronto," Maria said. "So far away, and I'm kind of glad about that; it'd be so boring to have to hang out with in-laws all day."

"How perfect. It sounds like you would have been very happy, Maria."

"Excuse me?"

"I said I'm sure you would have been very happy," Siyer said. "I'm just sorry it's not to be."

"What are you saying?" Maria said, puzzled. Then, as the peculiar menace of the words sank in, she stared at him with newfound suspicion. "You're not my father's friend, are you?"

"Not exactly, although I *have* met him a couple of times. It's such a small city, you know."

"What the hell do you want?"

"This envelope is actually a present for you." Siyer slid it forward across the ornate coffee table. "Please, take a moment to collect yourself."

Maria tore it open. There were glossy pictures inside, horrible, enlarged graphic pictures that had looked so sexy on the little phone screen. Blown up and printed, they seemed vulgar, threatening.

"That's not me," she blustered.

"Oh yes, dear, it is. There are head shots too, if you take a moment to look at the ones in the back," Siyer said. "Lovely pictures—I was so enjoying them in the car ride over. You have a stunning figure, so well groomed. Bengali girls tend to get so dumpy at this age."

"What do you want? Are you from Harun's family?"

"No, I do not know or care about the boy in Chicago," Siyer said. "Although of course, you'll have to give him up. I imagine his family would be rather horrified if these were released publicly."

"Please don't," Maria said in a dull voice. Everything seemed far away, inconsequential. This, she thought, was what true shock felt like.

"I am more interested in your previous affair. With Rais Khan Rahman."

"Did he give these to you? To get back at me?"

"No, he's probably not enough of a bastard. He was just careless, left his phone lying around. I suppose you can't blame him for not deleting the photos. They're so... useful on a lonely night."

"Oh god."

"I want you to go back to him," Siyer said.

"How can I? The wedding..."

"You'll call it off. Tell your parents you love Rais, or hate Chicago, or anything, really. They're indulgent, I'm sure you'll manage."

"And Rais?"

"Be seductive. I'm sure you can win him back."

"Why? Why do this?"

"To you? Because I can. Because you're temporarily useful. Right place, right time, so to speak. I want you to insinuate yourself back into his life completely. You don't have much time, so quite simply, go fuck his brains out. I want to know everything about him—where he goes, what he eats, who he talks to. At a later date, you will have to do more, but this is sufficient for now."

"Spy on Rais? Why? He's just... just a weird loser."

"Oh no, he's got a few large secrets he's been hiding from you," Siyer said. "Get him to tell you about djinns."

"Djinns? Like three wishes from a lamp?"

"Close enough," Siyer said. "Believe me, it's all true. I'd offer you proof, but really, what difference does it make? We both know you'll do precisely as I say."

"Okay," Maria said. She started to hand the envelope back, wanting it gone from her hands.

"Keep it, I've got copies," Siyer said, standing up. "Did I tell you about the video clips?"

"Oh god, no."

"You really are a pretty girl," Siyer said gently. "Now do as I say. I want to know what he's doing every second of the day. I'll be in touch."

Siyer's last visit of the day was to GU Sikkim's rooftop. Circumstances being much different now, the Afghan did not bother with niceties.

"You're finished, Sikkim," he said, towering over the old man. "It's all over. Your nephew visited Bahamut. *Bahamut.*"

"What? Impossible. He never said a thing."

"Matteras is upset."

"It's not my fault!" GU Sikkim said. "I've done everything Matteras wanted."

"You are incompetent," Siyer said. "I am to deal with the Khan Rahman issue now."

"You can't do that, we had a deal!" GU Sikkim said. "I'm a client of Matteras, for god's sake."

"Then do your fucking job," Siyer said.

"It's his damn mother," GU Sikkim said bitterly. "She's turned him against me. He's been lying to my face!"

"We need to send him a message to back off," Siyer said. "Matteras is on a tight schedule, and we don't want any complications, no matter how minor."

"What schedule?"

"The operation in the bay. Finally this cesspit of a delta will be cleansed."

"That's insane. Can he really do it?"

"He can and he will."

"Does he really have the support?"

"Forces are aligned behind him," Siyer said. "He has called an Assembly, but that is mostly a formality."

"God." GU Sikkim shuddered. "God. What's going to happen to me? To my family? We'll lose everything!"

"I would get out if I were you," Siyer said. "Liquidate. That's what I'm doing for the cabal."

"Fine. Fine." GU Sikkim grabbed Siyer's arm. "Look, Dargoman, we've known each other for years. Matteras was going to kill you that night. I put in a good word. I told him that you'd be more useful alive. You've got to help me. I've been loyal to you guys. Set us up somewhere—London, Sydney, anywhere. Let me into the cabal, for god's sake. I want to be a director in one of your offshore banks. And money. At least ten million. Plus you help us sell off and move whatever we can. In return, I'll deliver the boy to you. You can make him disappear like the other one."

Siyer smiled. "You're not cheap. The boy is protected by Barabas. We will not risk open warfare among the djinn."

"The mother then," GU Sikkim said quickly. "I can deliver her, I swear. That'll end it all. She's the real root of the problem."

"She is too well known in our world. She has become influential. She is intimately involved with the courts regarding her son's application. Many djinn correspond with her, many of them recognize her. *She is owed favors*," Siyer said. "It is not the right time to assassinate her."

"What then?" GU Sikkim looked desperate. He could feel his leverage slipping away.

"Matteras said to send a message. It has to be either you or the Ambassador."

"What?"

"I was going to kill you tonight," Siyer said, "but you reminded me of old times. So you can decide."

"What kind of choice is that?" GU Sikkim asked.

"You've run out of uses, Uncle," Siyer said. "Now choose."

GU Sikkim looked at the Afghan's face and concluded that the man was absolutely serious.

"Fine, fine, Vulu then, what do you expect me to say? He walks in the park two or three times a week, at dawn. You can get to him then. At least make it look like an accident."

"Excellent. I hope this will end the matter. Now, I've had a long day."

"Wait!" GU Sikkim wailed. "What about the money?"

"Ah yes," Siyer said. "I'll transfer a little something to your account when it happens."

"How much?"

"Two hundred thousand dollars should suffice."

"Two lakhs? A measly two hundred thousand? And what about moving us out?"

"What on earth would we want with a pack of Bengali refugees? Don't be silly. You're still rich, at least for a little while. Help your own damn family move."

CHAPTER 20
The Myrmidon Plan

Aside from training and the daily grind of survival, Givaras's obsessions were scholarly, much to the disgust of Indelbed. A large stack of plates was stored against one wall, each piece etched with tiny djinn script. This niche was called the Bibliotheca. Here, Givaras had put down treatises on the varied subjects he was master of, essays of rare insight and power, since the enforced isolation had allowed him to work unfettered for years on end.

Next to this space was another imaginary room called Cartography, which had maps etched on scales and bones, 3-D and beautifully carved. This room held endless fascination for Indelbed, not just because of the craftsmanship of the scrimshaw, but because the map room had a practical purpose. These were not flights of fancy or maps of distant galaxies Givaras purported to have knowledge of but, rather, maps of their prison, including a detailed 3-D working model.

Givaras had started this immediately upon his capture, with thoughts of tunneling out or at least exploring his environment. It had become clear early on that physical exploration in the wyrm tunnels was courting death, but he had fixed on an alternate, slightly safer method.

"You make the field a whisper, see, as faint as a cobweb, and you send it out like a tendril of smoke." Givaras demonstrated, and Indelbed marveled at the precise control the mad djinn had of his field, as if he could stack the particles like bricks into intricate shapes of his choosing. His talent was not brute force, but infinite finesse, and it struck Indelbed that in its own way, it was as much a superpower as the raw force of Matteras, more so perhaps because it was so underrated.

"It's hard," he said, after failing many times. His extrusions were clumsy, like fat sausages, as likely to bring down the wyrms on them as anything else.

"Practice, my dear, and you will surely master it," Givaras said. "For those of us without brute strength, precision is the path we must follow. If you cannot be the hammer, why then be the scalpel."

They pored over the existing maps and worked on the ever-evolving escape plan from what Givaras dubbed as the Myrmidon Prison. His early work had mapped the tunnel network, and the structure of this revealed the extent of Matteras's brilliance.

"You see, we are here, in the very central chamber. He has designed it so. The tunnels maze around us in irregular fashion, which indicates that the wyrms themselves made them. But look at the very outer rim."

"They're like ellipses."

"Precisely. The outer boundary has been shaped by him to create a closed loop. Somehow he used the wyrms themselves to create this circuit, and then he reinforced the sides with constructs so that they could not break out. Thus, these Myrmidon wardens of his tunnel endlessly within a fixed point, like flies in a jar."

"And to leave we have to break through the boundary."

"Yes. Initially I thought we could just force our way up, but if you manage to ever master the art of the questing field, you will eventually encounter what I call the Iron Dome."

"A construct?"

"Precisely, a very, very powerful one," Givaras said. "It stretches over us, fixed in the sand above the tunnel network. It cannot be broken through, at least not by either of us. Even if it were punctured by some burst of power, its release would drop the earth on us, burying the chamber. Ingenious, really, almost like a self-destruct button for the hasty."

"And trying it would bring the wyrms on us anyways."

"Right, right," Givaras said happily, "so you can see that the obvious way out, up, is certain death. Now the weakness of this prison, if any, is the soil. If we were inside pure rock, we'd be doomed. Luckily for us, the geology of the delta means we are in a very porous formation."

"You called it an Iron Dome, not a sphere."

"Clever. Yes, it is not a sphere. The construct is not present below us. Once I was done with the tunnels, I began to edge beyond the boundary, looking for natural fractures or passages in the earth. We are dealing with clay, sand, and boulders, mind you."

"You thought you could tunnel out?"

"I thought that I could train the wyrms, like a Myrmidon army, to tunnel in a line perpendicular to the dome, following this fissure here." Givaras pointed at a map. "I would goad them along the path of least resistance, until I reached the sea or the surface, whichever was quicker."

"But it failed."

"I couldn't goad them; the wyrms were brainless."

"God's Eye is not."

"No, so I propose we follow the same strategy. God's Eye will drill, and we will use the field to prevent the hole from collapsing and also to keep the groundwater from flooding us."

"What about the wyrms? Won't they chase us in the tunnels?"

"We will have to hold them off. God's Eye will repel them also, as the larvae will hesitate to attack a more advanced form, but will it be enough? We will be creating a terrific quantity of distortion in the field. In any case, we will pick a route where we cannot be attacked from multiple directions and thus prevent a convergence."

"You said the outer boundary of tunnels was artificial."

"I don't understand how Matteras made them, but he is a clever djinn and very powerful too. It is probable that those tunnels are reinforced with something to stop us from escaping. We will see whether it can withstand the might of God's Eye."

"You're really impressed with him, aren't you?"

"My dear boy, you don't know dragons. Nothing on this earth like them."

"Well, this one is stupid, lazy, and smells horrible."

"Shh! He's looking right at us."

CHAPTER 21
Wages of Sin

The submarine, it turned out, was perfect for hot-boxing. By dusk, they were cruising with the top down on the Meghna River. Boatmen greeted them hesitantly, puzzled by the open porthole with the two heads bobbing out. They didn't care because they were high and everything seemed particularly amusing, even the dead cow carcass that floated past and nearly collided with them. The wind was rushing past their faces, birds were flying overhead, and the bottle of whiskey they were passing back and forth was still half full. It was as good as it was going to get.

"You know what I've realized?" Rais said with all the profundity of the completely stoned. "I'm not cut out for this."

"Right, right, you're a terrible captain," Barabas said. "I mean the river is a mile wide and you keep bumping into corpses."

"Not that."

"Oh yes, you're also a terrible emissary," Barabas said. "I mean it's Emissary 101 that you're not supposed to flaunt this djinn stuff to the general public. But here you are, cruising down the river in a submarine for every villager to gawk at."

"No, no, I meant the bigger thing. The meta-thing."

"You're even worse at explaining things then."

"This whole heroic poseur thing," Rais said. "I mean I'm basically a lazy coward."

"Kaikobad was quite heroic," Barabas said with sudden glumness.

"He was a drunk, I thought."

"He was. But he was like a glamorous dark stranger." Barabas belched. "You're a drunk too, so at least you got that part right."

"What I'm saying is that I don't want to really do this fighting quest stuff."

"What? You can't just quit."

"Well, I want to be paid," Rais said, with the doggedness of the drunk. "Paid?"

"Not with this dignatas crap. I'm not falling for that fakery," Rais said. "I want material goods. Gold, dollars, pounds."

"Well, that's just ridiculous. Kaikobad never even dreamed of such a thing. It's an insult."

"Look, Barabas, I'm tired of being poor, living in a shithole, driving a piece of shit, going out to only shit places with you and then picking up the tab. How is it you've lived this long and not earned a damn cent?"

"I thought we were going to the cool, hidden-gem-type places," Barabas said, hurt.

"No, Barabas," Rais said. "We've been going to pox-infested dives. The only reason you haven't died of syphilis yet is because the fumes from the bathtub liquor you drink kill any germs within a five-meter proxitity. Proxicity. Whatever, you get the idea."

"So Ekram isn't a cool bohemian-artist guy?"

"He's a political cadre and a pimp who's illegally occupying housing in the university. So no, he's not a cool guy. And he's at least forty-five years old."

"And his sister isn't a student of human nature?"

"She's not his sister, no, and I'd say she's a hooker."

"No!"

"Why do I say that? Because, Barabas, she's presented me with an itemized monthly bill, which she expects me to clear."

"Kaikobad was a real shit, wasn't he?"

"What, for making you dress like a mullah, drink poisonous liquor, sleep with disease-ridden one-legged hookers, and hang out with the lowest underclass of criminals in the city? *Maybe you should pay your emissaries.*"

"All right, all right, I can see you've worked yourself up a little bit." Barabas finished the bottle and sent it spinning into the darkness. It bounced off a dead dog and came right back. "Kaiko and I had a lot of good times. I suppose you can do better, eh, Mr. High and Mighty?"

"Considering that even the drug dealers in the fourth-class workers colony are a better society of people than you're used to, yes," Rais said. "I declare, I can do better."

"All right, we'll go and hang with your uptight asshole friends then."

"Well, I'd take you, but... I'm actually so *fucking broke* that I no longer leave the house. And by house I mean the barely habitable dump in Mirpur."

"Hmm, why don't you move into Kaikobad's house? That's a bit of a mansion, eh?"

"What?!"

"He told me it was the best area in the city!" Barabas said, aggrieved.

"It was like thirty years ago."

"You know what's really irritating? The way you humans keep changing things around."

"Anyway, that place is a dump of epic proportions."

"Dump? The house is magnificent! I built parts of it myself. There are treasures there beyond human understanding!"

"What? It's full of random junk!"

"Ha! Junk indeed. Let me tell you, there are some pretty amazing things there."

"Barabas, are you trying to sell me my uncle's old crap as wages?"

"You'll see, my little friend," Barabas said. "Kaikobad didn't collect paper money, true. That doesn't mean he wasn't a shrewd operator."

"So people keep saying," Rais snorted, unconvinced.

The next day, tormented by the stabbing toxic brain rot that only the cheapest alcohol could achieve, they made their way over to Wari. The house had been boarded up, and as Rais forced the front door open, he found the interior even more derelict than usual. He remembered that day many years ago, his mother cleaning up the place to receive the emissary Dargoman and Indelbed cheerfully packing, perfectly willing to leave with a stranger, and he felt a pang of regret. For all their progress, they had achieved nothing on that front.

"This place is full of wards!" Barabas said, looking around.

"I don't see anything."

"Djinn constructs. Spells, you can say," Barabas said. "Protection."

"Fat lot of good it did my uncle."

"It's puzzling," Barabas said. "It would take a very high-level djinn to get Kaikobad in his own home."

"Matteras."

"Yes, but why would he bother? What was so important?"

"Perhaps he was pissed off with Uncle getting with his sister."

"Perhaps. Ah, this is what I was looking for. Take this. I told you there was valuable loot here."

Rais received the item and squinted at it in the dim light. It seemed like a pair of crude, rimless glasses, a simple steel frame affixed to thick circular blue lenses.

"Put it on," Barabas said.

He did, and the world suddenly bloomed into a latticework of smudged black lines, a mad Archimedean landscape twisting his vision into a Möbius strip, complex geometry shimmering in each available space, hanging menace like clockwork spiders.

"Now you see what we see," Barabas said smugly.

"Whoa. I'm tripping. What are these, like spells?"

"Crafters among us can use the distortion field to make stable structures of dark energy. These can be tied off and triggered by anyone, even complete humans. Kaikobad had a very faint power; he could sense the field and see the constructs, in a fashion—better with those glasses."

"Did he make all these spells?" The glasses were making his head spin.

"He could only do the simple stuff after he started drinking, but these wards are higher order. I made some of them. The larger ones were made by master craftsmen who owed him favors. I told you he was rich."

Rais was looking at Barabas, seeing for the first time the nebula of energy rippling around his corporeal form whenever he flexed his field. The djinn looked a lot less comical now.

"These glasses are pretty cool."

"They're a priceless artifact."

"Could I use spells?"

"Yes, anyone can, if you know the trigger words."

"And you can make spells?"

"Not very good ones. I'm not a master craftsman or anything."

"Couldn't you spell up a pile of cash?"

"No. Something cannot be created out of nothing. And before you ask me, the ancient alchemists can change things to gold, but I'm not one of them and they don't go around sharing stuff like that."

"Right. So there are djinns who can do a whole bunch of cool shit, but you aren't one of them, is that the gist of it?"

"I'm taking the glasses back."

"Okay, okay, sorry, jeez, way to be oversensitive."

"Come on, let's find some more goodies."

They worked well into the night, fueled by copious amounts of cigarettes and kebabs from the corner shop. Kaikobad had been an odd creature.

The most useless junk, not even worth thieving, turned out to be ensor-celled, sometimes baffling even the djinn. There were many things that em-anated power stashed carelessly all over the place.

"I'm done," Rais said finally, near dawn. "I can't see anymore. My eyes are killing me."

"Right, I should probably have warned you, those are experimental," Barabas said. "One of a kind. Me and Kaiko made them. We have a patent pending for it."

"And?"

"Well, prolonged use might burn out your occipital lobe. Kept happen-ing to the monkeys we tried them on."

"Great. What's this pile of stuff?"

"Oh, bits and pieces I'm thinking of reclaiming."

"Are you looting my uncle's house?"

"Nonsense, these are all things I had loaned him at one time or another."

"What does this pipe do?"

"Hrmm, it's the Never-Ending Pipe. Very valuable artifact."

"The what?"

"It makes a little quantum tunnel to the nearest smoking instrument and diverts it here," Barabas said.

"Are you serious?"

"You can't imagine the kind of weird shit you humans smoke. Kaiko once got a lungful of cow dung," Barabas said. "And it came from the most harmless-looking old grandmother..."

"Okay, I'm definitely keeping that."

"Now listen here—"

"Barabas, everything here is clearly Uncle Kaikobad's property, and you've already stated that you intend to remunerate me with objects from this house, so I don't think you have a leg to stand on."

"That's cheeky, coming from a fool who didn't even know what any of this stuff was."

"Do you want me to call my mother?"

"No, no, leave her out of it."

"That's right."

The next morning, they packed their bags, had coffee at Gloria Jeans with the last of Rais's monthly allowance (which was a beggarly amount given grudgingly by his father), smoked the grit out of their lungs with some tokes from the Never-Ending Pipe, and started off to find the reclusive djinn Risal.

"Last I heard, she was living in the clouds," Barabas said.

"Like literally?"

"Yes, we need an airship."

"I don't suppose Kaikobad had one lying around?" Rais asked hopefully.

"No, the airship club doesn't like unauthorized vehicles," Barabas said. "We try to keep a low profile. Don't want all your military folk getting uptight. And god forbid if Google gets wind of us."

"So do we just take a regular airline? What do you mean in the clouds exactly?"

"Don't worry. I know one housed in the old airport. Follow me."

They wandered into the old airport without anyone really stopping them, although it was purportedly under the control of the Bangladesh Air Force. Barabas had some bogus civil aviation badge, which he flashed around unnecessarily a couple of times. Eventually they made their way to a dark, abandoned-looking hangar, which had a couple of forlorn Fokker death traps lined up under patchwork tarps, pools of ancient oil staining the ground.

"I'm not going on those," Rais said, grabbing Barabas's arm.

The djinn whistled a couple of times, and from the back another disreputable-looking character sauntered out. Rais snapped on his blue glasses and saw the same telltale distortion field coming off him.

"Emissary-in-training Rais, meet the djinn Golgoras, captain of the airship *Sephiroth*, destroyer class."

"What do you want?"

Golgoras looked like a pirate. He had one normal eye. The other one had a brass telescopic eyepiece grafted on to the bone. He had four-inch walrus tusks growing out of his lower jaw. His hands were giant anvils of bone and gristle with a curved black talon on the end of each finger. He seemed ready to bite.

"He's an exotic," Barabas said, tapping his teeth. "Bit crazy, all the ones up there."

"It's an honor to meet you, Captain," Rais said. "The renown of the airship *Sephiroth* precedes you."

"Humph. Of course it does." He did appear mollified, however.

"We need a ride up. Orders from Himself," Barabas said.

"That oceanic bastard can go stuff himself," Golgoras said. "I ain't one of his damn clients, to be ordered about—"

"Remember '59?" Barabas said.

"Humph, fine. You using Bahamut's auctoritas?"

"My own is sufficient, I believe!" Barabas said.

Golgoras gave him a look intimating that no such thing was the case. "Where do you want to go? The Hub?"

"No. We need to find Risal. She lives in a sky house up in the remote quadrant. I have some last known coordinates."

"These are twenty years old, you fool!"

"She can't have gone far. It's a floater, not a damn rocket ship."

"All right, come then. Going to the Hub anyways. If this takes more than three days, it's on the big man's account."

The *Sephiroth*, actually, was quite enormous and sitting in perfectly plain view. The upper envelope was a torpedo-shaped blimp, rather predatory in a rakish sort of way, shark teeth designs running up the sides, the fabric something shimmery, lovingly etched with djinn-powered runes invisible to the naked eye. The ship part was a low-slung aluminum canister with complex wooden spars and rigging, complete with steering fins on either side, a couple of ship rotors at the end, and exhaust flues angling up from some kind of steam or combustion engine. The thing had an actual battering ram attached to the front in the shape of a gargoyle's fist. Moreover, there seemed to be cannons mounted on swivels at strategic intervals. Rais's estimation of the captain went up considerably; he really was a pirate.

"We have stealth tech, for when we're up there," Golgoras said as they boarded. "The Humes think we're a weather balloon."

"So, done any piracy lately?" Rais asked casually.

Golgoras glared at him. "No such thing as piracy up here."

"Awful lot of guns then."

Golgoras telescoped his eye threateningly, and Rais shut up.

The central control cabin was indeed crammed with peculiar-looking weapons, crates of contraband items, and nothing much in the way of furniture. The instrumentation was lovingly done in brass, in much the same fashion as the submarine, in what was possibly a signature style for djinn.

"Passenger cabins that way." Golgoras pointed to a narrow passage behind a reinforced wooden door. "Stay off the gun decks, stay out of the engine room. I have three crew members, they're my vassals, and they are under pain of death not to speak, so do not bother talking to them. Meals will be served in your rooms."

"Easy now," Barabas said. "You've become antisocial, wandering around all alone."

"In case of emergency, I'm throwing both of you overboard," Golgoras said. "Now clear off, I'm going to get airborne."

"Oh, we'd like to watch," Barabas said hopefully.

"The cockpit is off-limits to civilians," Golgoras said rudely. "At all times. Now move it."

They repaired to the cabins, which were little more than cramped alcoves with hammocks tied at intervals, creating a bunk bed effect. There were portholes at eye level, however, and once they were settled in things did not seem so bad.

"Bit tight," Rais said. "Beautiful ship, though. Your captain friend is a bit grumpy."

"The *Sephiroth* is famous," Barabas said, scowling. "Golgoras has gotten very high and mighty ever since he got it. How did he get it, you ask? Very dark deeds, I wouldn't be surprised. He says he won it in a race, but I don't know. He's become paranoid too. Doesn't want us around the cockpit snooping on his air charts and instrumentation. All these captains are so uppity. You'd think he'd let us watch from the wheelhouse."

"I'm happy hanging over here. You want a drink?"

"He's pretty low on crew. Just those three half-wit Ghuls."

"Ghuls?"

"Djinn, but an inferior race," Barabas said. "Poor fellows can hardly control their distortion fields. Not very smart either. Strong, though, and good workers—don't mind the nasty, dangerous stuff. Golgoras must be doing quite well if he can afford to hire three of them. Still, it's a big ship for just the four of them to manage."

"I'm amazed no one's noticed all these djinn flying around."

"Why should they? Sky's a big place, plenty of room for everyone," Barabas said. "Plus we've got fantastic stealth tech. Your radars probably think we're birds or something. Anyway, back to the point, this ship is seriously undermanned."

"What?"

"Theoretically speaking, I bet we could overpower Golgoras and take the *Sephiroth*. Imagine the dignatas!"

"Are you crazy?"

"Just a hypothetical plan. Not being serious, of course," Barabas said with relish. "We'd have to take down Golgoras by ambush and capture the cockpit. The Ghuls will be too stupid to realize what's happening, if we get him down fast enough."

"Yeah, sure," Rais said.

"Good, good," Barabas said. "First you take the Saber of Easy Cutting and strike through his distortion field. He'll be so surprised that—"

"Um, is that my uncle's sword?"

"Yes, of course, you did bring it, *didn't you*?"

"Er, no."

"What? Why? Why would you leave behind a one-of-a-kind magic sword particularly efficacious in fighting djinn? Why?"

"Well, it's really heavy and sharp—"

"It's a sword! It's a sword! It's supposed to be sharp!"

"Also"—Rais held up his hand—"the wires wrapping the hilt are kind of frayed and they cut my hand. See?"

"Well, at least tell me that you've brought the Invisible Dagger of Five Strikes."

"Ahem. We might have misplaced that."

"What?!"

"Well, it *is* invisible, and I distinctly remember putting it in my duffel bag, but..."

"So what the devil did you bring?" Barabas looked ready to cry.

"Cheer up, I've still got the pipe. Plus my glasses, of course. And also this bottle of whiskey from Uncle's secret stash."

"Is it a never-ending bottle?"

"No." Rais took a sniff. "Not a particularly good blend either."

"Oh, all right." Barabas shifted in his hammock glumly. "Pass it here. It's almost like you don't even *want* to fight..."

"Well, to be honest, hand-to-hand combat isn't really my thing."

"Kaikobad would have waded in with that thing—"

"Yeah, yeah, Kaikobad would have stuffed Golgoras into a lamp and conquered the skies with an army of Ghuls," Rais said. "You and me, though, we'd be Golgoras's bitch in two minutes max."

"Humph, if we had the sword we could have made short work of him."

"Cheer up, let's just enjoy the ride."

CHAPTER 22
Head in the Clouds

Two days into the journey, spent floating serenely from cloud to cloud, flying at deceptively fast paces, they were thoroughly lost with very little idea of up or down, or whether they had covered any distance at all. The portholes showed white, blue, and sometimes the gray of a thunderhead, the gentle curve of the rigid air envelope sloping up above like an avuncular sky god, dominating everything over the horizon. There were no reference points, no sightings of land, not even birds to keep them company, and they lounged in a trancelike state of timelessness, careless of measure or distance.

Golgoras too seemed infected by this languor; apparently satisfied with their harmlessness, he allowed them out of their hammocks and gave them a limited run of the ship, even tolerating their company for some hours in the cockpit, which was fascinating in all its steamer brass glory.

If Rais had found the submarine bizarre, at least that craft had had a modicum of human influence. The airship was fully djinn, with bizarre instrumentation and a subtle, needling sensation that everything was a little bit off. Rais's obvious admiration of the vehicle, coupled with his stoned, drunken harmlessness, appeased Golgoras to such a level that he was even willing, in short bursts, to expound on the many modifications and innovations found in the *Sephiroth*, which were completely unavailable to other, inferior ships.

Rais realized that even the most taciturn of djinns were, given the opportunity, prone to bombastic boasting.

"We could land anywhere. Anywhere. I've taken her down in the Russian tundra. On an Arctic glacier. In the Sahara. Tell me a fixed-wing monstrosity that can do that, eh?"

"Don't you ever see planes up here? How can they not know such an enormous—and beautiful!—airship is wandering around at will?"

"We stay above their cruising altitude," Golgoras said. "They all fly on autopilot anyway. At those speeds they can't see shit. They're so busy zipping around that they don't even know there is an entire world up here. And we have radar disrupters."

"Are we going to meet up with other airships?"

"Unlikely. This is a pretty remote area. We're now close to Risal's last known location," Golgoras said. "If we can't find her soon, we'll go to the Hub and ask around. You'll have run out of auctoritas by then, and I'll probably just maroon you." He winked to signal it was a joke, but as his remaining eye was a monstrous red thing that seemed capable of swallowing and ingesting small life-forms whole, it was hardly reassuring.

"Is the Hub like a floating city?" Here was the stuff of legends Rais had been expecting to find.

"Nothing so grand. It's more like a docking station and clubhouse for the Royal Aeronautics Society. No entry without membership. I'll have to pay a fee to sign you guys in." He seemed fairly disgruntled at this prospect.

"Yes, yes, it's a real secret hideout," Barabas sneered. "Let me say that of all the clubs, the RAS is filled with the most ridiculous, childish, purposeless members with hardly any use to regular society—"

"I seem to remember you applied once or twice," Golgoras said with a nasty grin.

"Yes, well, that was before I got to know you lot—"

"Got rejected too, didn't you?" Golgoras continued. "Not Aeronautics material, they said, if I recall. Memmion had a good laugh about that one."

"Memmion can go stuff himself!" Barabas said. "He's a fat bastard!"

"Memmion is a much greater djinn than that stupid fish you follow around!"

"You lot are nothing but a bunch of pirates!" Barabas said, thrusting his chin out.

"You're just a landlubber!" Golgoras said, leaning down toward the shorter djinn.

"Guys, guys, look!" Rais, who had now spotted the first thing for several days that was not a cloud, had to rapidly blink to clear the cigar haze from his eyes.

Spinning lazily in the middle of a giant cirrus was a pearly, opaque tube, several meters in diameter and over a dozen in length.

"It's actually a tube," Rais said. "How does it stay up?"

"Distortion field tech," Barabas said. "Risal was an important Marid. Quite a lot of auctoritas. Such a waste."

"It shouldn't be here," Golgoras said. "It's way off course. Where are its proximity markers? Or her little airship?"

"Look at that!" Barabas was, in fact, using the captain's telescope, so the others had to crowd around and jostle him to get a view.

"What is it?" Rais asked, after Golgoras had wrenched the instrument away.

"The hatch on the end is open," Golgoras said. "It looks like the pressure seal is broken. Something has happened."

"What now?" Barabas asked.

"I will hail her on the loudspeaker. Then we will try to dock."

Predictably, Golgoras's hail went unanswered. The tube seemed fully deserted. Docking was a problem. Closer examination showed that the docking mechanism of the tube had broken away, presumably along with whatever craft Risal normally kept in it. Golgoras maneuvered the airship over the spinning tube and then sent the Ghuls over the side with ropes.

It quickly became apparent that air-to-air docking was fraught at the best of times, a dangerous exercise in trial and error. After several attempts the Ghuls managed to hook the open hatch of the tube, gently slowing it down. Fixing a guide ladder to the hatch took another hour of tinkering. Finally, Golgoras made them sign waivers, and then equipped them with warm clothes, mountain-climbing harnesses, and an oxygen tank for Rais. The djinn, apparently, were not susceptible to altitude sickness, yet another sign of their superiority, as astutely observed by Barabas. The Ghuls gathered around to lower them into the hatch via a heavy iron pulley, their brutish faces lighting up with the simple joy of playing with a human yo-yo.

The air was austere at this height, disdaining the clutter of oxygen, and the cold was a gripping, numbing monster, instantly reducing Rais to a quivering wreck. He dropped like an inert package, bouncing around against Barabas and the guide ladder, unable to grab it or control his descent in any way. Luckily, the Ghuls, lacking in intelligence, were gifted with hyperspecialist physical attributes, which included, among other things, the apparent ability to thread a spinning needle in one go.

It was only a few seconds before they popped into the hatch, and the instant gratifying change in barometric pressure and heat told Rais that some remnant of Risal's magic remained. He steadied himself and saw that glowing runes still functioned all along the tube, holding in air and pressure despite the slow leak of the open hatch. Everything else was in disarray.

The tube was a simple white corridor, with living quarters in one end and a large open work area in the other, dominated by circular bookshelves spiraling the entire length of the structure, all the contents spilled haphazardly, torn and trampled, carelessly rifled. The bed was upturned, a simple table splintered, chairs askew, and everywhere the sign of long abandonment, a dusty coating of neglect and disuse.

"Not here then," Barabas said, poking around, obviously disappointed at the lack of spoils. "This place looks like it's been pirated several times. Funny, Golgoras found it pretty quick. I wouldn't be surprised if he looted it himself, before."

"She had a lot of books."

"Scholar, wasn't she?" Barabas said. He kicked an ancient almanac with disgust. "What a big waste of time. All that auctoritas, and she collects a bunch of useless books."

"What do you think happened to her?"

"Either she left, or there was an accident," Barabas said, bored.

"Or someone killed her."

"Djinn don't murder each other. Against the Lore," Barabas said. "It's what makes us superior to you violent fools."

"Okay, this is an expensive tube, right?"

"Ridiculously," Barabas said. He touched the walls appreciatively. "Humes couldn't make this. Not in a million years."

"It say's Hyundai on this plaque," Rais said. "This was made in Korea!"

"Well, that is, Humes might have made the components, but no way they could put it up in the sky," Barabas said. "Mind you, with prices these days, it must have cost Risal an arm and a leg."

"So it doesn't make sense that she'd just leave it abandoned. Plus she left all her books lying around. They were clearly her prized possessions. I doubt she'd just ruin everything like this," Rais said. "If we rule out that she just wandered away, that leaves accident. Maybe a storm or something hit her while she was outside."

"Had to be a pretty heavy accident," Barabas said grudgingly.

"Why?"

"Risal was powerful," Barabas said. "I mean like solid distortion field. She should have survived any kind of natural disaster."

"We might as well look through her stuff," Rais said.

"This is a hell of a wasted trip," Barabas grumbled.

Things continued in this vein for some time, with Barabas hogging the pipe and complaining, while Rais made a desultory search of the area. The documents and books were in many languages, some human, some djinn, and spoke compellingly of Risal's erudition. Then Rais found a calendar under the bed, and they spent some time giggling over Risal's faithful recording of daily caloric intake and bowel movements.

"This is over twenty years ago," Barabas said finally, finding the last entry.

"Nothing here is more recent," Rais said. "This soup can expired twenty-five years ago. There's some soda here that is over twenty years old."

"So she disappeared twenty years ago," Barabas said.

"Check her last few entries."

"She had a good breakfast, and her poop was regular," Barabas said.

"Is there nothing else in the damn schedule?"

"Oh, wait, I missed some bits."

"It would be a lot faster if I could read djinn."

"Kaiko could read djinn," Barabas said.

"Yeah, yeah, he was a real genius. He also farted lightning and slept on nails."

"Not really. He used the glasses."

"Oh." Rais had a go. "It works," he said stupidly.

"Of course."

"You couldn't have told me this earlier?"

Barabas shrugged. "I told you it was good loot."

Rais hit the books with renewed energy, dazzled by the sudden wealth of information. Something like the old curiosity and wonder fired through him, and he began reading feverishly. His brain started to operate once again at peak capacity after years of atrophy. It was not to last, alas. All too soon he realized that djinn writing, regardless of topic or author, typically exuded a bombastic, prevaricating, self-glorifying quality. Even the most trivial observations were presented as ground-shaking theories. Ludicrous assertions were made with casual disregard for logic. Evidence was that rare beautiful virgin—frequently alluded to yet hardly ever produced.

He found entire volumes of Risal's own work, ranging from djinn and human history to treatises on rare Amazon earthworms. She had a particularly pompous way about her, treating any foolhardy reader with punishing contempt, speaking in some passages as if to a child, and in others deliberately obfuscating the content until it was more or less gibberish. All her work was over a hundred years old, however. There was no sign of her recent studies.

"Really, I don't understand why you guys even bother writing anything down," Rais said finally with disgust. "I mean, does anyone actually ever read this shit?"

"Not me," Barabas said happily, having abdicated all scholarly pursuit to his trainee. "Not if I can help it. Dead bores, all of them. And Risal was more boring than most—legendary for it. She's written books that have not sold a single copy. Fact. No wonder she lived up here all alone. Probably pissed off all her neighbors."

"Bahamut told us to look at history," Rais said. He pointed dispiritedly at a huge pile of books and scrolls he had gathered by the bed. "This is everything."

"You get cracking," Barabas said. "I'm going to search for secret compartments."

"What?"

"Djinns love secret compartments. She's bound to have a few."

She did not, in fact, have any secret compartments. At the end of their allotted time, they were forced to admit defeat. Rais had found an index and gathered together as much of the library as he could find, an intimidating quantity of material, djinn glasses giving him a headache now, no doubt the early onset of the ocular disease promised by Barabas. Barabas himself had largely wasted his time, pilfering trinkets, drinking expired soda, and expounding outlandish theories.

"This book seems to be missing," Rais said finally, marking the catalog. "*Register of Kings: Gangaridai.* It was part of her rare manuscript collection. See? I've found all the other ones. They were secured in this humidor beside her bed. What are the chances that the rare book on Gangaridai is the one that specifically went missing?"

"What's your point?"

"It must be what Bahamut was asking us to investigate," Rais said. "Something happened back then that Matteras doesn't want people poking into. It must have references to the Great War in it. Did anyone else study this?"

"Not that I know of. It was long ago, boy," Barabas said. "Djinns don't go around dwelling on useless things that happened way back when. We prefer to focus on the present."

"Do you know anything at all about this Great War?"

Barabas shrugged. "A bunch of Nephilim and djinn fought with another bunch of Nephilim and djinn. Some people say that Gangaridai was destroyed in the war, and some people say that happened after, during the great flood. This was before the Ice Age. Personally, I think some nutcase like Kuriken probably *caused* the great flood by accident and destroyed the city."

"Nephilim?"

"That's how the nursery rhymes go," Barabas said. "I can't remember exactly. I think it's an old word for humans."

"It's from the Bible," Rais said. "Interesting. Kaikobad had a bunch of Bibles; he marked out passages on the Nephilim. I wonder what it means. What's Matteras's connection to all of this?"

"There are rumors that he's from a bastard line," Barabas said. "Royal pissing blood, apparently. He keeps that part quiet. Djinn don't like kings. We're all mostly republican, you see."

"There must be something more," Rais said. "We needed Kaikobad or Risal alive."

"We're stuck again," Barabas said. "And this stupid Risal had absolutely no good loot. Not even a treasure map. What's the use of studying history for hundreds of years if you can't muster up any good loot?"

"I'm taking all of these books," Rais said. He rubbed his face. Suddenly he felt a hundred years old. "I might as well read whatever I can. We might learn something useful."

CHAPTER 23
Broken Things

"So the Marid Risal is missing, and you found nothing useful," Golgoras said.

"No loot, that's for sure," Barabas said bitterly. "Bunch of useless books."

"This is a waste of time," Golgoras said. "I'm not using up any more fuel. I'm going to drop you at the Hub. You can find your own way back."

"Just a minute, that's not the deal. You agreed to help us find Risal, boyo," Barabas said.

"We. Found. Her. Tube," Golgoras said.

"She ain't in it, is she?"

"Is that my problem?"

"Other than the massive loss of dignatas in failing a simple commission..."

"You bunch of gobbets don't even know what happened to her!" Golgoras shouted. "Where do we go next, hmm?"

"Neighbors!" Barabas held up a thick hairy finger, as if this one word was self-explanatory. "She must have had neighbors. We track them down, have a chat, easy peasy."

"It is *not* easy peasy!" Golgoras roared. "There is no life here for a hundred knots in any direction."

"She disappeared maybe twenty years ago," Rais said, looking up from his reading. "And we know the tube has been adrift since then. Where was it originally moored?"

"The Aethrometer," Barabas said. "I know you've got one, Golgo old boy. Just trot it out, turn it on, and we'll follow the dots."

"We could try that," Golgoras said grudgingly after a few minutes.

"See? Easy peasy."

The Aethrometer was a device with numerous coils, valves, and meters, driven by a small steam engine belching coal smoke. There were intricate parts that twisted into eye-wrenching dimensions and a hint of incompleteness about the machine in the outlay of gears that moved but did not touch: metal hinges turning into themselves, bearings that burned through each other. The Aethrometer could track things. The distortion field left a trail in the ether, a faint rearrangement of quantum states, a misprobability that the device sniffed out like a faithful hound.

"It's been a long time," Golgoras groused as he fired up the engine. "But the tube distorts probability quite a bit and this place is remote, so it might work."

The compass and the altimeter began to twitch weakly, sniffing like dogs on the edge of winter, and slowly they eased into the hunt, even Golgoras finally taking an interest. There was daredevilry in following a scent nearly twenty years old and much dignatas to accrue in finding the lost historian Risal. In all things, finally, the djinn instinct always rose to the top, the old yearning for something risky, some oddity or wager to break the tedium of endless days.

"I found this book inside one of the other ones," Rais said. "It's very strange."

It was a thickish volume banded in old brown vellum, the edges rough cut, with illustrations in ink, of which there were many, of odd things that the glasses did nothing to illuminate. There was an altogether artisanal quality about the thing, as if the author had deliberately eschewed all printing technology to laboriously finish everything by hand.

"Title?" Golgoras asked.

"*Compendium of Beasts*," Rais said. "No author either. You know, the style of it looks so familiar. It was hidden inside Risal's ten-volume collection on Balinese snails. Had a different cover and everything. Only reason I found it was 'cause I dropped the whole case and it split open."

Golgoras looked at it, and his brass eye suddenly telescoped with some kind of involuntary emotion, an almost comical display of anger and disgust.

"The *Compendium*? Impossible! It doesn't exist anymore."

"It is handwritten. Even the illustrations are hand drawn." Rais flipped it open.

"Do not look at them!"

"What? What the hell is it?" Rais asked.

"The Maker wrote that," said Barabas, backing away. He seemed on the verge of crying. "How long have you had that? Why didn't you say anything earlier?"

"I told you, it was hidden. I have no clue what the damn thing is. Why are you guys overreacting?"

Golgoras stared at the pages and grew visibly paler.

"It's the *Compendium of Beasts*," Barabas said. He had one hairy hand clamped over his eyes.

"That book was destroyed," Golgoras said. "No copies should exist. This must be one the Maker made by hand." His disquiet was palpable, and it began to affect Rais, even though he knew nothing of this author or his dread book.

"Who the fuck is the Maker?" he asked, holding the thing at arm's length.

"You haven't heard of the Maker?" Barabas looked puzzled.

"I've only been an emissary for a few weeks..."

"Acting emissary," Barabas said absently. "He is the Maker of Broken Things. That's what they called him. Givaras—"

"Givar Abomination, Givaras the Madness," Golgoras snarled. "The Maker of Plagues, the Eye of Horus, Horus the Fallen, the Insane."

"Matteras fought him eighty years ago, they say," Barabas said.

"The only good thing he ever did," said Golgoras with a shudder.

The Aethrometer sputtered on, leading them in a gently meandering path in the sky, through white and gray clouds, a sea of water vapor and wind currents. The djinn sat huddled in the cockpit, debating in hushed voices. Their interest in Risal was waning. The Maker's handwritten book settled a cloak of dread over everything, a subtle cancer that seemed to dampen even the grunting sign language of the Ghuls.

In a few days they were floating in another patch of air, serene, lifeless, a desert in the sky. The Aethrometer twirled, twitched, and settled fast. They circled around fruitlessly, failing to stir it back to life; they had arrived.

"There's nothing here," Barabas said dumbly.

"Waste of time." Golgoras glowered, his brass eye telescoping as he swept his head from side to side. "Nothing here."

"What the hell was she doing here?" Rais asked.

"Marids like solitude," Barabas said.

"No neighbors then?" Rais asked with a smirk.

Barabas glared at him. "It would appear not."

The Ghuls found moorings with their preternatural eyesight, faint spells fading in the air, gear-like constructs that had once hooked the cylinder to the fabric of some other plane. The constructs had been sheered, deliberately severed like cut rope, edges frayed as the magic bled into the atmosphere at an imperceptible rate.

"Definitely no accident then," Barabas said, as they studied the moorings closely using a host of other arcane instrumentation.

"Any spell signatures?" Rais asked. "Something we can nail on Matteras?"

"Too long ago to tell," Golgoras said. "Whatever force cut the gears faded long ago."

"Damn."

"No sign of life for hundreds of knots," Golgoras said. "No witnesses. The perfect crime. The quest is over."

"There is the book to consider," Barabas said, morose.

"We should burn the fucking thing," Golgoras said. "Burn it, toss the Hume over the railing, and call it a day."

"He's a damn emissary," Barabas said after an alarmingly long pause.

"Er, guys, that's really not necessary," Rais said.

Golgoras ignored him. "Emissary, my ass. He's a damn trainee. There's no mention of him on the diplomatic rolls."

"He's Kaikobad's nephew," Barabas said. "Plus he's met Bahamut."

"You were a fool for taking him there."

"I've always been sentimental," Barabas said. "That's my tragic flaw."

"Er, guys? What's with this book? Shall I read it?"

"Do *not* read it," Golgoras snapped.

"And stop waving it around like that," Barabas said. "It's supposed to cause brain infection. We'll all get quarantined if anyone finds out you've got it."

"What difference does it make? We're all going to die soon anyway."

"What?" Golgoras asked.

"You haven't heard?"

"The Iso-Creationists have taken over the conservative faction. Matteras is threatening to flood the bay," Barabas said. "We're pretty sure he did Aceh back then as practice."

"That's only a little holocaust," Golgoras said. "Many Humes will survive, especially given the rate at which they breed."

"Oho, you're a Numerist?"

"Not as such, but you must admit there are a lot of them around," Golgoras said.

"What's a Numerist?" Rais said.

"Kind of club where they sit around moaning about how many Humes there are on this planet," Barabas said. "Lot of armchair generals. Never really get beyond vigorous fist shaking."

"Well, it seems like a straight-up political fight," Golgoras said.

"It gets worse. Bahamut has a device from Gangaridai," Barabas said. "Genuine article. He'll fracture time before he lets Matteras win. It's a Mexican standoff. What happens then is anyone's guess, but I'm not optimistic."

"Have you ever considered that Bahamut is stark raving crazy?"

"Frequently."

"Who exactly is supposed to stop this tea party? Tell me you've got some heavy guns lined up."

"You're looking at the A team."

"What about the Secret Archaeological Conservation Society?"

"Busy with some brouhaha in Kemet."

"Er, Kemet?" Rais asked.

"That's the black kingdom. Aigyptos, as you Humes call it," Barabas said.

"The Royal Anglers' Club?" Golgoras asked.

"They voiced their concerns, but they're a bit busy with their big Pacific whale-bashing contest. I think they promised to send Matteras a stern letter," Barabas said.

"Surely the Cabal for Zoological Variety will take a stand?"

"Well, sure, they're all for zoological variety, but Matteras has pointed out that his actions will only affect one particular species and might, in fact, promote zoological variety by freeing up space," Barabas said. "Solid argument, really, considering the extinction rate the Humes have racked up. Turns out that Zoological Variety is actually supporting him. Tacitly, of course. So it's up to us, really."

"We're doomed."

"Cheer up, think of the dignatas we'll accrue when we pull it off."

Rais, who had nothing to do, secretly attempted to read the book, despite the repeated admonition of the two djinns. They refused to touch it, and the Ghuls refused to even come into the same room.

He got through the first few chapters. It followed a loose format, part mathematical tract, part philosophical essay, and part bestiary of organisms that seemed pure fantasy. The drawings reminded him a bit of the Voynich manuscript, the famously mysterious fifteenth-century book in a gibberish language, which he had studied for a semester in university. It was only on the second pass that Rais understood some of the finer points, which progressively disturbed him until he actually put the book aside and went to the cockpit.

"This book," he said. "This guy. He's like... He's just... I mean, what the fuck?"

"I know," Barabas said. "Words are not enough."

"Goddamn right," said Golgoras. "What have you landed us in, Barabas?"

"Look, there's no reason to panic," Barabas said. "As I rationally explained earlier, there's no reason to think that Risal and the Maker are actually connected. I mean, she could just have his book—she was a rabid booklover for god's sake."

"Yeah, right. She just happens to have a book fucking banned by every fucking club and society in existence. The most fucking notorious and horrible thing ever written." Golgoras shook his great tusked head. "*And it's a fucking handwritten copy.* Givaras fucking gave that thing to her, I bet."

"You said Matteras fought this psycho djinn, right?" Rais asked, trying to think through a slew of strange mental imagery that seemed to have taken over large parts of his frontal cortex. It was as if the pictures from the book had crept up through his optical neurons and subtly infected random bits and pieces in his brain, recalling the time he had inadvertently taken three tabs of acid at the same time and spent a week hallucinating.

"Yeah," Barabas said.

"And then what?"

"He made him disappear," Golgoras said.

"They say that Matteras finally did him when they found some of the things he'd made were still living."

"So what did he do, anyway?" Rais asked.

"He made life. Tinkered with it, anyway. He was a bigwig at the Cabal for Zoological Variety, until djinns realized what kinds of things he was bringing to life," Golgoras said.

"He made the Ebola virus, they say," Barabas said. "Well, the virus is a by-product of creating the Ebola, which is a semi-invisible creature of rather horrific nature who actually feeds on the brain fluid released by the vic—"

"Okay, I get it," Rais said. "My point is first Matteras disappeared Givaras, then he disappeared Risal, and then my cousin."

"Hang on, we don't know about your cousin," Barabas said.

"Well, he disappeared, didn't he? And here we have a fucking expert at making things disappear, so I'd say that's a good lead, wouldn't you?"

"Calm down, I'm just saying you got to stick with facts and stuff—"

"Whatever," Rais said. "The point is, how come no one noticed all this disappearing?"

"Hmm, good point," Golgoras said. "The disappearances were spaced out over eighty-odd years. Hard to connect the dots."

"Frankly, we were all thrilled when Givaras got done, even Bahamut," Barabas said.

"Bahamut said all of this has something to do with the war," Rais said. "Risal had the *Register of Kings*, which is gone. And she had the Maker's book hidden. This is all connected to Kaikobad and my cousin. How?"

"The war was a long time ago," Golgoras said.

"It's a dead end everywhere," Barabas said, dejected.

"The funny thing is, *where are they? Where are the bodies?*"

"What?" Golgoras looked dumbfounded.

"I mean djinns don't kill each other, right? You guys are all la-di-da civilized..."

"Matteras is an archconservative," Golgoras said. "Djinn life is sacred. Murder is out. They take the Lore literally."

"Well, murder—aha!" Barabas said. "I've got it! I'm a genius! They're all in Matteras's murder pit!"

"That's kind of what I was leading up to..." Rais said.

"I've solved it!" Barabas was unstoppable. "We find the murder pit, we find all of them."

"They're all dead," Golgoras said. "That's the point of a murder pit. It's been years."

"Ha! It's Givaras. Wanna bet he's still alive?" Barabas said.

"So if this guy's alive, then my cousin's been stuck in a pit with this psycho djinn for the past ten years?"

"Yup," Barabas said. "Really bad luck, that. He's fucked."

CHAPTER 24
Kaikobad

Kaikobad stood on the seawall, staring out into the ocean. There were many others with him, watching. The city behind him was broken. The walls still held, her defenders still defended, but something vital had gone out: the sense of invincibility, perhaps; the insouciance that had characterized her lowliest denizen.

Six times, Kuriken had driven off the invading armies, scattering them, destroying their princes, taking the war across the world, to Kemet and Babylon, to high Lhasa and the plains of Harappa, everywhere djinn revolted, poisoned by Horus, who never fought, but whispered and cajoled, bringing madness in his wake. Kuriken had scorched the earth with his power, had extinguished tribes and ground to dirt nascent cities, yet nothing changed.

Six times, Memmion had returned, raising armies from god knows where, lately even raising the dead, animating them with power and hurling them like offal at the walls. Gangaridai had lost. The city might hold, might rule this land forever, but her dominion over the world was finished. The City of Peace was lost, the innocence and promise of the First Empire was gone, and with it came a peculiar sadness, as if a path had been shown and rejected: the djinn had chosen discord instead, had opted for violence, chaos, and random chance. For a brief period something wondrous had existed, but it was not the djinn way to bend the knee, to accept any master over their own desires. Peace was not to their taste. They had taught the world war, they had armed humans and Nephilim, and now there was no end to it.

The word of the day was Bahamut. Bahamut, the Marid of the Sea, was in open revolt, and every swell in the bay made the watchers flinch, as if he would emerge any minute and swallow them whole. No one knew what had turned him, this normally peaceable djinn who had slept for centuries. Ancient treaties of goodwill were broken. The lords of the First City had sailed ceaselessly into the deep, sending ambassadors, offerings, pleadings for parley. Bahamut answered only with rising waves.

There had been tremors underwater for many months now, small earthquakes that sent tidal waves up over the seawall, rattling the ships in the harbor. Bahamut was causing the earthquakes, testing some fell device. It was said that Bahamut taunted them, penned their great fleet in the slips, particularly galling as Gangaridai had been a maritime power, a far-flung network of trade routes, before the Marid of the Sea had turned against her. Ship captains despaired. Today, one old man, a famous navigator, had hanged himself from his top mast, unable to accept a landlocked world where he could no longer venture into the bay.

The Horologists still inhabited the basement of the King's Tower. The miasma of their sorcery had spread over more parts of the city. Food no longer rotted. Flowers bloomed for days, lending unearthly color and aching beauty to the scorched walls. Kaikobad could sense the uneasiness of the people as clocks stopped ticking, as confusion reigned over day and night, as hunger and thirst drew down, the urges of life fading, until they were like ghosts, going through the motions. Many fell into traps of repetition, playing the same game of chess over and over again, watching the same plume of smoke circling from mouth to hookah and back again, over the looping gurgle of water. The High King had unleashed some madness, some seductive alteration to the world, stealing upon them in their sleep, imperceptibly enough that they no longer recalled when it had first happened.

Kaikobad, drawn into the tale of the First City, now felt a gnawing despair. He battled to warn them, to tell them to flee, but the gate gave only memories. Perhaps somewhere there was another gate that would let him reach out and touch the skin of the world, but he did not know where, and it did not come to him, despite his prayers. Thoth consoled him in these moments. He had searched for the road himself, for as long as duration had no meaning. The road would take them back if only they could find it, the Charnel Road, the Bone Road—was blood and bone not the very essence of life?

When the watchers of the sea grew tired, they wandered off, and the waves got slightly higher every night, until they touched the lip of the wall and then regularly slipped over, creating a shallow marsh in the low end of the city, a flood at high tide that they had never seen. Unnerved, they barricaded the wall with their belongings, priceless furnishings tossed against the encroaching water, which moved like Bahamut's will, endlessly dripping, slow, inexorable.

Day after day, nothing happened, but the city drowned. The troubadours sang dirges. Wine was the order of the day, drunk in sorrow on the street corners, for they could all see that Bahamut would never come in cataclysmic fury. He didn't need to. He would kill them inch by inch, torture them with this slow, ceaseless deluge, and what army was there that could fight this? Young djinn and Nephilim played a game: they stood on the seawall with their field, holding back the water, reversing the tide, and it was a beautiful, noble futility, for their shield would hold for days, for weeks, until a single chink of exhaustion, a small faltering, would let in a drop, a trickle, and the strain would shatter everything, and they would have to start again, the water lapping at their feet half an inch higher. They faced their doom with smiles, with youthful bravado, as if there were nothing to lose.

"We will not fall," they said to one another, when the sun set and the campfires of Memmion's army in the burning fields grew oppressive. "The city cannot fall as long as we hold the walls. What does it matter if Bahamut sends the tides? We will be a city of boats."

Kaikobad wept for them, their lost innocence, and he wept for Indelbed, whom he could not see at all.

CHAPTER 25

Glandular Fever

Indelbed dreamed that wyrms were chewing on his extremities. This was understandable, given that Givaras kept talking about how his legs got eaten. Alternating with this nightmare was a second dream, which consisted mainly of a vision of Givaras sitting in front of a white background, taking a scalpel to his open brain. Indelbed would open his eyes and see the kindly face peering down, curious, enthusiastic, poking and slicing, all the time explaining things with excruciatingly boring scientific detail.

He explained this to Givaras, who dismissed it as his brain trying to cope with the close proximity to an actual proto-dragon. God's Eye was getting bigger, and the metamorphosis was visible now, with trills growing prominent around the neck, the jaws and snout elongating into something reptilian, the eyes glowing daily with increasing comprehension.

"The real interesting thing is this gland here," Givaras lectured, after the beast slept following a prodigious, cannibalistic meal. "In insects it would be referred to as the prothoracic gland. This creates the hormones that signal the body to prepare for change."

"Yes, that's interesting all right," Indelbed said from far away. God's Eye tended to thrash his head around if they got too close. He was getting an exaggerated sense of self now, an incipient megalomania and, with it, some awakening hostility toward his roommates.

"Do you realize that the hormones being released here are literally rearranging the insides of this creature? What wondrous things are occurring within? I wish I could cut him open now..."

"Hush!" Indelbed glared at his mentor. "*He can hear.* I swear he understands everything."

"It is very possible that the top of his spine is expanding. Here." Givaras pointed at the base of the neck, where iridescent scales were growing in beautiful patterns. "It is the beginnings of a higher brain. A perfect place to dissect... I know, I know, not another word on the matter. We can hardly throw away years of work on a whim..."

"Thank you."

"Ah, if you only knew what temptations I have been resisting," Givaras said mournfully. "Such opportunities for study..."

"Master, *please.*"

"Anyway, I have not been idle, like you," Givaras said. He brought forth a flagon fashioned from the inner membrane of a dead baby rock wyrm. They had, over the years, created a number of ingenious instruments from wyrm body parts, although Givaras tended to gravitate toward the head pieces. "I have been studying closely the incredible physiological changes occurring right in front of us—"

"Be careful he doesn't bite off the rest of you," Indelbed said. The thought of being without any company in the pit was horrifying.

"Life has been unfair to you, eh, Indelbed?" Givaras was looking down at him with something approaching compassion. "Losing your mother at birth, taken from your family at a young age and thrown into a pit..."

"I got to see the wyrms," Indelbed said. "And I got to see the distortion field and turn on the djinn lights."

"Do you still miss the living world up there?"

Indelbed shrugged. "I miss my dad. And Butloo. And the house. It's funny, when I was living there, I thought it couldn't get any worse. I guess things can always get worse. But at least I got to do magic. I'd never have seen magic living up there. I'd never have *known*, you know, for sure about this stuff."

"You're a good boy," Givaras said.

"Do you think we will really get out of here one day?"

"Perhaps, boy," Givaras said. "There is no knowing what an awakened rock wyrm will do. It was always a long shot."

"And you wanted to see a dragon, right?" Indelbed said.

"Yes," said Givaras. "I so desperately wanted to make one."

"So did I," Indelbed said. He patted the djinn on the shoulder. "Don't worry, if it doesn't work out. We'll keep trying."

Givaras hefted the flagon, passed it over. "I have been extracting the hormones from the prothoracic gland," he said. "A little at a time, while the wyrm slept. I have purified it with heat and the best of my art."

Indelbed looked at it blankly.

"I want you to take it," Givaras said. "In prescribed doses, it mimics the rate produced by the living gland."

"What?"

"I want to even the scales for you, boy," Givaras said. "I want to give you a fighting chance. Even if you survive the wyrms and escape the pit, how can you counter the wrath of Matteras? How can you fight off grown djinn who have lived for centuries? Who will protect you, when your own kin sold you out?"

"My kin?"

"Think, Indelbed," Givaras said. "Who gave you to the Afghan emissary? Who sent you away from your home, where the wards of your father protected you? What was the price for betraying a little boy, whom no one missed?"

Indelbed felt something drop in his stomach, a thick slug of metal in the gut, physically folding him in two like origami, and thoughts rushed through the careful fences of his mind, scattering defenses helter-skelter, and he felt anew every slight and turned face, every little sling, and the coldness of being alone. The natural cheer left him, leaving a yawning nothing, fingers of despair tightening around his throat, until he was convinced. Who left behind would have fought for him? The Ambassador? GU Sikkim? Aunty Juny? They had despised him one and all. His father? Was he even still alive? He tried to remember his face, but found that he couldn't recall anything much at all.

"What will this wyrm juice do?" he asked, his face tightened into a mask.

"I don't know," Givaras said. "I want to give you power. I want you to survive, to thrive in the world. The wyrm is becoming a dragon. What will you become, you offspring of human and djinn? Something hideous, perhaps. Or something beautiful, unique."

"Will you take it too?"

"No."

"Why?"

"Because I am afraid," said Givaras with brutal honesty.

"Will it hurt?"

"I do not know," Givaras said. "The wyrm appears content, yet he has no nerves in many parts of his body. I have never seen a wyrm change."

"But you've seen other things?"

"Insects go through partial or complete metamorphosis. Grasshoppers, for example, change from nymph to adult with a series of moltings, where they shed their skin and carapace for progressively larger and better-developed bodies. This is a gradual change; there is no need for a cocoon.

"The more advanced metamorphosis is severe. When a caterpillar pupates, the hormones liquefy the insides of the body, destroying everything to make building blocks for a new structure," Givaras said. "In such a case, the larva essentially ceases to exist and is rebuilt completely into a different creature."

"So my insides are going to melt, basically?"

"Nothing so drastic, I believe," Givaras said. "The wyrm, after all, seems to follow a process of partial metamorphosis—gradual changes rather than a complete pupation. Perhaps at some later time, it will enter a phase of radical change and create a chrysalis. For now, however, I believe that the change from rock wyrm to river wyrm will be gradual."

"And you have no idea what I will become?"

"It is a dragon hormone," Givaras said with a shrug. "I imagine you will become dragonish."

"If it hurts a lot will you be able to stop the pain?"

"I could probably turn off the parts of your brain that register pain."

"And what happens if I become something horrible? I mean like if my brain melts, or I become like some armless, legless slug?"

"I believe I can control the process somewhat, once the changes occur," Givaras said. "I will attempt to guide your metamorphosis. You have seen my skill with the field. If things are going badly, I will try to purge the hormones from your system. If you become something truly horrible, if you cease to be *yourself*, I will destroy you. But look on the bright side. You might learn to breathe fire!"

"You think I should do it?"

"You came in here a little boy. Look at you now, grown into a fine young djinn. A little undersized, but that's probably the diet. A nice, solid distortion field, and excellent fine control, if I say so myself. I have taught you mathematics, philosophy, biology, chemistry, and our djinn language, culture, and laws to the best of my considerable ability. You could not have had a finer teacher, I believe. Still, all of this will count for nothing when Matteras finds you. He will not accept you as a djinn—to him you are something loathsome. Both of us together couldn't make a dent in his field. He is *that* powerful. I think the hormone might be your only chance at survival. What have you got to lose?"

"Okay then, I guess I'll do it."

It took two days for his body to shut down. The hormone burned a track through his veins, like dragon flame in reverse, dripping through the fine hollow bone needles Givaras had whittled. Other needles had been placed strategically at acupuncture points, to relieve the pain and allow rapid spread of the hormone.

The pain was horrific. It was, for many hours, the only thing Indelbed could think about between screams, which at first he tried to stifle, and then let loose wholeheartedly, under Givaras's tender administrations. Something grew in his throat like a tumor, a scaly growth that set off panicked shouting, until Givaras took a dragon scale and cut his tongue out, scoring a bloody passage down his windpipe, draining out the blood carefully as it threatened to drown him.

"Don't worry, boy, you'll be able to grow it back later," he said. "Nothing to worry about. Just have to clear that air pipe a bit. Tongues are so useless anyway, eh?"

Each drop entering Indelbed's veins scoured him, and the progress of the hormone through his body seemed to destroy his organs; he imagined the tissue breaking up, the very cells melting under this virulent onslaught.

Givaras paused the drips occasionally, and this afforded him some temporary relief, although that was merely a dulling of the burning, a time to catalog the old horrors previously perpetrated on him.

By the third day, he had lost all faculties, and even the breaks were ineffectual, for his entire nervous system appeared to be revolting. Barely coherent, he begged his master in gestures to take out the needles, to reverse the process, to *hit him on the head with a rock*. Givaras explained in depth how it was better to stay awake as long as possible during the first shock, to avert the possibility of sliding into a permanent coma.

At hour eighty, he was delirious and time had no more meaning; he was an unmoored ship swaying on waves and waves of pain, not certain of his origin or his destination. Givaras's voice was a siren call of lucidity, far away and powerless to help, a mere reminder that he was not alone and this ordeal had some prior logic that was now lost to him.

The hormone itself was winding its way through him, puzzled at the lack of mass, trying to make chemical connections with parts nonexistent. Then, as fever took the host body and the temperature shot up to an almost unbearable level, the hormone began to experience minute alterations within its own receptors, a change caused by the searing heat, an upgradation to a different set of instructions.

At hour one hundred, things began to fit. Instead of the mushy, semideveloped organs of the larval rock wyrm, the hormones now began to recognize the sophisticated tissue of the new host body. They found the hormones of the endocrine system and hailed them like shipwrecked sailors floating in the ocean. They discovered warrior white blood cells, nerve endings, RNA signaling.

The heat-modified dragon hormones swept upstream, past the spine, avoiding the heart and lungs, until it reached the Turkish saddle at the base of the brain, where the pituitary, the master of all glands, quietly resided nestled against the hypothalamus, insignificant in size and demeanor, yet cunningly ruling the growth and subtle metamorphosis of the entire body.

When the dragon hormones reached the pituitary, there was a brief skirmish for control. Indelbed felt this conflict in the form of immense and varied agony in his skull. In the end, his pituitary capitulated shamelessly and allowed the foreign hormones to start making all kinds of changes.

At this point, there was a slight lull in the torture and Indelbed, with some slight calming cantrips from Givaras, was able to fall into a shallow, exhausted sleep. By hour 120, however, the pituitary was pumping out instructions in the form of new hybrid molecules, asking for big, big changes. In the near comatose state of the sixth day, the metamorphosis began in earnest.

CHAPTER 26
Moffat's Offer

Rais was in high spirits when Golgoras finally landed in the old airport hangar. Even though they had found nothing, he was sure they were getting somewhere. There was a mystery afoot, some strange web that connected all of this together. They had the name of a missing text and a second banned one. Besides, he had possession of Risal's entire collection, by dint of the laws of salvage, a truckload of books that would easily quintuple Juny's existing collection on the occult. At the very least, his mother would be ecstatic.

"Come on, Barabas, we're going to celebrate!" Rais said, grabbing the djinn around the shoulders.

"To your place!" Barabas said, cheering up. "Or do you want to hit the streets?"

"No, no, it's Thursday night, and we're going to my friend Moffat's house. I'm going to show you how they party in Gulshan."

"Rais, you choot!" It was midnight and their host Moffat was already drunk. This was no surprise really, for Moffat normally started in the evening or, on special party nights, directly after lunch. "And you've brought me a mullah. How charming. Can I keep him?"

"This is Barabas," Rais said. "He's a djinn. I've been meaning to get him some new clothes."

Barabas glared at him. "Thanks for having us, Mr. Moffat," he said in his most courtly voice.

"Any friend of Rais's..." Moffat waved them in.

Mofazzal "Moffat" Tareque was the hideously rich son of a now legendary real estate tycoon and MP who had allegedly buried a body in each of his ninety-three buildings, either for good luck or through a surfeit of corpses. Moffat occupied a duplex penthouse in one of these buildings, with his own elevator, bodyguard, and live-in bootlegger. His living room and adjoining garden stretched across half the roof, walled off from the hoi polloi, complete with a wet bar and a wading pool, which was empty now, but would soon be filled with naughty women. There was a grand piano under the shade in the patio, which Moffat played occasionally, when the drink made him maudlin.

Rais had met Moffat in kindergarten, when Moffat's father, rich but of awful birth, had shamelessly encouraged his son to befriend the scion of the Khan Rahmans. Moffat, a degenerate even at that age, hadn't given two shits about his father and had gone out of his way to kick the crap out of Rais at every opportunity. Almost inevitably, they had become best friends.

Decades later, Moffat was an expert at carousing, living off the rent from his innumerable properties, a modern-day raja with a court full of drunken sycophants and midnight nymphs. He threw ridiculous parties, and everyone came.

"What the hell, you fucker," Moffat said, leading them to the bar. "You never take my calls or what?"

"I've been up in the air a bit," Rais said.

"What do you guys want? Whiskey for Rais, just like his daddy. They say Khan Rahman blood is fifty percent scotch, ain't that right?" Moffat cackled. "What's the other fifty percent, I always wondered... something Anglo from the Welsh footman who raped your great-great-grandmother..."

"Fuck off, you inbred village hick," Rais said. "My great-grandmother used your people as footstools."

"A drink for the mullah? I've got pills, hash, pot, roofies, Viagra, cough syrup, Cheerios, Cubans, aaand coke. No yaba, I'm afraid—I don't allow that truck driver shit. One must have standards..."

"Hmm, Rais, this *is* much better than Kaiko's parties," Barabas said with a dreamy look in his eyes, as the bartender opened an old tea chest to reveal his cornucopia. "I'll take one of each, of course."

"Of course!" Moffat clapped him on the shoulder. "Good man! One of each for the djinn! Listen, dude, come with me for a second."

"What?" Rais let his friend lead him to a quiet part of the roof, where the music was a background hum.

"The djinn's a riot, man, I'm glad you brought him," Moffat said. "One of each..."

"You wouldn't believe some of the places he's taken me," Rais said. "Like slums inside slums. I wanted to show him a real party. Kick him out if he gets on your nerves, though."

"Nah, man, I love it." Moffat grabbed his arm. "Dude, I heard you've been cut off, kicked out, gone broke. You ever need some paper, I can cover you, you know that, right?"

Rais grimaced. "It's not that bad. Let's just say that my new line of work doesn't reimburse me in a regular way."

"I got some cash I owe you for that thing..."

"Forget it, dude, I'm okay for now." Rais pulled out a packet. It was an archaic gear the size of his palm, a soft-toothed, twenty-one-karat gold disk, which he had looted from Risal's home, where it had been connected to some plumbing device. Quite why such a mundane object was made of gold was a mystery, although Barabas had hazarded that djinn spells adhered best to the purer metals and the distortion field was best conducted through gold, which was the real reason alchemists so valued the metal. "Your dad still owns those jewelry stores in Chandni Chowk?"

"Yeah, I guess."

"Can you hawk this for me?"

"Solid gold, man." Moffat bit the gear in mock seriousness. "You into smuggling or what?"

"You wouldn't believe it if I told you."

"Try me, dude."

"It's supposed to be a secret."

"Man, look at me..." Moffat spread his arms like Jesus. "Do you think anyone believes a word I say? I'm like the ultimate junkie. Plus I'm your oldest friend, man. It's fuckin' weird not knowing what you do. Import-export? Like fuck. You don't know a sales invoice from your ass."

"I'm an ambassador to the djinn," Rais said. He pointed at Barabas, who was capering around under the happy confluence of hash and Pernod. "That dude—djinn. I just spent the last week or so on a djinn airship."

"What, you already get high before coming?"

"Moffat." Rais took his blue spectacles off and gently put them on his friend's nose. "Look around."

Moffat was already staring at Barabas, mouth open, smoke-slit eyes widening with excitement, so that for a moment he looked achingly like the boy he had been many years ago. His cigarette fell from nerveless fingers, and Rais put it out with a gentle tap of his heel.

"It's real..."

"Sure."

"Dude, I can see shit coming off of him... What is it, magnetic lines or something?"

"That's the juice."

"It's all real then..."

"What?"

"Djinns, magic, heaven, hell, *God*..."

"Djinns are," Rais said. He took the glasses back, put them on. "Not sure about the rest. By the way, your gardener is a djinn, I think."

"Whoa, what?"

"He's put little spells on each of the plants. To keep away pests, I imagine."

"That's awesome. I better give him a raise." Moffat swigged his drink. "So this is your life now? Hobnobbing with djinns?"

"It's not as exciting as it seems..."

"I'll give you fifty lakhs for those glasses." Moffat was abruptly serious.

"They are not for sale," Rais said.

"Seventy lakhs. A crore. Say a number."

Rais looked at him.

"There's the old haughtiness," Moffat said with a laugh. "Now I see the high-and-mighty six-year-old that I used to beat the snot out of. I missed that look. You've been so haggard lately."

"Fuck off, you idiot." Rais smiled. "Sell the gold for me, will you? I really *am* living on fumes."

"I'll send you the money tomorrow. If I remember." Moffat winked. "Where you living these days? I heard some terrible rumors about a flat in Mirpur..."

"I've taken over my uncle's place in Wari," Rais said.

"Dude, Wari?! You can live here, for god's sake. Hell, I'll give you your own wing..."

"Nah," Rais said. "But come by Wari sometime, if you're interested in this kind of shit. My uncle has some unbelievable stuff."

"Speaking of interested, some girls were looking for you."

"Fuck off, Moffat," Rais said.

"One of them was Maria," Moffat said with a sly smile. "She came by last weekend. I had a nautical-themed party. She wore a life vest and a captain's hat. That's it. Unbelievably hot."

"You're bullshitting," Rais said. "She's marrying some engineer in Alabama."

"Oho, so you *do* keep track."

"Yeah, yeah, Moffy, I thought I was in love, she was the one, blah blah blah."

"A common problem for you," Moffat said, "this pathetic descent into love."

"Well, you're a degenerate bisexual swinger," Rais said. "We can't all be perfect."

"Stick around, dear," Moffat said, smirking. "She promised to drop in."

Rais spent the next hour savoring Moffat's gold label, which, he had to admit, he preferred to the single malts lined up like venerable, slightly pretentious soldiers. There was something to be said for the smoothness of aged, blended whiskey that was better than the distinctive, slightly wonky taste of the malted stuff.

"I mean people act like every single malt is superior to every blended whiskey, but that's just ridiculous. Some of them taste like ass. And frankly, I don't really want a bunch of weird flavors in my scotch. I want it to go down smooth and not give me a hangover the next day. I'd take a gold label over a random eighteen-year-old any day of the week..." He was further expounding on this topic to another friend when a cool hand slipped around his neck and some kind of expensive perfume wafted over him.

"Random eighteen-year-olds been bothering you lately?"

"You smell different," Rais said, swallowing a mouthful. His friend smiled nervously at Maria and hurried off to spread the gossip that Rais and his old girlfriend were about to have it off.

"I tried to change a lot of things," Maria said, half throttling him before deciding to let go. She had always been deceptively strong. "But that doesn't always work out."

"Moffat said you've been stalking me."

"I need to talk."

"How's the engineer?"

"Gone back."

"So what is it? Getting cold feet? One last hurrah for us?"

"Hardly." Maria snorted in a most unladylike manner. In company she always affected a perfect textbook blend of well-bred demurity; with him she normally let loose her raucous, curse-filled, sarcastic harpy imitation. He had found it endearing before, had believed that he in fact was privileged to know her "real" nature, the lewd swearing an aphrodisiac. These tender thoughts had barely survived her unceremonious engagement to another man.

He waited for her to elaborate. She lit a cigarette, took a long drag, and blew smoke at him.

"I've left him."

"Why?"

"Because of you, asshole."

"Flattering as that may be..."

"Not *for* you, idiot, *because* of you."

"Why? He couldn't handle an ex-boyfriend?" Rais took a pull from the Never-Ending Pipe. He had played this same scenario numerous times in his head, had always come out of it vindicated and smug; now with Maria breathing fire in front of him, he just felt apprehensive and slightly wistful.

"Do you remember the pictures we took?"

"Yeah, that was your idea, if I recall."

"Well, asshole, why the fuck didn't you delete them when we broke up?"

"Er, I forgot?"

"Fuck you."

"Okay, I kept them for jacking off..."

"Ew."

"Joking. Really, I forgot."

"Well, did you give them to anyone?"

"Of course not," Rais said. "Look, I wouldn't do that, no matter how we ended."

"That's what I thought," Maria said. "Famous Khan Rahman honor. Well, some creep has them. Printed out in full HD color."

"Really? How'd they turn out?"

"You think it's a joke?" Maria spat out. "He came to my house, you fucker. He's blackmailing me."

"Why didn't you just pay him off?!" Rais asked. "Or called someone to have him taken care of?"

"Rais, he wasn't some street dude. He was scary," Maria said. "He knew everything about me. He knew everything about *you*. He wants me to spy on you. I'm supposed to get back together with you and then report everything to him. What the fuck are you into, you bastard?"

"What?" Rais felt the rapid sobering effects induced by fear. "So this wasn't some random sleaze? Describe this guy."

"He's old, like an uncle. He came in all suave and shit with an ivory cane and really expensive shoes. He said he was my dad's friend."

"What did he look like?"

"He had silvery-white hair, quite a lot of it, and looked very distinguished. He had an Oxford accent, like he'd actually been there and not just flown through Heathrow. He was tall, dressed really well, and was quite charming actually."

"Well, he seems like a catch," Rais said. "I'm surprised you didn't end up sleeping with him."

"Fuck off," Maria said. "And for your information, I never slept with the engineer while we were together either."

"How absolutely lucky for me. I can imagine his dismay."

"Actually, I was going through a virginal phase with him." She laughed. "You know, good girls wait for the wedding night and all that."

"Poor engineer. Well, what did this guy say about me?"

"Nothing," Maria said. "I told him you're a weird loser, and he said that you had a few 'large secrets.' He had this theatrical way of talking. And that god-awful cane."

"Wait, I have a feeling I know who this guy is," Rais said, as the composite details clicked in his mind and took him years back to the living room in Wari. "He wasn't Bengali, was he?"

"No, Kashmiri maybe? He didn't say."

"Afghani?"

"Maybe. You actually know him? Is this some sick revenge game?"

"No," Rais said. "And I'm sorry, Maria. I shouldn't have kept the pictures, although if this is the same man, he would have found some other way to get to you, I'm sure."

"Well, he's ruined my engagement," Maria said, grinding out her cigarette with unnecessary roughness. "And if he starts spreading those pictures around, my dad will just die. He's crazy too. He kept going on about genies."

"*Djinns*," Rais said. "He's the missing emissary Siyer Dargoman. He's a killer, never mind his accent, and he'll do a lot more to you than just ruin your chances on the marriage market."

"Ugh, you make it sound so vulgar," Maria said. "Arranged marriages are *in* these days. What the hell does this guy want, anyway?"

"He probably wants to kill me," Rais said.

"Good," Maria said.

"Fine then." Rais smiled. "I'm getting out of here. Thanks for the heads-up."

"Wait!" Maria snapped. "What the hell am I going to do? I'm supposed to be following you around like a retard girlfriend."

"I'd take the next flight to Chicago."

"And have that perv post my pictures everywhere?" Maria asked. "I'd never be able to come back home again."

"I'm kidding, you probably wouldn't make it to the airport anyway," Rais said. "I'm guessing he's having you followed, and me as well. As I said, pictures are the least of our worries."

"What the fuck is this all about? Are you like mixed up in some fundamentalist crap?"

"No, actually, I—*we* are mixed up with a bunch of djinns," Rais said. "Look, come with me, I'll explain everything and give you enough evidence to settle your doubts. We can figure out what to do afterward."

"Go where? It's the middle of the night," Maria said.

"Oh, come on, your reputation is in tatters anyway," Rais said. "And I'm hardly going to be forcing myself on you."

"Good," Maria said, flashing a butterfly knife from her purse, "because I've been wanting to stab someone, and it might as well be you."

"Remind me to give you the Invisible Dagger of Five Strikes," Rais said, laughing.

"And we better not be going to the dump in Mirpur," Maria said. "That place depressed the shit out of me."

"No, I've moved to my ancestral home in Wari."

"Wari?! Wari? Do people actually still live there?"

"It's a grand old house," Rais said with a perfectly straight face. "It was featured in the newspaper in fact. Come on. I'll drop you at home as soon as we're done."

They threaded their way across the now crowded terrace, avoiding invitations from various people, and had almost hit the door when Moffat came upon them with almost comical haste.

"Leaving?" he asked, slightly out of breath.

"Just giving her a lift home," Rais said. "Thanks, I'll call you tomorrow about the other thing."

"Er, good luck, glad you're on talking terms again." Moffat patted Maria's shoulder in an avuncular way. "Always rooting for you guys. You're not leaving your djinn behind, are you?"

"Oh shit, I forgot about Barabas!"

"It's just that he's taken his shirt off and he's lying on the piano and singing Beyoncé songs."

"You can keep him for seventy lakhs."

CHAPTER 27
Mata Hari

Maria was not, in fact, impressed with the ancestral home. She didn't like the fetid parking spot on the road, or the long, dusty walk through hawkers on plastic sheets and tea stalls peopled by undesirables who stared at her. She most certainly did not like the dilapidated disaster that was the front of the mansion, barely lit by naked yellow bulbs, if anything even more depressing at night.

They went inside, and Rais led her wordlessly to his uncle's suite, which consisted of the bedroom, a small living room, and a balcony, sparsely furnished, but the most heavily warded part of the house and therefore the safest, even though there was a large gash in the defenses where the intruder had struck, which was, miraculously, slowly healing.

"Well, at least you can tell that it was a grand house at some point," Maria said after a few minutes of awkward silence, which was strange because Rais had had many imaginary conversations lined up for just such a moment, yet nothing came out.

"Yeah, I might have exaggerated the grandeur of it a bit," he said.

"You think? It's a dump. Why the hell don't you bulldoze it and build apartments?"

"There's something in the will that prevents that," Rais said. "Gotta go to the next male heir intact, or whatever. In fact, I might even be the legal inheritor of this edifice, until my cousin pops up."

"Rais, he's been gone for like ten years." Her face softened a bit. "I don't think he'll be turning up anywhere. You've got to let that shit go, dude. What was he like anyway?"

"He thought he was a sterile mongloid freak," Rais said, and smiled. "He was just a regular boy. Never complained much, despite the shit people put him through. Anyway, to business. You want a drink? I stole a bottle of vodka from Moffat."

"Ugh. No."

"So here, put these glasses on."

"No."

"Humor me."

"I'll look hideous, Rais."

"Just look through them for god's sake."

"What the fuck? The room is full of spiderwebs! What is that shit? Invisible ink?"

"Spells," Rais said. "Made of dark energy or matter or whatever. Djinn stuff. This is one of the artifacts my uncle left. You can see all the hidden stuff with this."

"Wow. This place still looks like a dump."

"Look, it would be easier if you just believed me."

"Yeah, it would."

"Um, here, take a toke of this pipe."

"Hmm, not bad *shisha*."

"Now look inside, see, it's empty. I'm showing you actual magic. This is the Never-Ending Pipe. It steals smoke from the nearest living smoker. You're lucky with the *shisha*, by the way. Most of the time, in this house, I just get Bangla Fives. You ever smoked a Bangla Five? It's the harshest cigarette ever."

"Okay, that's interesting." Maria tossed the priceless pipe aside. "Look, Rais..."

Rais, fortunately, had thought of this eventuality, that one day someone would question his sanity and evidence would have to be furnished to back up any wild claims of flying djinns and underwater monsters. There were pictures on his phone, of Barabas leaning out of the airship, capering around the cockpit; of the aeronaut Golgoras in his bestial glory; even one of himself posing with the three hairy Ghuls. These were not hazy action shots in bad light, but rather well-composed selfies in full ten-megapixel close-up, where it was possible to distinguish each oily pore on Barabas's nose. The album was long, because Rais had been surreptitiously documenting his entire adventure, giant squid and all.

She went through them one by one, and her expressions told the tale, mocking at first, then frowning disbelief, and finally wide-eyed wonderment, an expression so unnatural to her face that Rais almost couldn't recognize her. She hadn't been impressed by anything since she was ten years old. He felt a rush of affection for her.

"So it's real," she said finally.

"Yes."

"And you are... what? Being haunted by them? Possessed?"

"My uncle, whose armchair you're sitting on, by the way, was an emissary. He's been in a coma for the past ten years. Emissaries are kind of like human ambassadors to the djinn," Rais said.

"And you're one of them?"

"I am trying to take my uncle's post. It is normally hereditary, but has to be ratified by a patron and a whole bunch of other courts and rules. Djinns love legal stuff. So I guess I'm an intern of sorts." Rais paused. "Oh, and my aunt was a djinn apparently. She died giving birth to Indelbed."

"A fine bunch of freaks in your family," Maria said. "You're the reason I'm in this mess—how're you going to fix it?"

"The man who's got your pictures," he said. "He's the one who took Indelbed. He knows what happened to him."

"No."

"What?"

"I'm not going to help you. Just fix this. I just want to get out of your whole sorry world once and for all."

"Maria, this man is a traitor and a murderer. He probably works for Matteras, the most powerful djinn in existence. Do you think he's just going to let it go at some dirty pictures? The second he thinks you're messing around, he'll torture and kill you."

"I'll just leave," Maria said. She was shaking, either from rage or fear. Almost certainly rage. "My aunt lives in London. I'll just take a flight out—you can have your stupid djinns all to yourself."

"What about your parents? Your little sister? Will they be willing to leave too? Will they even believe you? This is a man who kidnapped and almost certainly killed a ten-year-old child—a child who was half djinn. Do you think he'll hesitate to peel your dad's skin off and wear it as a cape?"

"That's sick."

"They're djinns we're dealing with, Maria!" Rais said, frustrated. "They don't follow any rules. And they don't care about humans."

"Okay, what's your plan then? When am I getting out of this mess?"

"When I do," Rais said.

"How, Rais? What am I supposed to do? Do you even have a clue?"

"I don't know, just play along," Rais said. "Try to find out more about him, where he lives, what he's doing here. If I could just get him alone, I could find out what happened to Indelbed, and maybe it would all make sense."

"What, you'd like ambush him?" Maria scoffed. "He'd kick your ass."

"Yeah," Rais said with a smile. "Probably."

"What am I supposed to tell him? He's going to want a fucking report."

"Just tell him you've managed, with great difficulty, to get me into bed..."

"Gross. You're enjoying this."

"Sorry, I really am. I would never wish you harm, no matter what, you must know that," Rais said. "I'm grateful you told me the truth."

"I wouldn't lie to you," Maria said. "I mean, I'm not a liar."

"Look, buy some time. We can figure this out. Tell him I'm hanging with Barabas."

"The creep you brought to the party? He's a djinn?"

"Yeah."

"God. Why am I always stuck with losers? Where are all the cool fucking djinns?"

"Ah, so, you can sleep over if you like. I'll take Indelbed's room."

"I'd rather sleep on the pavement. Just drop me off at home, asshole."

CHAPTER 28

Brokers

"A billion billion worlds spin like tops all throughout the darkness, according to your own science," Givaras was saying, as he dripped water into Indelbed's cracked, parted lips.

Indelbed had achieved consciousness through a haze of delirium, guided by the drone of his master's lecture. He felt as if he had come out on the other side of death. Memories were tenuous, his understanding shaky. The pain had abated somewhat from before, at least in his brain, which throbbed and twinged still, but with less urgency. His other great realization was that he was paralyzed from the neck down, and something was horribly wrong inside his mouth and throat; specifically his tongue was gone, leaving blinking and eye swiveling as his only method of communication.

"Who knows, then, how many awful things have arisen?" Givaras continued. "How many terrible random creations, how many old horrors lurking in corners? When I realized that we ourselves are an accident of mutation, then what other fantastical powers could elsewhere arise? Hmm? And what would be our defense? Look here, our abilities are manifold compared to the rest of unitary life that has developed on this world, making us superior beyond comparison. But what of other worlds, other dimensions, hmm? Would we, similarly, be outmatched one day? Crushed beneath foot like a cockroach? And let me remind you that the basic study of evolution reveals a constant natural struggle between life-forms for scarce resources, often leading to the outright extinction of the losers. What then awaits us? And remember, we were never numerous. The most successful forms of life can replicate quickly and continuously. Complex, long-lived creatures like us are prone to extinction."

Indelbed, who had heard much of this before, tried to communicate that he was now conscious and extremely concerned. Givaras eventually noticed his frantic blinking and smiled down benevolently.

"Yes, your tongue, unfortunately, had to be removed. Something was changing in the structure of your throat, and I was afraid you'd choke," the mad djinn said. "And subsequently, *really* impressive changes occurred inside your trunk, which put you in convulsions, caused by pain possibly, which I feared would kill you, so I took the precaution of paralyzing you by breaking your spine."

At this point Indelbed, knowing full well that Givaras was not joking, nearly ruptured his eyelids trying to voice his extreme distress at these remedies.

"I suspect by now you would have gone mad from the suffering had I not paralyzed you. I will keep you in this state until I am certain the worst is gone. Of course this method of pain control is extreme and not precise. Please let me know if you start feeling things again."

Givaras pottered around somewhere and then returned. "You're wondering whether I can reverse the process and fix your spine, no doubt. I have had extensive experience, I'm afraid, in grafting tissue and healing various injuries. Part of my time has been spent as a zoologist. I have, of course, experimented on hybrid creatures before, but never one such as you. Human-djinn offspring are regrettably few and far between, and your lineage is particularly interesting. Also, not many of you consent to my little experiments. Now no more conversation, dear, I must concentrate."

Whatever Givaras was doing didn't hurt, and as Indelbed couldn't see anything anyway, he was, after a period, in the bizarre situation of actually being bored while in the middle of what was possibly the most horrible medical procedure in the history of man or djinn. As the panic died away, he entered a period of calm where he accepted that it was better to be paralyzed than tortured, and if the next remaining step was a painless death, it was not such a bad thing. He was just drifting off into a Zen-like state when Givaras again prodded him awake with further news, demonstrating conclusively his ability to torture with his voice alone.

"Of course, you're lucky that I am prepared with instruments," the djinn said, waving wyrm bone utensils that, horrific enough to begin with, were rendered even more nightmarish by the gore dripping off them—gore that had up to this point existed peacefully inside Indelbed.

Indelbed blinked his assent to how lucky he was.

"I'm afraid I've not been candid with you," Givaras continued. "You may be wondering how I have magicked such equipment out of the blue. When my colleague Risal was expiring, it was in fact a long and drawn-out affair. Marids, you know... very difficult to finish off. I tried to save her, indeed I did. My knowledge of the wyrms was limited then. I tried to introduce their bile into her system, to see if I could balance the humors. It did not work, of course. She was terribly weak, not healthy like you. Also of course, I had no knowledge of or access to the wonderful hormones of a growing wyrm. Still, I believe I have learned a lot from my failure. There are now poisons building in your blood, which will eventually destroy your organs. It is necessary to purge them from time to time. I made the error of bleeding Risal. In her weakened state, she went into a coma. After that she was never quite the same. I believe now that we have to burn the poison out. I will try a technique of heating your blood, essentially boiling it. The pain is going to be rather horrid; I think some of the sensations will get through despite your damaged spine. However, you should survive, which is the main thing. It's only pain, eh?"

Indelbed, who had at this point given up on survival as anything to be thankful for, blinked a few times and tried to add a silent scream to the discourse for good measure: *No. No! NO! No, it hurts, it hurts, ow, ow, ow, stop...* Givaras was not one to wait around with scientific endeavors, and once the blood started boiling, the pain indeed managed to overcome the block and once again flood Indelbed's neurons. Instinctively, spurred into concentration by agony, he tried to pull together his distortion field, if for no other reason than to smash Givaras into atoms, but in this too he failed miserably, leaving him with no other option but to lie back and pray for the oblivion he had so foolishly left behind.

Rais woke up saturated with nightmares. It was as if Givaras's book had opened some kind of door in his brain and destroyed some filter, allowing a torrent of random, horrible things to assault him. This dread followed him throughout the morning. He wandered around the veranda aimlessly, brushing his teeth, drinking cold water and trying not to puke it back up. Hangovers were getting much worse. He tried to recall the conversations with Maria, whether he'd made an ass of himself. Some of the memories made him cringe. On the whole it was nice having her back in his life, even though she had left in a huff.

The bell rang soon, and Butloo scurried to open the door. It was a messenger, Moffat's old driver, another hoary family retainer with three dozen years of service. He and Butloo knew each other somehow—they had a few quick words—and Moffat's man was content to leave the package with him.

"Moffat Sahib sent this," Butloo said, and handed over a paper bag. It was filled with ten bricks of cash, new notes in the original bank rubber bands. "He said the gold was very pure. If you have more, he will take it."

"Good." Rais took the packet. He threw one of the bundles at the butler. "You haven't been paid lately, have you, Butloo?"

"No time in the past twenty years, sir," Butloo said.

"Oh," Rais said.

"Nor has any of the bills, sir," Butloo said. "They do not cut the electric or water lines because they are afraid of the house, sir."

Rais kept a bundle and handed over the rest. "You better keep it then. Just pay out as little as you can, I don't know when I can get more. Buy some decent food for us, for god's sake."

Butloo blinked in surprise. Kaikobad had never even attempted to pay his bills. It seemed an insult to his memory to start throwing money around. "This is far more than enough."

Rais's next visitor was not so welcome. He had barely finished lunch when Golgoras stomped in, his disguise imperfectly placed so that Rais could see half a tusk each superimposed on his otherwise unremarkable bottom lip. Barabas followed him, looking disgustingly healthy and rather smug. Rais blinked, trying to clear his vision. His eyes were always tired now; it felt like Kaikobad's glasses were rotting his brain.

"Get ready," Golgoras said. "You're coming with us."

"I'm sick," Rais said. Hangover and distortion field were combining for a very unpleasant feeling.

"These humans are so weak." Golgoras glared at Barabas.

"It's not my fault," Barabas said. "Kaikobad was the real thing. This one won't last very long."

"Okay, guys, what's the big rush?"

"Captain Golgoras here has joined the team!" Barabas beamed. "We are like the three muskets!"

"Musketeers," Rais said.

Golgoras held up a hand. "I have been chartered by the Royal Aeronautics Society to formally investigate the disappearance of the Marid Risal.

That's all. It's a stretch. As a sky dweller, she could be considered a de facto member of the society."

"Won't hold up," Barabas said knowingly. "Society rules only apply to moving vehicles."

"Ordinarily, yes, but the sky tunnel was unmoored and therefore drifting..."

"Okay, guys, please," Rais interjected. He knew these conversations could carry on for hours. "I've found the missing emissary. Or rather, he's found me..."

"The one who took Kaikobad's son?" Barabas suddenly looked rather keen.

"The minor hunt boy?" Golgoras asked. "I remember that. I tried to get him myself. No one claimed the reward in the end."

"We can finally find out what happened," Rais said. "Help me capture the emissary Dargoman, and Barabas can torture him until he talks."

"You can't just kidnap emissaries left and right," Barabas said. "Bad form. Of course, if you really want to..."

"Later," Golgoras said. "We have bigger squid to grill. Matteras is having an Assembly. I will attend, as the ranking member of the RAS in this area. I got the invitation last night. You two will accompany me. This is important. It might be our last chance to gauge the mood before he goes ahead and does what he's been threatening."

"Well, it's so rude not to invite me, seeing as I am Bahamut's most particular client..." Barabas was huffing.

"Bahamut ain't what he used to be," Golgoras said. "Get ready, Hume. You're the closest thing we have to an emissary. I believe the Hume point of view will be in short supply."

"Er, guys, what am I supposed to do in this Assembly?" Rais asked.

"It's between a debate and a press conference," Golgoras said. "You keep your mouth shut and look stupid. We want to test the mood first before trying anything. You know what happens to oversmart emissaries?"

"What?"

"They get squashed, like Kaikobad."

The same morning, while Rais trembled through half-remembered nightmares, his father, the honorable ex-ambassador, was taking his morning constitutional around Baridhara, enjoying the crisp air and general lack of traffic. Schoolkids aside, this was the best time of the day. He had just sat down on his customary bench in the little strip of park when something sharp poked him in the back.

He yelped and turned in outrage, when someone slapped him across the face, hard enough to send him sprawling. The emissary Dargoman stepped into view, casually dangling the cane sword in one hand, a thin trickle of blood dripping from the point.

"You!" Vulubir Khan Rahman shouted, recognizing him instantly. The man had hardly aged.

Dargoman hit him again, this time with a closed fist. The Ambassador found himself on the grass, his head spinning, the sun suddenly hot, blood leaking from the stab wound in his back.

"You people just don't know when to stop," Dargoman said.

"What the hell? Uncle Sikkim told me everything was fine..."

"Everything. Is. Not. Fine." Each word was punctuated with a slap. "That old fool has lost control. Your bloody son is not backing off."

"Stop! Stop. We did everything you said!" The Ambassador lay sprawled on the ground, reeling. "What do you want me to tell him?"

Dargoman stood over him, the sword point hovering like a wasp.

"Nothing," he said. "You *are* the message."

The Ambassador cringed away as the sword came down, stabbing through his upraised hand and punching into his chest with disturbing ease. He had a heart attack at the same time, the organ seizing from sheer terror, so that by the time the blade actually penetrated, it was rather a moot point. The cane sword was a civilized weapon, the exit leaving a narrow kiss of red on the Ambassador's white shirt, and as he flopped to his side, a thin quantity of blood discreetly watered the grass. From far away he looked like a man taking a nap on the grass, and it was only an hour later that the park caretakers bothered to investigate. By that time Dargoman was far away, and no one had noticed a thing.

The Assembly was in the ballroom on the second floor of the Westin, the exit from the lift discreetly protected by a couple of humans with concealed guns. It was hardly necessary. More than thirty senior djinns from all over the world were attending; the power of their combined distortion fields outweighed the Russian nuclear arsenal.

"Oh god, they're all in suits," Rais said with a groan. "It's a formal event."

Barabas was also looking somewhat dismayed. "You could have told us," he said accusingly to Golgoras.

"Never mind," the pilot said. "There wasn't time. Matteras's invitation arrived 'late.' He doesn't want us here."

"I'm going to get you guys makeovers after this is over," Rais said. "We look like assholes."

As they neared the double doors, the nauseating hum of a field generator hit Rais, making him gag discreetly. He slipped on his glasses and reeled back from the intricate spheres of power pulsing from the entrance.

"It's a phase shifter," Golgoras said. "Matteras isn't messing around."

"All the top djinns must be coming," Barabas said. He sounded nervous and starstruck at the same time.

The security here was a bit more serious: a dapper djinn with a jackal head stood tall, sleek and black furred, red eyes scanning the crowd restlessly. His field was clenched tightly around his body, almost like armor, a pearlescent shimmer of potency.

"It's Hazard," Barabas squeaked. "The Iso. They say he's the best duelist in the world. He's never lost a fight! Retired undefeated! Oh my god!"

"Listen, do you want his autograph?" Rais asked.

"Hazard." Golgoras nodded. "You're running the door now?"

"Captain," Hazard said in a guttural growl. "Last-minute thing. Matteras wanted it discreet. Some important folk coming down for the palaver." He flicked his glance lazily toward Barabas and Rais. "Not sure about your friends, hey?"

"Emissaries welcome, surely?"

"Of course," Hazard said. "Quite a few attending. Not sure your man is really up to standard, hmm? No offense." He threw the last line at Rais with mocking politeness.

"None taken," Rais said.

"He's one of Bahamut's," Golgoras said.

"Ah, yes, isn't he some kind of giant fish these days?"

"Hmm, yes, aquatic," Golgoras said.

"Perhaps you knew my uncle Kaikobad," Rais said.

Hazard glanced down for a second. "Yes, of course," he said in a more normal tone. "I was sorry to hear about his accident. Is he still alive?"

"Yes," Rais said. "And you heard that his son went missing all those years ago?"

"Yes, of course. The minor hunt boy."

"I'm Kaikobad's de facto heir," Rais said. "I understand Djinn Lore supports such a claim until formal ratification of the post."

"Perhaps," Hazard said.

"And in such a circumstance one might say his auctoritas would accrue to me, only in the dispensation of professional services, again pending final ratification."

"That is highly debatable. Personal auctoritas would not—"

"As such, would I be the highest-ranking ambassador in the room?"

"Well, Kaikobad would have been," Golgoras said with some amusement. "I think he's got you, Hazard. I will formally extend the support of the RAS toward seconding his motion. We can convene a hearing right here—you look like you have a quorum. We can postpone the Assembly a bit."

"Debatable, yet within the Lore." Hazard bared his teeth. "Matteras won't be amused by a motion delay. It will take weeks of argument to sort out his legal status. We can dispute this another day. Welcome, then, nephew of Kaikobad. I hope your term as an emissary is less eventful than your uncle's."

They walked into the field generator, which was a beautiful brass machine puffing out dirty white smoke like an errant cigar, along with belching noises, none of which seemed to bother any of the Ghuls climbing over the gears and levers. The aperture was similar to a metal detector, and they crossed it single file, passing a threshold that twisted reality by a quarter inch, a subtle shifting of time and space that permitted the djinn absolute privacy. To the outside world, everything within the field was simply not there, it was an empty room.

The djinn inside the field were not bothering with disguises. Thirty of the most peculiar shapes were walking around guzzling wine and food, from a thing made entirely of leafy branches to a walrus-man, who resided inside his own bubble of water and made life inconvenient for everyone by shouting commands through a loudspeaker inserted into a periscope-like opening. Distinguished men of varied races walked among the djinn, emissaries come to represent different interests. With a sliver of fear, Rais made eye contact with Dargoman, who lounged across the room attended by a flunky, his cane tapping his foot restlessly. The Afghan raised his fingers in acknowledgment. Rais could see spells circling large parts of his body, caterpillars inching around an apple core.

"Everyone here is very, very important," Barabas gushed.

"I see him," Rais said. He couldn't take his eyes off the Afghan.

"And look, Matteras is serving caviar and everything," Barabas said, stuffing himself. "I mean Bahamut is the stingiest host ever, never even gave us a fish."

"Hush," said Golgoras to Rais. "We can't get to your enemy here. You have to wait. Matteras is about to speak."

"Welcome, friends," Matteras said, tapping his glass. Hazard stood behind his shoulder like a dark specter, his jackal face grinning mindlessly. "Thank you for coming."

"Really, Matteras, it's a damn shame, dragging me down here," a white-haired djinn grumbled as everyone settled down. "I mean, we appreciate the whole Givaras thing, but—"

"I assure you, Beltrex, this will interest you. The question at hand—"

"Just get on with it," Beltrex said.

"The question is one of real estate," Matteras said, "or the alarming lack of it."

"The old Numerist argument," Barabas whispered to Rais.

"Beltrex? I've heard that name somewhere..." Rais said.

"For thousands of years, we have shared this earth with human civilizations, guiding them, helping them, living among them," Matteras said, raising his voice to cover the room. "As many of you are aware, after the Great War, a decision was reached to practice a policy of Seclusion. The destruction wrought in that war precipitated the final ice age, causing the near extinction of both man and djinnkind."

"Surely you are not arguing against Seclusion!" Beltrex bellowed. "You're mad!"

Several other djinns hooted their approval.

"He hates humans and wants to take us to war!" Walrus shouted. "Look at me! I'm too old to fight wars!"

"Not at all," Matteras said. "I assure you—"

"Look at Hazard, he's pointing his teeth at me!" Walrus interrupted. He began rolling toward the center of the room in martial fashion. "I say, I've got teeth myself. Put up your sphere, little jackal, let's put that undefeated record to the test!"

There followed an immediate outbreak of odds calling and side betting, and demands for better lighting and an impartial referee.

"Wow, these guys are all crazy," Rais said.

"There's a reason djinn prefer to live in isolated places," Golgoras said. "Too many of us in one place always leads to fighting."

"No fighting, please, Walrus," Matteras said, fending off his bubble with one foot. "Look, we all know your tusks are bigger. Poor Hazard can't help where his teeth point—he's got a damned jackal head for god's sake. I've asked him a hundred time to be a bit more orthodox, but there you are, can't have everything, eh?"

"Hmm, yes," Walrus said. "Perhaps. My own teeth have been known to point askew."

"The warmonger Matteras has riled up poor Walrus!" Venerable Beltrex, who was hard of hearing, appeared to have trouble following the proceedings. "Shame! Shame!"

A coterie of djinns, who seemed to find it funny to repeat Beltrex, now took up the chant with aplomb.

"Look, everyone, *I am not a warmonger*!" Matteras shouted. "I just want to discuss the issue of space. Beltrex, you're always complaining about how crowded California is these days."

"Yes, true, those boys keep slapping roads everywhere..."

"And, Walrus, am I right in thinking the arctic ice is giving you trouble?"

"Can't find a patch without a bear taking a shit on it," Walrus said.

"Well, all I'm saying is that for the past thirty centuries, human civilization has just kept on growing. They've literally used up all the space. I mean, it was great when it was a couple of villages by the two rivers, but now they've spread everywhere! You can't even go into orbit without bumping your head on a satellite. Right, Golgoras?"

"Hmm, well, it *is* getting a bit harder to fly around," Golgoras said.

"There isn't a single square mile left where they don't have a drone or a beacon or an outpost," Matteras said. "Even poor Bahamut living in those ruins keeps getting harassed by oil drills and scientific probes. We can't hunt whales anymore, can't race giraffes, can't blow up volcanoes because there's always someone living underneath them."

Everyone was nodding along now, even Barabas. Rais kept waiting for some of the emissaries to speak up, but none did. Many of them looked bored, genuinely unconcerned. Others slunk around Dargoman, paying circuitous homage to the man; he had dealt with the ones who counted, and Matteras had removed the recalcitrant ones from the board. Whatever was happening, it was clear that this Assembly was intended to be a formality.

"You gotta have seclusion, you know..." Beltrex butted in weakly.

"What I propose does not violate the policy of Seclusion one iota!" Matteras said.

"He's smart," Golgoras said quietly. "No way he can overturn Seclusion in one sitting."

"What is it?"

"It's been the cornerstone of our human policy for the past fifteen thousand years," Golgoras said. "After all those disasters following the war of Gangaridai, the elders decided to retreat completely into the background and deny our existence. Humans kept trying to worship us. You were corrupting us with power—good djinns getting tricked into becoming godkings and cult leaders—and the rest of us would have to band together and deal with it. It was exhausting. Or so I'm told. I wasn't alive then, of course."

"You're lucky the Seclusionists won the day," Barabas said. "I heard that the other options put forward were exterminating humanity altogether, or rounding them up and raising them like cattle."

"How generous of you guys," Rais said.

Matteras was continuing meanwhile: "I have long studied the global effects of human civilization. Suffice it to say that I have the full backing of the Weather Channel Enthusiasts' Club when I say that the climate is nearly wrecked beyond repair, and almost all flora and fauna are facing extinction in the next fifty years if the poisoning continues at this rate."

There was a murmur of agreement. The Weather Channel Enthusiasts' Club was a very well-respected organization, which reflected djinn fascination with weather channels. Many of the renowned weather girls on TV were in fact members of the club.

"Given their current predicament, humans are fully expecting natural disasters to strike them down," Matteras said. "Recall Katrina? I assure you, all natural."

"Is that the girl on NBC?" Beltrex asked.

"Er, no, that was a hurricane, Beltrex."

"And that big tsunami in Aceh?" a dapper djinn in a suit called out.

"That one had a bit of help," Hazard said with a grin.

"Aceh was a test," Matteras said. "Our apparatus can create a tsunami five times greater. Our proposal is this: we will utilize the device in the Bay of Bengal to start with. The following earthquake damage, tsunami, and hurricane will effectively depopulate the entire coastal region, possibly the entire subcontinent, as well as Indochina. Humans in this area will return to the Stone Age, which is, I must say, where I much prefer them to be."

"To start with, you say?" asked Beltrex.

"Yes, I would naturally make it available for anyone else who wants to use it." Matteras smiled. "In California, for example? They have a lot of earthquakes, I believe? Surely a really big one wouldn't surprise anyone..."

"Hmm, well, yes, I'm not sure I'd go that far..."

"The simple math is this: there are too many of them. They breed faster than we ever thought possible, they occupy every inch of earth and sea, and their rapid technological advancement means they are beginning to change the natural order of things. They're already living longer. The rich ones will stop dying altogether pretty soon. I know of an emissary right in this room who's had fifteen liver replacements. Fifteen! God knows what else he's changed!"

The emissary in question, an old Australian gentleman, had the good grace to look abashed.

"A few small accidents, and we set back the clock. We keep them manageable. Otherwise, sirs, you will wake up one day from a good long nap and find our world completely unrecognizable. I am not heartless. I am not a murderer. But humans are reckless vermin. We have stood by and watched, and they have slowly destroyed the very fabric of our culture. If we continue on this path, there will be no djinnkind anymore! Only fragments, riding human lucre, lurking in corners, stripped of all natural majesty—a race of charlatan street magicians doing tricks for a living. We were kings, and now we are interlopers in our own lands, pushed out by our own mercy, our own belief that we must somehow preserve our inferiors!

"A worthy sentiment, my fellow djinns, a civilized stance, but woe to us that we daily grow more human than djinn, broken, our princes and kings mere figureheads, our great patrons swimming in disinterested seas, clinging to some ancient past, our days of glory gone. Young djinns grow up debauched, with their drugs and their rap music, content to wallow in luxury. Where is the Lore, I ask you, where is the Mos Maiorum? Where is our dignatas, when they prefer simple human currency, filthy human specie backed by empty promises, a fraud perpetrated by the rich on the poor? What will happen when our generations abandon their ways? What will we become but another kind of human, occultists, shadowy figures plotting, all remnants of blood gone, all memories lost?

"They are too many! They drown us in temptations. Every year, more of the djinn breed with them, producing the sickly, sterile, broken offspring of neither race. Every year, our youth dwindle, and these febrile hybrids, these abominations, litter the earth—drooling, disabled creatures, neither djinn nor man, but loathsome beasts. We are the chosen race! Are we to end our days in obscene couplings with jumped-up monkeys? Chosen by God, I say! Chosen by fire! And have we maintained the purity of fire? No! Take care, gentlemen, lest the flame dwindle into idle smoke.

"They are too many, sirs! They are too many, and they are advancing too rapidly! We accepted them into our kingdoms, and they have become the masters, unaware of our very existence. If we do not act, we will cease to be djinn. We will become them! We will be swallowed! In fifty years they will be too many, they will be too advanced! Already their physicists hypothesize about the field. One day some patent clerk or other will make a machine to manipulate it, and then where will we be? We will have given away our birthright to apes with thumbs!

"They are too many, I tell you, and we are too few! If it comes to war, in fifty years, we will lose! It is our survival, and we must clear for us some space. As their nature is to occupy every inch of land, we must make it so unpleasant that they leave of their own accord.

"This is a mere interlude, sirs, a slow war of occupation. We were willed these lands! We were given these by God! From the dawn of time, we have nursed these humans like pets, raised them like dogs, and now we reap our harvest. We have squandered our superiority, our divine power. It is a sin! We were created to rule, sirs, and what do we rule? What dominion do you now hold, Beltrex? A few dusty grapes in a vineyard? Do you remember what it was like to roar in the plains, to tremble the endless herd of bison? How many subjects do you have, Kuriken, in your hollow kingdom? You once ruled all things Rus, from the taiga to the sea. If times were better before, then let us go back to them. If you are too squeamish, then allow me, sirs, to strike for you, allow me to act, give me this one chance to turn back the clock!"

If he had any further admonishments, they were drowned out by tumultuous applause.

CHAPTER 29
Final Solutions

They took a break for refreshments, as djinn were wont to do, which gave everyone time to mull over things. Djinn being naturally cliquish, no one was willing to voice an opinion until he had gauged the general mood of the Assembly. Rais circulated the crowd, picking up snippets. He was somewhat notorious due to the legal wrangle he had incited by his application, and several people hailed him, asking after Kaikobad. One indigent-looking djinn even inquired about his mother and surreptitiously asked for a loan.

He came into the orbit of Dargoman once, and the Afghan gave him a cold bow and tapped his cane suggestively. The old emissary had a reckless violence about him, barely constrained, as if only the smallest nod to etiquette was stopping him from running Rais through.

"We're fucked," Barabas said glumly, as Rais joined him and Golgoras next to the buffet line.

"It's the numbers thing," Golgoras said. "I'm not averse to humans, but it's perfectly clear that we're getting to a point of no return. Lots of the younger djinns feel that way."

"And that drooling hybrid thing got me," Barabas said. "Those things give me the creeps."

"What happens here? Do we get a vote or something?" Rais asked.

"More of a feeling-out process," Golgoras said. "Any major objectors are supposed to voice their opinion now, preferably with legal backing. Any serious points, and it gets kicked to the courts. If everyone goes along, then he can do what he pleases, and damn the consequences. His dignatas is big enough to handle it."

"So like are you going to object, or pussy out?" Rais asked.

"What?"

"Big bad pilot, you haven't said shit yet."

"I'm biding my time. And best watch your tone, Hume."

"'Cause it looks a bit like you're intimidated."

"Shut up," Golgoras said. "There's a way of handling these things."

"And Barabas, aren't you Bahamut's right-hand man?"

"Er, yes, but I might have exaggerated my auctoritas. I'm not sure these big guys will pay any attention to me."

"I can see that," Rais said. "Bahamut really wants to use his bomb, I guess. I can't believe he's not going to put up a fight. I'm beginning to wonder if he *can* actually fight."

"Bahamut is a legendary fighter!" Barabas said hotly. "He fought in the Great War!"

"It's funny that everyone keeps talking about the Great War."

"Well, it's the Great War. Much greater than any of those puny wars you Humes have fought."

"It's just weird that no one seems to know any actual facts."

"What do you mean?"

"Well, I keep asking around, but no one can give me any details. Who fought who, exactly?"

Golgoras looked puzzled. "Well, djinn and men, obviously."

"Against each other?"

"No, no, they were allied," Barabas said. "Remember that old song about men and djinn marching off?"

"Right, Gangaridai, the original one, that was djinn and men living in harmony, the golden age, the eternal city, blah blah blah," said Golgoras.

"So djinn and men fought who? Who were the enemy?" Rais asked.

"Er, I guess another bunch of djinn and men? I'm not a damn historian," said Barabas.

"And Gangaridai was one of the cities fighting? It was like one of the main sides?"

"Yes, yes, we all know the famous battle in which Gangaridai got wrecked," Golgoras said. "Remember that song about the Spires of Ganga?"

"Battle? No, no, Gangaridai got wrecked after. I thought it was the lords of Gangaridai that blasted the ice age and ruined the world," Barabas said. "Must have been Matteras's forefathers, come to think of it, that royal bastard."

"So there was a war fought by djinn and men against other djinn and men, involving Gangaridai in a grand battle that might or might not have set off an ice age," Rais said. "See what I mean about everyone knowing fuck all?"

"Well, it *was* twenty thousand years ago," Golgoras said, aggrieved. "You can't even remember what happened two thousand years ago."

"So who won the war?"

"What?"

"Who won?"

"You know, I have no idea..." said Golgoras. He stared at Rais. "You raise a good point."

"Bahamut *told* us to look in this direction." Rais said. "In fact it was pretty much the only lucid thing he said."

"It was a holocaust. Nearly destroyed both man and djinn," Golgoras said. "It birthed the policy of Seclusion. It was twenty thousand years ago. It is no wonder that we don't dwell on it. But surely someone has records."

"Like Risal?"

"Like Risal," Golgoras said. "Who is gone. Hmm, I see. Bahamut might not be senile after all. We will speak further on this. Matteras is ready to continue."

The interval was over, Hazard having kept strict control over the bar. It was a well-known fact of Assemblies that should any interval spill over into the third drink, the audience would certainly become unruly and the entire day would be lost. Matteras, mic in hand, was motoring on.

"Friends, friends, come, hear me! I have the solution, but alas, I am only one djinn. I have merely offered to make a bit of space for my fellow djinn, a tiny little adjustment to the landscape, and for that reason I have been hounded by Bahamut, threatened by his lackeys, my auctoritas attacked by the full weight of his clients! In fact, there is one of his minions now, come to disrupt this august Assembly!" He was pointing directly at Barabas, whose hapless face was trying to desperately convey that he had no intention of disrupting any Assembly, august or otherwise.

What? Barabas mouthed, thrust suddenly into the wrathful gaze of thirty senior djinn.

Matteras ambled over. "Look at this pathetic specimen," he said, pulling Barabas toward the center of the room by one ear. "Look at this bedraggled djinn, come to ogle his betters. Look at the contempt Bahamut has for us, to send such a creature as his cat's-paw!"

"No, I mean, sirs, I am merely observing—"

"Where is *your master*?"

"Er, look, he's a fish, isn't he?" Barabas said, spraying out a crumb of éclair.

"Exactly!" Matteras looked around mockingly. "Not just *one* fish. He's a whole school of fish. I'm being hounded by a school of fish. I am being threatened by a creature without two brain cells to rub together. I'm be-ing—"

"Hold on now," Beltrex said. "Bahamut's been around. No need to go off on him..."

"Where is he then?" Matteras asked. "If he's so civic minded, where is he? If he's so ancient and venerable, where is his wisdom? If he's so damn powerful, why hasn't he protected us against human encroachment? Time after time, I've asked for his guidance, for the support of his auctoritas. Always, he has thrown it back in my face. I offered him my allegiance, and instead he threatened me with destruction."

"What? Doesn't sound like him," scoffed Beltrex.

"You, insignificant Ifrit," Matteras snapped at Barabas. "What does Ba-hamut have in his possession?"

"Um, the giant squid?"

"No, you idiot, the fractal bomb! The bomb! That thing he looted from the ruins of Gangaridai!"

"Hang on, hang on, he didn't loot nothing," Barabas said, stung. "I don't know who your ancestors were, and I don't much care either. If you wanted to preserve your precious Gangaridai, it should be you down there rotting in the ocean instead of him!"

"Boy's got a point," Beltrex shouted. "Well said!"

"He has a fractal bomb, you utter brainless fucks!" Matteras was fairly frothing now. "What this witless hick isn't communicating clearly is that Bahamut is stark raving mad, and he has explicitly threatened to discontin-ue time with his bomb if we don't comply with his every wish!"

"Humph, fractal bomb just a rumor," Walrus said. "Bahamut big exag-gerator. Probably. Very bad for all of us otherwise."

"Oh, for god's sake, let him set off his fractal bomb," said Kuriken, the dapper djinn. He was coolly lighting a cigar, blatantly ignoring the no-smoking policy of the ballroom and not the least bit worried about ash-ing on the floor. "At least it'd put an end to this interminable debate. I for one would love another ice age. Carry on, Matteras. What would you have us do? Assuming we agree in principle to your little proposal."

Rais stepped forward finally, casting a disgusted look at Golgoras.

"Ah, sirs, sorry to interrupt," he said. "I would suggest that Lord Matteras's proposal to depopulate most of Asia is not at all a foregone or desirable conclusion."

There was an instant hush in the room.

"Hazard, who exactly is this human, and what is he doing in our Assembly?" Matteras asked with deceptive calmness.

"Your sister, sir, was my aunt," Rais said, taking some advantage of the lady djinn he hardly remembered.

There was pin-drop silence in the room now. One did not bring up Matteras's sister to his face without serious repercussions.

"He is, in fact, the emissary Kaikobad's nephew," Hazard said with a note of apology.

"Ah, yes, our replacement," Matteras said. "You, whose application has caused so much amusement and entertainment for our courts. Still, I do not recall inviting you to speak."

"I am surprised, sir, that with so many august emissaries in this room, none see fit to object to your proposal to cleanse the entire subcontinent of humanity."

"Perhaps they are wiser than you," Matteras said. "There are, after all, many more humans in other parts of the world. Who would miss a few?"

"Would you allow me to speak on behalf of my uncle, who lies in a coma?"

"I am sorry, I am not one of those impressed by borrowed dignatas. Kaikobad would have been most welcome to speak, but what possible use could *you* have in this debate? Do you have any experience in our politics? Do you know any of the social axioms? Do you have any advantage over these other emissaries who have served us for decades?" Matteras asked. "Silence, boy! Be satisfied that I do not disperse you into fairy dust as you stand."

"Let's just get on with it," Kuriken said, bored. "Throw this poor fool out, Hazard, for god's sake. I thought this was an exclusive gathering. If I knew you were going to invite every beggar off the streets to speak, I wouldn't have come."

"That's the Siberian king, Kuriken. He's as bad as Matteras," Golgoras whispered to Rais. "Don't worry. I have a plan." He stepped forward, shouldering Rais aside. "Never mind the boy, I've got other concerns."

"Oho? And what does the Royal Aeronautics Society have to say on this? I was assured you were a mere observer," Matteras said.

"Your fetish for earthquakes is a matter of indifference to us," Golgoras said coolly. "As is your apparent desire to slaughter millions of people. I'm concerned about a missing djinn."

"What? What nonsense is this?"

"I'm not a human, Matteras," Golgoras snapped. "Moderate your tone, or I will leave, and you can speak to the society lawyer."

"Why don't we settle this right here, bird boy," Hazard said, ambling forward.

"Ah, Golgoras, so delightfully brusque," Matteras said. "Please, no need for duels or lawyers. If only you'd be a bit clearer, Golgoras, perhaps we would know what you're talking about."

"The historian Risal," Golgoras said. "She's gone missing."

"She wanders around; she's probably somewhere remote."

"It has been twenty years," Golgoras said.

"So what, then? What the hell does it have to do with me?" Matteras looked around. "What does it have to do with Royal Aeronautics, for that matter? She wasn't a member, was she?"

"No."

"Then this is clearly a trivial waste of time. Kindly allow us to continue."

"She was a tenant," Golgoras said. "She lived in a sky tunnel. We built it for her and held her moorage contract. She is missing. The tunnel was drifting. We are legally bound to investigate."

"Fine, fine, investigate," Kuriken said. "Why are you boring us with it?"

"We are investigating," Golgoras said. "And thus we are here."

"What does that mean?" Matteras asked.

"We found her home abandoned, deliberately sheared off," Golgoras said.

"I must ask, once again, what this has to do with me? Is it my fault that your society builds shoddy sky tunnels?" Matteras asked.

"We thought you might know where she has gone."

"I do not, nor do I care."

"You did care about the Maker, though, didn't you?"

"He put the mad djinn down," Kuriken said. "Your own society gave him a medal, if I recall. Why are you bringing up that cursed episode again?"

"Yes, he put him down," Golgoras said. "In a murder pit, was it?"

"I did what I had to," Matteras said. "I don't recall the RAS being particularly helpful during those dark days. In fact, no one wanted to know any details back then."

"You're a bit of an expert on murder pits," Golgoras said. "Famous for it."

"What is your fucking point, pilot?"

"Risal was in touch with Givaras, wasn't she? One of his friends?"

"The Maker had no friends," Matteras said. "Not any sane ones, at any rate."

"We found this." Golgoras held up a lead-lined box and threw it at Hazard, who instinctively caught it one-handed, jackal teeth snapping. The box unlatched and the vellum-bound book spilled out, landing on its spine, pages flaring open like a carnivorous flower. Hazard stumbled back with an animal cry and there was dead silence.

"It's a first edition," Golgoras said, carefully looking away.

Matteras stared at the book, transfixed. "This is impossible. It was destroyed."

"It's handwritten," Golgoras said.

"I can't see it," Beltrex complained in his quavering voice. "What is it?"

"It's the *Compendium of Beasts*," Golgoras said. "An original manuscript. Anyone want to read it?"

The crowd flinched back.

"You found this at Risal's?" Matteras was quiet now, an intense stillness about him that was much more frightening than his vitriol. "You three?"

"Yes."

"I should kill all of you just for touching it, just for *seeing* it," Matteras said. He shook his head. "I destroyed every scrap of paper Givaras ever touched. How the fuck can it exist?"

"Matteras," the pilot said quietly, "are you quite sure he's dead?"

"No one could survive where I put him," Matteras said.

"It's the Broken," Golgoras said. "Are you quite sure? I'd check if I were you..."

Walrus began to roll out of the room surreptitiously, gray water in his bubble sloshing, spouting an impressive stream of protective wards. A susurration rose up behind him—"*Givaras, Givaras, Givaras*"—emissaries clucking like penguins, more than thirty ancient djinn in the full maturity of their power flexing their fields, the air suddenly so thick with magic that Rais could barely stop himself retching. Kuriken stood in the middle smoking, an island of calm, a hard smile on his face. The discord rose, as djinns fought to preserve the book, or destroy it, or study it for the hidden magics of the Maker. In ones and twos they started to leave, plotting. The great Assembly was over.

CHAPTER 30
Kaikobad

It had been months since they had seen Memmion. The golden giant invoked atavistic fear in the First City these days. Every so often some out-watcher would claim to see him over the horizon, and the citizens would quake. There were effigies of him burning on every street corner, at the foot of every tower. The port quadrant of the city was permanently flooded now, a sloshing, stagnant marshland, the streets largely abandoned. Ships still braved the ocean, bringing food and supplies to the beleaguered empire, old trading partners maintaining alliances.

Rumors abounded, hope and despair jumbled together in manic-depressive splendor. The rebellion had ended, the enemy were scattered. Givaras the Broken was raising an army against them, the likes of which had never been seen. Memmion had made an airship and was going to attack from the skies. Kaikobad wandered the cafés lining the raised ocean promenade, now level with the sea. The patrons still came to lounge here in defiance, smoking their pipes, even though their feet got wet with every swell, and the bamboo furniture was all rotted with seawater. He knew all the regulars, had heard their stories.

Actual news from Lhasa was dire. The one true rumor was that the Ghuls had abandoned them. The djinns were not only one race, but three that Kaikobad knew of. Possibly there were more, or once had been, but as with so many things djinn, the knowledge was lost or deliberately obfuscated. The Ifrit were the most numerous, and the Marid more powerful, although it was unclear whether they were simply a type of Ifrit or a separate race altogether. The Ghuls, more numerous than the Marid, were distinct in several ways. They were physically stronger and faster, and typically held to be less intelligent, almost beastlike. It was rumored that they could not control their fields, although this was probably bigotry. They were taciturn and uncommunicative even to other djinn, and shunned contact with humans and Nephilim. The central culture of the djinn, dominated by Ifrit, treated the Ghuls as a subservient race.

Certainly, as a political unit, they were weak. They served in a largely menial capacity in the djinn world, as crew in ships, as builders, porters, and artisans, a cross between guildsmen and indentured servants, often working for food and a pittance. Gangaridai was built on Ghul labor, and they had received scant reward for all of that. Individual Ghuls did not seem to have dignatas, or at least so little that it was hardly worth acknowledging. Rather, the dignatas accrued to each Ghul tribe, of which there were many, the largest being centered in Lhasa. Their inner workings were secretive, and it was unclear to outsiders the exact hierarchy.

Over the past months, Ghuls had been leaving the city, more and more disappearing every night. This had been dismissed as the normal attrition of war: trade drying up, workers leaving for safer pastures. But now news came that Horus, named Givaras the Broken by the Ghul, had been spotted in Lhasa, that he had offered an enormous contract to the tribes of Ghul, so large that it tripled the collective dignatas *of the entire race*. It was unprecedented. He offered something amazing, a gesture that beggared him and at the same time enriched him beyond measure.

It was one more ally gone, a dire psychological blow for the city. The High Lords of Gangaridai, in their arrogance, had never considered that the Ghuls would take sides, that a race of servants had to be appeased and cosseted. Those few Ghuls who remained in the city were now viewed suspiciously, shunned and abused, further exacerbating the problem.

The High King was engaged in sorcery with the watchmakers. He had not yet come out of his tower, had barely left it since the first attack, not even during the last assault, when Elkran had beheaded the captain of the infantry outside the eastern gate, his rippled black sword so thin that it disappeared when viewed sideways. Elkran, undefeated in duels, equal perhaps to Kuriken himself, was lithe, his blade a whispering death. The two were destined to meet, although for now, Kuriken's challenges went unanswered, and even he could not be in many places at once. It was the nature of Horus to direct his attacks in multiple fronts, always harrying, harassing, whittling down the far-flung outposts of the First Empire. Day by day, Kaikobad watched as the caravans and trade ships shrank, the noose tightening around the city, and the little luxuries dried up, like ice in the summertime, lemons from the north, the emeralds and rubies from Lanka that the djinns loved to etch with spells.

But the Horologists had not been idle. Perhaps it was apparent only to Kaikobad, for the citizens already lived in a kind of dream state, a fugue of semi-timelessness, but parts of the city had been disappearing, buildings winking out of sight overnight, entire streets turning to mist, then returning again, subtly altered, eerily empty. He noticed when Barkan's tower disappeared, which had been a favorite haunt of his. It was not so much gone as inaccessible, a peculiar state of half-life, as if something could exist and still be completely removed at the same time. Then an entire corner of shops went—fruit and incense sellers, a milliner, a florist, all gone—and a kind of suspended grayness remained there, a smudge the eye flitted over, and people walked on past as if nothing had been there ever, or perhaps they saw it still, and it was Kaikobad's eyes that were deficient.

As he followed this phenomenon, he noticed people disappearing too, ordinary folk vanishing, and it was assumed by their friends that they had just left in the night, perhaps fled to some safer place. Kaikobad, who could not sleep, saw them fade in front of his eyes, dissipating into a kind of alternate existence, or some purgatory. It was more worrying to him than the war. The magic wafting from the King's Tower stank of something unearthly, something very old and beyond the ken of mortals. He wanted to warn them all that their lords were making deadly waves, were fundamentally betraying the world somehow, but he could find no one to listen, no djinn or man who could even see him.

Even incorporeal, he could not approach the King's Tower. The wards there were strong enough to warp space itself, the ways to it locked by some combination he could not turn. So he watched and wandered the city as it slowly slipped away, the visions now crowding his mind with such pressure that it was impossible to differentiate one from the next, nor even to find respite in Thoth, for he could not find him or his quiet words. If the djinn was still speaking, those words were lost in the ether; Kaikobad had become the city, his mind melded together with its brick and mortar, and he was certain that he would now share in its doom.

CHAPTER 31

The Boy Who Would Be Dragon

When Indelbed woke up the pain was gone. Or rather, the dentist's-drill-on-exposed-nerve torture was over. What was left behind was a dull, pervasive ache and bone-deep exhaustion, and the weird feeling that his insides had been rearranged. There were no compensatory powers. He felt pitiful, scarred.

"Don't worry," said Givaras. "You're a dragon on the inside."

Indelbed couldn't speak because he had no tongue. His eyes were gone too, vision dialed to black, optic nerves rearranged by a bone scalpel. He had dreamed that maybe: Givaras bent over his face, playing tic-tac-toe on his retinas. He saw stars rushing through the abyss, his eyeballs scratched by ancient light, and he saw the ghostly lines of the distortion field: the trails of the wyrms, simple and brutal; the bizarre complexity of Givaras, all etched in shapes that had no geometry. The light hung behind the djinn's shoulder, no dirty blue smudge but an orbit of whizzing lines, as fascinating as an anthill. Is this what dragons saw? he wondered.

"You've done so well," Givaras said, pleased. "I didn't expect you to survive. Now we will try to grow back your tongue."

And so Indelbed did, molecule by molecule, patiently stitching together the tissue using minute touches of the field; paralyzed from the neck down, he had nothing better to do. He could never have done this before, even with Givaras's guidance, but his blind eyes could now see a grid, faint contrails of vibrating energy, and with all the time in the world he lay down the pieces. He had not believed the tales of regrowing limbs or changing shape, but now he saw it could be done, and it was a balm to his scarred mind.

Days passed, and he grew some misshapen thing in his mouth, an alien piece of elastic flesh, horribly odd, but it worked, and he could utter sounds and then words.

"Thank god," Givaras said, when intelligible words finally came out. "I was going mad for conversation."

"You're insane," Indelbed said. "That was worse than I had thought. I'm blind and paralyzed. And I remember the pain. Every bit. You broke my spine. I can't walk."

"I will repair that," Givaras said. "And you can see the field, can't you?"

"I have no idea what I'm seeing. Ghosts, it looks like."

"I've made you better," Givaras said. "You can see what no one else can. I believe you can see the actual particles themselves."

"There is nothing better about this!" Indelbed hissed. "Nothing! You promised me power. Where is it?"

"You're alive, that's the main thing," Givaras said. "I've done this sort of thing to grown djinns, and they never made it. It must be hybrid vigor or something."

"I was better off before."

"Perhaps. Things might look dark now—"

"Haha."

"—but I assure you, significant changes have occurred. If you could just see..."

"This is going to get really old."

"Your feet have turned into flippers!"

"What? Oh god!"

"Ha! Got you!" Givaras cackled.

"Put me back in the coma. Please."

"I will, briefly, to repair your spine. I hope after that you regain full functionality."

"Oh god, another operation."

"My operations have kept you alive, young man," Givaras said. "While you should be congratulated on surviving what has killed three grown djinns, I assure you, it is my skill that—"

"*Three* grown djinns?"

"Ah, yes, you recall Risal of course. There were two inhabitants in this prison before her."

"You said the wyrms ate them!"

"They ate them *afterward*."

"So what happened to these djinns?" *Did they go under the knife voluntarily? They must have been fools, all of them, if they did.*

"The first one was an Ifrit named... I forget his name now. He was a friend of mine. I gave him the wyrm hormone. Of course, it was not a mature wyrm like God's Eye. Within minutes of the infusion, he went into deep convulsions, accompanied by horrific pain. This did not stop for days, until he quite simply died of exhaustion. This is the reason I paralyzed you. The second djinn was a Marid like Risal, powerful. He died in the most useless way. Asleep in a coma, his mouth and jaw started to liquefy for some reason, and he drowned in his own blood quicker than I could let it out. To prevent this, I cut out your tongue and inserted a bone breathing tube. Finally, there was Risal. She almost made it. In the final stages, she began to suffer hallucinations as her optic nerves began to change. Essentially she went mad. She released her full distortion field and tried to change her body by force. The swarm, as you can imagine, tore her apart. This is why I have blinded you. Do you understand now how carefully I have nurtured you?"

"You can't be serious," Indelbed said. He wondered again how willing those previous djinns had been to Givaras's administrations. "I expected to be maimed. But this is horrible. You've made me into a monster." *I am truly not a little boy anymore. Will anyone recognize me?*

"Yes, perhaps," Givaras said. "You came here a frightened little boy. I have indeed made you into a monster. You said you wanted to survive. This is the price. There are no knights in shining armor in this world, boy. When fighting monsters, what else can you do but become one?"

"You said we would escape!" Indelbed said. "I thought that I would fly! You promised me a dragon."

"And I shall make you one," Givaras said. "Come, boy, it's not over yet. Did you know that in a certain light I can see the most remarkable scales under your skin?"

When he woke up again many days had passed. He remembered flashes of lucidity, discomfort. He remembered hanging upside down, suspended in a niche, splinted with the bones of Risal, encircled by her, a bone cocoon. He remembered looping nightmares. He could feel below his neck: pins and needles on his legs, soreness along his elbows, the stretch and play of tendons. Something had been fixed, something worked again. He staggered to his feet, fell, then got up again, head spinning, arms and legs weaker than a newborn's, but he couldn't recall ever feeling happier. The chronic pain was on a low ebb, thrumming away in the background, below anything scream worthy; and the legs worked, arms worked, everything seemed normal. He could see the faint outline of bones, and there were things whizzing around inside.

"Oh, good, you're up." Givaras brought some food, the ubiquitous chunk of wyrm meat.

Indelbed ate and realized that his regrown tongue had no taste buds. A blessing, it turned out, although his new body appeared to welcome wyrm meat.

"I rebuilt your spine," Givaras said. "I took the opportunity to look around a bit. Remarkable things are happening to your bones."

"I'm glad you're enjoying yourself," Indelbed said. "At least I can walk."

"And your eyes are remarkable," Givaras said. "I suspect that I have achieved something wondrous."

"Everything looks weird," Indelbed said. "I can't see colors. I can see whorls and lines inside God's Eye. If I spread the field thin, I can make out solid surfaces."

"Can you see my face?"

"I can see *inside* your face," Indelbed said, squinting. "But if I kind of squeeze my eyes together and make the field really thin, I can sort of see the outside. It's giving me a headache."

"Good. Instead of light, you are using the field to see surfaces. You must experiment with it—I cannot teach you how. As you get better, I believe you will be able to see the surface world as well as ever. I think I have improved you. You can't see them yet, but there are scales under your skin, almost invisible. The evolution in you has become slightly garbled. Final-stage wyrms have the scales, according to legend."

"Great, I look like a fish."

"Not at all," Givaras said. "The scales would give immunities to the great dragons. You have to be annealed in great fire to achieve this."

"Are you going to set me on fire now?!"

"No, we need a hotter kind of flame," Givaras said. He looked around speculatively. "It will have to wait."

"Thank god."

God's Eye came sniffing around, circular maw reeking, and coiled himself loosely around Indelbed's cot.

"He is confused," Givaras said with great satisfaction. "Because your distortion field is no longer fully djinn."

"He's bigger," Indelbed said. "I can see... *inside him.*"

"He has begun to grow exponentially since your ascension to dragonhood," Givaras said. "It is fascinating. I believe brood competition is making his body develop faster."

"Givaras, am I still your apprentice?"

"Yes, of course."

"And so you wouldn't kill me, would you?"

"No, child, I would not kill you in any case," Givaras said. "For you are of noble djinn blood on one side and an emissary on the other. Nephilim. To me, both are valuable and worthy of respect."

"You're not just a third-rate scientist."

"Third rate?!"

"You know what I mean. This place... this *prison*... it was built for you. The things you know... the things you can do, they're not *normal.*"

"You've been in a cave with wyrms for the past ten years, boy, what do you know of normal?"

Indelbed snorted. The dragon in him made him brave. To be honest, he was so tired and pain addled that he didn't really care if he lived or died. This was, he supposed, what old people felt like before they pulled the plug.

"You know, I preferred you as a sweet little boy."

"What were you, Master, that Matteras took so much trouble over you?"

Givaras smiled. "You are my first and only apprentice for a thousand years."

"*A thousand years?*"

"In 1066, there was Matteras."

CHAPTER 32
Horus Rising

"Well, that was horrible," Rais said. They were now in the second-floor lobby of the Westin, returned to the real world, and djinn in various levels of disguise were milling about before making their exit, under the gaze of some very puzzled hotel staff.

"Not that bad," Golgoras said.

"No one else opposed him," Rais said. He was actually shocked. In the back of his mind, he had been expecting a few allies at least. "None of the emissaries. It's like everyone is perfectly fine with him drowning millions of people."

"At least they did not reach a consensus," Golgoras said. "Now they're worrying more about the Maker than anything else."

"How much time does it buy us?"

Golgoras shrugged. "Depends how much dignatas Matteras is willing to risk. The room was bad. If Kuriken goes all in with him, it might still be enough."

"Tell me about Beltrex," Rais said.

"Old guard," Golgoras said. "Saner than most. Known to be a legal expert."

"How old is he?"

"Really old," said Golgoras. "Thousands of years. Not polite to ask."

"Is he antediluvian?"

"He might be." Golgoras shrugged. "Djinns don't advertise age. He's pro-Seclusion."

"He likes Humes. Fact," Barabas said. "Owns vineyards over in America. Majorly into wine making. Won some Hume award once. Wouldn't shut up about it. Why?"

"He was in Risal's journal."

"No shit!" Barabas said.

"Yeah. Risal was asking him stuff about the war. She had a partial bibliography for her paper drafted in her journal. She listed him as a primary source," Rais said.

"That's interesting."

"It doesn't say what exactly he answered. Can you help me corner him?" Rais asked.

"We'll invite him to lunch," Golgoras said.

"Is he going to agree to meet us?" Rais asked.

"Oh yes, he's a miser. Never passes up a free meal," said Golgoras.

Beltrex, in fact, was hanging around the elevator muttering darkly, and he very quickly agreed to Golgoras's proposal of lunch at Prego, courtesy of the Royal Aeronautics Society. The Italian restaurant was near the top floor of the Westin, cheerfully lit and almost empty at this time of the day. A life-size poster advertised a Filipino band in fishnet stockings and half-price drinks during happy hour. An absence of waiters dispersed quickly as they entered, the staff members studiously pretending to work in various remote corners of the restaurant.

"Pretty poor show, for Matteras," Beltrex huffed as they sat down. He proceeded to order two of everything and several exorbitantly priced cocktails. "In my day we used to open Assemblies with a cocktail party and close with a ten-course banquet."

"Well, don't worry, the society has an account with the Westin. Let's see if we can put together a feast for you, eh?" Golgoras said. Rais had never seen the pilot this amiable.

"Humph, well. And you know that Matteras got us here flying commercial? China Southern. Cheapest airline you can find. I had a six-hour layover..."

"Well, don't worry, Beltrex, I'm flying out that way. I'm sure I can drop you off," Golgoras said. "No charge."

"My thanks to the society."

"Well, you know, we believe our interests coincide somewhat. You're known as a peaceable djinn, and we at the society think this thing Matteras is doing is a little bit much."

"Well, I sure as hell ain't for it," Beltrex said. He turned rheumy eyes toward Barabas. "This is your new protégé, huh?"

"Ahem, that's the djinn Barabas," Golgoras said.

"Right, right, sorry, where's that new emissary?"

"Well, emissary-in-training, really," Barabas said with a huff. "Kaikobad's nephew."

"In my day it was pretty careless, losing your emissary like that," Beltrex said. "You'd have lost an ass-load of dignatas."

"I did, I did," Barabas said angrily. "You can't imagine what I'm going through. I can't even hail a taxicab these days. It was so careless of Kaikobad!"

"You're the new whelp," Beltrex said to Rais, "the one creating the ruckus in the courts?"

"Well, my mother's handling that part of it," Rais said.

"Scary woman," Barabas said. "You'd better stay away from her, Beltrex, if you were smart."

"Why don't you boys take a smoke break?" Beltrex said. "I want to talk to our emissary for a bit."

The old djinn's field flexed for a second, and the other two almost flinched back. For a brief moment, his power was so luminous that even Rais could feel it. Golgoras nodded shortly.

"I knew your uncle," Beltrex said, when they had left. "Good man."

"Yeah, so says everyone," Rais said. "We knew him as a crazy drunk, but apparently he was pretty solid out here."

"You won't be stopping this clusterfuck, boy," Beltrex said. "They've thrown you to the wolves."

"It does look that way," Rais admitted.

"Matteras is a different kind of djinn," Beltrex said. "New breed of 'em. Aggressive. Younger ones, the ones who've forgotten the war, they follow him. Think he's some kind of royalty."

"Beltrex, might I ask a question?"

"Sure, son."

"How old are you?"

"That's a personal thing for us djinn. An emissary worth his weight would have known that."

"Is there *anyone* alive from back then?"

"I'd be careful, boy, asking about the war. Djinn don't like that kind of talk."

"I've noticed. I can't figure out why."

"A lot of powerful folk went crazy," Beltrex said. "It was the time of high magic, the golden age of djinn, and the war put an end to that and almost to everything else—men, djinn, this world, perhaps more. It was a holocaust, an extinction event. It ended the First Empire of Djinn. Ain't no surprise no one wants to think about it. The young guns like Matteras, they don't know what it was like, can't really understand why we are the way we are."

"Bahamut told me to look at the war."

"Bahamut is old and strange."

"Was he active during the war?"

"Almost twenty thousand years ago?" Beltrex shrugged. "Hell, he might have been. I don't know, he might have been around back then—no one brings that shit up. Look, boy, I knew your uncle, I owed him a favor or two, so I'm gonna warn you: some waves you can't surf. Matteras will end you, your family, your entire damn race if he wants to, there's not a damn thing you can do to stop it. Now you be smart and get outta here with your folk. You all need help, hell, bring 'em to Napa, I'll get you green cards."

"That's generous of you, sir," Rais said. He thought for a moment of living with his parents in a nice vineyard, making wine for tourists, far away from all of this, and it was seriously tempting, to see his parents close together again, like olden times. Then he thought of Moffat, Maria, their parents, all his own friends and relatives, and the hundreds of acquaintances—his whole world of people, really—blotted out for no reason. He thought of lonely Indelbed, maybe still alive somewhere, stuck in a murder pit, and the urge to surrender went away. He had to do *something*, anything.

"And don't go digging into the war thing. Sick shit happened back then is all *I* remember. A lot of Marid died, a lot of 'em went to sleep after."

"Sleep?"

"Sure, a lot of djinn hibernate. Sometimes we skip centuries when it gets boring. All I'm saying is any folk still around from back then, we probably don't wanna be running into 'em. Djinn were a different kind of breed back then. Nasty, arrogant. Uncivilized. Didn't have the laws, didn't have our Lore. I'll say no more on this, except I don't much like the way we're heading. Mind you, that was a clever trick with that fake book."

"It wasn't a fake."

"You must be mistaken, boy."

"It's real. Hand drawn by him too. Found it at Risal's."

"Bad news to have that thing floating around," Beltrex said with a grunt. "Even worse if that bastard is still alive."

"I still don't get why Givaras is such a big deal. I mean, what exactly did he do?"

"Givar Broken killed more men and more djinn than the plague," Beltrex said. "And he's *old*. He's one of the founder djinn. They called him Horus in ancient Kemet. The things he's done over the years are strange even for the ancients. He has theories that are a little hard to take. He's known as the father of the evolutionary school for a reason. Plenty of nasty things crawling around that we owe him for. Some of the djinn follow him because he's, well, the closest thing we have to a champion of science. The Creationists hate his work, always have. Me, I don't care much either way."

"And this terrible book? The *Compendium of Beasts*?"

"They call him Maker because he makes things. Living things." Beltrex leaned forward. "Matteras destroyed all the books. I never read it. But, of course, I've heard bits and pieces."

"From Risal, by any chance?"

"What?"

"She's missing. Has been for twenty years."

"The historian? I don't know her."

"Are you sure? We found the *Compendium* at her place. It was cleverly hidden. Her home was ransacked twenty years ago, all of her original work taken. I have the rest of her library."

Beltrex stared at him. There was very little of the absentminded djinn about him now. "So you have stolen her library. Theft is punishable by death, according to our laws."

"It was not theft," Rais said. "I have the documentation from the RAS. Salvage rights. Her home was unmoored, spinning freely, and the door was unsecured. I filed a claim for discovery of an abandoned vessel."

"Very careless of Risal, to leave her house up for salvage."

"The funny thing is she mentions you in her journal."

"She kept a journal?"

"Yes."

"You've read it?"

"It was mostly full of bowel movements and what she ate. All nine volumes."

Beltrex smiled. "That seems like Risal. Perhaps I did know her a little."

"Was she asking you questions about the war?"

"She might have been."

"You spoke to her then?"

"I might have."

"But not about the *Compendium*?"

"Oh no, not that. Never knew she had it."

"I've read it, you know. Thrice. It's strange, some of the drawings in the book are in Kaikobad's notes, I swear."

Beltrex sighed. "I don't know about Kaikobad's notes. Givar was before his time. Maybe he found a few pages, who knows? That book was banned, and some people can't help rooting around forbidden fruit. You really should have kept the book hidden, boy," Beltrex said. "Owning an artifact of Givar's marks you for death nowadays."

"I've got a damn good memory," Rais said. "Near eidetic. I can recall whole passages even now. It seemed like he was giving very detailed instructions on how to *make* djinns."

"Hush now," Beltrex said. "That kinda talk might get you killed around here. God made djinns. *God.* We are the chosen people."

"Right," Rais said. "The Creationist creed."

"You might think Creationists are some lunatic fringe, but a lot of djinn believe it, inside," Beltrex said. "Anything that says otherwise is anathema. You never know who's going to turn on you if you start spouting that Evolutionist stuff."

"Yeah," Rais said. "I think Risal knew that. The *Compendium* was hidden, as I said, and it wasn't in the catalog."

"Catalog?"

"Risal was very organized. I found her catalog, and I matched it to every single book in her library. There was only one book missing: the *Register of Kings*, from Gangaridai. It was part of her rare book collection."

"And?"

"I want Risal's missing book."

"Why?"

"Because Bahamut told me to look into it." *And because I'm not going to fold like everyone expects. Maybe I'm my mother's son after all.*

"Typical Bahamut," Beltrex said. "Reading books while the world is burning. Now I hate to tell you, boy, but I don't have her book, whatever it's called, and I don't know what happened to her either."

"It's called the *Register of Kings*, by the djinn Mohandas. Did she say anything about it?"

"I can't remember any specifics. Risal used to talk a lot of gibberish."

"Are there any notable libraries where I might find a copy?"

"Gangaridai had a big one."

"Destroyed and underwater, of course," Rais said.

"Mohenjo Daro had one. The old city, I mean, the djinn one."

"Again, destroyed."

"The Bayt al-Hikma had one."

"The House of Wisdom? Burned by the Mongols in 1258 when they sacked Baghdad. The Tigris ran black with ink from all the books they dumped into the river."

"I'm sorry, boy, not too many djinns interested in old books these days. Kuriken's got a library in his castle up in Siberia. Probably the last one left in Russia that wasn't sacked by the Bolsheviks. I once sold him all my first editions for a cartload of Cossack bones."

"I've got to ask... Cossack bones?"

"Medicinal value," Beltrex answered, and winked. "Gets the juices flowing, ahem. When you're as old as I am, m'boy..."

"Right, right." Rais shuddered. "So *Kuriken* might have a copy?"

"I wouldn't go asking him," Beltrex said. "Hates humans. Barely tolerates his own emissary and that woman is a bloody Romanov princess."

"So again I hit a dead end."

"I'm sorry, boy."

"Did my uncle Kaikobad know Risal well?"

"Hmm, you know, I think I remember seeing them together once or twice. He knew a lot of djinns."

"Beltrex, what do you know about Nephilim? Kaikobad was obsessed with them. He had a collection of different Bibles."

"Nephilim are a myth," Beltrex said shortly. "You're wasting your time."

"Thanks, Beltrex. One last question. Do you know anything about haplogroup R?"

"What is it, some kind of STD?"

"No, never mind. Thanks for talking to me, Beltrex, I appreciate it."

"Sure thing, son. I owed Kaikobad a favor or two. If he wakes up, tell him I tried to help."

CHAPTER 33

Kiss the Ring

Rais was in the lobby when he checked his phone. It had been on silent the whole morning. There were eighteen calls from his mother and finally one short message: "Your father is dead. Apollo Hospital. Come quick."

When he got there, everything was already done. Uncle Pappo, the heart specialist, had taken care of business. Even though it was a stabbing incident, the hospital had issued a certificate saying heart attack. The men who had found him in the park had been paid off. The officer in charge of the Gulshan police knew Juny personally and had come to pay his condolences and offer any required assistance. The home secretary, another friend, had called. There would be no autopsy, no formal investigation. His body was taken out discreetly in a minivan, straight to the mosque for a quick prayer. It had been strongly advised that he be buried as quickly as possible, to avoid any complications.

Numb with shock, Rais followed the steps, stumbling through the rituals, shouldering his end of the coffin through the rain and slipping in the mud, his father heavy in death as he had been in life. He was surprised at what he felt: the rawness of grief. He had drifted away from the Ambassador lately, or, rather, his presence had dimmed in his secret life, like a guttering candle, but the loss felt immediate, like a cut limb, and he realized that he wasn't finished with his father yet, and now never would be.

They were in Banani, in the most coveted of graveyards, where burial plots were the most expensive real estate in Dhaka. Old families and the rich had plots here, where they could bury their dead on top of each other (it was common wisdom that buried bodies decomposed within seven years, so it was possible to reuse the plot). With most old families, the previous generations were much more numerous, and thus there was plenty of space to go around. The Ambassador's grandfather had had three wives (not simultaneously) and seventeen children surviving to adulthood. His own father had produced only four, and the Ambassador himself had managed only one. Thus, when Rais passed on, he would have his pick of ancestors to be buried with.

The Ambassador was laid to rest on the long-decayed bones of his father, and everyone praised the profound rightness of it, a fitting end to a great man. This was the prized spot, and his elder brother grumbled under his breath and would later complain to his wife that it was typical of Vulu to selfishly take everything for himself. The graveyard was leafy and pleasant under the light rain. Rais got into the rectangular hole barefoot, lowering the corpse, turning the head sideways so it would look to the west, this job reserved for the closest of kin. His father had never been religious. He wondered whether facing west would give him much pleasure. The cemetery officials up top kept up a steady stream of advice, as professional buriers of men, each one sure of the precise formula required to appease God. Plus they wanted to be remembered for tips.

Thankfully the body was swathed in white cloth and tied up; there was nothing to see, it felt like a doll, a mannequin being put to rest. Rais felt weird manhandling it, wary of hurting it somehow. When everything was perfect, he said a last whispered prayer on his father's forehead, resisting the urge to kiss it. His cousins pulled him out, an undignified scramble. Everyone grabbed a clod of dirt and threw it, reciting a prayer, the last ritual of the burial itself. This was a job deemed unsuitable for women, so they stood afar, watching, clustered around Juny, who stood ramrod straight in the rain, umbrella high, her face inscrutable. By now everyone was soaked, white kurtas plastered across skin, saris beginning to droop, but no one minded because of the heat. All told it was considered an efficient funeral, a clockwork thing typical of Juny, and most of them were grateful to be away so quick. In less expert hands these things might eat up the whole day.

It was only family at the graveyard, for the Ambassador's vast pool of friends and acquaintances had not yet been notified. Over the next week there would be obituaries and wakes, laments and paeans, but no mention of that trickle of blood from the sword wound in his chest, nothing shady at all about the august Ambassador, only grief.

Rais got into his mother's car, the old Mercedes tooled by the equally old driver. Several relatives looked like they wanted to get in—it was customary to be suffocated by family during these times—but Juny motioned the driver to lock the doors and drive, and just like that they were gone into a pocket of space, leaving behind a trailing menagerie. Rais looked up at his mother's face and saw no sorrow, only rage.

For four days their apartment was a carnival, a revolving door of mourners bringing food, eating, drinking, gossiping, and praying—endless rounds of it. Juny was the perfect hostess. She accepted condolences with grace, provided round-the-clock snacks and meals, shed tears on demand, was cosseted, petted, hugged, and comforted beyond normal human endurance without displaying a single crack. Everyone left eventually, vaguely dissatisfied but not sure why, saying things like, "She's taking this well," and "I'd have thought she'd be a bit more upset."

Of course, in some corner of their hearts, despite their genuine good wishes, they wanted to see her broken, just a tiny bit; wanted to see a faltering of the dynamo, any kind of stutter, any sign at all that she was human, that she could be brought down a peg or two. Rais, who could read his mother, saw nothing in her face other than the opaque obsidian gaze of the raptor, cold, waiting, waiting, and he was frightened.

When they were alone she had the house cleaned. She could never abide the clutter of other people, the tracks of their shoes, their dirty plates and crumbs, the indentations of their bodies on her chairs. Rais knew she had held back before, out of consideration for the Ambassador, but now she let loose on a massive scale of reordering, and he thought this was perhaps her way of expressing grief, of coping. He rose to comfort her, or at least assist her in some way, and she forestalled him with a glance.

"It's not grief," she said, somehow reading his mind. "I prefer the house like this. Your father was more... casual, but it was also his house, so I compromised."

"That must have been hard."

"It is what people do for one another. I am sure I had annoying traits he forgave. He was a good man."

"He was murdered," Rais said, savoring the words, the ability to say them out loud to someone. "I can't believe it."

"Stabbed by a sword hidden in a cane," Juny said, "carried by an Afghan emissary."

"How do you know?"

"I know."

"What will you do?" Rais felt hollow inside. He wanted to shout; he wanted to run and rage and bluster. He wanted to ram his fist into the smug face of the frightening old man. But his fury had never been enough, never been lengthy enough or strong enough or cold enough, to carry through to action.

"What can I do? I'm just a widow now." Her face was a mask.

Rais snorted. "If I believed that, I'd be the biggest fool on earth."

"It's true," Juny said. "Your father was killed because of us, because of what we started."

"That's bullshit," Rais said. "You and I both know he wasn't innocent. He knew Matteras, he and Uncle Sikkim both."

"This is the one thing he never confided in me," Juny said. "I think he felt guilty for whatever he and Sikkim did. There was remorse in him the past few years."

"If he worked for them, why did they kill him?"

"He didn't work *for* them," Juny said. "I suspect Sikkim did, at one point, and your father got sucked in. They killed him because of you, because you're getting closer."

"It's strange—I never thought they'd do that, even Matteras," Rais said. He balled his fists into his eyes, abruptly tired. It seemed so far away now, the submarine and the airship. This was real life again, ugly, uncertain. "They're so lofty... Killing *isn't their way*."

"It's unlike them," said Juny. "I think it's Dargoman, mad with power. He works for Matteras now. He has vast resources—he sits at the head of a cabal of businesses that span the world. I've been looking into him."

"You knew he was here? For how long?"

"He has been here on and off for the past three years."

"You didn't tell me."

"I didn't want to face him yet," Juny said. "I was scared of him."

"Scared? You?"

"Because of you!" Juny said. "We weren't ready yet, Rais. We still aren't. They have too much money, too much power. They've been setting up their companies for hundreds of years. Dargoman could crush us without his djinn masters even twitching."

"He's certainly started the process," Rais said bitterly. "I have Golgoras, Barabas. But Bahamut won't move, won't leave the bay. I met another of the old boys, Beltrex. He basically told us to pack our bags. Maybe we should. We're all alone now, Mama. Maybe we should just get out."

"No! No." Juny's eyes were two black Dobermans snapping at the leash, and it warmed him. "I think we'll stay."

"You'll fight back?"

"Oh yes."

"So, what do we do? You said he was invulnerable."

"This is my city," Juny said. "He's strong, not invulnerable. Not now. He's not safe from *me*. So far I've been waiting, watching. He doesn't think we can hurt him. Well, if we're going down, we'll go down swinging. If it's war, we will need a war chest."

"How much do we have? I have claim on a sky tunnel full of gold fittings. Risal's library's pretty valuable if we sell it off."

"We're not selling off a djinn library. Your father made me cosignatory to all his things: the house, the fixed deposits, and some public shares."

"I didn't know he had any money."

"He left enough for us to live well, not enough to start a war."

"Then what? Sell the flat?"

"Don't be silly. There's one account he didn't tell me about. A joint account. We're going to pay your old GU Sikkim a visit. We need the power of the Khan Rahman trust."

"Oh yeah? I haven't seen him around. Heard he was in the hospital."

"He had a heart attack when he heard about your father."

"Really?"

"Not really. He's faking. I think it's time he finally retired. I've been preparing for this day for a long time."

"You're not going to kill him, are you, Mama?"

"No. I'm going to take his family away."

GU Sikkim was holed up in a superior room in Apollo Hospital, a bulky attendant adorning the door, an ex-military man with a holstered gun. He moved to block them, recognized Juny, deeply salaamed instead, and ushered them in. GU Sikkim was sitting in bed watching TV, looking perfectly hale despite his advanced years. He had unhooked all the tubes and sensors. On a tray nearby were the remnants of a hearty lunch—home-cooked rice and curry—smuggled in via tiffin carrier.

"Mutton, Uncle?" Juny sniffed. "It's *so* bad for your heart."

"Juny!" He collapsed back into his bed, clutching his chest. "Sorry for your loss. I'm so shocked. I had a heart attack. Is it visiting hours already? Abdul! The doctors said no visitors, you idiot!"

"Oh, leave poor Abdul alone," Juny said, sitting down on the edge of the bed. "Abdul and I are old friends. If you don't recall, the Ambassador found him for you, and I found him for the Ambassador."

"I should have guessed." GU Sikkim looked at her with loathing.

"In fact you'll find that most of the servants in the entire family were placed by me," Juny said. "And they all keep in touch. Your cook, for example, told me just the other day that you still eat three mangoes a day during the season, even though Pappo has forbidden it."

"Pappo? That fat oaf! Fine for him to go around forbidding this and that. You don't see him eating boiled chicken and vegetables all day," GU Sikkim said. "I tell you, doctors are the worst hypocrites..."

"We heard you were sick," Rais said. "Naturally we rushed over to visit you as soon as the mourning period was done."

"Naturally," said Juny.

"Terrible business, your father," GU Sikkim said. "Stabbed by muggers in Baridhara of all places. The country is going to the dogs."

"He was stabbed, yes," Juny said, "by a very thin blade. He was not robbed. He apparently knew his attacker because someone saw them talking briefly."

"There was a witness?" GU Sikkim looked terrified.

"A maid on the roof of one of the apartment buildings," Juny said. "Did you think I was not going to investigate the death of my own husband?"

"Did she see the attacker?"

"No, she was too far away," Juny said. "All she can say is that the attacker was a man, and he probably walked with a cane."

"Dargoman!"

"You didn't know?"

"Dammit, woman, do you think I had my own nephew killed?"

"It wouldn't be the first time."

"What the hell do you mean by that?"

"Many years ago you and my husband sold Indelbed to that djinn. From that day onward you set this family on a course that will end in the destruction of all of us."

"That's a lie!"

"Dargoman works for Matteras now," Rais said. "He wears his mark. I've seen it. In fact he is widely known now as the emissary with two tattoos."

"You stupid fool! It's because of your meddling that this has happened! Your father's death is on your head! And your mother's! I told you to not mess around with djinns. I begged you to leave everything alone. Why didn't you trust me?"

"Ever since he died, I've been looking back at the day we first met Dargoman," Juny said. "And something always struck me as strange. At first my husband loathed the man on sight. Yet overnight he changed his mind and insisted we send the boy off with this unknown person. He resisted my most *stringent objections.*"

"You mean he defied you, the poor henpecked wretch," GU Sikkim said bitterly.

"It was unlike him to discard my advice," Juny said.

"You mean you bossed him around."

"He knew what I was when he married me," Juny said. "He was perfectly happy letting me manage his meteoric rise in the civil service. You ordered him that day, to let Dargoman have the boy."

"You have no proof of that!"

"This isn't a court, Uncle, I don't need proof. I presume Matteras got to you. The question is how and why?"

"I'm not answering your questions. I'm sick. Please leave me alone."

"I was going through my husband's papers. You'd be interested to know that I was his joint signatory on everything."

"He was a fool."

"He relied on me heavily."

"So now you've got all his money," GU Sikkim said bitterly.

"Everything except for an account in Singapore, set up ten years ago. There is no mention of it anywhere, no checkbook, no statements, no deposit slips. There was, however, a letter from the bank sending the first debit card and pin number," Juny said. "I was in charge of his finances. I do not believe he had an alternate income large enough to be kept in Singapore. As you are no doubt aware, Citibank would not service an overseas investment account without a minimum balance of a few hundred thousand dollars. How much was the payoff? How much did Matteras give you?"

GU Sikkim stared at her with a deflated, helpless rage.

"Tell me, Sikkim, or I will fly there with his death certificate and find out myself."

"I'm telling you, Juny, you don't want to get involved in this. I'm on your side. I've been *protecting all of you.*"

"When the family finds out you took blood money for killing a child, you'll be finished anyway."

"You'll ruin your precious husband's memory doing that too!" GU Sikkim snarled.

"I don't care," Juny said. "You ruined everything anyway, when you took away Indelbed."

"Five million dollars," GU Sikkim said finally. "Matteras gave us five million dollars in a joint account."

"How much is there now?"

"A little over six," GU Sikkim said. "We didn't touch the money. We were afraid to use it. You think we did it for the money? You don't know Matteras. When he wants something, there's no way of refusing."

"So you felt a little guilt at least."

"Vulu didn't want to do it," GU Sikkim said. "Matteras had me by the balls, though. He would have destroyed me, destroyed the entire family. I had to protect everyone. One little boy in exchange for our entire clan. Who really cared about him? He was nothing to anyone. Vulu agreed in the end."

"That decision ruined Vulu. He wasn't the same person after Indelbed disappeared," Juny said. "How did it start? With Matteras?"

"How does anything start?" GU Sikkim asked. "I made some bad bets around the time Indelbed was born. Industries went under; we had bank loans. I borrowed from the family trust to cover. I was the chairman, I could do it with a couple of fake witness signatures. I invested trust money into the factories, but we couldn't turn them around. I was ruined, and the trust would have lost over half its value. Then there were the lawsuits. I would have gone to jail. Everyone was laughing at me. Matteras came with an offer. It was too good to refuse. He wanted me to keep an eye on Kaikobad, to report everything. That man was a drunken sot, he rarely left the house, so I agreed. Matteras never seemed interested in the boy. They don't care for family, you know. Later, of course, I was hardly in a position to refuse."

"You could have told us."

"You think you know djinns, but you don't know Matteras," GU Sikkim said. He turned to Rais. "I begged you to stay out of this. If you had reported to me like you promised, I would have been able to intervene with Matteras. Instead, you've angered him. He's killed your father and now he'll come after us. After *me*."

"I don't think so," Juny said. "I think Matteras is too busy, and you are too minor a detail for him to bother. I doubt Matteras would order the killing of a man. He is far too high in auctoritas. Dargoman runs his human businesses here, and it is Dargoman we have to deal with."

"Dargoman controls a financial empire that stretches from Brazil to Malaysia," GU Sikkim sneered. "You're going to deal with Dargoman? You're just a housewife."

Juny smiled. There was something distinctly unpleasant about it.

"Even a housewife could lead this family better than you," she said. "I think it is time you retired, dear Uncle. The strain is too much for you."

"What the hell do you mean?"

"I mean you will step down as chairman of the trust and appoint me in your place. You will permit me to audit your assets and I will reclaim what I see fit, including the six million in Singapore. Finally, you will handwrite a letter announcing your intention to retire, which I will circulate throughout the family. You may cite health reasons."

"I will do no such thing," GU Sikkim scoffed. "Don't be a fool."

"It is the easiest way, I assure you."

GU Sikkim jeered, "Rais, please take your mother out of here. She is overcome with grief and talking like a madwoman."

"Interesting you should say that," Juny said. She brought out a thick hospital folder. "Since you are the gentleman suffering from Alzheimer's."

"What?"

"Here are reports from neurologists from Apollo, Square, and United," Juny said. "Oh, and one from America."

"One of my college buddies teaches at Johns Hopkins," Rais said apologetically. "He thinks I'm playing a joke on you."

"What are these lies?"

"Conclusive proof that you suffer from dementia and early-onset Alzheimer's," Juny said. "And here is a statement from your very own personal physician."

"Pappo!"

"Turns out he's not that fond of you," Rais said. "Particularly after he found out what *really* happened to my father."

"That traitor! I got him this job..."

"Oh, I've done far better," Juny said. "He's been offered a post as chief cardiologist at Square Hospital. Mostly on merit, I must say—he's actually a very good doctor. His last task here, in fact, will be to sign the legal documents required to declare you insane. As he is the only doctor you've ever consulted for the past twenty years, I think his word will carry the day."

"This is ridiculous. We are in Dhaka, not some village. You can't just lock someone up by saying so."

"Oh, it's done already. Go on. Read the reports," Juny said.

"My family will save me. You think I won't speak out?"

"You won't, in fact, speak at all." She opened her purse and started lining up little vials of intravenous medication like toy soldiers. "Dear Uncle, you have checked yourself in here with the symptoms of ischemic stroke following acute myocardial infarction. A suitably severe diagnosis, no doubt useful in case you had to pretend incapacity. However, it works both ways, of course. These vials contain the medicine for your condition. Sedatives and antidepressants for your insomnia and depression. Alprazolam for anxiety. Neuroleptics and Valproic acid for agitation. Frankly, a cocktail like this will keep you under for most of the day and severely confused for the few hours you do manage to stay awake. Certainly no one will understand a thing you are saying."

"You think the hospital will just medicate me without my permission?"

"It's already on your chart. These are standard treatments for your condition. You signed off on it when you checked in," Juny said. "Pappo secretly told the duty nurse not to administer them. An instruction I will reverse on the way out."

"Abdul! Abdul!"

Abdul popped his head in, received a frown from Juny, and closed the door hastily, refusing to meet his employer's eye.

"Don't blame him," Juny said. "We've told him that you've had a stroke and will not make sense a lot of the time."

"It seems you have thought of everything," GU Sikkim said heavily. "You would really do this? Poison me with medicine, for what? Some kind of petty revenge?"

"I blame you for my husband's death," Juny said. "But he was a grown man, able to make his own decisions. Indelbed is a different story. He was just a boy. He was our *family*."

"You hated that whelp as much as the rest of us."

"You took him from *my* care."

"My, my, my! All you care about is yourself. What about me? What about my daughters?"

"I will leave you enough to live on. Your daughters are busy working, with families of their own. They will hardly notice."

"You just want the money," GU Sikkim said. "All this, just for cash. I always said you were a gold digger. A vulture, that's what you are. Poor Vulu's corpse isn't even cold yet. You think you can run the trust? The other directors will never accept it!"

"You've been using it as your piggy bank for the last twenty years," Juny said. "I think some spring cleaning is in order. I will, of course, have your express recommendation. Remember to put that in the letter. Oh, they'll kick up a fuss, but when I go through the real accounts with them, I think you'll find that everyone will calm down. After all, they are all criminally negligent and accessories to your embezzlement. As executor of my husband's estate, I could put the lot of them in jail."

"You'll drag my name through the mud!"

"Not if you cooperate," Juny said. "Treat me like your successor, act in good faith, and I promise you, I will deal with the djinns."

"And Matteras?"

"I'm not going to roll over for him, if that's what you're asking."

"We are doomed. No one can save us."

"Yes, we are on the verge of extinction," Juny said. "Dargoman will wipe us out for sport. You know that I am the only one with the knowledge and ability to deal with this. Help me, and I swear I will ensure some of your precious Khan Rahman brood survives."

"I have no choice."

"Excellent. Now start writing what I say..."

CHAPTER 34

Just a Poor Boy from a Poor Family

Indelbed was weak, crotchety, and easily exhausted. Gone were the days of scampering around hunting wyrms. He could barely keep the light on. The distortion field came and went like a signal in a storm. He spent his time lying in the coils of God's Eye, letting the rumble of the wyrm's deep heart lull him to sleep. The creature had come to some conclusion about him, treating him as a sort of runty kin, a useless pack mate who should nonetheless be preserved out of some dimly understood evolutionary precept.

God's Eye too had morphed in subtle ways, which was more of a sharper delineation of existing features than anything else. The immature wyrms were all maw and teeth: blind, thrashing things, snouts like rock drills, hides battered. God's Eye was acquiring a lacquer to his carapace, a gleam in his eye, the hint of a jawline, an elongation of the skull, the possibility of a nose, a sort of potential grace. The frills around his neck were growing, scaled in soft patterns, the root of some unknown apparatus. He was a pickier eater, but, in compensation, had developed better hunting skills, the patience of a deep-lying predator. He would wait still as death in front of a tunnel, jaws open, a mantle of calm around him, a deadening of pheromones and whatever else wyrms used for sensory matter. Givaras would light a beacon for the hapless wyrms and the first would blunder unwittingly into those jaws, now powerful enough to easily snap infants in two. God's Eye was good. He shared his kills. He understood the concept of cooperation.

Indelbed, of course, watched these activities from the sideline, further irritated by not being able to take part. Things continued to go awry inside him, bringing fever, aches, and sometimes episodes of searing agony that inevitably caused blackouts. His memory was patchy, and sometimes he forgot words. He eyed Givaras suspiciously and tried to avoid him for a time, before relenting out of sheer boredom. It was difficult to give your nemesis the silent treatment when there were only the two of you. For his part the djinn chattered on, having one-sided conversations and continually monitoring Indelbed, poking, prodding, even bleeding him on one occasion.

"You know what your problem is?" Givaras said, on day fourteen of the great sulk. "You've never been loved."

"Yes, yes, you've mentioned this before."

"No, just think about it. Your father blamed you for your mother's death; he certainly didn't love you. You had no siblings. The Ambassador and Sikkim, they sold you out. Your Aunty Juny, Rais, they never loved you. Think about it. They must have all known. Imagine them sitting around their dining table, deciding your fate. They let you, a little boy, go away with a stranger. They *sold you* to Matteras. Even your mother didn't love you. She was djinn, and let me tell you, we have no familial feelings whatsoever."

Indelbed had no clear picture of his mother, but he was moved to object. Surely all mothers loved their offspring! And his father? He had cared for him. He had tried, at least, to protect him.

"I can't say about your father, but djinn aren't like humans," Givaras said. "I mean, we are *fundamentally* different. We aren't pack animals like you. I suspect we were solitary hunters in an evolutionary sense. It makes a huge difference, you know. Society for us is a burden, a continuous series of transactions. You see, we don't have families or tribes. Djinn do not have children often, and they do not require such an enormous amount of care. It is rare for parents to raise children."

"So what, you just throw them back into the ocean?"

"Often they are entered into patron-client relationships," Givaras said. "Or master-apprentice, if they show aptitude in something. The point is that concepts such as love, loyalty, familial bonds, do not work very strongly with us."

"So even my mother didn't love me—that's your whole point?"

"My point is you're thinking like a human. But you're half djinn, so you must be capable of thinking like a djinn. I am trying to help you do that."

"And how would that help me? You all sound mentally disturbed. No offense."

"Well, it would stop this prolonged bout of sulking, for starters."

"It hurts, Master."

"Pain can be borne, every djinn knows that. And it has not been wasted."

"Was it worth it? I'm a freak."

"You already were one, half man," Givaras said. "You are unloved, unwanted, and no one will ever, ever help you."

"Thanks."

"Except for me."

"Yeah, being the recent recipient of your help, I can safely say that—"

"What I'm showing you is that the world has characterized you as a loser, and you will never be permitted to rise. It is a valuable lesson I learned long ago."

"We're both in a cave, left for dead, on the constant verge of being eaten by wyrms," Indelbed said. "I don't think you've actually learned any lessons at all."

"I am alive, when the world thinks that I am dead," Givaras said. "That is enough for me. And I kept you alive, you ingrate."

"Yeah, thanks for that. So what's the big life lesson?"

"You see, it's quite simple. To win, you must cheat."

"Cheat? That's your big revelation?"

"Cheat."

"Like in a game?"

"In everything! Cheating is the secret! Understand that every rule, every law, has been made by someone to keep you in line. You cannot win. The world is designed to keep you in one place, to maintain the status quo. To overturn everything, to get out of your spot, the only answer is to cheat." Givaras was more animated than normal now. "I have already set you on this path. You have cheated death twice already, for neither the wyrms nor I have killed you."

"Yay."

"You have cheated your fate. You were destined to die ignorant and weak, whereas I have made you enlightened and strong."

"Ahem, I'm actually a blind, vomiting cripple who couldn't light a candle." *And I'm beginning to wonder whether there ever really was a plan to escape. Maybe you just wanted to experiment on me to pass the time...*

"Yes, well, you might recover, you know, no need to be so pessimistic."

"Sure," said Indelbed. "You know, Master, what I really like about our chats is how wildly flexible you are with the truth."

"See? Cheating..." Givaras beamed. "Now, back to our lessons. Matteras isn't going to off himself, you know."

Somewhere over the Pacific Ocean, about five hundred miles off the California coast, the *Sephiroth* started to lose power. Tiny iron shavings suspended in the engine lubricant had been eating into the seals, shafts, and bearings, constant friction chewing holes into the parts, allowing fuel and lubricant to spread throughout the two main engines. Normally the magnet under the oil pan would have prevented the larger shavings from moving around, but this had been removed, and curiously, the Ghuls had not noticed. In fact they had not checked a lot of things, a gross and unusual dereliction of duty.

When the engines started slowing down above the Pacific, several other things happened as well. A minuscule tear next to the heavy air intake valve on the right side of the main envelope spread far enough that the valve began to malfunction. The *Sephiroth*'s outer envelope was essentially an airtight composite skin laid upon a lightweight skeletal frame. Inside this vast space was a complicated array of smaller envelopes and balloons. At the base were reinforced tanks where the helium was kept in a compressed state. When the helium was released into the lift envelope, the *Sephiroth* would rise, as the air inside of the envelope became considerably lighter than the atmospheric air outside. To lower the *Sephiroth*, the helium was compressed back into the tanks, and the two heavy air valves on the outside of the envelope were opened, to let normal air into the ballast envelopes, thereby making the inside of the *Sephiroth* heavier in comparison to the outside. Descent was controlled by the ratio of heavy air to helium.

When one of the heavy air valves began to malfunction, it started leaking in air at an uncontrolled rate. This, coupled with sluggish engines, caused a serious imbalance in the *Sephiroth*, making it list and lose altitude at the same time. The strain caused the fabric around the valve to open farther, letting in more and more ballast. Increasing the humiliation for Golgoras, the *Sephiroth* began to spin as it fell, due to one side of the airship now being considerably heavier than the other. He could have stopped all of this with the use of his engines, but as they continued to fail, he could not get enough power to the compressors to inflate the inner helium envelopes, nor could he straighten course as his propellers were now useless.

Being a fair way up, he could still have rectified this problem by physically patching the valve and then rigging a smaller spare engine for limited movement, but the Ghuls were being remarkably inefficient. Golgoras sent two of them to fix the critical leak by climbing the maintenance struts deep inside the envelope. He waited in vain for an hour. The leak did not lessen, and the Ghuls never returned to deck. The third Ghul, in charge of engine maintenance, was sent to bring the spare machine online, but he never returned either, despite repeated calls to the engine room. Golgoras, unable to leave the cockpit, was forced to fight the spin and attempt a controlled descent.

The hull and substructure being designed for water landings, the airship was effectively a sea-worthy vessel. While there was some damage to the hull during the crash, neither Golgoras or Beltrex was hurt, except for the former's pride. By the time Golgoras had steadied the ship, ensured it was holding watertight, and started fully deflating the envelope, the three errant Ghuls had decamped with the lifeboat. He couldn't even hold them for breach of contract, let alone mutiny and obvious sabotage, for they had left him a note citing the primary rule of maritime landings, the gist of which was "every djinn for himself." Thus, bruised and humiliated, he and Beltrex limped into an abandoned part of the California coast several days later, where Golgoras was forced to physically pull the *Sephiroth* ashore over rough sand and rock, splintering the beautiful wooden hull, a final fuck you from the saboteurs, which was enough to make the djinn roar and shake with apoplectic rage.

To make things worse for the pilot, once safely onshore, Beltrex promptly abandoned him, saying, "Thanks for the ride. Good luck with your ship. Fortune is clearly against you—kindly inform everyone that I have seen the error of my ways and will not be opposing any future motions brought forth by Matteras."

In the darkness he could hardly see her. She had not aged. Oh, there were wrinkles on her face, around her eyes and the corners of her mouth, smile lines, although he could hardly remember her smiling much over the past twenty years. Perhaps they were sarcasm lines, etched into her skin by the acid of her words. Her hair was immaculately dyed—she had grayed early, and his father had teased her mercilessly about it, one of the few instances, he suspected, that the hapless Ambassador had scored a point.

He missed his father with a sharp pang, moments of yearning so heavy, it seemed impossible that the seconds would pass, would put the corpse back into the dull safety of the past. Hapless Ambassador: the man had been mocked in his inner circle, where everyone assumed that Juny had run his life. It was not that he had been incompetent or particularly comical. Left alone, he would likely have succeeded on his own, for he too had had an ironic wit, a distinguished manner, and a degree of drive. It was just that in every category, for every merit, his wife surpassed him by a measurable quantity.

They had been natural allies, Rais and his dad, forged from a very young age, when it quickly became apparent to both father and toddler that to preserve a measure of independence, to enjoy some illicit pleasures, they would have to join forces. When Juny was going through her dental hygiene phase, his father would smuggle him big triangles of Toblerone chocolate, purchased in secret from airports and smuggled back in his briefcase with the same diligence he normally reserved for bringing back duty-free liquor. They would eat it in the guest room and then gargle with mouthwash to prevent detection.

When she had ruthlessly fixed him to be an engineer at age twelve, and enforced this dictum by buying him only Lego Technic toys meant for sixteen-year-olds, the Ambassador had quietly bought him a guitar and hidden it in the garage. On Wednesday nights when she used to play bridge with other Foreign Service wives, they used to sneak out there with plastic chairs and his cigars, and Rais would practice chords.

The Ambassador hadn't been a bad man, hadn't even been greedy or vainglorious. His ambitions had been reasonable, given his starting position, and he had more or less achieved his wins fairly. One mistake, so many years ago, had cost him dearly: his conscience, his luck, most probably the love and respect of his wife. But it had never cost him his son.

They had not been demonstrative. The natural awkwardness between father and son had risen up between them too, some imperceptible curtain of reserve, during the teenage years and beyond, until Rais had returned from college, aimless, to live at home, and they had once again fallen into gentler routines. There were no special memories; they had not climbed a mountain together or gone fishing. It was more an accumulation: five thousand cups of tea drunk together, the wordless division of the morning newspaper, heated political debates over minutiae, exchanged glances whenever Juny did something particularly funny.

Then there were the annual shoe-shopping expeditions during summer holidays, because the Ambassador insisted every man should have a pair of polished oxford brogues, and since his son could not be trusted to not stray instead into loafers or Nikes or whatever atrocity was being peddled as footwear these days, it behooved him to ensure this one thing. It had been a point of pride for him to be well shod. He had also taken Rais every two years to his tailor, so that whatever else, he would always have at least one good suit. He had taught him to buy cuff links and bow ties, even though Rais had never worn either.

This haze of memories was powerful by dint of their very vagueness, for Rais couldn't take one down and relive it with any great depth. He couldn't remember what words were said, or any particular action. They were ephemeral; they disintegrated into nothing upon examination, only to re-form in the back of his mind as a mental clutter of half-snatched conversation, a grunted exchange, some unfunny joke. He stared at the jasmine tea in his mug, thrust there by Butloo not five minutes ago, and wondered if it was the aroma triggering olfactory memories, these half dreams of nothing. His eyes were full of tears, so he wiped them, drank his tea, and waited, as his mother finished her prayers in the dark part of the room.

"You wonder that I don't grieve," she said after several minutes, still sitting in the shadows. She had noticed his tears, as she did every little thing. Only the lamp next to Rais cast a cone of light. Juny hated the overhead bulbs; she rarely turned them on.

"I miss him," Rais said.

"I miss him too, truthfully," Juny said. "How can you not miss someone you've spent thirty-five years with? But I never knew what good crying ever did anyone."

He stared at her. She seemed more vital somehow, as if some psychic burkha had been lifted from her form. "No, Mother, crying never helped anyone." What else could he say? There was only one right answer with Juny.

"All my life, I worked in proxy," Juny said. "Around him, through him. It feels strange to come out of that."

"It must be refreshing, to stop having to maintain that fiction."

"He wasn't an empty fiction. He was a shield, a buffer, a filter. He had a thick skin. Insults, slights... they just rolled off him, he was impossible to puncture. I would be howling in rage, but he'd just keep rolling on, amused by the uncouth peasants. Khan Rahmans breathe rarified air, because their noses are tilted so high up—isn't that the old joke? He sheltered you too, you know, cocooned you in money and privilege," Juny said. "And I followed his lead in that. It was not always one-sided between us."

"I know that."

"You were always *like* him. When you were little, you used to sit like him, pretend to read the paper like him. Your mannerisms, your words, he was so proud of those little things," Juny said. "You have to be stronger now, Rais. You have to be more like *me*."

"I feel hollow. And skinless."

"That's the feeling of childhood falling away."

Later on, Barabas came to offer his condolences.

"Listen, we're seriously outgunned here," Rais told him. "If you guys want to help, how about pumping in some cash and muscle?"

Barabas balked. "Ahem, I suppose I could return some of the loans..."

"What loans?" Rais asked.

"Your mother..."

"What about her?"

"You don't know?"

"Obviously not."

"She's the Black Banker. We all owe her money."

"What?"

"Look, I don't know if you realize it, but it's quite expensive getting around town these days. And things like trains and buses don't accept dignatas."

"Of course I realize it, you fuckers don't pay me a damn cent."

"Well, we had a network in place, but after Kaikobad got in the coma, and Dargoman switched sides, all the credit started to dry up. It got pretty embarrassing." Barabas shuddered. "I mean, I've blasted quite a few Humes in my time, don't get me wrong, we all have, but you can't go around doing that for rickshaw rides and restaurant bills, eh?"

"I suppose that would be awkward," Rais said. "Plus you'd run out of restaurants pretty soon if you killed the owner every time you had to pay a bill."

"Precisely. And then there's Seclusion, you know." Barabas tapped his head. "Long story short, turns out many of Kaikobad's contacts were approaching her to find out what to do, and she just sort of... took over. She set up a bank, started lending us money. Microcredit, apparently, because we don't have collateral. Community policing. If anyone slips up, well, everyone pays."

"She made a Grameen Bank for djinns." Rais smiled. "Didn't breathe a word of it to me..."

"It's all small amounts, but it adds up, I tell you. She's sitting on a huge pile of dignatas right now, believe me," Barabas said bitterly.

"I can imagine. Where's Golgoras? He was supposed to do a deal for me. Plus I was hoping to borrow a Ghul or two, set up some protection for my mother."

"You didn't hear?"

"Um, I've been busy."

"He and Beltrex crashed over the Pacific. Sabotage."

"Damn. Where's Golgoras now?"

"Just got back. He's fixing the *Sephiroth* in the hangar. Pretty pissed off. Serves him right. I offered to help if he'd make me first mate, but he told me to eff off."

"So it's just us now?" Rais frowned. "In that case, you *have* to help directly."

"What?"

"Barabas, please, we're about to be destroyed. Khan Rahmans have been the emissaries in Bengal for two thousand years. Do you want the massive loss of dignatas involved in seeing us extinct?"

"Hrrmm. All right, fine. What do you need?"

"My mother's moved her base to Wari. The old spells are damaged. I need you to repair the perimeter. And then you're going to sit there and make sure no djinns attack the place."

"That perimeter's going to take days," Barabas grumbled. "And what are you lot going to do while I'm slaving away?"

"Mother's taking over the trust and then going to war with Dargoman," Rais said. "Me? I'm going to stop Matteras. By the way, do you remember Kaikobad ever talking to Risal?"

"I shouldn't think so. She was a bit uppity. Never invited *me* to her fancy sky tunnel."

"Was he writing to her, perhaps?"

"He was always writing letters," Barabas said. "I never paid attention to any of that."

"Think, Barabas. How do you even send letters to someone up in the air?"

The djinn frowned. "There is an air courier. A Ghul. Kaikobad would have known him."

"Can you ask him, please? I really need to know."

"Okay, okay," Barabas said. "I'll call him down."

"Let me know as soon as you can. One last thing. You ever heard of haplogroups?"

"Sure, I love their music. I'm up to date on all the obscure stuff. Moffat said he was going to help me become a hipster. That means someone very cool. He said I've got the right kind of beard."

"Never mind."

The house in Wari was already on red alert. Abdul lounged incognito in the tea stall at the entrance of the alley, winking as they crossed, his gun bulging clearly under his shirt. Two or three other ex-army subedars stood at strategic points, armed with pistols. The shopkeepers in the street knew Juny by this point, had already been recruited to her cause. They kept an eye out on who came and went. This was a Khan Rahman bastion, and despite the peculiarities of the doctor, almost everyone was a loyalist.

The gate was reinforced with iron bars, and a further gunman stood on the roof, armed with a rifle and other various small arms, not enough to stop a djinn, but proof enough against a man with a cane sword. Butloo still manned the front door. The stalwart was quivering with pride. He had somehow dug up an old army uniform, some kind of Gurkha rig from the British era, complete with the heavy-bladed knife. He snapped a salute, and then shook hands with Rais for good measure.

The house was a beehive on the ground floor, clerks at small wooden desks counting money, accountants poring over ledgers, and a clutch of lawyers around the dining table, smoking cigarettes and making lists of dirt they had on each other. Juny had refurbished the place. Every moldy surface had been scrubbed, painted, or, in some extreme cases, replastered. She had fitted the kitchen with equipment that actually worked: a gas stove, a microwave, a restaurant-grade refrigerator. Her carpenter had fixed all the windows with new netting, preventing the mosquitoes from coming in. The library had been restored to its former glory, shelves polished and straightened, for Juny had moved their entire occult collection back here, replenished with many of Kaikobad's old books, whatever the used-book shop owners had been able to track down for her. Rais's own haul of books, secured from Risal's sky tunnel, had spilled over to a second room.

Upstairs, the entire second floor had been polished and painted, all the old junk furniture thrown out, the guest bedrooms made inhabitable, one of the sitting rooms cloned into a hospital room, prepared to receive the comatose owner of the house. Kaikobad, still in his long sleep, was coming home at last. Juny had taken the Doctor's old bedroom suite, converting part of it into her office. The only room untouched was Indelbed's. His aunt fully expected him to return one day and insisted that he should find all his meager belongings exactly as he had left them. It was perhaps a blind spot for her, and many of her allies whispered about it behind her back, speculating that she was losing her mind, but as she conducted the rest of her business with chilling precision, it was left alone.

Pappo was there when Rais returned, setting up a holding room for Sikkim, as were a dozen or so of the family, relatives already co-opted to the cause. Rais greeted them, left Barabas to work, and went upstairs. His mother was in Kaikobad's room, going over papers with the family barrister, an elderly relative who had an encyclopedic knowledge of the trust.

"I brought Barabas," Rais said. "He's fixing the spells. Might not stop Hazard or Matteras, but at least we'll get some warning."

"I think Dargoman is the real threat anyway," Juny said.

"All the guys with guns... it seems a bit excessive."

"Look, my first job is to keep everyone safe," Juny said. Her face softened. "No more casualties."

"I see you've moved in GU Sikkim."

"I had to. He's one of our best resources right now—I want to make sure no one sticks a knife in him. Matteras has had his hooks in this family for a long time. I need to know who else is suspect."

"Uncle Pappo?"

"He's with us. Everyone downstairs has been vetted," she said. "For the next few days, we won't leave the house until the dust settles. I've also moved Kaikobad back in here, with full round-the-clock nursing care. That clinic was atrocious. He's still completely nonresponsive, but who knows. I feel better having everyone under one roof. It's not safe out there. If you need something, send for it. If you must go out, take Abdul and the driver. The cars are parked on the main road. Barabas must stay here."

"He'll stay. We just have to keep him drunk."

"I've already stocked six cases of whiskey. We've called a board meeting for the trust tomorrow. It's going to be held here. You better attend. We might have to show off Barabas to convince some of them that djinn are real. Can you believe they've not had an actual board meeting for the past thirteen years? Sikkim used to send the minutes by mail and they'd just rubber-stamp his diktats."

"And now they'll rubber-stamp yours."

"You better believe it," Juny said. "Now, did you bring a copy of the *Compendium*?"

Rais brought out a sheaf of papers bound in blue plastic. "Matteras has the original. I made a copy of course. I think the manuscript actually had spells woven into it. It's possibly dangerous to readers. The djinn claim people have lost their minds reading it."

Juny was already flipping through it.

"This is fascinating," she said, propping open a page of the bestiary section. There was a picture of a minuscule catlike creature with wings. "He's actually giving instructions on how to make this thing, I think."

"Most of the theories are in the appendix," Rais said. "Genetics and evolution."

"Anathema to the conservatives."

"Correct. Unpalatable to most djinn, in fact. Deep down they're all convinced of their own superiority. How can you not be, when you're the only ones that can manipulate the field?"

"Do you think he could actually make these monstrous things?" Juny asked after reading a few more minutes. "It's disturbing..."

"I know," Rais said. "He's claiming almost godlike powers. I can understand why the other djinn wanted him put away."

"So, son, what's the plan? How soon is the storm going to hit? Should we be packing up and getting out of here?"

"Not yet," Rais said. "Okay, here's what I'm pretty sure about:

"One, it starts with Gangaridai and the Great War. That was twenty thousand years ago, and no one remembers any of the details. Two, Givaras wrote a lot of books. Matteras has destroyed all of them. Givaras created awful things, new forms of life. I think he actually fought in the Great War, but there's no proof. Three, Givaras is in a murder pit with Indelbed and Risal. They might still be alive. Four, Risal is the missing historian who was researching the Great War. Her work is gone. I have her journals. There are nine volumes of bowel movements and minutiae. Teased in between are hints of her work. Five, also missing is Risal's copy of the *Register of Kings*, possibly the last copy of a book chronicling the kings of Gangaridai. Six, the air courier just confirmed that Uncle Kaikobad was corresponding with Risal. He sent her a package. This is huge, because: seven, Risal mentions in an offhand way somewhere in volume seven that she has sent a sample for genetic testing and is waiting for the results."

"You read all nine volumes?" Juny asked. "I couldn't get through even half of one."

"Reading vast quantities of useless things"—Rais smiled—"that's my superpower."

"I know," Juny said. "Vulu and I used to laugh about that. You were a very frustrating child." Her face softened. "You've done well, Rais. You didn't give up. You didn't run away. I'm proud of you."

"Surprised?"

"Not at all," she said. Then she laughed. "Your father and I worried a lot, you know, that you never finished anything. I'm glad you've found your calling."

"Back to business," Rais said, slightly embarrassed. "I don't have the correspondence between Kaikobad and Risal. I think Kaikobad hid his own work, and Risal's got stolen. But I have both of their notes. They're talking about genetic drift and haplogroups, epigenetics and mutations. She started out researching Gangaridai and ended up working on genetics."

"Why?" Juny asked.

"She had some genetic studies done, on mitochondrial DNA and Y chromosomes. As far as I can tell, it was only one sample. Why? What did she find? The original data is gone. I tried to track down the lab, but it shut down long ago. I gleaned some information from her offhand remarks, but I need to talk to a specialist and run some tests of my own. I've found a guy. Only catch is his lab's in Nevada."

"It's not safe to go outside right now," Juny said.

"I visited Uncle Kaikobad in the clinic, you know," Rais said.

"What?"

"Yeah," he said. "They told me you used to go there every month."

"I made sure he was not being neglected," Juny said. "Why did you go there?"

"I took a DNA sample—a cheek swab, a little bit of blood," Rais said. "I also got a swab off Barabas. My friend Roger in Nevada is testing them both right now."

"Why?" Juny asked.

"What do you know about haplogroups?"

"Nothing," Juny said.

"So haplogroups are genetic groups descended from single ancestors. See when humans replicate, the DNA from the father and the mother get recombined. The kid gets a mixture of genes from each parent. Except for Y chromosomes and mitochondrial DNA. Y chromosomes come from the father intact, because women don't have Y chromosomes, and the mitochondrial DNA comes from the mother's body. In effect, *all* mitochondrial DNA in the world is matriarchal and all Y chromosomes are patriarchal."

"Okay," Juny said.

"Hang on, it gets interesting. Now any single nucleotide mutation in the Y chromosome gets passed on from father to son, so it's possible to track entire populations to a hypothetical Adam, right? The first guy in Africa had Y chromosome A, let's say, and then a few hundred years later, we had a mutation in one of his male descendant's Y chromosomes, and *his* offspring became A1. Get it? Now on the mother's side, there's mitochondrial DNA, and you can track Eves like that. It's useful in figuring out migration patterns and how original humans spread across the world. For example, we know that humans crossed the Bering Strait to populate the Americas because of haplogroups."

"Is this relevant to us somehow?"

"Yeah, see, that's what I thought. It's really fucking boring. So why was Risal obsessed with human haplogroups?"

"She was?"

"Tell me something, how common is it for a djinn to work on human genetics?"

"As far as I know, most djinn disdain human science," Juny said.

"She was studying something called the R2D. It's a variation of one of the big haplogroups out of Central Asia. I started looking it up, except there's no mention of R2D anywhere," Rais said. "Not on the web, nothing in science journals, nothing in my university library. So I sent it to my doctor buddy in New York. He's a Jew—they know this shit 'cause they're always doing genetic research to get rid of hereditary diseases. Anyway, he got me in touch with Roger. I got him interested in the R2D subclade. That's not the official name, of course, because it doesn't actually exist. What he did have, though, was a working list of peculiar or unresolved haplogroup errors, or just plain oddities—there are plenty of them—and they go unresolved because there isn't enough money or inclination to study them. This is the kind of stuff that crackpots use to make theories on alien intervention, or biblical origins of man, or whatever."

"So Risal believed in aliens?"

"Well, single cases of this haplogroup, which she calls R2D, has been found four different times. The first time was in a Siberian tar body, which was carbon-dated to around 14,000 B.C. A second time was partial remains near the Gobekli Tepe region, where the Y DNA was inconclusively tested. Gobekli Tepe monoliths were dated around 8000 B.C., mind you. The third was in North America, among the Iroquois in a recent study of the Bering Strait crossing, but the sample was thrown out because it made no sense. The last was in India during a routine study trying to establish that Brahmins are a super-race descended directly from God. Anyway, the point is that it appears to be an old mutation of the Y chromosome that a) still exists, and b) has a very unlikely spread."

"So Kaikobad sent Risal a genetic sample, what, twenty years ago?" Juny asked. "They were looking for this R2D group?"

"Kaikobad could do magic," Rais said. "How?"

"Well, djinns have distortion fields," Juny said. "As far as I know, that isn't really magic. The field itself exists everywhere, it's a part of physics. They have the ability to manipulate it within a certain range."

"Right, so say Kaikobad had the same thing. The ability to manipulate the field. I mean, how else can we explain it?" Rais said. "What if it's just a physical trait, like height or intelligence? What if it can be passed on genetically?"

"Let's say it can be explained in scientific terms," Juny said. "Then the real question is: How closely linked are humans and djinn genetically? Is the field ability independently present in humans as well as djinn? Or is it linked? Think about it. Humans and djinn are actually close enough genetically to reproduce. We know that for sure."

"Indelbed."

"Right," Juny said. "He's twenty years old now, you know."

"The sample?"

"It might have been him."

"Okay," Rais said, getting excited. "What if humans and djinn are just related species, or even just mutations of one species? What if the R2D mutation is the genetic marker for the field ability? Most djinn don't believe in evolution or genetics. They wouldn't like this at all. I mean, it might tear them apart."

"Say it's true," Juny said. "Djinn believe they are superior. This is a deeply rooted belief. Even the most tolerant, humanized djinn think they're inherently better. Imagine if there was irrefutable proof that they're just like us? I don't think they could accept that, as a species. Say this is what Kaikobad discovered."

"It would certainly explain why Matteras got rid of him and Risal."

"Could we use it to stop Matteras somehow?"

"I don't know, but we have to try," Rais said. "If we can embarrass the Creationists, if we can set back Matteras somehow, it might be enough to negotiate. You have to get me to Nevada somehow."

"It's too risky."

"It's only Dargoman we have to worry about. If I can give him the slip, I'm safe enough from djinns. They won't gun down an acting emissary officially investigating Risal's disappearance."

"Officially investigating?"

"That's my next stop. Golgoras can deputize me if I twist his arm enough."

"Good. That's smart. You can't go alone."

"I was thinking Maria."

"Do you trust her? Or are you infatuated?" Juny stared at him. "Because if you get it wrong, and she tells Dargoman, you're dead."

"I guess I'll think about it then."

"Okay, give me two days. I have a plan. I hope it works."

CHAPTER 35
Kaikobad

The luster was gone from the city: the marble walls dark and grimy, the trees lining the central avenues listless, even the breeze reeking, laden with ash. Everything outside burned, and the stench tormented the remaining citizens. The noose had tightened sufficiently that essentials were scarce now—bread and rice, vegetables, oil, salt, fish—shortages that were unthinkable even a year ago. It was not so much that their gates were encircled, for the enemy did not have the forces to create an airtight siege; Horus had simply destroyed the hinterland, all the farms and settlements that supplied the city, possibly all the farms and towns in the entire continent. It was the first time they faced total war, a war devoid of champions or honor, most of the time even devoid of fighting.

Kaikobad, for so long trapped in the eternal city, felt its pain as if it were his own body under siege. He was no longer certain that he was seeing visions. It seemed more like he was actually living in the city, that it had somehow accreted around him. He wandered aimlessly and was drawn to a simple house in the brandy quarter adjacent to the outer wall, where the distilleries had once thrived. There was a broad courtyard in front, where caravans used to unload.

In the open terrace, shaded under an old mango tree, sat Kuriken, smoking a hookah, looking curiously peaceful. It was jarring to see him in such mundane surroundings. He wore his armor, the gleaming white *kavach*, and his power waxed with the morning sun, so that his field was a thing of gleaming beauty. It was said that Kuriken was incorruptible, implacable, that his armor could never be pierced, that the city would never fall as long as he stayed true. Watching him, Kaikobad could well understand the faith of his followers. He remembered the wasted version of this djinn from the real world, the bitter, mocking king whose field was black, whose fingers dripped blood, and he wondered what had happened to this magnificent champion, what dire path he had taken to arrive at his current fallen state.

A lady djinn appeared across the gate, covered in veils, and Kuriken rose in greeting. It was apparent he had been waiting for her. She approached with a nod, perfectly at ease, as if this was part of a regular routine. He poured wine for her and offered her a plate of fruit as she sat across from him, two intimates sharing a respite, a scene so incongruent, so normal, that Kaikobad forgot the horror they were living in. She removed her veils, and her beauty staggered him. It was perfect yet warm, animated even while she sat still, her hands held placidly on her lap, her field powered down to an inch of her flawless brown skin.

"Davala," Kuriken said, savoring the name.

"Peace, Kuriken."

"You risk much to come in person," Kuriken said. "To enter this place is easier than leaving."

"I know," Davala said. "The paths are still open, my love. I have come to bring you back."

"You have many loves," Kuriken said with a smile and a genuine warmth Kaikobad had never seen in him.

"You were always my best," Davala said. Her face grew fierce, black eyes sparking with the lithe grace of a leopard. "Come with me, love. I will forsake all others. We will forget this war in some icy mountain, some northern wilderness where neither man nor djinn will disturb us. We will spend eternity together, contemplating the sky, and you will not be violent, and I will not be restless."

"I cannot," Kuriken said. "I will not betray my word."

"You are doomed," Davala said. "You will die here."

"I cannot die. I think I would welcome it."

"This city is finished. Obstinate djinn! What that sorcerer brews inside his castle is anathema to life. He will destroy the world with his hubris. Will you stay and watch this happen?"

"And what will Horus do to this world, or bloody Memmion?" Kuriken asked. "I have seen them slaughter thousands. I have seen Barkan level mountains with his hammer. What will Bahamut do but drown the world one day? You are in bloodthirsty company, Davala, these are all monsters. None of us are innocent, love, none of us are right. But at least let me keep my honor. I alone am not an oath breaker."

"The devil take your oath," Davala said. "What do oaths mean to djinn? We are made of fire! I have lived a thousand years. What oath can last for the span we are expected to live?"

"We could live twenty thousand years, and still I would not relent," Kuriken said. "Do not ask me this again. Remember you loved me once, the best parts of me."

"I love you still, fool," Davala said. "The shining knight of the First City. The great champion. You were always the best of us. But that city is gone now, Kuriken. That beauty, that grandeur, is ashes now. The time of champions is over. Horus wages a different sort of war. You must be able to see that, you must be able to change."

"I will not."

"And if you faced me on the field, would you run your spear through me?" Davala asked.

Kuriken looked at her for a long time. "If you stood across from me on that field outside, I would cut away my armor and let you kill me."

"I believe you." Davala shuddered. "Your insanity is contagious. Do you think I could ever harm you?"

"Your friends have sent you here for something," Kuriken said. "Ask me now, and I'll give it to you."

"I came of my own accord," Davala said sadly. "I had to try."

"They call Elkran the Black Whisper. Where is he, this killer of djinn? Where is blood-soaked Memmion, who has traded his love of gold for gore? Where is Givaras, the breaker of Ghuls? I can see them from the walls. I grow hoarse calling to them. Why do they not come and fight?"

"You fool, do you think Givaras fights duels? Did you think you would face him in glorious combat and one of you would fall in heroic death, while the minstrels sang?" Davala asked. "You alone think this is a play, Kuriken, an epic song. Is your precious High King fighting duels? Is he thinking of honor and sacrifice in his tower?"

"Your friends are cowards."

"They are playing to win this time," Davala said. "The rules have all changed. Only you don't understand that."

"I am simple," Kuriken said. "Too simple for you."

"You are singular," Davala said. "And you underestimate yourself. I must leave, dearest. It will be too late soon, even for you."

"I was never tempted to leave," Kuriken said. "Until you came."

She drained her glass and walked away, through the gate into the haze outside, where the demons lurked. Kuriken sat for a very long time, staring after her. He made no sound, although it seemed to Kaikobad that he wept.

CHAPTER 36
Starvation Diet

"This is hopeless." Givaras flopped down next to Indelbed.

They had been crouched in front of a promising tunnel for five hours now, flickering the field on and off. Hunting had dwindled in the past weeks, slowly petering off, until their reserves of the awful meat were low and putrid. For some reason, the wyrms weren't coming.

"It's God's Eye," Givaras said.

"This is part of the plan, right?"

"I wasn't sure this would happen," Givaras said. "It seems as if God's Eye is now giving off pheromones that are repelling the wyrms, despite the lure of the distortion field. We will have to act soon."

"So, to the maps!"

They hobbled to the Cartography, unaccountably excited. The 3-D model of the tunnels had been expanded greatly since the early days. Over the years they had mapped each tiny crack and geological layer with the thoroughness and scientific rigor typical of Givaras. They had calculated collapse pressures, drilling rates, and aquifer conditions with a degree of mathematical detail that had caused Indelbed sleepless days and nights. By the end of it, Indelbed knew a lot of math, and the geological survey was extremely accurate.

Their escape plan had come with a lot of complex problems. Surprisingly, water had been their greatest one, the fear of flooding from the aquifers above, as well as some slight chance of gas ingress. They would have to create a casing from the field to prevent the tunnel from collapsing.

A second problem was provisions for God's Eye. He was their engine, and they would start with a limited quantity of fuel, with little likelihood of restocking along the way. The proto-dragon would starve while he tunneled the path, but if he made it close enough, they would live.

Their route was 3S27, the designation of the third tunnel from the bottom of the map, following a direct route to the S curve of the outer boundary that sank below the iron dome. It was the twenty-seventh route they had mapped, the one finally settled on. During this first phase they would be using preexisting bores, requiring just a degree of enlargement to fit the wider God's Eye, which would save precious energy. If they were attacked by a convergence in these tunnels, they would be dead, for even God's Eye would be a sitting target, unable to turn. The entire success of the plan depended on Givaras's theories on dragon evolution and the strength of whatever dominance pheromone the giant wyrm gave off.

The S curve was phase two with its own dilemma. The outer curve was definitely sealed off by some construct, creating the self-contained prison network. They would have to break through. If they failed, they would face a long and futile return leg back to the central chamber.

If they succeeded at the boundary, finally, phase three would start: a last desperate, grinding, crawling dash to the sea, moving through unknown sand and clay formations and possible bedrock. They would be starving by this point, wholly reliant on God's Eye's instinct to complete his metamorphosis in water. Here again they depended on theory, for no one living had ever charted the evolution of the giant wyrms, either underground or in the seas. No one had even seen the mature, final iteration of the dragon, the mythical creature of air. They were gambling that the earth wyrm, the sea wyrm, and the airborne dragon were the same creature. If these were in fact three different animals, they were dead.

"This is the worst possible timing," Indelbed said, after the initial euphoria had dissipated. "I'm blind and sick, and you haven't even regrown your legs. We won't even make it to the boundary."

"Ah, I'm not bothering to regrow. I'm using these."

Indelbed touched something hard, and through field vision he saw the ghostly outline of Risal's shin bones, held by the djinn like relics.

"I'll walk out wearing Risal this season, haha."

"Can you even do that?"

"Why not? She's not using them. I just have to liven them up a bit and reconstruct my knee joints."

"We'll look like a pair of real sick bastards if we ever get out, won't we, Master?"

"Trust me, boy, we will see daylight again."

"And then?"

"You're a dragon, and I'm Givaras the Broken. The world outside is full of awful things that I've made. Men and djinn will weep when they see us."

"Good."

"You got any food in this shithole? I'm starving."

"Shit, Maria, how did you get in here?"

"You're kidding, right? Your security is Abdul. Relax, all your guys know me. They think we're getting married. They practically handed over the house keys to me."

"Fuck off."

"I heard you did something to your uncle."

"He's out of the trust. Mother is taking over."

"Sorry about your dad. I liked him."

"He used to hit on you."

"Yeah, a little bit, but not in a gross way."

"Seen your boyfriend lately?"

"Not personally, thank god. He sent word. He wants progress, and he's not being subtle with his threats."

"What did you tell him?"

"Shit, Rais, I told him everything, what do you think?"

"He knows we're holed up here?"

"He knew that anyway."

"You know he killed my dad, right?"

"Yeah, he told me," Maria said. "He also threatened to kill my parents. He wants an exact log of where you're going to be for the next week. I think he might be thinking about grabbing you or something."

"You can move in here, you know. He can't get in as long as Barabas is here."

"Yeah, and we can live happily ever after humping in your cousin's shitty room with your mother next door." Maria swept around. "Why isn't there any goddamn furniture in here? What was he, a monk?"

"He was like ten years old when he left," Rais said. "He was poor. Never had any stuff. He never complained. My mom won't let anyone change the furniture."

"Guess you guys are shit at looking out for family. Fucking Khan Rahmans."

"Yeah, I guess we just kind of blipped over it."

"You liked him, though, right?"

"Yeah, the little I knew him. He was funny," Rais said. He looked around. "You want lunch? I can get Butloo to bring something."

"That weird old dude? No thanks."

"No, my mom's cook is here. He's taken over the kitchen."

"Oh, okay then, yes." Maria sat on the bed, which, other than Rais's plastic chair, was literally the only option. "Rais, this stress is killing me. When are you going to deal with this guy?"

"My mom's working on that."

"Thank fuck at least one of you has balls."

"You know, you're a really pleasant person."

"Yeah, whatever. So I'm going to be hanging around here spying on you. Just go about your business."

"I was going to take a nap."

"Well, you'd best take the floor then."

"I'm beginning to envy the engineer."

"Do you want me to tell your mother why I'm here?"

"She knows about the pictures. She already tore me a new one." Rais snorted. "I'm sorry, Maria, but you have to pick a side. You can't tread water anymore. If you're with us, you've got to be with us, you've got to *help*."

"Can you beat them?" Maria asked. She didn't sound sarcastic anymore, just tired and frightened, and Rais felt a surge of affection for her. It was easy to forget that none of this was her fault. "Can you even hold them off?"

"I'll keep trying. You have to trust me. We have a shot, I promise. Come over tomorrow for the meeting. We'll tell you everything."

"What if I blab it all to Dargoman?"

"If you do, you do. What am I gonna do? Hurt you? This is me showing trust."

"All right, I'm all in."

CHAPTER 37
Last Supper

They gathered in Kaikobad's library, now restored to its former glory and more, the old rattan chairs tossed out, replaced by good leather armchairs behind a walnut-colored coffee table. Indelbed would have been amazed at such wealth. Rais remembered going through this very room with his cousin, searching the dusty shelves for magical texts, and felt a lead ball of regret in his gut, that peculiar combination of cringing sorrow and shame that came with the memory of past failures. Next door, Kaikobad's even breathing rattled their ears, a steady in and out for the past ten years, seemingly untouched by time, but his ghost lurked in this room, dampening their cheer at this most dire hour, reminding them that their losses were many, their successes very few.

Even Barabas was cast down by the varied dooms hanging over them, from the murderous threat of Dargoman, to the cataclysmic promise of Matteras, down to the insane final solution that lurked in the bay. They huddled around the table nursing mugs of hot tea, Moffat proposing outlandish solutions to the Dargoman problem.

"Why can't we just kill him?" Maria asked finally. "He's only human."

"He's protected by a lot of spells," Rais said. "His entire body is crawling with constructs. I saw them in the Assembly."

"I've got the invisible knife. The Five Strikes thing," Maria said. "Won't that cut through all his spells? I can get in a room with him..."

"It probably would," Rais said.

"He's very well protected," Juny said. "I've had him followed before. He's never alone. He's got at least ten bodyguards at all times. Even if you somehow got him in a room alone and stabbed him, Maria, you wouldn't get out alive. We are not going to risk any of our people just to kill him."

"Barabas?" Rais asked hopefully.

"Can't touch an emissary," the djinn said. "We'd lose every shred of dignatas we've got left. Matteras would take us to court and keep us there for the next hundred years."

"Why don't we take *him* to court?" Rais said. "We've got him dead to rights for murder."

"Not murder," Juny said. "But you might have a good idea."

"Why not murder?" Maria asked. "My dad's a secretary. If you've got evidence, we can get Dargoman remanded before he knows what's happening."

"I don't think remand would hold him," Rais said.

"We won't take him to human court, dear," Juny said. "We'll take him to the Celestial Court of the djinn. Unfortunately, in the Lore, an emissary murdering a human isn't that serious a crime. Not enough to stop him."

"Loss of dignatas, though," Barabas said. "Not that anyone's counting. Matteras is so popular now, even his servants are strutting around commanding this or that."

"No, but I think we can get Dargoman for something else," Juny said with a rare smile.

"What?" Rais asked.

"Breach of contract."

"What?"

"Thank god for your uncle Kaikobad," Juny said. "I don't know if you recall the conversation the day we first met Dargoman. Kaikobad hired him. They had a verbal contract in which Dargoman explicitly agreed to protect Indelbed."

"I remember you making him say that," Rais said.

"Same thing. He went along with it, he *acted* accordingly. *Well*, I think we can show enough to imply that he deliberately broke the contract," Juny said.

"Is that really serious?" Maria asked.

"Breach of contract is the most serious crime in djinn law," Juny said.

"Will it work?"

"It's serious enough that they will call for a hearing, and he will have to personally attend," Juny said. "I know the judge. He's a conservative, but the good kind. Breach of contract won't sit well with him. Remember, Dargoman switched patrons. That kind of thing is unacceptable to conservatives. Once Dargoman comes in, I can tie him up with legal arguments for at least a month."

"Clever," Barabas said, and laughed. "If you can actually prove breach of contract, he's going to be in big trouble. You'll beggar his dignatas."

"Let's say we occupy Dargoman for a while," Juny said. "The question is, can you make it count, Rais?"

"Matteras."

"Yes, Matteras," Juny said.

"He's gone to Siberia, to see Kuriken, I heard," Barabas said. "The Assembly didn't reach any decision, but the way it was going, well, not too many objections by the big guys. We're hanging by a thread, I'd say. If he and Kuriken come to terms, they probably have enough clout to get this thing done."

"And Bahamut?" Juny asked.

"Look, I can't say what Bahamut will do," Barabas said. "I don't know why he lives in the ruins of Gangaridai, I don't know why he won't come out of the water. I have no idea if he's really got a bomb that works, or if he's going to set it off."

"What's your gut feeling, Barabas?" Rais asked.

"He does, and he will."

"All right, we don't have much time then," Rais said. "I think the only way out for us is to negotiate a peace with Matteras. All that stuff he said about living space sounds like bullshit to me. Or at least not the whole thing. He's got some personal stake. I need to get to the lab in Nevada. If everything works out there, I think we can get to Beltrex and convince him to step in. That should be enough clout to get a sit-down with Matteras."

"Vegas!" Barabas said. "I want to go there!"

"Er, Barabas, you need to stay here and protect the house," Rais said. "No way anyone is going to attack it with a djinn inside, even if it's just you."

"Hey!"

"Joking," Rais said. "Maria and I are going to Nevada. The rest of you stay here and deal with Dargoman. If we don't make it back, well, it means we've failed, so get ready to run like hell."

"Maria," Juny said, "that knife of yours. Do you know how to use it?"

Maria bared her wrist. It shimmered on her arm and then slowly winked out of sight. "I'm ready to use it. Readier than Rais, anyway."

"Good," Juny said. "Good. You'll do."

"What about me, Rais?" Moffat asked.

"You're going to stuff Barabas with every kind of pharmaceutical product you can get your hands on," Rais said. "Whatever it takes. Just make sure he does not leave the house."

"Sure," Moffat said. He winked at the djinn. "This dude is a beast. I'm not sure I can keep up."

"What about the RAS?" Juny asked.

"The *Sephiroth* crashed, apparently. I'm going over to see Golgoras next," Rais said. "We'll need him with us and the full weight of the society."

"When do we leave?" Maria asked. "I've got to make up some excuse for my parents."

"In two days," Juny said. "We'll file the lawsuit tomorrow. I'll hit him with some other things I've got lined up too." She took a deep breath. "I just want to say that this is dangerous, and we might not win. Dealing with djinn is always dangerous. I am proud of all of you, however. Maria, Moffat, I have prepared an evacuation plan. You and your families have been factored in. I want you to make arrangements and give them the heads-up. If we fail, things will become very chaotic in this city. I will do everything I can to ensure their safety. I hope you trust in that."

"Thanks, Aunty," they chorused. It was easy to believe in her competence. Juny then proceeded to stick with time-honored aunty tradition and fed them tea and a plethora of heavy snacks.

Later, as Moffat was seeing him into the car, he slapped Rais on the back of the head. "Do you actually have a plan, or are you just trying to take a honeymoon with Maria?" he said. "You spent half the damn meeting smiling at her. Do I have to remind you how bad it was when she dumped you? She is the antichrist, man. You need to remember that shit."

"I was smiling," Rais said, "because we're flying coach to L.A., China Southern. She's never flown economy before. It's going to be the worst thirty hours of her life."

CHAPTER 38
Fire Horse

Indelbed had always dreamed that their escape would be explosive, the dragon thrusting out of the water, soaring above the people as they gaped in astonishment on the bank. The reality was more of a slow grind through rock and sand, a dusty, exhausting process that strained his every ability with the field, yet still left time for long stretches of utter boredom.

In surface life, he remembered seeing a picture once of the two great machines that had drilled the Channel Tunnel, connecting France and England. His father had studied in England, and of course the house was full of memorabilia from the colonial age; their family had prospered during the British era, being part of the traitorous land-owning class.

He had always thought England was somewhere vaguely north, close to Sylhet. When he had finally seen it on a map, he'd been astonished to find it more than halfway across the earth, an island so remote that it seemed a very peculiar thing that those people had come all the way to Bengal. But then, perhaps their island had been very cold and unpleasant?

The tunneling machines, however, had impressed him no end, and seeing God's Eye in action finally, he realized that the giant wyrm worked in a very similar fashion. His rotating jaws were filled with different kinds of teeth, some to crack rock, some to grind, and a final, flatter set that drilled through sand. He produced copious amounts of saliva, which seemed to serve a lubricating purpose, and there were channels in the bone along the sides of his face, where the cuttings were shunted aside. Indelbed wasn't sure, but he seemed to be eating some of the rocks. He would have asked Givaras, but he wanted to avoid another lecture.

Givaras was using a goad on him, leading the wyrm by manipulating certain spots on his skull. He had seriously considered trepanation to better access the brain, but Indelbed had persuaded him out of it. It was unlikely

God's Eye would take kindly to having holes drilled in his head, regardless of the benefits.

The first part of their escape was simplest, as they were using an existing tunnel, and God's Eye merely had to enlarge it. The wyrm did this with sullen ease, often just using brute force to collapse layers of sand and pebbles. Indelbed's job was the least glamorous. He was the rear guard, which meant choking on a steady stream of cuttings and wyrm shit, itself composed mostly of rock. He had to pull the travois, full of their stockpile of wyrm meat and water, which was unbearably heavy, but could be slid along the tunnel floor with relative ease once he cleared the way. Far harder, he had to form a protective casing with the field around the area being drilled, to prevent the dreaded cave-in, and then to gently collapse the tunnel behind them, to prevent pursuit by other wyrms.

This strategy had created some friction between them, because Indelbed had wanted to preserve the route back to the cavern in case this attempt failed. In reality, the thought of existing in a little traveling pocket of dust-choked air for god knows how long had steadily frayed his nerves, but Givaras had pointed out that leaving a giant tunnel behind them just begged for a convergence, and the untested deterrence value of God's Eye's tail was a rather thin sliver to hang all their hopes on.

For twelve days they continued along the tunnel. As they approached the periphery of the network, wyrm incursions became frequent, and their progress slowed to a crawl. They were in a deep pocket aquifer now of wet gray sand, and the roof of the tunnel required constant propping up. This was the riskiest portion of the route, for aquifer water filled the tunnels here, and they had to extend the field in a bubble to the front and rear in order to keep from drowning. At least they were able to replenish their water supply.

God's Eye was hungry and irritable by this point, taking longer to start up after each rest, snapping angrily at them during feedings, agitated, suspicious, barely allowing Givaras to approach his great head.

Then, as they neared the edge of the boundary, disaster struck. God's Eye bored too hard at a clayey layer, collapsing the tunnel above, burying them in clay, sand, and squealing wyrms. Indelbed felt the field constrict under the weight, suddenly hammering him to his knees, water seeping up quickly from the edges, until he was moments away from being crushed or drowned. Over the roar of God's Eye he could hear the panicked hissing of wyrms thrashing around in the light and a rancid maw snapped near him, and he had to fight the instinct to collapse the field altogether. Things crumbled around him, and he felt the thump of God's Eye's tail clubbing him in the stomach, flinging him back.

Givaras shouted a command in djinn and fire spurted from his outstretched hands, a horrible liquid flame that coated everything and sucked the air out of the tunnel. God's Eye roared angrily, but his carapace was thick; the plates blackened and blistered, but held. The juvenile wyrms popped in the heat, their chitin literally cooking them alive inside their own skin, the softer parts just melting. It was over in seconds, an awesome display of power that flashed across Indelbed's altered vision, erasing the delicate lines of the field completely.

He staggered in fear, seeing only white, and fell against God's Eye's smoking body, scorching his palms. He heard Givaras hobbling over.

"I can't see the field!" Indelbed shouted. "It's all white. My field is gone!"

"Hush now, boy." Givaras righted him. "Your field is intact. You are still holding us up. Be calm. The white will fade, and you will see the lines again."

"What was that?" Indelbed asked. "So much power... You said you were weak. How could you do that?"

"It was a spell," Givaras said. "I was saving it for Matteras, but this seemed like an appropriate time to use it."

"Oh. I didn't know you could do that."

"There are many things you do not know, apprentice," Givaras said. "I said my field was weak. It does not mean I am ineffective."

"We're buried. I can feel the weight above my field. It's cracking."

"You've got to keep calm. Just hold it together."

"We can't go back. The tunnel has caved in for real."

"You did well keeping us alive," Givaras said. "Things are not so bleak. We are now very close to the outer edge. Can you not feel the presence of the construct? I suspect two or three more days will get us to the wall of our prison, and the first part of our journey will be done. And these wyrms have unwittingly reprovisioned us."

"Yay, more wyrm meat. At least you cooked them."

It took them three days to get to the seal. It appeared to Indelbed as an enormous wall of light hanging somewhere over the dark horizon, pulsing as they got closer, until he could see the individual strings making up the structure, something beautiful and horrific with power, on a scale beyond his imagining, a display of force that beggared Givaras's fire. Not for the first time, he questioned what crimes his master could have committed to warrant such an exhibition.

Finally, their tunnel broke through to a stone chamber made of ancient monoliths, and they could go no farther, for the wall of light was now within touch, curving up around them, and the heat from it was enough to shrivel their eyelids. God's Eye gave a long, plaintive moan, unable to turn and flee, and turned a great sad eye at Givaras, an accusing glare, as if to question why he had been goaded so far to certain death.

"What do you see?" Givaras asked.

"Light!" Indelbed said in wonder. "Strings of light woven together."

"You can see the field," Givaras said. "Can you see the fire behind it?"

"Fire?"

"Channeled from the earth's core. Do you not feel the heat? That, despite the field barrier containing it. Imagine how hot it is in the center," Givaras said. "An ingenious seal by Matteras."

"I don't get it."

"The seal is not the barrier. Any barrier made of magic can be broken, given enough time. You see, constructs decay over time, and even if they are renewed with power, they are still dependent on structural logic."

"So what is this thing?"

"The field you see is merely a double layer surrounding us," Givaras said. "The real trap is what is held in the middle. This is core fire, mined from the center of the earth, as hot as the surface of the sun. Clever, clever trap."

"So it was all for nothing." Indelbed sat down inside the wyrm's coil. The plates were already warm from the heat. God's Eye shivered nonetheless.

"Not so."

"We cannot cross this barrier."

Givaras was standing within touching distance of the barrier, fieldless, his naked fingers stretching toward the fire, blistering, the skin roasting.

"You're burning!" Indelbed shouted, far more scared, he realized, of being left alone here, trapped in this blazing room, than any other kind of doom.

Givaras retreated. "The barrier repels my field, like two magnets pushing against each other. But if I go naked, I burn. Clever, clever Matteras.

How tempting, to step inside the flame." The djinn was smiling, a manic grin lighting up his face. His charred hand smoked.

"Let's go back, Master, please." Indelbed had visions of Givaras diving into the fire, of some suicidal madness claiming the djinn. To be trapped here was bad, but to be alone would be much worse. He would die then, he decided, just step into the fire and let the core fire have him.

"If the dragon were more mature, he would have flown through," Givaras said, petting God's Eye. "They do that when they are older, you know."

"He hates it," Indelbed said. "He's cowering in fear."

"He does not have the scales for it yet."

"Scales." Indelbed was preoccupied with many things, but he was not slow. Givaras's inflection of the word had a peculiar resonance.

"Dragons anneal themselves in the hottest fires they can find. There is no fire hotter than this. Matteras has provided us with a gift."

"I have scales."

"You have scales."

"No!"

"It is what you were made for."

"No! I'm not walking into fire."

"Come with me. Just stand next to it. I promise you, you will not burn. You cannot see what I can see. Your skin is reflecting the flame like diamonds."

Indelbed got up as if sleepwalking. The djinn led him to the barrier, pushed him on. The heat was great, but it felt weak against him, like tides hitting a distant shore.

"I was broiling when I stood this close," Givaras said. "I felt my skin cracking. Yet nothing happens to you."

"Did you know this was the trap?" Indelbed asked. "Core fire?"

"Yes," Givaras said. "Or rather, I suspected. I could not be sure until I saw it physically."

"This is why you gave me the dragon hormones."

"I suspected it would be useful."

Indelbed stared at the wall of light. So close, the weaves mesmerized him. "You think I can just walk through?"

"The layer only repulses the field. It's permeable if you're just meat. Turn off your distortion field and let the fire take you."

"And then?"

"Get to the center, make a spherical shield, and push down. The fire runs in a circuit, like electricity. You have to make a bubble and cut the loop. It should give us a tiny window to cross over."

"You think I'm going to survive in the middle of this core fire long enough to do all that?"

"Don't worry, it just has to be for a couple of seconds. Just make a shield and hold on as if we were dueling. I bet there's a device on the other side, some kind of field generator that keeps the fire going."

"You're betting now?"

"I will turn it off, and you're home free."

"I'm just going to walk out of there..."

"A little crispy maybe. You'll be fine."

Indelbed walked in. It was not fine.

The seal of light had been holding back the true heat of the core fire. Once inside, the flame washed over him like an errant wave, the nascent scales beneath his skin shriveling—pathetic, iridescent insects—the scream boiling away in his throat, as he pushed down with some primal instinct, down with his faltering field, core fire licking around the edges of his ragged bubble, threatening to engulf him.

He felt the whisper of space around his body, a slowly disintegrating pocket of superheated air, and with a terrible effort he turned his head, saw the vague outline of the wyrm lumbering toward him and then balking, cowering before the flame, his massive head throwing off the djinn's goad, his high-pitched wail making an unearthly sound that penetrated the veil of fire, making clear his extreme unwillingness to proceed.

Indelbed felt hope draining out, the pocket starting to collapse in earnest, and then Givaras dived through the gap to the other side, moving fast like a mantis on stilts, borrowed legs burning to a deep burnished ebony as the heat flared at the intrusion. The bubble collapsed behind him. Indelbed's field guttered and shrank to an ethereal second skin, the dragon blood singing inside him, yearning, not nearly enough proof against core fire, but still he lingered, a stick figure spinning arms akimbo, a little bit of hope tethering him to life, as all around him the fire roared, and that brief window snuffed out.

"I made it," Givaras said, his voice so very distant, marred with pain. "You did well. I knew you would."

"I'm burning, Givaras! Get me out of here!"

"How am I supposed to do that?"

"*Stop the fire*. Turn the machine off!"

"There isn't a machine, I'm afraid."

"What?! No machine?"

"None."

"There never was a machine," Indelbed whispered. "Help me, Master... It hurts."

"The pain will pass if you let go. You have succeeded, after all. I am free."

"You raised me like cattle..."

"My fire horse," said Givaras. "Matteras thought I would kill you, but I built you into something... wondrous. Be thankful. I gave you far longer than I should have. After all these years, I found that I enjoyed... teaching."

"Please, I beg you, Master..."

"Your apprenticeship is ended, I'm afraid. All that is left is to burn."

"Burn?"

"It is a noble death."

Indelbed shrieked as the final patina of the field dissipated, those ghostly particles vanishing, and the terrible heart of the core fire, hotter than the sun, roared through him, a brief flash of something so exquisite that it made up for the complete abyss of dissolution. "Then let all djinns burn with me, I pray to God!"

"That's the spirit," said Givaras, as he walked away.

CHAPTER 39
Last Ride

Rais drove across the city, looking out through the back window, protected by tinted glass. His mother's driver wasn't cut out for the jungle traffic outside the tristate: the thrust of rickshaws, pedestrians dashing across in front of them glaring, buses slowing in the middle of the road, desperate passengers hurling themselves into the open doors. He spent too long switching lanes, never cut off the other cars fast enough, was, in short, too polite to really survive out here. He was also afraid to get the Mercedes scratched, the old car polished as always to a beautiful shine. It took them two hours to get to the old airport hangar, longer than normal, but today was an exam day, literally thousands of students pouring out of every nook and cranny, trying to get to their halls, trailing harried parents.

He saw the kids in blue-and-white uniforms, hopping out of cars, buses, vans, rickshaws, human haulers—every sort of transport possible—and wondered if they knew about djinns, if they dreamed strange dreams. He felt an ineffable sadness and realized that he loved this city on a basic level, the sheer scrambling vitality of it, the insane confidence of sixteen, seventeen million people that it wouldn't all collapse. He imagined it being swept away, obliterated by water and wind, as countless other cities had, and wondered where then he would belong, which place would claim him, and thought that this is what a refugee was, someone rootless, unwanted. *Maybe I'll go down with the ship. It's the least I can do, isn't it?*

"You are sad, Rais *bhai*," the old driver said, staring at him from the rearview mirror.

"What would you do, Uncle, if there was a big flood?"

"There have always been big floods," he said. "You don't remember them? In 1990 we took boats out of Gulshan."

"What if everything washed away, all the buildings," Rais said. "What would happen to you, to your family?"

"Some would live, some would die," the old man said with a shrug. "Juny madame already sent my sons to Rome, to work. They used to sell flowers there, you know? My youngest one speaks Italian. He works in a café now. They send me more money than I know what to do with."

"Mama sent them?"

"Your mother has sent every single child of every single staff to school. She has gotten them jobs, or sent them abroad, or gotten them married," the driver said. "If everything washed away, she would find us a new house."

She takes care of people, Rais thought. *They are so sure of her, so certain that she'll put everything right. At some level she must genuinely care what happens to everyone. Whereas I don't. Or can't. Perhaps I've misunderstood her for all these years. It's not the toughness she wanted from me. It's more empathy. Less selfishness. Yet empathy is the last thing anyone would ever associate with her.*

What is this confidence these servants have? He felt he lacked the quality that engendered such loyalty, such blind faith from people. There was, at his core, something solitary, something that prevented the gathering of followers. In moments of painful introspection, he could recognize this truth. He wished now that he had made some effort to know Kaikobad. That man had been a successful emissary, a famous one, yet a drunken recluse at the same time, a mélange of glaring contradictions. *Uncle Kaikobad never gave a fuck about anyone. Maybe I need to be more like him. There isn't much time to pick mentors, really. Golgoras is our last reasonable ally, and I'm gambling everything on the fact that Risal and Kaikobad were onto something good, rather than wasting time on some mumbo jumbo.*

Rais found Golgoras covered in grease, sitting among the dismantled pieces of two great engines, fuming with rage. The airship was a bedraggled sight, 80 percent deflated, the outer envelope of the blimp gashed along a two-meter span, flapping open like indecent skin, the air valve a broken nipple torn off, hanging. The wooden hull was gouged and nicked where engine parts had struck, the entire rear blackened by smoke and flame; the smell of salt water permeated everything.

"Three hundred years!" Golgoras shouted. "Three hundred years without an accident!"

"Where are the Ghuls?"

"They've disappeared," Golgoras said. "Broken contract, which is unheard of. Fucking Hazard." He looked past Rais at the old Mercedes parked outside. "You've got bodyguards now?"

"Dargoman killed my father," Rais said. "You must have heard."

"Yeah," Golgoras said. "Sorry. It's a fucking disgrace. He ought to be in court for that."

"Can't prove it anyway," Rais said. "How long are you out of commission?"

Golgoras spread his hands. "The starboard engine suffered a cataclysmic failure. Iron shavings in the lubricant. The grit broke some of the bearings and pistons, the engine caught fire. The port engine seems fine, but I have to take it apart anyway to make sure. That's the problem with sabotage: you have to check every single thing now. I'll probably have to take apart the entire envelope to check the seams."

"You can't get help?"

Golgoras shrugged. "I've sent word to the society for more Ghuls. Let's see. Not sure I trust anyone at the moment."

"My cousin has a workshop."

"Do they repair airships?" Golgoras asked skeptically.

"No, but you could send the parts out in pieces," Rais said. "They'd never know what they're working on. The principles are the same. It'd be a hell of a lot faster than doing everything yourself."

"All right, thanks," the djinn grunted. "What can I help you with?"

"I was doing some research," Rais said. "You ever heard of haplogroups?"

"Nah. What the fuck are they?"

"Human genetic groups descended from single ancestors," Rais said. "Risal was into it. Have you ever heard of any other djinns studying it?"

"Human studies are not of great interest to us," Golgoras said. "If Risal was pursuing this, she might have been the only one."

"She didn't have any colleagues, or students, or like any other scientists she collaborated with?" Rais asked.

"There is no science club," Golgoras said.

"Why don't you have scientists? It's fascinating. You have technology, some of it married to the distortion field, that is quite advanced, and if Bahamut is to be believed, some devices that can alter time and space entirely. You have a very well-developed legal system, and a financial system that could be described as post-currency, almost. But where are the theoretical physicists?"

"Perhaps our knowledge of the universe is more advanced than Humes'. We are the superior race, after all. We are more powerful, we live longer, there is nothing on this world that can harm us—"

"Yes, hmm, you are in a way the apex predator. I can see how that would retard your growth. Have you considered that you have reached an evolutionary dead end?"

"Have you considered that you might fall out of an airship sometime?"

"Ahem, sorry," Rais said. "No offense."

"Human science is of no interest to us," Golgoras said. "Don't forget, five hundred years ago you thought the earth was flat. Three hundred years ago you were riding horses. There are djinn alive now who remember you as cavemen. Do not think we are impressed with your physics."

"Okay, okay, I see your point. However, I think there *are* a few djinn interested in science now." Rais lowered his voice. "I have some ideas on what Risal found. Let's say I figure it out with some proof. Do you have any objections?"

"You're free to look into the matter as de facto emissary."

"Will you back me up, though? Will the RAS officially endorse my investigation?"

"Let's say we do. If you actually find something controversial, I get first look at it. If it's big enough we'll get Memmion involved. We say how and where the information is used."

"How old is Memmion?"

"You're obsessed with age," Golgoras said with disgust. "He's old, okay? Bahamut old. Gotten a bit strange, but not nearly as bad as Bahamut. It's best to use him as a last resort."

"And what about Bahamut?"

"The RAS and Bahamut are temporarily aligned in this matter. Memmion and Bahamut are old friends, they've always seen eye to eye. It's your decision whom you want to talk to. If you want to take all this to a giant school of fish, well, good luck to you."

"I see your point. We have a deal."

"I hope all this running around is worth it. I heard your clock is almost up. If Matteras and Kuriken are dickering over how to split up the world after they've drowned half of it, you've hardly got any time left. There's not a penny's difference between them when it comes to humans."

"I'm trying. Oh, can you sign this please?"

Golgoras frowned. "Hell is this?"

"Salvage rights on Risal's house."

"What? You can't do that—"

"Why not? We found it. You were only commissioned as transportation. Maritime law gives us full salvage rights as the first party."

"Maritime law?"

"My mother has a copy of the full charter of the RAS too, if you want further references."

"I'm beginning to hate that woman," Golgoras said.

"Okay, look, I'll cut you in, twenty percent human currency on top of haulage fees for bringing stuff in. You personally, not the RAS."

"I could have thrown both of you clowns out of the air lock. Twenty-five percent, and I can't be soiling my hands with human coin. You'll have me as a silent partner for whatever investment you do and kick in the returns in kind. Oh, and I want my account cleared with your mother. What the hell do you want from there anyway? You already took the books."

"I want all the plumbing and anything else that's solid gold. And then I want it reaffixed at a location that only we know about," Rais said. "If things go south we might have to hide."

"All this human fixation with gold. Fine. Equal shares in auctoritas. That means both our names for initial discovery. That's not negotiable," Golgoras said. "No way I'm losing out to a cretin like Barabas and a Hume."

"Auctoritas? Does that mean I have auctoritas now?" Rais smiled. This had not really occurred to him yet.

"Confirming Risal's disappearance? Breaking up the Assembly? Finding the *Compendium of Beasts*? Yes, I'd say you have auctoritas."

CHAPTER 40
Celestial Court

Shofiullah was leading a convoy of three container trucks out of the customs yard in the port city of Chittagong, sitting in one of many thousands of trucks in line, except that his goods had no manifest, no bill of lading, no tax clearances, no papers at all, in fact. They were dark containers, unloaded in secret, unrecognized by the ship that had carried them in from the eastern ocean, waved through by a chain of corrupt officials. This was the very thing that was never supposed to happen, the thing a hundred safeguards had been made to prevent, yet Shofiullah drove in and out of the yard with a swagger, cigarette dangling from grease-stained fingers, driving one-handed, his twelve-year-old assistant capering like a monkey from the passenger-side window, trying to shout a way through heavy traffic.

These were routine shipments from Thailand, containers filled with Yaba tablets and other pharmaceutical products that were sold at huge markups to the addicted fashionistas of the capital city, plus boxes of cocaine, ecstasy, speed, diet pills—everything packed in oilcloth and sunk in sealed barrels of motor grease, just a brief nod toward security, for it was actually unthinkable that any official would interfere. It was a part of cabal business, a very lucrative part, not least because of the influence it allowed the cabal to wield among the city's elite, selling upmarket supplies to high-end people.

Shofiullah and his fellow drivers had barely gotten a hundred meters out of the gate when plainclothes investigators stopped them, flashing papers too fast to read, pulling guns, sweating in the heat beneath large dark glasses and black bandannas. One or two shotgun-wielding, jackbooted RAB were behind them. Shofiullah had time to flick away his cigarette and reach for his trusty Nokia before they pulled him down, face against the tarmac. There was something perfunctory about their refusal to talk. The gunshot was casual, once in the back with a six-chambered revolver.

"Trying to escape," one of them said, as they began to walk away. "Cross fire."

He bled out on the road, but the drug haul was large enough that when his body made the eight o'clock news, he was promoted from hapless driver to international drug runner and armed terrorist with links to Salafi groups worldwide.

In an apartment in Old Dhaka, three elderly women spent all night gumming new labels onto cans of expired milk powder bought on the cheap and distributed as fresh inventory all across the city. Each lot took a week to clear, and the women were paid well and allowed to live in the apartment, a marked improvement from the slums that would have been their more natural milieu. They had worked here unmolested for three years now, had literally grown fat off the expired milk, for no one minded if they consumed a few tins of their own supply. This was cabal business, the cabal being one of the greatest net importers of food, although to be fair, the trade in expired goods was only a small part of its genuine distribution; still, profits were profits, and this was a highly lucrative side business.

Three A.M., and the police busted through the door, splintering the flimsy plywood down the middle, and then proceeded to lay waste to everything. The women had money set aside for this, phone numbers, secret handshakes. These cops were peculiarly deaf. They still took the money, but pretended not to hear anything else. They had notebooks full of serial numbers that they matched to the tins, tracing shipping documents to original letters of credit. Finally, a magistrate came in with his own stool and little folding table, set up shop, and began writing his report. A journalist with a video camera started filming everything. It was then that the old women realized the cabal had finally failed them.

At the crack of dawn, long before any respectable tax officials ever rose from their beds, the guards of an office building in Motijheel, the city's financial district, were rudely awakened. Ministry men from the National Board of Revenue came out of two hired vans, escorted by plainclothes police. They didn't bother speaking, for their orders came from up high, and they had received very specific instructions on what to find. The office doors were hastily opened, books of accounts ransacked, laptops confiscated. This was a cabal office, a part of the real estate business that formed the bulk of its assets, and there were important documents here: land deeds, tax files, sales figures. Dargoman himself sat here sometimes, for the stock exchange and the bank head offices were all nearby.

They would find nothing great. The cabal had accountants and lawyers, after all, who were adept at hiding wealth. Taxes were filed on time, bribes were made, paperwork was kept up to date; in many ways they were model citizens. The NBR men had their own skills, however, from countless hours poring over handwritten accounts: hard-won instincts for weakness. And it wasn't long before they identified one of their bread-and-butter targets, the VAT on rent. The land deeds were fine, income taxes paid, licenses renewed, but the office was rented, one of the many the cabal kept around the city, and the office manager had neglected to pay VAT on the rent, a newish rule that was normally overlooked and settled out of hand.

Once the chink was found, further NBR accountants and lawyers were drafted in, notes were written back and forth, until the file, now several yards thick, appeared on the table of a director of the VAT wing, a relative of the Khan Rahmans, a once indigent boy whose schooling had been paid for by the trust, whose passage to this very post had been eased by a series of calls made by old Uncle Sikkim. While his inspectors waited patiently for him to cut a deal, the director did the exact opposite. He marked it for immediate prosecution, applied the highest possible penalties, ordered an eight-year tax investigation of all related enterprises, and then promptly went on his preapproved annual leave to visit his daughter in Canada, basking in the peculiar glow of having, for once, done his job.

"Where is Matteras?" Dargoman tapped his cane impatiently, thrusting aside the doorman. His bodyguards were on either side, ex-army men with shotguns and vests, no real attempt at hiding their purpose. The emissary was a worried man these days and had dispensed with the niceties of civil society altogether. He had an ex-cartel armored car with bulletproof glass, one of only three in the country, reportedly.

It was not his patron djinn he found in the conference room, but rather Hazard lounging in a swivel seat, smoking a long brown cigar and apparently contemplating the city traffic through the tinted French windows.

"He's gone north," said the djinn without looking up. "To Kuriken."

"I need him," Dargoman snarled. He flung himself into a chair.

Hazard motioned for the varied flunkies to leave. "Humans." He blew out smoke. "What use are you? *You* need. *You* want. Need I remind you, emissary, that you work for us?"

"I work for *Matteras*," Dargoman said. He modified his tone, however. Hazard, if anything, was even more rabid than Matteras, barely reined in at the best of times. He had spent very little time in the human world, was unused to the hustle and bustle, the constant irritations of daily life. He was one of those who yearned for the untamed vistas, the vast reaches of gray sand and ocean, and he was willing to depopulate entire nations to improve his view. "Still, perhaps you would deign to advise me."

"Unburden yourself, by all means."

"You are aware that Matteras entrusted the company assets in Bengal to my care?"

"Yes, his cabal, this great human plaything," Hazard said. "Each of us must pass time the best way we can."

"I was given the impossible task of liquidating and removing our wealth. Millions of dollars' worth of land, interests in industries, proxy shares in banks and insurance companies..."

"I assure you, I have little to no interest in this."

"It was proceeding," Dargoman said, "at a reasonable pace. I was happy with the progress."

"My delight knows no bounds."

"Until recently. Everything has reversed. We are being blocked at every turn. The National Board of Revenue has opened an investigation on us. Money laundering. On *us*. We damn near wrote the tax code for the last budget. Naturally I summoned my clients in the NBR—"

"*Our* clients, you mean," Hazard said. "Humans do not have clients."

"Yes, fine, I summoned the clients of Matteras and the many officers in my pay. They could do nothing. The dealing officer will not take bribes, he cannot be threatened." Dargoman held up his hand. "In isolation, this is nothing. But three days after, our trucks were seized by Narcotics Control, trucks without bills of lading or invoices, carrying hard-earned Yaba pills worth eighteen crore in the Dhaka market. Last week, seven sales of property failed to go through, seven guaranteed buyers who inexplicably canceled their contracts. No explanation given. No phone calls returned."

"So, bad luck?"

"It's that damned woman!" Dargoman said. "She's thrown out that senile fool Sikkim, she's taken over."

"You killed her husband, did you not?"

"Yes."

"Well, you can hardly expect her to sit idly by. Are you telling me
this much-vaunted cabal of yours cannot handle one irate middle-aged
woman?"

"We are wealthier," Dargoman said. "But she has hundreds of relatives.
They're like weeds. And she's cultivated the most peculiar contacts. She
has servants everywhere—peons, guards, drivers—they all seem to belong
to her. Our files are vanishing from tables, information lost, titles and deeds
stolen from safes. The SEC peon who keeps the mail register has inexplicably lost two of our applications, setting us back a year. The land registry
office has lost three of our original deeds. The sitting minister for land has
apologized, there's nothing he can do. Thirty million dollars put at risk,
because some land clerk owes a favor to that bitch!"

Hazard was amused. He was always amused, even when he killed men
like cockroaches.

"I know where she is hiding," Dargoman said. "I want your help to
smash them."

"I am hardly interested in humans smashing each other. Kill her yourself if you can."

"They have that djinn there, you fool!"

Hazard stared at him for a moment, and Dargoman saw madness spiraling in the turn of his pupils.

"I apologize," Dargoman said hastily, dropping to one knee. "My ardor
has betrayed me. Forgive the impertinence."

"Quite."

"The djinn Barabas is holed up with them. He does that infernal pup's
bidding, that upstart emissary. To destroy the house will be difficult using
our more... regular forces."

"I will not kill Kaikobad's nephew, and certainly not Barabas," Hazard
said. "He is a very old friend."

"They're all very old friends," Dargoman said despairingly.

"We are not low men, murdering each other for scraps. We are made of
fire, human," Hazard said. "You would do well to remember that... before
I am forced to chastise you."

"Matteras wouldn't like that," Dargoman said. Humiliating, debilitating fear spread from his bowels. He had seen Hazard chastising people before.

Hazard smiled his jackal grin. "Matteras does not speak for me."

"I beg forgiveness, my lord," Dargoman said. He prostrated himself for good measure. "I am a humble emissary."

"That word," Hazard said. "It is tossed around a great deal. You seem to think it confers some sort of privilege upon you, some mantle of djinndom, as if you were *more* than human. You are a servant, Dargoman, plain and simple, and sometimes servants require a good beating. Matteras indulges you."

"Yes, Lord."

"Forget your petty misfortune. You have been summoned to the Celestial Court."

"Me? Why?!"

"A case has been lodged against you. By the woman."

"She's a civilian!" Dargoman snarled. "By what right can she file a case?"

"The court has accepted her complaint," Hazard said, "possibly because so many of our jurists owe her money."

"Her husband was not an emissary," Dargoman said. "I am within my rights in killing him. It was a personal matter, between humans."

"Quite. I regret to inform you, emissary, that the complaint is not for your little murder. It is for something much more serious. Breach of contract."

"What?"

"Apparently you signed a contract with Kaikobad, undertaking the safety of his son. A commission you failed terribly at." Hazard smoked his cigar. "Did you undertake such a contract?"

"A verbal contract at best."

"Did you take custody of the boy?"

"You know I did."

"Then off to court you go. I suggest you hire a good barrister."

"You must help me—I did it for you."

"Oh, I'm a terrible lawyer. My talents are... slightly less academic."

"Matteras then?"

"My dear boy, can you imagine Matteras going to court to defend a human, much less his own cat's-paw?"

"I'm his emissary, for god's sake. He can get the case dismissed. His auctoritas is enormous."

"Best ask him then. Only don't go tearing off to Siberia. If you think I'm bad, you should see Kuriken. He'll hang you on a spike and light a lamp inside your gut. I've seen him do it."

"Has Kuriken blessed our cause?"

"They are negotiating. He leads his faction of the conservative party. We must see why he delays. He has been vague. Matteras no doubt will convince him. His auctoritas joined to ours will be enough."

"And then?"

"Then comes the storm."

CHAPTER 41
Storm in an Urn

There was an apartment building in the middle of Old Town Gopibagh, purportedly haunted, which rattled during storms with ghostly shrieks. The building was old, before the real estate developers really got going in Dhaka, and thus had not been designed properly. Rather, it had the appearance of an old six-story house partitioned into a dozen or so separate apartments, sharing a common stairwell and wraparound balconies that served as passages.

The house was haunted because one of the apartments belonged to Matteras. He never visited, and no one lived there. The green wooden door was fixed with a very heavy padlock on the outside, impervious to the attempts of a generation of children trying to break in. The apartment seemed to have its own internal climate, which did not correspond to the greater weather patterns of the nation. It gave off great heat and cold alternately, so that sometimes the door was rimed with ice and sometimes steaming with heat.

Ironically all the Old Town people believed in djinns, and had Matteras actually come down and explained what he was about, they would have been perfectly satisfied with him. Instead, it was the cause of continuous speculation, the source of a hundred urban legends, until every lame dog, every missing child, and every unexplained pregnancy was blamed on the apartment, despite it having never manifested any hostile intent whatsoever.

Inside, the apartment had floors stained with red oxide, a very old way of decorating cement. The place was completely empty. Hieroglyphs marked the walls, carved into the plaster, almost invisible to the naked eye, but crowding dark and thick for those with djinn vision. These spells made the interior freezing cold. The source of the heat came from a room farther inside. The apartment was disused except for the central bedroom, which was locked. The door was too hot to touch, and only the efficacy of the spells carved into the wood stopped it from combusting. The heat turned the ice into steam, and the door smoked continuously, adding to the otherworldly atmosphere.

Inside this room were the only two objects in the entire apartment: a large urn made of grayish clay, set upon a low wooden table. Every surface within was covered in hieroglyphs, done in the same hand as the rest of the place, done by Matteras personally in fact, for no other djinn or man knew of this room. These last sets of spells were exhaustive, the work of a master, and the dignatas of Matteras would have gone up considerably had his fellow djinn ever seen them.

The urn gave off great heat, and sometimes it made rattling noises, but it had never moved an inch from its base; in fact it was gripped there by forces unimaginably complex and would never even contemplate moving. The urn was currently full of dirt, good black loam, pebbles, sand, and water. There were hints of odd stuff in there: a hot line of fire, a handful of worms, a few other things.

The urn was ancient and had been subject to huge quantities of magic over the years by various hands, so much so that it was almost sentient now. Its thoughts were glacial, which was good, because it barely had time to register surprise before its innards started shaking and then expanding, and then some strange quirk in quantum space allowed an odd-looking foot to smash through its body and land on top of the table, a foot attached to misshapen legs, and the urn had time to reflect indignation before a second foot also came out, and everything shattered into a thousand shards.

A fully grown djinn stood on the collapsed table, careful not to move, a slight smile on his face. His skin was burned crimson and black, like a striped beast, and he had horns on his head.

"Fucking Solomon," he said, as he looked at the remnants of the urn.

He sat on his haunches and studied the surrounding glyphs for many minutes, until he found the one he needed. One picture, carved deeply into the floor, was cloven in two, a particularly far-flung piece of clay bisecting it. Thus divided, the meaning of this glyph changed entirely. It was just about enough. He put his finger to the spot and the spell started to unravel. A little white dervish swept through the runes, breaking them down, opening a safe path to the door, then out across the living room to the main gate.

The padlock popped open. Givaras the Breaker of Things balanced himself on someone else's legs and walked out.

Several days later, the urn had almost reconstituted itself into some proximity of a vessel when another body flopped out of n space, shattering the wretched thing once again. This time, used to near-death experiences, the urn did not panic, but resorted instead to a stoic reflection on the generally ill nature of man and djinn.

Indelbed fell to the ground, a smoking carcass, held together by will and a vestigial wisp of the field. After an interminable amount of time, he sat up, because even though he was sickeningly injured, he was not dead. Skin and scales flaked off him, but pain was a distant drum. He was used to pain, and the absence of core fire was a relief to which all other sensations paled. At first he saw only darkness, but when his eyes adjusted to the field he saw black lines surrounding him, trees in a winter forest, stretching in all directions, and superimposed, tessellations of force, tiles of icy power. The field roiled all around, disturbed. There was no way through, only a terrible, leaching cold, frost rimming all the surfaces, forming now on his fingertips.

I was burned and now I will freeze, Indelbed thought. He did not really want to move. The cold was slowing down his thoughts, lulling him into stupor. Idly, he gathered the shards of clay around him, piling them up. It took him a moment to realize that they were like puzzle pieces, glowing with power, the edges literally straining to reconnect. He joined them together, and the urn re-formed, slivers of clay flying back through the air in a temporary reversal of entropy. Indelbed's blind eyes could see the thing very well, an ancient vessel glowing with power, its field fluctuating as it regained form.

"Hello?" He spoke on whim, not really expecting an answer.

"Thanks," said the urn. "Really. It would have taken me ages to do that."

"Ahem, I'm talking to a jar then? A bottle?"

"We prefer urn. Although Solomon, of course, called us amphorae."

"I suppose I've finally lost my mind."

"There were twenty thousand of us created. I can't imagine there are too many left. I am an ancient, unique—"

"Was I *inside* you?"

"Of course. You, the wyrms, the other one. It's all to do with folding space. You could fit anything into anything, if you know how, which of course Solomon did, being the premier magician of his time. However, they say that those are lost arts now, although if you ask me—"

"Other one?"

"He's the one who broke me the first time. Walked funny."

"Givaras!"

"Very abrupt fellow."

"Where did he go?"

"He found a path through the spells. I was shattered at the time, but I believe I got a good look. That's the interesting thing about me—"

"Can you show me out? Sorry, it's just that I'm freezing to death."

"Oh yes, of course. Would you mind just gathering everything together and really sweeping all the little pieces in? I'd like to come with you; it's not very interesting over here, although I once spent several thousand years on the ocean floor, but there were crabs, and fish, and sponges, and—"

"Look here, I've got it. Hang on, there's a big piece over there. Okay, I think you're whole. Hey, so that entire murder pit thing was built inside of you?"

"Yes, it's all to do with n space. When you start unraveling some of the dimensions, you get different kinds of geometry—"

"So my wyrm is still in there?"

"Well, he certainly did not come out."

"Good. Come on, urn, you're up. Show us the way through these spells."

"Right. I'm on it, Young Master! One false move will destroy us! Well, destroy you. I'll probably just reconstitute. Still, I'm going to try my hardest! We have to be careful now—the odd-legged one took a long time getting out, I think first left, and then—"

"You're the best urn Solomon ever built."

The urn would have beamed had it the facial mechanism to do so.

At four o'clock, while Rais and Maria were speeding across the Pacific, Indelbed was limping from the apartment building in ill-fitting pants and a flood relief blanket, the urn clutched protectively in the crook of his arm. His current ailments were innumerable, and the small cache of adrenaline that had fueled his escape from the ensorcelled room was soon used up. On top of everything, he was suffering from massive sensory overload. The noise hit him like a sledgehammer when he approached the main road—the cars ringing in his ears; the ceaseless street-side conversations;

the hollering, shouting, and swearing—the grinding pressure of humanity buffeting him along, keeping him upright even as his feet stumbled over unseen obstacles. His vision was overwhelmed, all that hard-earned skill gone; he was just another blind boy walking the beggar's road.

When he finally couldn't will himself any farther, he fell to his knees and let the heels and knees of irritated passersby push him toward a wall. He sprawled there in a daze, burned feet bare, head and body covered in the stolen blanket, shivering. Someone stopped, pressed a two-taka note into his hand. Another man tossed a note at his head. A dog sniffed at him and then ran away barking. After some time, a nearby tea stall owner grabbed him by the arm and dragged him into an alley.

He slapped him a few times, asked him some questions, but Indelbed couldn't speak coherently, his regrown tongue flopping in his mouth like a dead fish. The tea seller noticed his sightless eyes and stopped shaking him.

"Are you blind?"

"Yeshhh."

"Beggar?"

"Yes," Indelbed said after a moment.

"Where are your people?"

"Orphan," Indelbed said. *Not true. I have a father. I had one. I'm going to find him. And if he's dead, I'm going to kill everyone who did it.*

"You look sick."

"I was burned. It's not contagious."

"You can sit in this corner for a bit," the tea man said. "You can't beg here. If you come near the stall I'll beat the shit out of you. You're scaring away my customers. How much money do you have?"

"What?"

"Do you think taking care of sick people is my job? Give me your money. And that jar. What's in it?"

Indelbed handed over the crumpled notes he had collected.

"The bottle." The tea man cuffed him lightly. "Come on."

"No."

This time the kick was in earnest, battering him in the ribs. "Give the fucking bottle, beggar."

"It's an urn," Indelbed said. "You can't have it."

The tea man laughed, slammed him twice in the stomach, wrested the urn away, and promptly dropped it as it nipped his fingers with frostbite.

"Djinn." Indelbed grinned through cracked lips. He dribbled out the distortion field, letting the light sparkle on his palm in pretty colors. It was pretty much the extent of what he could do right now.

"Djinn!" The tea man staggered back in fear. He was a believer.

"Where are we?"

"Motijheel, Master. Please, I have children. Don't..."

"Possess you? Eat you?" Indelbed bared his teeth, stained red from his own bleeding gums. "I'll take your right arm."

"What?"

"Cut it off and give it to me. Or do you want me inside your head? I'll wear your skin like a coat."

"God save me..." The man started to mumble prayers. He was on his knees now, hands clasped, the very picture of supplication. People were looking at them funny.

"Oh, shut up," Indelbed said. "Your broken Arabic has no effect on anything. Do me a service, and I will forgive you."

"Anything, Master, anything."

"There's a house in Wari I must get to. Take me there, and your service is done."

"Yes, Master."

"Oh, and get me a cup of tea."

By the time they got to Wari, Indelbed was thoroughly lost. The old houses were gone, supplanted by tall, cramped apartments. The streets were unrecognizable, the roads full of cars now, the old shops gone, replaced by newer, swankier efforts. He knew no one, and no one knew him.

They overshot his road a couple of times, back and forth, the tea seller too frightened to object, until some remnant of decade-old topiary clicked in his head, taking him back to the last time he had left this street. Indelbed stood at the narrow mouth of the alley, feeling very small. It was quieter here, cooler, and his fledgling sight returned, the field stealing around him like a whisper, until he could see the contrails again.

He walked toward his gate finally. There were ley lines of power clustered around the house, physically pulling at him, but he hit a barricade long before that, plainclothes ex–police officers fingering shotguns, bored. They turned him away with a push and a shove, one of them recoiling in disgust after getting a good look at his face. Indelbed wanted to say that it was *his* house, that he belonged there, that he wanted to go home, but there was no one to talk to, no one the least bit interested. With a terrible pang, he longed for the old days, when it was just the Doctor, Butloo, and himself, their peculiar three-pronged family that had just about lurched along, oblivious to djinns, magic, and dragons.

He looked in vain for someone he knew and remembered Mr. Karim, who lived in the neighboring apartment building and had sent them a fruit basket every Eid. He tried the gate, but a guard blocked his way, and when he mentioned Mr. Karim of flat 4B, the man laughed and said that Karim Sahib was not in the business of talking to diseased beggars. When he didn't move off the step quick enough, the guard whacked him with a stick halfheartedly. Loathe to give up, he found a shady spot by the electric pole and sat on his haunches, waiting for at least a familiar face. People passing by avoided him, but otherwise left him unmolested.

After several hours sitting still, he had his patch of the road sewn up, his power spread painstakingly thin, until he could track every mongrel rat that strayed into his path.

At last he saw Ali, his old friend from two houses down, grown tall now, walking with a backpack but still with that telltale shuffle, surrounded by a gaggle of other boys. Ali Baba would remember him—they had spent hours playing marbles, poring over a solitary dirty magazine; he had often thought of Ali in the cave. He called out Ali's old nickname as he passed, softly enough, and Ali's head jerked around in recognition, but his eyes dulled as they crossed Indelbed's huddled form, like a curtain falling, and he walked on without slowing, not seeing anything that might possibly interest him.

Indelbed almost despaired. Was it Ali? Might his sight be off? He wanted to run after him, to ask him about marbles and magazines, but the moment had passed.

Then he saw an old man walking toward the corner store, slightly stooped, wizened, but not really that much worse off for a decade's worth of living. It was a man absently walking the same steps he had done for the past forty years. Butloo! Indelbed squinted hard, tracing every familiar plane on that face, every wrinkle, until he was absolutely sure.

Then he called out in joy, he stood and waved his arms, forgetting everything. Butloo turned and stared at him, perplexed. "It's me! It's me!" But the old man saw something fearful, for he made a warding sign and backed away, brow furrowed, a look of horror on his face. Indelbed croaked out again, voice breaking, but there was only confusion in Butloo's face, and it occurred to Indelbed that perhaps he didn't look like himself, not like little Indelbed, not like anything human at all. He wanted to speak, but no words were coming out, only a lot of blubbering tears. It was too late anyway. Butloo was hurriedly walking back, and the shopkeeper, irate at this disturbance, was already coming out from behind his counter with fists clenched.

Indelbed retreated, gathering his tattered blanket around him, casting his face back into the shadows, adopting the shuffling gait of a beggar. Givaras had promised him dragonhood. Instead he had made him into a misshapen outcast.

He wandered aimlessly for a while, walking off the despair in his gut, until he came to a railroad market—hawkers with baskets of tired vegetables, ripe-looking fish eyeing the tracks with longing, their ghost souls contemplating annihilation, and clothes piled on racks—a sort of impromptu shopping center that scattered every time the train came and then amalgamated again on the tracks. It was dark now, and even these inveterate traders were winding down, heading for nearby shanties, or just finding a good spot on the ground. Indelbed was tired, hungry, and desolate, his distortion field guttering out so that he could barely see two feet in front of him, and he had no money for food or water, so he found a quiet space and lay down inside the cocoon of his rotten blanket, trusting in the dark.

He woke up in the weak light of predawn, found himself propped upright and tied to a pole naked somewhere behind a tin shed in another section of the tracks. His hands and feet were loosely bound with cables, enough give that he had slid to his knees. A younger boy sat on a stool nearby, watching, a thin strip of bamboo in his hands.

"Water," Indelbed said. He raised his face and gave his captor a ghastly smile.

The boy took a plastic Coke bottle full of tube well water and poured it over his face, keeping a fair distance. Most of it dribbled into his mouth.

"Bless you," Indelbed said. "Where am I?"

"They brought you at night." The boy nodded toward the shed. "The night guard from the market and Ramiz."

"Why?"

"They were going to rape you, but when they looked at you with a flashlight they thought you were diseased, and no one wanted to have a go." The boy picked up a brick. "Listen, do you want me to hit you on the head?"

"What?"

"Trust me, it'll be better. The guard is not so bad, but Ramiz likes hurting people. He'll beat you for hours and then set you on fire. That's what he said last night. He did a retard beggar like you last month. The guard filmed it and showed it to me."

"I'm not a retard."

"You're a freak. No one's gonna come looking for you."

"They let you live."

The boy shrugged. "I'm not diseased. Have it your way. You'll be begging for the brick soon."

"Won't the market people come when I scream?"

"Scream?" The boy laughed. "No one came when I screamed. They're protecting the market, see, catching thieves. Everyone knows little boys are thieves."

"They're going to burn me..."

"With kerosene."

"Stick around then," Indelbed said, and grinned. "You're going to enjoy this."

When the men came out finally they found him napping. The night guard was in his uniform, replete with stick and whistle. From the stains it seemed to be his only set of clothes. He came and cracked his truncheon against Indelbed's shin, hard.

"Look at this thief, Ramiz," he said. "Sleeping like a baby."

Ramiz was a chubby, bearded man with a checkered scarf around his head and a spiffy Arab-looking outfit. He had a three-foot length of rod in his hands, which, up close, Indelbed identified as a product of the BSRM steel company. A second later it slammed into his arm, hard enough to fracture human bone.

"Look at his eyes," the night guard said. He had his phone out, filming, an avid, obscene gaze on his face. "He's blind."

"He's still a thief," Ramiz said. "You know what I do to thieves."

"Yes, Ramiz," the guard said.

"We're going to break your arms and legs, boy, and then I'm going to cut your hands off."

"And then we'll burn you," the guard said. "Don't forget the burning."

"He already looks burned," Ramiz said. "Disgusting. He ought to be killed before he spreads his filthy disease."

"Don't touch him, Ramiz," the guard tittered. "It might be catching."

"Don't worry," Ramiz said, "the only rod I'm going to use on him is iron."

They laughed a bit at that, and then Ramiz started cracking Indelbed's arms and legs with a well-practiced swing. The blows got harder progressively, but Indelbed was dragon inside, and his bones wouldn't break. He cried from the pain, though, screaming with each terrible hit, and that seemed to please Ramiz well enough. The guard watched from the sidelines and shouted instructions. Ramiz started bashing Indelbed's knees, stomping on his hands and feet, working methodically for an interminable amount of time, until he was faint from the pain and his voice reduced to a whisper.

Inside he was laughing, because this was nothing compared to the madness Givaras had inflicted. It seemed as if his master had trained him well for life on earth.

"Fire!" he shouted, letting the laughter bubble out. "Bring the fucking fire, enough of this tickling."

Ramiz didn't like that. He set to with rage, aiming for the head, trying to blot out the unexpected intrusion.

"He's going to pass out!" The guard pulled him back. "He's not going to enjoy the kerosene!"

"Fuck this." Ramiz tossed the rod aside. "This freak actually wants to die. Get the kerosene, boy."

The boy brought a jerrican and splashed it all over Indelbed, shaking the last few drops directly on his face.

"Wish you'd taken the brick now?" he whispered.

Ramiz lit a book of matches and threw it into the puddle, fanning the fire with a piece of cardboard until it caught properly. The three of them stood back to watch. The flames shot up with the kerosene, covering Indelbed almost completely, igniting the scales beneath his skin. It was nothing like core fire. He was dragon, and kerosene fire was like a mother's embrace, a hot breeze on a summer's day; it energized him, taking away the pain and the exhaustion. It burned off his bindings, freeing his arms and legs. He surged up, arms spread wide, fire dancing on his skin, and he embraced Ramiz, holding him tight in a lovers' grip, and kissed his face until the fire caught his clothes, his hair, his mouth, until his eyes shriveled and his ears crisped, and he fell in a wet mess, thrashing in animal pain, trying to slough off his own skin.

The night guard tried to run, but the boy tripped him, ramming that bamboo stick into his legs. Indelbed set fire to his ankles, holding on for a good minute, until he could feel the bones turn to charcoal. He left the moaning guard for the boy. They seemed to belong together. He felt the urge to leave this filthy place, but everything was distant, subservient to the roaring exuberance of the dragon. Indelbed whistled as he walked along the tracks to the market, carefree as a bird, arms alight, setting fire to everything he touched.

CHAPTER 42
Of Apes and Men

Roger was socially awkward. He was a big, pear-shaped man with sparse hair and a scraggly, miserable-looking beard. He had made an effort, putting on his best clothes, but this amounted to a slightly crumpled white shirt and beige pants, the ubiquitous semiformal attire of his fraternity days, which he subconsciously reverted to whenever he was unsure. Nor was the venue conducive to his comfort—it was too fashionable, the food too fusiony, the waiters too good-looking, the drinks tinged with exotic fruits, the whole thing just off. Rais, never having set eyes on Roger before, had misjudged the entire evening. The most unhelpful part, however, was the glowering Maria, sitting opposite poor Roger and making him thoroughly anxious, for she was bored and, as often followed, entertaining herself by being cruel.

Roger was not good with females, and one of Maria's caliber made him very jittery, so that he spent half his time flicking his eyes toward her before quickly returning his gaze to the misery on his plate. Roger, it turned out, was also not good at reading the menu, for he had mistakenly ordered an assorted seafood platter, hoping for some combination of shrimp and scallops, and had been served instead a sea urchin and octopus gumbo.

What Roger was good at, however—pretty much the only thing really—was thinking. Specifically, he was a near-genius geneticist with far-reaching theories on human evolution, work that he pursued in his free time, while fulfilling his near-menial day job at a middling lab in Vegas that catered mainly to vanity family tree haplogroup testing. This was a fad now, so middle-aged men and women giddy with excitement could go off to Ireland to finally find Great-Uncle Harry.

"Look, Roger, just order something else. They've got burgers here, I'm sure..." Rais said, trying to make up for Maria's utter, unconcerned rudeness.

"It's okay, I like this, er, octopus soup thing."

"We should have just gone to a bar," Rais said. "We'll do that, yeah?"

"I don't drink."

"Of course you don't," Rais said. "Do you want some ice cream, perhaps?"

"For fuck's sake he's not four years old," Maria said.

Roger, whose face had lit up, now stared back at the table morosely.

"Look, we'll just have a bunch of dessert." Rais signaled the waiter. "Can't go wrong with that..."

"Our house special, sir, is bacon ice cream with a pumpkin mousse..."

"No, no, we want something normal. Like cake. You have any cake?"

"Cake? Cake?" The waiter stroked his beard in contempt. "Sir, we have a Thai-Austrian fusion of mango sticky rice with Sachertorte, if you wish to be conservative, haha—"

He stopped talking because Maria had grabbed his tie and yanked his head down, literally, to her level.

"Listen, dickhead, my friend wants cake. The food here is garbage, as you well know, so please, for the love of god, get us something fit to eat so we can end this miserable night."

"Miss, we don't... we don't have real food."

"I'll give you fifty bucks if you go to the bakery down the street and get us something."

"Yes, madam." The waiter straightened up. "Of course."

"That—that was great!" Roger said, speaking coherently finally, his admiration overcoming his natural reticence.

"Thanks," Maria said, thawing slightly. "I'm the muscle." She was always a sucker for genuine flattery.

"Roger, man, thanks for helping us out," Rais said.

"Sure, man, anything for the Jew—"

"Er, Rog, we try not to call him that anymore," Rais said, as conversation in neighboring tables diminished noticeably. "You know, it being racist and all."

"Right, right. Well, the J-E-W throws a lot of work at me, so when I got your skin cells I did the karyotype right away. G-banding, right? It condenses and stains the chromosomes so they can be studied under a microscope.

Standard stuff. Anyway, the results were so weird that I repeated them a bunch of times, using different techniques, and now I've been working on them the *whole* week. Like *voom*! I can't think of anything else."

"Well, that's great, Roger."

"You gotta tell me, man, what the hell are they?"

"I will, I promise, but why don't you give me your theories first?"

Roger, talking about work, was a different man now, far more animated and articulate enough that even Maria was interested.

"Sample B and sample K, right? Well, right off the bat, we got something majorly weird. B has twenty-four chromosomes. Humans have twenty-three, right, in diploid pairs, so B has gotta be a great ape. I have a look at it, and sure enough, chromosome two is split in two, just like a great ape would have it, except the sizes are a bit different, and then I scan it for some common gorilla or chimp or bonobo markers, and nothing there—I mean, there are major differences in genes, they're further away from the great apes than we are, despite the twenty-four. So it's an unknown branch of great ape, am I right? I mean, that's mind-boggling, because there just *aren't* any unknown offshoots we know about."

"Okay, back up a bit to the chromosome two thing."

"So humans have twenty-three pairs of chromosomes, and all the other apes have twenty-four chromosome pairs. This was a major problem for evolution, because we're supposed to be related to a common ancestor, so how the hell did we lose a whole chromosome pair and still be functional, right? And we know we lost a pair, because what are the chances of gorillas, chimps, and bonobos *all* gaining an extra pair by chance? Well, the obvious answer turned out to be the correct one. We didn't lose any genetic material at all—turns out somewhere along the human branch, two of the chromosomes just fused together. There's evidence of this on chromosome two, which clearly has the centromere and telomeres and genetic information of two smaller ape chromosomes. It just all fits together perfectly. So that's kind of the big circumstantial evidence for evolution of man from ape, but of course, the weird Bible guys froth at the mouth thinking about it. Anyway, this thing still has the twenty-four, which means it split from the common ancestor before the humans. Our closest relatives, the Denisovans, had twenty-three pairs, and most likely Neanderthals did too, so sample B has to be an ape offshoot."

"He certainly looks like one," Maria said.

Roger gave her a puzzled glance. "However, that's not even the most remarkable thing. The really strange thing is that this thing isn't diploid. See most mammals are diploid, meaning the chromosomes come in pairs, one from each parent. This sample is tetraploid. That's four chromosomes per set. This happens in plants and some rare animals, like frogs or salmon or reptiles. It almost never happens in mammals. The only case I can think of is the viscacha rat, in Argentina. There are most definitely no unknown species of great ape with viable tetraploidy. Therefore, I believe this is a joke sample, although I have no idea how it could have been made. I must conclude that this is a birthday present from the Jew, because my birthday is coming up. It is the day after tomorrow."

"It is not a hoax."

"It's a living sample? You're sure?"

"I swabbed B's mouth last week while it was passed out in its own vomit," Rais said.

"Okay, okay, I explored that possibility." Roger was visibly excited now. "Look, it could be a massive, massive mutation. It's possible that when this thing was being conceived, the two gametes doubled for some reason, creating a true tetraploid, and then that carried on through mitosis. This is possible. It happens in humans sometimes, but the fetus normally miscarries, or if it's born, it doesn't survive long. Gross congenital defects. Sample B is an unknown ape with gross congenital defects."

"It is not an ape. I will tell you what it is later."

"It's definitely got gross congenital defects," Maria said.

"This brings us to sample K. Sample K is a human with twenty-three chromosomes. It seems like a normal human, although there are some possible anomalies. The majorly strange thing is in the Y chromosome. Now in normal humans the Y chromosome is about a third in size to the X chromosome. Why is that, you ask? 'Cause it's lost a lot of genetic material over the past few million years. Parts got miscopied, left out, whatever. The Y has fewer functional genes than other chromosomes, but it's important because it determines sex, right, it essentially makes males. It carries the SRY gene, which starts off testicles in men. It also has genes that create sperm. Now this is the curious part. Sample K has a longish Y chromosome. It's like got twice the amount of information. That's not supposed to happen, right, the Y chromosome tends to get shorter with time, because it doesn't recombine during meiosis—"

"I'm losing it a bit," Rais said, raising his hand.

"Meiosis is when the cell divides to make the sex cells, with like half the chromosomes, dumbass," Maria said. "Like the sperm has twenty-three and the egg has twenty-three, and you put them together and get a perfect forty-six? What? I took bio."

"She's right, of course," Roger said. "And during meiosis, normal chromosomes kind of swap DNA—it's called recombination. It means the eventual offspring benefits from greater genetic variety. Getting back to it, the Y can't take advantage of recombination because it doesn't fit with the X anymore, except right at the ends, because it's lost a whole lot of genes. This means the Y gets passed on pretty much intact from father to son. That's important."

"Yeah, that's how you trace family patrilineage," Rais said.

"Yeah. So anyway, this sample K has a long Y, which is strange, but could just be a mutation. I was curious why, though, so I went ahead and used FISH to light up the Y. That's basically the technique we use to look at individual genes on a chromosome. What I think this guy's got is called sperm heteromorphism."

"That sounds bad."

"Not really. It's common in moths and butterflies."

"Rare in humans?"

"Never found in humans, as far as I know. It means the body makes two kinds of sperm. In this case, I think he makes haploid sperm and diploid sperm. Normal sperm for humans is haploid, right, it sends just twenty-three chromosomes including a single Y or X, which combines with the ovum's X, and you get an XY or XX zygote with a combined forty-six regular chromosomes. Then there's the bigger diploid sperm, which sends forty-six chromosomes, including a YY or an XX. Now you get YY or XX sperm sometimes, but it's an accident, and normally those fetuses abort naturally. In a human, this kind of thing leads to major birth defects. This guy is making them on purpose. It's just strange."

"It's actually beginning to make some sense now."

"Owfff, can you just get to the point?" Maria said.

"Not yet," Rais replied, and smiled. "Rog, keep going. I want to hear your theory first."

Roger took a deep breath and drank some water. "Okay. Logically, these two cases are related, since you sent me the samples together. Sample B is a tetraploid male with twenty-four by four chromosomes. Sample K is a diploid male with twenty-three by two chromosomes, a seemingly normal human, except for the strange Y chromosome, which appears to allow it to mate with tetraploids. If I could get a sperm sample from sample K, I guess I'd find that he makes both haploid and diploid sperm, probably in equal proportions, which, theoretically, would allow him to have viable offspring with either normal humans or the tetraploid ape thing. See, the sperm with the extra chromosomes would be bigger, thus a different shape. I'm guessing the shape itself would ensure that the correct sperm would get into the correct egg. Of course we also have to look at the epigenetic side of things. It's possible that something environmental triggers the production of either kind of sperm. It's actually pretty common for an outside stimulus like temperature or something chemical to switch genes off or on."

"What about the extra chromosome?" Rais asked. "Won't that lead to a mule-type situation?"

"You'd think that, right? I was worried about it, but then I looked at it another way. The fusion of chromosome two was a mutation, right? I mean, it happened to one guy first. So how was he able to pass it on? He must have had offspring with a regular ape with twenty-four chromosomes. The answer is that no genetic material was lost in the fusion. The two smaller ape chromosomes just lined up against the bigger human chromosome, and you got viable, fertile offspring no problem. Of course, it's not that simple. Every gene codes for different numbers of proteins. There's most likely an RNA signaling system that works on top, which directs which protein exactly is being made. Basically DNA is a lot more resilient than people think, and mutations often stick around for millions of years, until they actually have some impact. Anyway, in short, it just works."

"Say that you're correct, and our sample K mates with a tetraploid twenty-four-chromosome ape creature like sample B. What would the off-spring be like?" Rais asked.

"Well, everything says they'd be grotesque, unviable, sterile deformities."

"Supposing they weren't."

"Then you'd have tetraploid hybrid creatures with genes from humans and some branch of great ape descended from our common ancestor. A creature that could be mostly human or mostly ape in look, but able to fully mate within the tetraploid community, as well as with human males carrying the anomalous Y chromosome," Roger said.

"Which brings us to our original contract, the haplogroup study."

"Well, we look at SNPs, which is *single* nucleotide polymorphisms, meaning just one nucleotide is out of place, whereas this is a major, major genetic difference in the chromosome. I mean, the magnitude of this is mind-blowing. I broke sample K's Y into a bunch of snips and looked for them, and they match the historic samples I told you about before, plus some notes on unlikely-looking Y chromosomes, which just about confirms that this is a peculiar mutation that has been with us for a very long time and spread out over a very large land area."

"Okay, let me tell you the secret. Sample K is my uncle, the emissary Kaikobad. Sample B is Barabas, a djinn."

"Like an actually djinn?"

"Yup."

"Woohoo! Yessss! Woooh! I knew this was something cool!"

"You're going to believe him, just like that?" Maria asked. "You're not going to like ask for a rational explanation?"

Roger leaned forward, his eyes big, sweat beading his forehead, a vein popping on his neck. "Hey, I've waited for this moment my whole life. I *knew* magic was real. I *knew* there was more to life than chairs and tables. I was raised by Wiccans. I've seen magic."

"So, Roger, what's your best guess now?"

"So first off, looking at djinn DNA, we appear to come from a common ancestor, except for the tetraploidy. Can you imagine what this means? This is proof of another intelligent species on earth! Wait, they are intelligent, aren't they?"

"They're either complete idiots or they're psychopathic mass murderers," Maria said. "Take your pick. Guess which ones are on our side."

"If we assume that we are all descendant from the great ape line, at some point there was a tetraploidy mutation. The chromosome count matches up, but no other branch off the ape line has any kind of polyploidy. The break-off must have been distant," Roger said.

"What kind of time frame?" Rais asked.

Roger began to sketch on the tablecloth with a pencil.

"If we make a third hypothetical djinn line, that split must have occurred *at least* eight hundred thousand years ago. The djinns could have split off the main line as early as that or much earlier—there's no way to tell without more study. The other issue is the whole tetraploidy thing, which is not really present in great ape genes. However, it *could* be. People think DNA is like eighty percent garbage, but that's wrong of course. We carry a lot of useful mutations, and they only get expressed when it's relevant. That's the whole point of epigenetics. That's how animals can adapt so fast to environments. So it's entirely possible that tetraploidy is carried somewhere in the great ape line, and for whatever reason it got switched on with the djinn branch. Hell, even humans could be carrying the genes—we just don't know enough to rule it out.

"If I could map the whole genome, I could get a better idea. You have to give me a live sample..." Roger was now practically grabbing Rais by the neck. He was surprisingly strong, seemed well capable of strangling him out of excitement. "I need to see it, man. You can't keep me out of this!"

"Relax, Rog, trust me, I'm not trying to keep you out. We might have trouble finding a djinn who'll actually cooperate with this. I don't think they'll be exactly thrilled by your ape theory."

"Well, give me your uncle then, let me verify the Y chromosome issue."

"He's in a coma back home."

"Let's fly back there then," Roger said. "I'll charge it on the lab. I'll sell all the equipment if I have to."

"We can't, we're a bit pressed for time," Rais said.

"Wait, he's your real uncle, right?"

"My father's cousin."

"So let me run the tests on you. You might have the same condition. Ys get passed on intact. If it runs in your family, well..."

"What?"

"Gimme a sperm sample, man, let me check if you've got the goods."

"Ugh," said Maria. "This is just getting ridiculous now."

"Like right now?"

"I can't sleep knowing all this, man. I've got to see djinns, man. This is like a Nobel Prize–winning type of breakthrough in genetics, dude. We'll pop over to the lab and you can get some out."

"You want to come and help me?" Rais asked Maria.

"Is stabbing you in the eye going to help?"

"No, psycho..."

"Then no."

CHAPTER 43
Entourage

"Congrats! You've got tetraploid sperm. About fifty percent. You wanna see the little suckers?"

"Can we just *stop* waving his damn sperm around?"

"So that confirms one part."

"It's almost like someone engineered a kind of human that can mate with djinns," Roger said. "It could have occurred through natural selection if there was a large population of tetraploid djinn females sometime in the past, and the dual sperm humans would double their chances of creating offspring. Or something triggers the production of tetraploid sperm at the right time. If only we had a genuine hybrid..."

"Well, my uncle married a djinn, and they had a child," Rais said. "My cousin was perfectly formed—there were no deformities—and he wasn't retarded—"

"Well, bring him over then!"

"Can't. He's dead."

"Oh." Roger scratched his head. "Can we exhume his body and get some DNA maybe?"

"No, Roger, we can't," Rais said.

"We could get a dead djinn body, though, couldn't we?" Maria asked. "What about your aunt? Didn't she die at childbirth? Isn't she buried in your plot?"

"There's an empty headstone for her at our graveyard. Matteras took her body. I asked Mother about that," Rais said. "Look, actually, Roger, I might have placed you in a bit of danger with this whole thing. I have a feeling if the wrong djinn finds out about this line of inquiry, he'll kill you and burn down the lab."

"A lot of danger, actually," Maria said.

"I don't care. I need to see djinns. I have to physically know they're real. I want to see magic," Roger said. His eyes were fixed far away. He was remembering hours of Dungeons and Dragons in his parents' basement. Their game master had always had a fondness for djinns. One of their recurring story lines had been set in the desert.

"How old is the haplogroup for the long Y chromosome, Roger?"

"If this is part of the R2D subclade, and if all four of the cases I told you about actually do belong in one subclade, then the oldest was the Siberian one at 14,000 B.C.," Roger said. "If I could get those samples, I could establish the subclade very easily, because the long Y is so distinctive. I guess I could write to those labs and try to get some reports."

"Okay, Roger, you're going to come with us," Rais said. "We're basically following the same line of inquiry as the historian, and she got yanked out of the sky and offed, so we can't risk that happening to you. Take all your stuff—you can do the research while we travel."

"Like right now?" Roger asked.

"You want to see djinns or not?"

"I'm ready," Roger said.

"You can pack a bag, Roger," Rais said. "And maybe take some of your kit."

"Where are we going now?" Maria asked.

"Beltrex."

"Rais, we don't have much time," Maria said. "They just issued a hurricane warning in Teknaf. I don't think it's natural. What if Matteras has already started his shit?"

"I can't possibly stop a hurricane, or an earthquake, or anything else Matteras throws at us," Rais said. "No, our only shot is to negotiate a peace. We don't have any leverage, but something is going on with this whole genetics and Great War thing, and if we figure it out, we might have some chips. Beltrex is part of the solution. We need some serious dignatas backing us to get Matteras's attention."

"Your mom sent me a message. They've accepted a preliminary hearing on the breach of contract. Looks like Dargoman's going to court," Maria said.

"You're texting with her now?"

"Hey, looks like I passed the Juny test. A few years too late, but whatever."

Roger, suffering from growing bewilderment, was now raising his hand and waving it around. "Guys, these are djinns we're talking about, right? What about the magic? When do I get to see magic?"

Rais frowned. "You know, they don't do too much magic actually." He glanced at Maria. "You ever actually seen Barabas do anything useful?"

Maria snorted. "Is drinking, puking, and passing out useful?"

"Yeah, I think you're going to be a bit disappointed, Rog. They mostly talk shit and sue each other," Rais said.

Roger's face fell. "They don't have magic swords and armor and stuff?" he asked.

"They mostly wear regular clothes," Rais said. "The rich ones wear suits."

"Magic carpets?"

"They ride rickshaws and cars," Rais said. "Oh, wait. They have airships. You're going to like the airships."

"Can we ride in one?"

"Yeah," Rais said. "You'll love Golgoras. He's got tusks and a telescopic eye."

"What? Like a pirate?"

"Yeah, pretty much exactly like a pirate."

Later, sitting in Roger's house waiting for him to pack, Rais called his mother. She answered on the first ring, as she almost always did, blessed with the supernatural power for anticipating phone calls.

"Still alive," he said. "How's it going on your end?"

"The djinn court is... interesting," Juny said. "It's packed with Matteras's clients and the conservative faction, but these guys take their contracts very seriously, so it's not over yet. Breaking contract is worse than murder apparently. We're stuck now on the finer points of the validity and strength of a verbal contract."

"Will you win?"

"No, but I can tie him up for a long, long time."

"Good. I think we can flip him if you keep the pressure on."

"You want to sit with him?" Juny sounded skeptical. "I don't think he'd agree."

"Maria might be able to convince him."

"Was this her idea?"

"Nope. She still wants to stab him with the invisible knife."

"He killed your father."

"I know, but we can deal with that later. Right now we need to put him to work."

"He'll never believe we actually want to negotiate."

"He will, if you let him know that you two were estranged, that, in fact, you hated my father."

"I'm not sure I want that."

"Mother, you're not one to become sentimental after all these years. Let him know that you're happy enough with your coup and that I'm sick of looking over my shoulder."

"He'll think you're a coward."

"What do I care if he does what I want?"

"Everyone else will think that too."

"I'm counting on it."

"You're getting better at this game," Juny said. There was a faint note of smugness in her voice.

"I've had a hard teacher."

"Okay, what else?"

"I need to see Beltrex, but he's not taking my calls."

"Why?"

"I want to test out my theory on him."

"Beltrex is difficult to pin down. Be careful, son. I think he's the djinn referred to in legends as Barkan. He's spilled a lot of blood in the past, no matter how senile he comes off now."

"He said he owed Uncle Kaikobad a favor or two."

Juny laughed. "They all say that, only because they know Kaikobad isn't going to claim anything. Djinns are the biggest frauds around. I've got some markers with Elkran, Beltrex's cousin. He spends a lot of time out in California."

"I didn't know djinns cared for family like that."

"Between you and me, I think they are lovers."

"Oh."

"What else?"

"I'm going to need the airship. Can you ask Golgoras to meet me somewhere near L.A.?"

"That miser is going to charge us. He's expensive. You better make it count. And, Rais, don't dawdle."

"I'm not. Why?"

"It's starting to rain over here."

They took Roger's white van full of equipment to the airport in Reno and a cheap flight to Oakland, California, and then a rented suburban to the Sonoma Valley, where Beltrex owned three old properties, cabernet vineyards, under different names. He normally stayed in his compound in Sonoma, although he had other fields in different regions. There was a time when he had owned most of California, apparently. His main vineyard was on rolling acreage that seemed to stretch to the mountains, with perfect rows of grapes and winding roads, eerily quiet. A house sat in a dip in the ground flush against a hill, almost hidden from view, until they got close enough for security cameras to stir to life. There was an electronic gate and, carefully disguised behind foliage, an electric fence. A camouflaged militia-type man popped up, seemingly from underground, and informed them that this was not a tourist vineyard, there was no wine tasting, and they should get the hell off private property. He was tense, his walkie-talkie kept crackling, and he gripped his semiautomatic with white knuckles.

"Not a good time?" Rais asked.

"Man, turn that car around, I ain't asking twice."

"Relax. I'm an emissary. Get Elkran on the phone."

"He ain't here. And the big man in the house ain't here either."

"Okay, Josh? Josh. Look, I'm supposed to meet Beltrex, I've got an appointment with Elkran. Why don't you relax and tell me what's going on."

"You know all of 'em?" Josh asked finally.

"I'm *one* of them, if you get my meaning."

He turned away, consulted with someone who spoke in rapid-fire Spanish, and then pointed his gun. "Okay, you're probably gonna regret this. Inside, the three of you."

The gate started to retract slowly. He couldn't see them, but Rais got the feeling that more than one rifle scope was now trained at them.

"Drive in slow, pull up to where them Escalades are parked."

"Er, Josh, why are you taking orders in Spanish?"

Josh looked aggrieved. "'Cause them Baja mob've come up here for a meeting, but Mr. B and Mr. E took off earlier in the incident, leaving me in charge, *knowing* I've got a bad back, and how am I supposed to protect the ranch against all them killer Mexicans, huh?"

"Baja mob?"

"Gangsters, man. Baja fucking cartel." Josh dropped his voice to a whisper. "The Aztec himself is here, and that means he's gonna kill everyone. He eats their livers, man. Didn'tja learn that in school?"

"Tough luck, man."

"I don't even speak Spanish," Josh said miserably. "They got me out here as cannon fodder, in case someone comes in shooting."

Roger drove very slowly over the pebbled driveway to the hacienda-style mansion. The courtyard up front was indeed filled with haphazardly parked Escalades. There were gunmen on the roof and loud music coming from inside. Men and women in bathing suits were unloading crates of liquor and plastic floaty toys from the back of a van.

"Welcome to *el rancho*," a guard similarly attired to Josh said. He had a bruise on his cheek, and someone had apparently taken away his sidearm, because an empty holster flapped against his hip. "The Aztec would like to welcome you as his guests and invite you to join the party."

The front door led to a massive marble-floored hallway with high ceilings, at the far end of which was an open terrace leading to a central courtyard complete with swimming pool, wet bar, grill, and a dozen deck chairs. The party was in full swing here, people in various stages of undress draped around the deck lounging and dancing, men flipping burgers, dogs barking, Tupac at full blast, a Thai chef making satays and smoking a cigar, and a plump nude woman swimming laps.

A waiter thrust some champagne flutes at them, and several steps later a woman in a lime-green bikini stuffed a cigar into Rais's mouth and lit it, laughing and chattering in Spanish, and then proceeded to somehow disrobe Roger without him noticing, his body bobbing like a pasty white flag among the tanned good health of the party crew.

The lady led them on, grabbing Roger by the hand, pulling them through various parts of the house, the music fading with each step, until they found themselves in a wood-paneled study. A shaven-headed man sat behind the desk, reading a book, his thin, ascetic face furrowed in concentration.

"Oy, Tenoch, your guests," she said, kissing his forehead before sauntering out.

Tenoch rose courteously, shaking hands and ushering them into seats. He had the slightly distracted air of an academic, the holstered .33-caliber on his waist incongruous.

"I hope you did not find the party too obnoxious," he said. "My colleagues are... exuberant. Would you like a drink? Coffee perhaps?"

"No, these are great." Rais raised his cigar.

"Excuse the guns, people expect that sort of thing," Tenoch said.

"That's an Aztec name, right?" Rais said.

"Nahuatl," Tenoch said. "My aunt christened me so I kept it, although it's a terrible name for a cartel boss. Everyone else is called El Tigre, or El Chapo, or Serpiente or something."

"The guy at the gate called you the Aztec."

Tenoch sighed. "I can't stop them from making up stories. They think I'm some kind of shaman because I read books."

"He said you eat livers."

"What?" Tenoch looked disgusted. "What kind of barbarity is that? I studied engineering in college, for god's sake. I wanted to join NASA."

"So what happened?"

Tenoch frowned. "What do you think? I came back for a vacation and somehow my dad suckered me into a month-long internship, which has stretched to eighteen years now, and he's gone and died in the middle of it of course..."

"You guys are what, the Sinaloa? Josh said something about Baja."

Tenoch bowed slightly. "We are an offshoot of the infamous Sinaloa. My family deals in some specialized aspects of the trade, beyond the regular business of MDMA, heroin, and cocaine." He leaned forward. "We are what you could call a boutique firm."

"Really? I wasn't aware there were different kinds of cartels."

"Well, you see, there are market segments naturally, in such a large economy. When I inherited my position, I exchanged our bulk processing assets for a more advisory role. Quite simply, we provide technical assistance to the Sinaloa and to the others, upon request. Our main portfolio offers solutions for surveillance, communications, cloud ware, and exotic weapons. And, of course, the specialty services, like alternate dispute resolution. That's a very popular one. The murder rate among gangsters has gone way down since we started up."

"That's fascinating. I guess cartels can't just walk into Microsoft and ask for cloud space."

"They can't take each other to court either." Tenoch smirked. "Now, forgive me, but let us get to business. You are associates of Mr. Beltrex. I assume you are here to explain his absence?"

"Ah," Rais said.

"No, we've come to find him, just like you," Maria said. "Where the hell is he?"

"That is unfortunate," Tenoch said. "We were counting on Mr. Beltrex."

"Anything we can help with?"

"Are you able to magic items in and out of the country?" Tenoch asked. "Or perhaps you can return to me the astronomical sum I have paid in advance to Mr. Beltrex for such a service? I sincerely hope, for both our sakes, that you can answer yes to one of those questions." The gun was somehow in his hand and pointing straight at Rais's forehead.

"Okay, relax," Rais said.

"You claimed to be *one of them* at the gate," Tenoch said. "Now *be* one of them. Perform the job Beltrex was contracted for."

"Look, what exactly was Beltrex supposed to do for you?"

"Mr. Beltrex arranges dark shipments of exotic items. He has ways to avoid radar, which, quite frankly, I want to know nothing about. We have been working on acquiring some military drone technology for the past eighteen months. To procure such a thing is difficult. To actually remove it from U.S. soil is practically impossible. I am here to hand it over for export. Imagine my regret, then, to find both of them gone under such peculiar circumstances."

"Peculiar circumstances?" Rais asked. "Like what?"

Tenoch made an impatient gesture. "They were taken. Homeland Security? The CIA? Who knows. We will get to that later. First let us discuss how exactly you are going to solve my problem."

"Do you mind if I confer with my colleagues?" Rais asked.

"By all means," Tenoch said. He gestured to the couches at the far end of the room. "No violence, please. Just to clarify, there are men with submachine guns outside the door, watching through the closed-circuit camera. I myself am considered something of a marksman. You appear peaceful people, but in this line of work..."

"Of course," Rais said.

They huddled together at the far bookcase. Roger was a pool of nervous sweat, more out of excitement than fear. Like many educated white men of his class, he seemed to expect everything to work out in his favor and considered the possibility of Tenoch actually executing him to be nil.

"I've got the Five Strikes," Maria said. "It's weird, I know it's there, but it's kind of hovering out of sight, waiting to be used. They didn't find it when they searched me. I'm pretty sure I can kill him before he shoots all of us."

"That plan seems to include at least one of us getting shot," Rais said.

Maria shrugged.

"You got a magic weapon?" Roger asked. "Can I hold it?"

"What about Golgoras?" Maria asked, ignoring him. "You said he's waiting for us. Call in an airstrike. Let's bomb these guys."

"Let's not," Rais said. "I think we can make a deal. Golgoras is running solo. What if we hooked them up? The *Sephiroth* can run Tenoch's shipment, and Golgoras gets some free crew—he doesn't trust Ghuls anymore. It's a good deal for Tenoch; Golgoras can probably swing a clientship. What do you think?"

"Can't hurt to ask," Maria said. "I can always stab him if he refuses."

"Look, Tenoch, I have a proposal," Rais said, as they returned to the desk. "One of my partners has an airship. He's waiting off the coast for us, he should be able to get over here pretty fast. I can't guarantee it, but if he agrees to terms with you, he can get anything in and out for you without detection, one hundred percent."

"Airship? Like a blimp?" Tenoch looked skeptical.

"Not really. It's faster than any blimp you've seen, and it's completely stealth—I mean radar-proof, sonar-proof. It could be floating in front of your eyes and you wouldn't see it," Rais said.

"I find this very hard to believe," Tenoch said.

"Beltrex was probably using the same method," Rais said. "I understand your disbelief. But the real issue is I don't think you know exactly what you're dealing with here."

"I'd be very careful how I phrase the next sentence," Tenoch said softly. "If I were you."

"Beltrex, Elkran—what do you think they are?" Rais asked.

"Scary old men," Tenoch said. "I don't care how they do their shit, I don't want to know. Elkran particularly. The dude is evil."

"They're djinns, man!" Roger said. "Djinns. They do magic! Can you believe it? Actual djinns!"

"Thanks, Roger, that's probably enough," Rais said.

"Djinns?" Tenoch asked. "Are you serious?"

"Like spirits, demons—"

"I know what the word means," Tenoch said. "I can't tell if you're joking or insane."

"All right, take a look at these pictures on my phone."

Tenoch looked. "I see men in fancy dress."

"The underwater ruins? The giant squid?"

Tenoch shrugged. "I've seen skinny-ass bitches turn themselves into JLo with Photoshop. Who trusts pictures these days?"

"Okay, you said Beltrex and Elkran were taken. From where?"

"He has an underground bomb shelter," Tenoch said. "It was locked from the inside. I had to blow the wall. I had a peep inside, couldn't find anything. I am waiting for my forensic expert to have a closer look."

"Well, can we go see it?"

"Are you a forensic expert?"

"If I can't convince you he's a djinn, I promise I'll take out my own liver."

"All right, I'll play along," Tenoch said, getting up. "I'm openminded, but you're really stretching it here."

The basement was a bunker running under the house and partially into the hill behind, a large suite of rooms protected by steel doors, still intact. Tenoch had blown a hole in the reinforced concrete wall instead. Two men in Kevlar guarded the wreckage.

"The staff swear that Elkran and Beltrex were both in here. They woke up in the middle of the night to strange noises. They came down but found the door locked, with no one answering. They tried the phones, the coms, the walkie-talkies—everything. Then they went back to sleep. We came yesterday, couldn't get in either. I sent to San Diego for explosives, my people got in this morning. I just blew the wall an hour before you got here," Tenoch said.

"Did the servants throw up that night? When they came to check?" Rais asked.

"Yes. All of them apparently," Tenoch said, surprised. "How did you know that?"

"Distortion field," Rais said. "Aftereffects of djinn magic. When they use it, we get sick. I puked every day on the *Sephiroth* until I got used to it." He put on his glasses. The visible surfaces were covered with runes, all of them pulsing, potent. There were no breaches on the outside; the lines continued unbroken even over the hole in the wall. "See."

Tenoch took the glasses, saw, and then cursed in Spanish.

"Believe me now?"

"It's giving me a headache," he said finally. "What are those?"

"Spells. Protective runes. Permanent structural changes to the matrix that djinns call the field. The djinn can see these markers with the naked eye. Beltrex didn't need protection from men—normal weapons can't really kill him," Rais said. "These wards are to keep djinn out, and I'm pretty sure it's djinn who took him. Let's go inside. I'm guessing we'll find a breach."

"Is it booby-trapped?"

"Not for humans. Beltrex wasn't worried about us."

The rooms inside were undisturbed: a luxurious foyer, followed by an office, a kitchen, and several bedrooms, this inner sanctum furnished more in the djinn style, with brass and polished wood, many ancient artifacts scattered haphazardly, a few rooms filled like a museum. The annex reeked of magic; wherever Rais looked, dark powers crowded his eyes. Beltrex had been potent.

"Thousands of years of loot," Rais whispered, thumbing a scrimshawed mammoth tusk, shaped into a horn.

The others were ambling around, awestruck despite themselves. There were priceless things here: jeweled swords, old porcelain, several chests of bullion, a head of Anubis with glinting emerald eyes. In one alcove was a gigantic double-handed war hammer resting on the ground, the oversize flat head balanced by a thick, curving spike on the other side.

Rais followed the runes, unbroken lines of protection, until he got to the final room, burrowed flush into the adjoining hill, the walls and ceiling of the room fashioned from the actual volcanic rock that formed most of the geological structures in Sonoma. The breach was here, the wards weakened or unraveled, creating an impossibly perfect circular hole in the middle of the roof, as if someone had drilled down through the hill above.

"Are you trying to tell me that you think the U.S. government somehow drilled through the hill into this room and snatched Beltrex? Without him noticing?" Rais asked.

"It's that or djinns." Tenoch borrowed the glasses again. "I guess I'm leaning toward djinns now."

"See the breach?"

"Yup."

"The runes were weakest here, because Beltrex thought he was safe. On account of the hill on top of his head."

"So djinns came down this hole? And what? Kidnapped them?"

"No signs of a struggle," Rais said. "Beltrex was a beast, and Elkran was a famed duelist. I don't know how they could be overpowered."

"How powerful are we talking about?"

"I don't know. They keep saying they're more powerful than nuclear bombs," Rais said. "Not sure whether that's just shit-talking or they're being serious."

Everyone passed around the glasses, until they were all convinced by the breach. Then they sat on the thick carpet like children and just stared at the hole.

"Wow. Christ. So it's all real," Tenoch said. "Djinns are real. So spirits, demons, angels—everything is real?"

"Blows your mind, right?" Roger said.

"I don't know about angels," Rais said. "I don't think djinns are supernatural. I think they're just like us—wandering around lost, trying to make sense of everything."

"Are you guys going to sit here all night looking at the hole, or are we going to get the hell out of here?" Maria asked finally. "This place is just creepy."

"You still inclined to kill us, Tenoch?" Rais asked.

Tenoch shrugged. "Safest thing to do, really. Djinn or not, I still have a drone sitting over here I have no way to get out. Getting caught with it means a one-way trip to a dark room in Gitmo, no trial, no lawyer."

"Let me make the deal then. The airship is hovering over the Pacific as we speak. I'll take you and your shipment out, drop you in Baja, same way Beltrex would have. And you get to see a live djinn."

"What's the catch?"

"Golgoras owns the ship. He's going to want something," Rais said.

"What, like cash? I've already paid."

"He won't take cash. Djinns don't take human currency normally. What deal did you have with Beltrex?"

"All kinds of weird drugs, women, men, electronics, you name it," Tenoch said. "Those dudes had appetites."

"You have men here, right? *Sicarios?* Got any you can spare?"

"What?"

"Golgoras needs crew that he can trust. I'm guessing you guys can help each other. Give us a few men, it should square it," Rais said.

"Hey, man, most of 'em are family, okay? What do you mean give him a few men? Where the hell would they be going?"

"Relax, they'll just be crewing the airship. It's mostly routine work. Where are we going? Well, I think I know the djinn who took Beltrex and Elkran. He's making some kind of move," Rais said.

"You know where to find them?"

"I'm pretty sure they've gone to Siberia."

"I'm not going to Siberia."

It took a day to convince Golgoras. Tenoch was sold the minute he saw the *Sephiroth* slowly take form in front of his eyes, shedding her chameleon tech. Even with the hasty repairs, she was a beautiful, rakish ship, low and predatory. It took Golgoras quite a bit longer.

Golgoras was not a happy djinn. It was bad luck having a woman aboard the *Sephiroth*. He did not want Tenoch and his armed *sicarios* wandering the deck. He did not like the idea of transporting a coffin-size crate full of unknown drone tech. He most certainly did not enjoy Roger following him around like an imprinted duckling, asking minute questions about his physiology. But most of all, the one thing he *definitely* did not want to do was go to Siberia. "I'll drop you off at the Hub; you can charter something else there."

"We don't have time, Golgoras," Rais said. "Matteras has kidnapped them. I'm sure of it. Who else could it be? Who's powerful enough and cunning enough to get past Beltrex's defenses like that? Kaikobad's house had wards like these, and Matteras somehow took him out ten years ago."

"And where's the proof of that, hmm?"

"Well, do you think Beltrex broke his own protection and drilled a hole up the hill? Why? 'Cause he's afraid of doors all of a sudden?"

"Beltrex is batshit insane. It's not impossible that he did just that," Golgoras said.

"It's on you if they end up in a murder pit," Rais said.

"I am not his client and therefore not obliged to act."

"Well, *I* am an emissary, and it is well within my remit to investigate any suspected kidnapping, regardless of who it is," Rais said.

In the end, they dropped Tenoch off in Baja and signed six of the *sicarios* as crew. The contract was 386 pages long, and Rais had to spend half a night explaining it and the intricacies of djinn law to Tenoch. The gist of it was that, in return for providing a minimum of six crew members and round-the-year maintenance and refueling support, the *Sephiroth* would dedicate every tenth contract to a shipment of Tenoch's choosing. The remainder of the time, the crew would serve Golgoras in whatever capacity he deemed fit, including combat conditions, although they would receive additional recompense as hazard pay if they did in fact come under fire.

Six men volunteered, officered by Tenoch's cousin Raul, and were duly inducted. They signed the contract in blood, and Golgoras placed constructs on them to prevent any possibility of sabotage or mutiny. Tenoch also signed the contract in blood as the main beneficiary, and then had the honor of being offered patronage by Golgoras, which he accepted. As Rais explained to him, he was now tied to Golgoras by bonds of honor and clientship, and he was expected to serve his patron in any way possible, with the understanding that in times of dire need, he would be able to call upon a powerful djinn captaining a deadly airship. For the Sinaloa, this was a major coup, and Tenoch disembarked the ship a well-satisfied man. As part of their agreement, he readily supplied the ship with assault rifles, submachine guns, concussive grenades, RPGs, and a stock of six surface-to-air missiles that could be fired from a modified torpedo tube. Two of the new crew members were snipers, and they set up shop at each observation deck, manning cannons that had not been fired in years. Mines were cleaned, the bow and prow guns primed, the grappling hooks waxed and coiled.

The *Sephiroth* had never been this fighting fit, and Golgoras was pleased with Rais's negotiations. Any upgrade to his ship was a balm to the captain's heart, and he was mellowed enough to offer his three passengers a cask of amontillado on the bridge in celebration. He was, however, still adamant. There would be no Siberia.

"Be reasonable, boy," Golgoras said, clapping him on the back. "One does not simply barge into Kuriken's castle without an invitation. There are protocols."

"I'm not telling you to barge in. I'm asking you to just get us there."

"That's the same bloody thing."

"You are under contract. Do you, at this time, formally renege? I will require that in writing, if you please."

"I do not please!" Golgoras snapped. "And shut up with all the legal talk."

"Not so fun when you're on the other end of it, eh?"

"You did good with the Mexican contract," Golgoras said. "Fair terms, and it gets me out of a jam. Frankly, I don't trust *any* Ghuls right now. There are strange noises coming out of Lhasa. If the deal with the cartel works out, we can crew a lot more ships with Tenoch's men. I'm going to recommend it to Memmion. You'll get a lot of dignatas out of this. You should be pleased with yourself."

"Thanks," Rais said. "I still want to chase after Beltrex, though."

"I will take you to the Hub. We will see Memmion. You will explain your case to him."

"We can catch them, Golgoras!" Rais said.

"And then what? He must have come with an airship. Do you think we can take him in the air? With an untested crew? Do you know how strong Matteras is? For all we know he has an army of Ghuls. And what if we get to Siberia? How exactly do you intend to storm Kuriken's castle? It's a fucking castle. Kuriken isn't some senile ancient. He'll peel the skin off you."

"Delightful. And how exactly will Memmion help?"

"Oh, if you can convince Memmion, you're sorted," Golgoras said. "He has a fucking dreadnought."

CHAPTER 44
Pipe Dreams

It rained for three days before the first tsunami hit the coast. It was a small wave, only five feet high by the time it crashed into the mangrove forest, which served as a storm wall for the southern coast. There were only a few casualties, more from acts of idiocy than the actual tide. In Bangladesh, there were always a few casualties. The worst affected were the trees. The aftershocks were felt in the countries surrounding the Bay of Bengal. It was unusual seismic activity, underwater somewhere in the Indian Ocean, far from traditional fault lines. Scientists termed it an aberration and vowed to study it further.

Indelbed didn't mind the rain. It kept him cool. He had fled Wari after the fire in the market. Many people had died. He went back two days later, walking through the remains of charred wood, blackened tin sheets, scraps of cloth, and rotting vegetables, everything laced with ashes and the lingering smell of burned bodies. He knew that smell. Nightmares haunted him from that night. He was struck by remorse and the certitude that there was something alien inside him, some urge to destruction, because he remembered vividly the joy of loosening the fire, the fierce bloodlust, and could not deny that he would do it again, no doubt, if pushed. He almost turned back then, but it was the urn he needed, the jar of earth stacked somewhere in the night guard's hut of horrors, which contained his cavernous home and his blood brother, calling incessantly to him. It was a desperate idea. He wanted to return to his prison, a place cool, dark, and peaceful.

The hut was abandoned. The boy and his keeper had both left. Police had taken the body of Ramiz. The hut was padlocked from the outside, and a notice hung on the door, declaring the place off-limits pending a court order and investigation. Indelbed broke the lock with a brick, the metal so brittle that it snapped like honeycomb. The room inside was basic, with a bed, mosquito net, cupboard, table, and chair. A small boxy television sat in a corner, a table fan; tin plates, cups, and bowls were stored in a chest. The place had been ransacked a bit, the police looking for any cash, perhaps, but otherwise left intact. The urn was under the bed, rolled to one corner.

"Ah, Master, I knew you would return!" the urn said as soon as he touched it. "I knew it! I said, 'The Young Master wouldn't leave me on this dirty floor, rolled up like a flower vase...'"

"Sorry about that, I had a bit of a problem with the locals," Indelbed said. "In fact, I wanted your help with that..."

"Master! Why, I would be delighted to help! I can name the ninety-nine djinn Solomon kept in perpetual slavery, I can give you the recipe for the special Halwa he ate on Wednesdays, I've got a pretty good idea about the technique he used on his favorite concubine, which used to make her squeal, I can—"

"It's a bit of a rush, actually. The police might be after me. I want to go back inside."

"Back inside?"

"Into the murder pit. You said it was deactivated, right? Does that mean I can come and go? Without breaking you, I mean?"

"Well, theoretically..."

"Can't you teach me?"

"You'd have to master folding n space," the urn said doubtfully. "It took Matteras years to prepare the cave and even longer to fold core fire."

"I can see the field. Not just spells and runes and permanent constructs, I mean I can actually see the free movement of particles, even when they're not being distorted," Indelbed said. "My eyes use the field particles to see instead of photons."

"Oh. Well! What a stupendous talent, Master! Even Solomon could only see with regular light! If only I had eyes, I would use them to look into your magical orbs—"

Indelbed was forced to stuff the urn into his blanket at this point, because people were looking at him funny. His clothes were ill fitting because he had stolen them, and his blanket was covered in soot and very likely worse things. He walked barefoot and stank. He looked like a beggar, not one of the prosperous ones either, but the mentally ill kind who were covered in filth and really homeless. It rankled. His house was right there, occupied by djinn, and no one even remembered him, not even Butloo. It was as if he and his father had been erased, their home, their lives, just brushed out. He was obsessed with the house, felt a visceral need to retake it.

Without it, he supposed he *was* a beggar. Over the past three days, all of his food had actually come from begging. He loitered around the street stall restaurants at night, and they often paid him to go away; he never took money, asking instead for the food left over on the dirty plates—invariably they gave him that and more, disgust warring with pity. He supposed long ago he would have died of shame rather than eat like this, but he had spent the last ten years eating wyrm meat, so leftover rice seemed like a step up.

Food was harder to come across during the day, however, and there was a greater chance of being recognized as the blind black boy who started fires. He walked swathed in his blanket, despite the heat, and avoided lingering anywhere. He had found an empty lot that was stacked with large concrete pipes, kept there by contractors installing new storm drains. He slept inside one of them. It reminded him of a tunnel. The second night someone attacked him, trying to drag him out by the foot, but a quick shove of the field sent the assailant sprawling. He slept badly, the darkness crowded with nightmares of burning men, the field always on, a whisper of madness, but he was used to that.

He did not go to the pipes until dark. It was dangerous to stay there for too long, because while the night guard tolerated street people sleeping in them at night, the road contractors during the day would most definitely not appreciate people setting up permanent habitation. By the third night in the pipes, he had set out his route, identifying several shady spots where sympathetic vendors let him sit on the footpath and two abandoned buildings where he could sneak in for a nap. Food and water were from begging and in meager portions; he was not too disturbed by a diet that would have caused starvation to more prosperous persons.

That night, he took stock inside his pipe.

I have nothing, he said to himself, *other than this urn. Ironic, that my only possession was given to me by Uncle Matteras, who imprisoned me for no reason. I am at an absolute zero. I fell into that hole with my luggage and a cell phone. I have left those behind too. I have nowhere to go, and soon perhaps my escape will be noticed, and the djinns will start looking for me. If I stay in the street for too long, I will eventually get into trouble. Someone will try to rob me, or rape me, or beat me. I will hurt them, and then the police will know it was me who set the fires. I am all alone in this world. My father is dead. He must be. He would never have voluntarily left the house. Or he is still in a coma. It is all the same, I am truly an orphan.*

My family sold me to the djinn. My master left me to die. No one recognizes me, not even Butloo. There is no one in the whole world who will help me, and many who will gladly kill me.

I wish I could go back to the murder pit. I wish God's Eye was beside me. It is pathetic, that I am free and long for my prison. That's the little boy talking. The little boy is no good. He's just going to crawl back into the hole and hide. I'm going to be the dragon. Givaras thought I'd burn, but I lived. I am the dragon. I'm going to take back my house. I'm going to kill the djinn inside. I'm going to find Matteras and kill him. And then I'm going to find Givaras and stuff him back in the urn. I'm going to feed him to God's Eye. I am the dragon. You're all going to pay.

He went to sleep cradling the urn and dreamed of burning in core fire.

The second earthquake hit the bay early that morning. Tremors were felt all the way to Dhaka, waking up infants and setting the dogs barking. The pipe adjacent to Indelbed swayed alarmingly and finally rolled off, nearly crushing a little street boy sleeping nearby. Indelbed himself was cocooned inside his field and did not feel anything. In the bay, near the underwater ruins of Gangaridai, a great school of fish watched the disturbance with obvious irritation. The epicenter was at the northern subduction plate near the coast of Myanmar, where for aeons, one plate had been slipping under another with little fuss, at a rate slow enough to be largely unremarked.

The school had sacrificed some of its members to investigate the phenomenon, and before they died, they had reported a large field disruption at concentrated points along the fault line, causing periodic eruptions, where thousands of tons of rocks were ejected from the overlaying plate, ultimately creating the tsunamis. The second of these great waves, generated by a quake measured 7.8 on the Richter scale in Myanmar, was much larger than the first, measuring over twelve feet from trough to crest and traveling over 250 kilometers per hour from the center, a wall of energy that shot through the ocean like a cannonball, wrecking itself on the already storm-ravaged coast.

This time, the trees were not the only casualties. Over a thousand people died in the coastal region, either drowned by the wave, or buried by the tremor, or destroyed by the ensuing storm. Geologists and oceanographers came from all the neighboring countries, fitting the current activity to their working models, trying to predict the next big one. Reputations were made as this paper or that proved to be correct; the consensus was that the hitherto peaceful fault line had built up intolerable stress over time, and this was far from the end. Excited historians claimed that this was exactly how Atlantis, or the great antediluvian civilizations, had gone down, and *National Geographic* discussed sending a dive crew to see if it could spot any sign of volcanic activity.

Government agencies rushed about, provisioning storm shelters, sending warnings, collecting stocks of biscuits and saltines and blankets.

Bahamut, who had seen the power being expended underwater briefly with his own eyes, sat in his watery home with his fin on the trigger, and patiently waited for someone to come rescue him from his intolerable predicament.

The journey to the Hub was long. Roger spent the entire duration following Golgoras, watching his every move. He volunteered for every task, proving to be something of a mechanical savant, even coming up with a new calibration of the gas ratio, forcing the captain to grudgingly acknowledge that he was a useful fellow. By the end of the journey, he would be widely recognized as de facto first mate, even by the cartel crew.

Maria spent the journey learning to fire a gun, with off-duty *sicarios* happily teaching her how to strip and load assault rifles. In private, she and Rais explored the workings of the invisible knife. This was their secret weapon, their ace in the hole, for it was clearly a djinn killer, an assassin's tool, probably the only thing they had that could hurt Matteras in case it came to a fight.

Knife was a loosely accurate name for what was essentially a formless, invisible object. As Maria had observed earlier, it seemed to hover not just out of sight, but out of existence entirely, a sort of potential lethality waiting to be called into being. She kept it leashed to her wrist, for it was liable to get lost altogether. The weapon itself was almost like a whip. It seemed to hit about a foot in front of her fist when she threw a punch, making five little ripples in the air, micro-disturbances that Rais could see using his glasses. They had tested this once against Barabas from a safe distance, and the knife had shredded his field. It was similarly efficacious against mundane objects, shattering wooden posts, even gouging five deep rents in a steel plate.

"Last resort, right?" Rais said, watching her attack the decking from a safe distance.

"Yeah," Maria said. "Like Raul said, no point having a weapon if you can't use it."

"Right," Rais said. "Please take it easy on the ship."

"This thing is awesome," she said. "I'm going to stab Dargoman with it when I get back home."

"Yeah, but right now you're about to make a hole in the hull. If Golgoras comes in here he's going to have a heart attack."

"Rais, there's been more storms at home," Maria said. "I've been getting updates."

"Dhaka?"

"Streets are flooded, but no extensive damage yet," she said. "There are hurricanes and tsunamis hitting the coasts, though. A lot of casualties in Cox's Bazar."

"How many?"

"Estimated twenty thousand according to the *Daily Star*."

"That many?"

"They're having trouble explaining what's causing all this," Maria said. "Underwater earthquakes in the bay seems to be the consensus."

"Fuck. We're really running out of time."

"You best be persuasive with Memmion then."

The Hub was somewhere in the tropics, invisible to the human eye, approachable only through the route mapped out in Golgoras's prized RAS charts. It had been created long ago, with magic not easily replicated today, for it occupied a slant of space slightly altered from reality. Precise turns and maneuvers had to be made to enter this pocket universe in an invisible four-dimensional lock; one wrong step would send you spinning back out to empty sky. At last, after an hour of careful navigation, the port flashed into view through the haze of distortion, brilliant from the sun, a series of interlocked giant spheres made of reflective burnished copper, like droplets of fire, moored airships dotting their circumference.

They were all awed, standing on the deck, marveling at something completely alien hanging in the sky in plain sight, the first real evidence of the superiority and might boasted by the djinn. The Hub had three central spheres made of crystal, each large enough to contain a city block, connected by wide tubes. Inside were the functional habitats for the djinn and Ghul who crewed the airships, warehouses for stashing loot, and manufactories for repairing and, indeed, assembling the ships themselves. Long ago there had been great foundries and shipwrights for making everything, but nowadays, they mostly just ordered the parts in from Hyundai.

The bottom halves of the spheres were given over to nature, giant trees growing upside down, the canopy trailing earthward, teeming with a riot of confused birds. Further, smaller spheres and tubes spoked out from the main circumference, forming docks and ancillary structures, some with obvious functions. Rais counted something like fifty airships of various sizes moored, about half of them small pleasure craft.

"I can't see the dreadnought." Golgoras's eye telescoped alarmingly. "Something is wrong. Memmion hasn't left the Hub in two centuries..."

The Hub was strictly for use by the RAS, an avowed egalitarian club espousing strong republican views, yet there were still some perks for seniority, because Golgoras made straight for one of the choice central berths around the largest sphere and was permitted to moor the ship with minimum delay. There were no officials at hand to greet them, just a uniformed Ghul leaning expressionlessly against a wall. Everything was apparently self-service.

"Where is the harbormaster?" Golgoras said. "Something is wrong."

The pilot hurried Rais and Maria down, leaving Roger and the crew with the ship. They followed a winding, sunlit corridor to the club bar, where a smattering of djinn greeted Golgoras in a variety of tongues. This was not the captains' bar, which was much nicer, Golgoras explained, but sadly out of bounds for visitors. Even at the club bar, there was a large book at the door where he had to sign their names and expend a minute quantity of his auctoritas to gain them entry.

"What's going on?" he asked the bartender. "Where is everyone?"

"Over at Memmion's."

"I was heading there next."

"Half the sphere's there," the bartender said. "He's gone."

"What?!"

"He got some visitors, and then they got into the dreadnought and flew off."

"He took the ship? Left? Why? With who?"

The bartender shrugged. "Who the fuck knows? Between you and me, Memmion's been acting odd the last fifty years. Erratic as fuck. Time we think about a new chairman for the society, maybe..."

"He built the Hub," Golgoras growled, turning to leave. "And bartenders don't get a fucking vote."

"He's going to spit in our drinks next time we come here," Rais said. He had to run to keep up with the djinn.

"He's an Ageist cunt. That's one of those neo-clubs where they sit around talking shit about the Lore. There've been more and more of them around. I'm going to tell Memmion to sky a few of them when I see him."

By the time they reached Memmion's door, it was fairly clear that he had left abruptly, and the crowd of djinns thronging the corridor had no clue where. Golgoras interviewed a few of the higher-ranking ones, including the chief mechanic of the sphere, who claimed that the dreadnought had left with her full complement of Ghul crew, but none of the Ifrit officers. Three visitors had come in the night with a hired craft, which too had left with the dreadnought. No one had noticed them; they had apparently known the ward keys for entering the sphere undetected through Memmion's private dock, a backdoor entrance into the Hub long unused and mostly forgotten. Memmion's own security of interlocking spells, brutally powerful, were undisturbed.

The dreadnought, properly named the *Sublime Porte*, the pride of the fleet, the largest, most dangerous ship ever built by the Royal Aeronautics Society, had not slipped moorage for over a hundred years, the last time being when it had accidentally come loose from its ties during a rare conjunction of telluric disruption and a thunderstorm. Now, both the elder djinn and the dreadnought were gone without a trace. The steward of the Windward Sphere was visibly distraught, and people were looking at him accusingly, as if he should either produce the missing edifices immediately or furnish everyone with a ready-made explanation.

The hall was now completely crammed with onlookers, the entire sphere jammed up like the site of a major disaster, the djinn being much addicted to gossip and conjecture.

"Full Assembly of all captains present in twelve hours!" the steward said, brushing aside Golgoras. "I will present my findings then."

The steward promptly locked himself in his office and refused to entertain any further visitors. Fuming, Golgoras led them back to the ship.

"It's Matteras! They said three djinns—it must be them," Rais said as soon as they were back on the bridge. "He kidnapped Beltrex and Elkran, and now he's taken Memmion."

"How, hmm? Memmion is four hundred pounds, with a field that's like a brick wall at a hundred yards."

"I don't know how!" Rais said. "With threats, or blackmail, or ambush. You said yourself Memmion hasn't left the Hub in hundreds of years. How fighting fit was he? Maybe he was asleep and they just carted him off wrapped in a carpet..."

"And the *Sublime Porte*?"

"They took the ship, Golgoras. It's Matteras, for god's sake—he's smart and ruthless, he's running rings around everyone."

"We should wait for the Assembly," Golgoras said. "Find out what the steward knows."

"He doesn't know shit! Did you see his face? He was shitting his pants. What will the Assembly achieve? They're going to dither around for a bit and then eat canapés and get drunk. We've got to fly! We can catch them, Golgoras! We're just a day behind!"

"Ah, Your Excellency, what are you going to do once you catch them?" Maria said. "Like don't they have the big ship now with all the guns?"

"*Sephiroth* can take her, maybe," Golgoras said doubtfully. "If we can sneak up above her. It's going to be tough, though. We'll take casualties."

"We've got the rockets," Roger said. "Tenoch's snipers are really good. We could probably hit a bunch of them before they even see us."

"Guys, don't worry, we're not going to fight," Rais said.

"They'll just give up and hand everyone over, I suppose?" Golgoras asked.

"We are going to negotiate."

CHAPTER 45
Kaikobad

Kaikobad stood on the north wall, where defenders silently manned scorpions armed with iron-tipped bolts. Bougainvillea had grown along the ramparts here, decking the heights with purple flowers, back when defenders and scorpions had both been unthinkable. The vines were long dead now, flowers pulped underfoot.

The last besieging army was outside, a pathetic force compared with what had come before, testament to the staggering losses on all sides. The remaining names had arrived at last, the original instigators finally ranged against the city. Memmion was in the sky in his new floating warship, raining down missiles. Bahamut churned the waters of the bay, ever threatening. The famed Gangaridai armada was nearly gone, battered to kindling by repeated hurricanes smashing the seawall.

Barkan, Elkran, and Davala commanded the Nephilim armies, circling the northern walls in a double line. Behind them was Horus, named the Broken by the Ghuls, leading his client army at last against the First City, the Ghuls armored in black, carrying their fifteen-foot-long spears. It was the end, and the mood of the city befitted the gravity of the moment.

Buskers were gone from the drowned promenade; minstrels, poets, playwrights all silent. The town crier, who used to go to every plaza and park shouting his news, sat at home in a drunken stupor. No one wanted the news anymore; people could smell it in the air, feel it in the water sloshing at their feet.

The city was flooded. Almost all the streets were ankle-deep in water, black with ash, mud, and sewage—a rank wartime soup. The famed mosaics of the old district were chipped and damaged, some of them deliberately vandalized with chisels. People did strange things in wartime. Dead dogs floated on the grand avenue, abandoned pets unable to fend for themselves. It was a full degradation, a complete collapse of civic duties. Almost all services were suspended, except for the breweries, which continued to churn out cheap alcohol. The taverns did roaring business: it seemed as if half the city was crammed into them.

There were rumors that Kuriken had left. He had gone outside and not returned. Watchers on the wall claimed to have seen him meet Givaras on the field. Some claimed that he had killed their nemesis. Some claimed that Kuriken had lost heart—he was a coward. Kaikobad knew that it was a moot point anyway. The First City was fading away at an increasing rate now. Entire quarters were so tenuous that they could not be approached, their inhabitants insubstantial as ghosts, seemingly unaware of their own condition.

The High King at last walked the bones of the city, surrounded by dark-eyed Horologists, stalking some pattern through the ancient ley lines, laying the final nails of his crowning work. This had been his intention all along, everything else mere posturing, all the fighting and the bloodshed just the interlude to the main act. Perhaps Kuriken had recognized that, understood his own role as the joker of the pack, and decided to walk away. He, at last sight, had at least still been one of the living, still a physical presence, his vitality too strong to fade so easily.

Kaikobad followed the High King with professional interest, appreciating a true master. The exhausted Horologists were marking the cardinal points in the city, the exact spots that aligned with the sacred constellation, the three stars of Orion, and the High King himself was doing the final spell work. He was, in fact, the only sorcerer, Nephilim or djinn, capable of such a thing. Kaikobad watched him in awe, only now understanding the full scale of what was being attempted here. The sheer hubris of it, the impossible ambition, made something sing inside him, and he understood the nature of the High King's war, how small the enemy outside was, how insignificant and petty. This High King was fighting against reality itself, Horus, Memmion, and the others just ticks on his back that he did not have the time to swat away.

The High King sensed him, but there was nothing he could do. Kaikobad existed on a level below the surface; there was no way to pry him loose. In the end, the High King visibly shrugged, the red-masked face showing wry amusement. In a way, perhaps he was glad for an audience, a lone witness to his brilliance. This would, Kaikobad realized, literally be his last act on earth, the last hours of his existence, in fact. That he would spend it with a ghost from another time was poignant.

When the work was finished, the High King sat on a stool in the middle of the central plaza and breathed in the gentle mist from the last fountain in the city, a river dolphin made of bronze, gurgling water out if its mouth, on occasion spraying it high in the air. Once, children had played here, racing boats in the runoff drain, while lovers pitched coins into the water. Those people were long gone now, stored away someplace safe. One by one, even the Horologists went, either back to the tower or fading to some other world, it was impossible to tell.

The High King sat for a long time, and Kaikobad waited with him in companionable silence, as all around them the city began to unravel and spin away like cobwebs in the wind.

CHAPTER 46
Gangs of Old Town

Indelbed woke up inducted into a gang. It wasn't something he had scheduled. This was his first encounter with the monthly migration of the street boys: feral juvenile drug dealers who used a rotating circle of habitats, the entire city their home, the garbage dumps their pleasure domes, the bridges their secret roads. The pipe yard was next to a Water and Sewerage Authority pump house, a spacious plot containing the tube well that supplied water to the block. WASA owned pumps and wells all over the city, under the rule of entrepreneurially spirited pump operators. The pump operators here had erected a phensedyl bottling factory in the extra space. Phensedyl was a cough syrup that people took to get high. It worked. The original cough syrup had a slightly higher codeine content, which was enough to attract an early user demographic of recreational substance abuse aficionados.

Ironically, it wasn't the extra bit of codeine that was making them high initially, but rather the promethazine, which, among other things, served as an anticholinergic, an overdose of which caused hallucinations. It was like a Dramamine high, only milder, suitable for unregulated, continuous abuse. Of course, as soon as phensedyl became a massive money earner, pharmaceutical factories in West Bengal had started churning out special batches with extra-high codeine content, thereby proving that customer service was alive and well.

All month, the phensedyl factory in the WASA pump house diluted and bottled their product. On the last weekend of each month, the boys descended to resupply. They lived in the pipes for three days, settling accounts; mapping out routes, distribution points, and where the dangerous spots were; marking a ledger of all the beat cops, who was greedy and who was nice; noting who was missing, who'd been hurt or killed. At the end of the conference they left with the new supply, a month's worth of benediction for their clients.

The leader was a twelve-year-old who looked ten, a mass of old scars on a short, compact body and a close-cropped head. His eyes were ferocious, black, almost cross-eyed with intensity, and he was somewhat jowly, unusual in a street kid, possibly the very source of his power.

This was the face Indelbed saw, staring at him upside down. It was impressively ugly from either direction.

"You too big to live here," Boss Kid said. "Pipe too small."

"Yeah, I know."

Indelbed was now aware that a knife was hovering around his throat. It wasn't a kitchen knife. This one looked small and professional, a stabbing instrument.

"I'm the djinn of the pipes," Indelbed said with a grin. Knives made him laugh, unless they were made of bone.

"You djinn?" Boss Kid didn't give anything away, ever. You could tell him the world was ending, and he'd ask a phlegmatic "When?" and then recalculate his margin.

Indelbed reached out with his field. The knife got hot, too hot to hold.

"Djinn," Boss Kid spat, refusing to drop the knife, even though his palm was smoking. "Plenty djinn in slums. You go there. This is pipe. No such thing as pipe djinn."

"Now there is."

"Then I'm your boss. You live here, you work for me."

"You sell those bottles? What is it? Cough syrup?"

"Hundred percent top-quality foreign phensedyl, *pacca*, no cut." Even Boss Kid's sales pitch was atonal. "You drink it, I kill you."

"That all you guys deal?"

"Ganja, hashish, heroin, beer, Viagra," Boss Kid counted off on one hand. "My boys best in Dhaka. I give food, protection, salary, free housing, and insurance. Also holiday every six months. Go home to the village."

"Insurance?"

"Health insurance, motherchode, like the multinationals, no? One bottle phensedyl a month. No cough, no runny nose."

"You want me to go around peddling all this stuff?"

"No, you too big." Boss Kid measured him up with a practiced eye. "Police get you quick."

"Maybe I can stay here protecting your stash. Look menacing."

"Hmm. Maybe. Half salary, you sit on ass all day."

"I'm a djinn!" Indelbed protested. "I should get double."

"You weak djinn. But first djinn in crew. Okay. Basic salary. You follow me one week. Trial period. Eid bonus if fighting."

There was no fighting. Boss Kid was an extraordinarily savvy leader. He saw the world as a desert, and he hopped from oasis to oasis, cannily nursing his resources while his enemies floundered in the sand. Everyone owed him a favor; he ate for free in restaurants, ran the bar for the Wari football club, kept his drugs stashed in the ward commissioner's house. He worked for the police and RAB as a valued informant, and when they were off duty, he got them booze and drugs. He murdered and robbed, and for a fee he got rid of bodies. He was an ace disposal guy. He didn't give a shit; if there was a profit, he'd do it. But Boss Kid never peddled in flesh. His face darkened whenever propositions like that came up, and if anyone took his boys, he made them pay with blood. This one redeeming factor in his fast-receding humanity was enough for Indelbed. They were kindred souls, more or less.

When the week was up, Indelbed suggested that they take over the pump house. It was a question of higher economics. Boss Kid controlled distribution, but not supply. In this case, supply was easy to manage, because Boss Kid already knew the broker at the Benapole border who supplied the barrels of concentrated stuff, and moreover, he also knew the ward commissioner whose nephew actually sanctioned this pump house. The pump operator was simply a middleman, eating up precious commissions.

"He's got big guys," Boss Kid pointed out. His own boys, while tough, ranged from twelve to four. The four-year-old was particularly mean.

"I'm a djinn."

"Four big guys. One pistol. You little blind djinn."

Indelbed made a small flame dance on top of his palm. "I'm enough."

Boss Kid shrugged.

The massacre at the pump was not like the night market. Indelbed had been practicing. He did not intend to lose control like that again. Killing random people made him weepy afterward. They planned the ambush meticulously. The pump operator and his men did not expect anything, least of all from Boss Kid, who was their most reliable ally. In actuality, while they had all peddled in violence years ago, these days it was more the bluster of force, with their vests and truncheons, brass knuckles visible in their breast pockets, the single revolver held prominently in a holster beneath a see-through shirt. These men were used to pushing and shoving, open-handed slaps, a few choice words: bullies rather than soldiers, their single prized weapon destined to remain unfired.

Indelbed was rigged out as a blind beggar, with Boss Kid as his helper guide. This was a common sight on the streets, duos of cripple and child roaming in tandem, pulling at heart strings and wallets. Indelbed had his field out, tendril thin like his master had taught him, and in his fist he held five coins, the edges lovingly sharpened by Boss Kid.

"Oyo, Boss Kid, you're leading the blind now?" the day operator said, when they hobbled into the yard. He peered at them. "Is it the kid from the pipes?"

"My retarded cousin. From the village," Boss Kid said.

"Born blind, or did you help him along?" The operator laughed, because this was the sort of thing he found funny.

"Born blind," Boss Kid said. "Going to be beggar champion."

"Oyo, Boss Kid, he doesn't even have a bowl."

"But I have some coins," Indelbed whispered. The serrated coins flew out of his palm. The operator looked puzzled for a second as he toppled over, the metal slicing through his trachea before lodging entirely into his spine, popping out a vertebra and slotting neatly into its place. Two of the guards had been in their customary seats, and both died sitting down, throats slit. Two more were sleeping inside the pump house. Their deaths were messier. Indelbed had to fly the coins in through the window, around distances he couldn't really judge properly, so he ended up sawing at the guards' necks with them, spinning them back and forth, opening up everything with great gouts of blood.

It was over in less than thirty seconds, over before the operator's body had stopped twitching on the ground. Indelbed and Boss Kid stood still the entire time, hands out, staring in apparent astonishment as the men keeled over. Finally, the screaming started, as the more alert bottlers began to notice the five simultaneous deaths by coin. By the time the pandemonium had subsided, Boss Kid's boys were in firm control of the site, having appropriated the gun, occupied the pump house, and secured the body of the operator, who had the keys to all the locks and a cell phone full of useful numbers.

Boss Kid was a thinking kid. He had added his own flourish to Indelbed's plan. They had left alive one last person of authority, the foreman of the factory, a man universally hated by all, but especially by Boss Kid, because he was also a child trafficker who would bring girls from remote villages to the city, before sending them north to "work" in India. Sometimes he would break them in, in the pump house. This man, also sleeping, suddenly woke to find himself covered in blood, his mouth gagged and his hands bound, being led like a dog outside by a couple of urchins, scraping on his hands and knees.

Here, he shook with outrage as Boss Kid told all the gathered workers that this man, their hated foreman, had in fact killed all the others using the bloody knife found in his hands, the very knife he normally carried on his belt and had used more than once upon his fellows with sadistic flare. They took his gag off and commanded him to speak. At the same time, Indelbed sent a fist of air into his mouth, preventing this very thing. The foreman strained until blood vessels in his eyes popped, but he couldn't get a word out, nor could he get loose as fists and sticks and feet mobbed him, the workers baying, a rough and ready execution for the perceived murder of five men in broad daylight. Boss Kid simply stepped out of the way and watched with his normal lack of expression. Old scores were rarely settled so smoothly.

When naught but pulp remained, the boys gathered up all the dead bodies into jute sacks found miraculously at hand. It was, in fact, very easy for Boss Kid to take charge, seeing as how the bottlers were by and large a docile lot, and Boss Kid had a natural authority and was known among the drudges as a mover and a shaker. Moreover, the workers were scared. Their protectors were gone, and they had just beaten a man to death. Many were inclined to run away at this point, but Boss Kid calmed everything down by handing out the daily wages in cash, ordering a round of hot, milky tea for everyone, and then informing them that it was going to be business as usual. By lunchtime, the blood was scrubbed out, the coins were back in Indelbed's pocket, and everyone was diluting phensedyl and capping bottles. Productivity for the rest of the day went up by 10 percent, in fact.

"Aren't they going to send someone?" Indelbed asked, as they relaxed in their new rattan chairs, slightly speckled with blood, but who cared about that?

"Three days till the next resupply," Boss Kid said. "We do bumper production. Explain to the big man. Ask for the job. Production plus distribution, one shop. Easy."

"And the new pump operator?"

"We cut him out. New guy comes, he operates pump. We pay rent. He keeps mouth shut. He want anything more, you coin him."

"Good. What are you doing with the bodies?"

"Construction site. We put in cement."

"I have a better idea. I want to try something with them."

"You eat them?"

"No!" Indelbed said. "I want to put them in my jar."

"Burn them?"

"No, by folding them really small. There is a way. I'm trying to learn the technique. I need bodies to practice on."

"How many you fit inside jar?" Boss Kid asked, dubious.

"Well, they won't stay there long. I have a foolproof method of disposal on the other end."

"Okay, we try. New business. They pay big money to get rid of bodies. You get rid of body, we bring five, ten every week, how much you want."

"Good. I have a giant wyrm in there to feed."

This information did not faze Boss Kid. "You good djinn." Boss Kid patted his arm.

A week later, they had, indeed, negotiated a reprieve. The MP's nephew did not care who exactly ran his factories as long as the money rolled in. There were three other layers between him and Boss Kid. Boss Kid simply paid his money up, greased everyone a bit more, and people just forgot about the six missing men. The workers were happier, because the foreman had been a bastard, while Boss Kid was merely a frightening robot, someone who left them alone unless production fell.

"We need to make the gang bigger," Indelbed said at the next resupply, when the yard was again crawling with kids.

"Bigger."

"Every kid in Wari. So we can take over all the phensedyl bottling in the area." He clinked the coins in his hand. "Same way."

"Three factories in Wari. No one rule all three. Two bosses tried. Both dead. We try, we dead too," Boss Kid said. The prospect didn't seem to bother him too much.

"They didn't have a djinn, did they?" asked Indelbed.

"No."

"So we can do it."

"Kill too many, police, RAB, come *fatafat*."

"People disappear all the time. No bodies, no murder. Who's going to suspect a blind boy and a ten-year-old?"

"Twelve and a half."

"I'm going to make you rich, Boss Kid."

"Rich and dead." Boss Kid seemed to find this funny.

"And start recruiting adults. We're going to need more than eight-year-olds for what we have to do."

"Oldies? Why you want?"

"Cannon fodder. You understand cannon fodder?"

"Them that die first." Boss Kid grinned. "Why you want cannon fodder?"

"There's an old house there on road eight," Indelbed said.

"Khan Rahman house."

"You know it?"

"Everyone know it. Old house. Haunted."

"It's well guarded," Indelbed said.

"Police, RAB, everything."

"Also there's a djinn in it."

"Your friend?"

"No. I'm going to kill him."

"Why?"

"Because it's *my* house."

"I heard djinn don't kill djinn."

"I'm not a djinn. I'm a motherfucking dragon."

CHAPTER 47

Kaikobad

Kaikobad slammed back into clarity. It was like being dragged through very cold water.

"Thoth!" he shouted. "Are you still here?"

"Yes," his friend said. "I had feared you lost."

"I think I know where we are," Kaikobad said, once he had collected himself.

"We are in a dark river with no markers," Thoth said. "I am glad you have returned."

"I saw it, Thoth. I saw him complete the spell."

"You saw Kartiryan? At the end?"

"I believe he permitted me to watch," Kaikobad said. "Look, you told me that these were visions, or memories from the gate. I don't think so. I think we are somehow experiencing the real events as they occur. This place is timeless, so the actual sequence of events doesn't matter."

"You believed earlier that we were ghosts in the field," Thoth said.

"I was wrong," Kaikobad said. "I think we have somehow stumbled into the nuts and bolts part of the universe. I think the world we lived in, the physical world, is a projection of this one, a kind of skin or surface. This is the layer beneath, the working part."

"A skin? What does that make men and djinns?"

"I don't know," Kaikobad said. "Bugs crawling on a piece of fruit? Specks of dust? I don't know. This place is fundamental. When we access the surface projection from here, we are literally experiencing life on earth. I think we could alter everything out there, even the laws of physics, from here."

"Are we then inside the mind of God?"

"Thoth, I never knew you were a deist," Kaikobad said. "Even here, you believe?"

"Belief does not depend on circumstance," Thoth said stiffly. "I would have lost hope long ago otherwise. Have you learned how to escape this place, how to unlock the gate?"

"I think the gate is a hole, a pinprick in creation," Kaikobad said. "I was on the other side of it. I believe that was the field, that my mind was somehow translated onto it. See, I used to study the science of distortion. My theory is that the field actually records the existing states on the surface world, and distortion is a kind of rewriting of that data. This place is something else. If the field particles are like strings, perhaps this is the bottom end of the string. I believe this part is supposed to be inaccessible to the surface dwellers. I believe conditions here determine the nature of the field and in turn the laws of physics on the surface world itself, the very interactions of what we believe to be fundamental matter.

"These two layers should be discrete. The gate is artificial, it shouldn't be here. Thoth, I don't know how to say this, but I think you *are* the gate."

"What?"

"You're locked in place," Kaikobad said. "I saw the High King punching the hole. But he had to keep it open somehow. I think he used you. Do you remember nothing?"

"I remember the city," Thoth said sadly. "And the road. I don't know. Did I dream my whole life?"

"I want to explore this place," Kaikobad said. "I think there are deeper layers here with actual physical stuff. We haven't gotten to the bones of the universe yet. We can find your road here somewhere. In fact, I think I can find that bastard Kartiryan here, and he's the only one who can show me how to get back."

"You are determined to return then? We have the chance of learning the true nature of reality itself."

"My son is still there, somewhere on the surface," Kaikobad said.

"If what you say is true, then the world out there is just a projection. Is your son even real? Is anyone up there real? What if the universe dreams, and the world is just that?"

"We are real."

"According to you, only because our minds have somehow been translated onto the field," Thoth said.

"This isn't the right question," Kaikobad said. "We are real because we believe it. In this place, the energy shifts to our will. We have agency. Indelbed is real to me. I don't know if he's dead or alive, but I have to find him. Matteras put me here by accident, I think, and unwittingly, he's increased my power tenfold. I'm the ghost in the machine, and I'm going to find a way to wreck him."

CHAPTER 48
Siege

They flew low across the Sakha Republic, through cloudless skies, with miles of taiga forest below, endless gray larch broken by the occasional glinting stream, emerald seams in a giant's scalp. It was easy to imagine that this land had stood still for thousands of years. Their path would take them farther north, into the subarctic tundra, and then finally to the true arctic permafrost, vast uninhabited lands, a virtual continent encased in ice and ancient secrets. Kuriken's castle was marked on their oldest chart, drafted on vellum over two thousand years ago, the last time the great djinn had officially entertained visitors. Even more than most elder djinn, he was known for a pathological desire to be left alone.

It was cold now, well below zero, and they huddled in their cabins, Maria bundled in furs, flicking endlessly with her knife, slicing apples. The wonder of the airship had largely worn off for everyone. Golgoras was going fast, but not too fast. He was in a bit of a dilemma. Finally convinced that it was Matteras they were pursuing, he was honor bound to try to rescue his patron. At the same time, he had no desire to actually catch the dreadnought and precipitate an airborne battle that he was pretty sure of losing. Thus he scanned the skies with his instruments all day, and any stray bird or threatening-looking cloud made him take ludicrous evasive measures.

Eventually the forests ran out, and there was just permafrost: a featureless, dreary, soul-sapping whiteness, devoid of landmarks. It was here they finally approached the castle, and in the end, despite their fears of getting lost, it was not that hard to find, for the entire structure was encased in a glowing bright blue force field, visible for miles as a pinprick of winking light, like some fallen star.

"I don't know what the hell is happening. We go down slow," Golgoras hissed.

Roger, now fully versed in the workings of the ship, began turning on the compressors. Slowly, the dirigible started to sink. As they got lower, he cut the engines, and everything went quiet.

They were on battery power, which fueled only the command center and air ventilation. The heat from the engines, used to control the climate throughout the ship, began to dissipate, plunging them into an icy hell. Pretty soon they were all huddled in the cockpit, shivering in their furs, miserable and buffeted by drafts. Golgoras had his lone eye glued to the main telescope, an ornate djinn-powered device crowded thick with successive layers of enchantments put on by various captains. It had originally belonged to Sinbad the Sailor, apparently, and was a prized artifact that Golgoras had "salvaged" from a downed airship.

"I can see the dreadnought," he said finally. "Airborne over the castle. Why is she not moored?"

"What?" Rais crowded him. He had his own mini-telescope, but he couldn't see shit. The *Sublime Porte* was only a speck in the air from this far away, and the castle a blue smear on the ice.

"It looks like she's firing a broadside. I can see flashes of powder. Those cannons haven't been fired in a hundred years..." Golgoras said. He frowned. "Why are they shooting at the castle?"

Rais finally got a look through the big telescope.

"They're definitely pounding the castle," he said. "That blue thing is a shield of some sort."

"Why, hmm? Why is Matteras hitting his closest ally?" Golgoras thrust his face into Rais's. "Something very screwy is going on here. I'm not going near that thing with the *Sephiroth*."

"We have to investigate," Rais said.

"That dreadnought has one gun turret fore, two aft, and three broadside. At our current angle of approach she can hit us with at least five turrets," Golgoras said. "That's twenty fourteen-inch bores. We only have twelve-inch bores. She's got range *and* size on us. If she gets off even one salvo, she'll shred us before we can even get within firing range."

"So then what's your plan? I'm pretty sure Memmion is in that ship..."

"Those guns have an effective range of maybe three kilometers. We put the *Sephiroth* down, offload you there, and get back up. You Humes can walk over to the castle and investigate all you want."

"What? Come on, Golgoras, I need a ranking djinn. They'll blow us to pieces otherwise."

"I'm not taking my ship into firing range until you confirm what's going on."

"How about we park the ship out of sight and all go? You are sort of honor bound to rescue Memmion, aren't you?"

"What do you mean park the ship?"

"We put it down on the ground with the power off and stealth tech on, so no one can find her."

"And leave her all alone?!"

"It's the fucking arctic! There's no one else here. Tenoch's men can keep watch. The rest of us wave a white flag and trek over."

Golgoras pulled him aside. "You want me to leave her unguarded with a bunch of drug dealers?" he asked in a furious whisper.

"Can't you lock it up or something? They're hardly going to fly off with it themselves... you think just anyone can fly a djinn airship?"

"Humph, that's true."

"You can take your charts with you. That thing is useless without your charts."

"Pfft."

"Look, Tenoch's signed a contract with you. He needs your help to move his cargo. I explained how you guys are about contracts. Trust me when I say that these men are not going to mutiny in any way. I don't think Tenoch wants to be hunted down by djinn lawyers for the rest of his life."

"Just as well."

"So we going?"

"Give them landing instructions, Roger," Golgoras said. "Keep it stealthy."

Roger took two hours to stow the ship, and they spent a further hour getting rigged out in snow boots, parkas, and walking sticks, plus ancient-looking backpacks with wooden frames, filled with a variety of camping gear, including tents, bedrolls, and a lot of expired canned food.

The expeditionary party was Rais, Maria, and Roger, none of whom had ever trekked over ice, all three of them in fact having a strong aversion to nature in general. Luckily Golgoras was an inveterate explorer of remote, hostile places and had, for reasons unknown, spent some years living in Antarctica. He was the windbreaker, plowing a furrow through the ice with his field, smoothening the path. It was a three-kilometer trek over fairly level ground, theoretically an hour's worth of serious walking for Rais and Roger, and hardly a fifteen-minute workout for Maria, who clocked four minutes a kilometer easy at the gym.

It actually took them over three hours to close the distance. The air was thin, sucking out oxygen from their lungs, and the temperature bitterly cold, and the ground deceptively slippery. The packs were awkward and heavy, and they were forced to take frequent breaks. The dreadnought loomed over them, seeming to take up half the sky, the pounding of the guns far from comical this close. Feigning unconcern, Rais was all too conscious of the fact that they were now within range, and any of the airship crew could pick them off if they were so inclined. Fortunately he always carried a white flag in his kit, and he was now flying this as high as he could. Other than Maria's knife, they were conspicuously unarmed, even Golgoras giving up several of his choice weapons, although an unarmed djinn was an oxymoron, as the field was his chief weapon, and the captain packed a powerful distortion ability.

This close, it was unmistakable that the ship was besieging the castle. The cannonballs rippled the force field with each salvo, sometimes making it falter, but it was holding for now. It was a peculiar, lonely siege, just the ship and the castle, two monolithic structures playing out a lifeless game.

When they crossed the final rise, directly in the shadow of the great ship, they saw the most incongruous sight. There were no trenches in this battlefield, no army of men, or guns, or horses. The ground operation seemed to consist of a few yurts and a campfire with a number of folding deck chairs. From this distance, if Rais was not mistaken, the attacking army appeared to be lounging around the fire smoking and drinking.

"Memmion!" Golgoras huffed, as they staggered into the perimeter. "What the hell is going on?"

Rais, following on his heels, saw an enormously fat djinn turn toward them. He was, indeed, smoking a hookah and had one paw wrapped around a priceless bottle of Lucien Foucauld 1847 Cognac. Sitting beyond him was Elkran, Beltrex, and, at the end of the line, an old lady djinn smoking a cigar and carrying a formidable-looking revolver. They all seemed remarkably hearty for victims of kidnapping. There was an empty chair in the middle.

"Pilot," Memmion rumbled. "And emissary. Welcome to our siege. We had bets placed on when you would finally catch up." He made a face. "I lost."

"Catch up? You knew we were coming?" Golgoras asked.

"Of course. Nothing takes flight without my knowledge," Memmion said loftily. "Although hearing you brag incessantly about the speed of the *Sephiroth*, I'm surprised it took you this long..."

"Well, to think we've been tearing after you for days, racking our brains on how to rescue you." Golgoras was getting peeved now.

"Rescue?" Memmion looked puzzled.

"Excuse me, Memmion, Beltrex, Elkran, er, lady djinn," Rais said, stepping forward into the fire, not least because he was freezing. "Were you not, in fact, kidnapped by Matteras?"

"Eh?" Memmion asked.

"What the devil is he saying?" Beltrex, hard of hearing, asked the ancient-looking lady djinn.

"Apologies, emissary." Something nightmarish came out of the yurt. He was burned black, the skin split and riven with great bloody trenches, a careless spray of blood mist clouding him, eyes shining through it all with manic intelligence. The wounds were raw, everything about him an elongated, pent-up scream. His legs were wrong, the shin bones inverted and much too long, so that he strode forward with the gait of Pan, a gunslinger's walk, and too soon he was inside the circle, staring down with amusement at Rais. "It is I, in fact, who kidnapped them."

"Who the devil are you?" Rais asked, rapidly losing equilibrium.

The burned djinn smiled. "Why, I believe I *am* the devil. One of them, in any case. Givaras the Broken, at your service."

It would be churlish to say that Golgoras fainted, for he did no such thing. He only staggered a bit, enough that Rais had to prop him up.

"You're supposed to be underground," the pilot said, his mechanical eye rotating wildly.

"Ah, yes, I escaped," Givaras said. "And seeing the state of the world, I felt it necessary to call my... more mature brethren for a gathering."

"Givaras!" Rais shouted. "You were in the murder pit? My cousin, ten years ago. Was he there with you? What happened to him?"

"Ah, you are then the emissary Kaikobad's nephew," Givaras said. "Your cousin indeed joined me. Indelbed, he was called. A skinny little boy. He survived for a long time. He died just days ago, while we were trying to escape. I am sorry."

Rais slumped. "He was alive all this time? How did he die?"

"Why, I believe he burned."

"Did he suffer?"

"No, I don't think he did."

"Did you kill him?"

"Strange to say, I did not. I taught him. I enrolled him as my apprentice. I was fond of him. He spoke to me much, about your mother, Juny, for example, and your uncle Sikkim. He thought you all hated him and had sold him to the djinn," Givaras said.

"No one hated him," Rais said.

"We were escaping through core fire," Givaras said. "You see that I am hideously burned. I survived barely. He was destroyed instantly. I doubt if he even felt it."

Golgoras rounded on Memmion. "What are you all doing? Why haven't you restrained this criminal?"

"The situation has changed, pilot," Memmion said. "You would do well to pay attention."

"Beltrex, what the hell is going on?" Rais asked.

"What?"

"Oh, stop pretending to be deaf," Rais said. "We visited your vineyard, found the big gaping hole in your bunker. We thought Matteras had gotten to you. Clearly we were way off."

"Yes, right, Givaras here felt the need to pay us a visit." Beltrex scowled. "Why he couldn't take the front door is beyond me."

"I had no desire to announce myself to the world," Givaras said. "Considering I've spent the past eighty years in a prison, you can surely sympathize."

"But why on earth did you and Elkran go with him?" Rais asked. "I mean, I thought he was the most reviled, dangerous djinn to have ever existed..."

"Because he made some good points, boy," Beltrex said. "When you're as old as we are, well, nothing is black and white."

"Oh, stop your waffling, Beltrex," the lady djinn said. She looked at Rais with a toothless smile. "Beltrex was always a big coward. He'd never refuse Givaras in the flesh. I am Mother Davala, emissary, the Fury, Bringer of Vengeance, Sacker of Ancient Sumer and Babylon. Your spirit is weak. There is no fire in you. Kiss my hand and tremble before my majesty."

"He's trembling from boredom," Beltrex said with a snort.

"At least *I* am not a hypocrite," Mother Davala said. "*I* did not applaud and cheer when Matteras put Horus away in that murder pit."

"I didn't see you protesting much either, Davala," Beltrex said.

"I sent a strongly worded letter."

"Six months after."

Givaras looked at his army mournfully. "Such is the nature of my alliance," he said. "It's no wonder I keep losing."

"Mother Davala, an honor." Rais grinned. "Beltrex, I'm sure you're very brave. Can someone please tell me the rest of the story?"

"Givaras gathered Elkran and Beltrex. They came to me next," Memmion said in his deep basso. "Convinced me to get the big ship out. We came to pick up Kuriken, but as you can see, we were a bit late."

"I thought we came here to find Matteras," Maria said. "Where the hell is he?"

"Take a look." Memmion tossed a telescope her way. "Top of the tower."

Rais, Maria, and Roger took turns looking. There was a figure on top of the tower, nailed to a cross. On closer inspection, it turned out to be Kuriken. The expression on the djinn's face was one of priceless fury.

"Did Matteras do that?" Rais asked. "Is he mad?"

"No more than the rest of us," Memmion said.

"But they were allies... Kuriken wanted even more earthquakes than Matteras," Rais said.

"Matteras has plans beyond the simple desire to make living space," Givaras said. "You humans, unfortunately, are only a small part of the picture. In his thirst for knowledge, he has perhaps discovered certain essential truths about elder djinns that would lead him to consider Kuriken an enemy."

"Elder djinns?"

"The ancient ones," Givaras said, spreading his arms wide. "You see us here now, this haggard lot, alongside Kuriken on his tower and Bahamut in the sea. So few of us left."

Mother Davala snorted. "You mean so few of us answered your summons."

"Many are sleeping," Beltrex said, "or wandered far off the mortal path."

"You say Matteras is fighting *all* the elder djinn?" Golgoras asked. "By what mathematics is his auctoritas greater than Memmion's, or the Mother's or even Beltrex's, much less all of you combined? What can he hope to achieve?"

"You perhaps underestimate his following. I must inform you, pilot, that the Hub fell two days ago," Memmion said.

"Fell? To whom?"

"To the younger djinn, members of the so-called Creationist Party, in partnership with the Ageist Society."

"Nonsense, Memmion, I left the Hub barely a week ago. The steward was firmly in charge."

"He has since been defenestrated," Memmion said.

"Kemet has also fallen," Mother Davala said. "Hazard has taken the Great Pyramid. Karnak too is in the hands of the Isolationists."

Golgoras's eye telescoped alarmingly. "How can this be? Matteras is defying the Lore."

"He is perhaps not so orthodox as he once believed," Givaras said. He seemed to be enjoying a private joke.

"He has caught us unaware," Memmion said. "But we too have caught him out. He is locked in that castle, surrounded, far from aid."

"Surrounded?" Rais asked. "You guys maybe have the campfire surrounded. The castle looks far from worried."

"I could pound that thing into rubble!" Memmion shouted. "I have air superiority! I could separate that thing into atoms. No fortification exists in this world that can resist the *Sublime Porte!*"

"Yes, and unfortunately, Kuriken is nailed up on the roof. You would end up atomizing him as well," Givaras said. He looked at Rais. "As you can see, junior emissary, we are at an impasse. Matteras cannot leave the castle, and we cannot take it without destroying Kuriken. That field you see is being generated entirely by Matteras. Despite the claims of my old friend Memmion, I do not think we can win this battle very easily, even if we *were* to sacrifice the czar. Remember, of you all, I alone have faced something of his strength before."

"I have a weapon much stronger than any of you," Mother Davala said, patting the amphorae beside her. "And I'm not afraid to face that little runt."

"I could knock down his gate from here," Beltrex declared. He considered it for a bit. "At least dent it badly."

"Well," Mother Davala conceded, "it *is* a heavy gate."

"Well, you are lucky that I am here then," Rais said. "It seems like you need an emissary to negotiate a settlement."

"What?" Memmion snapped. "Negotiate with that upstart?"

"Why not?" Rais asked. "It looks like you're actually losing, to be honest."

"Yeah, guys," Maria said. "If you've lost the Hub and Kemet and all those weird places, won't Matteras's friends be on their way here soon? With like an army?"

"Winning and losing are immaterial to those of us who have lived for twenty thousand years," Mother Davala said. "For you antlike creatures, victory and defeat are absolute. What does it matter to us, who have seen thousands of such turns? One day we win, and one day we lose. It's all the same in the end. I've slept through twenty Matterases."

"Nonetheless, losses accumulate," Givaras said. "Thresholds are passed. And we are perhaps at a node of change. We must not sleep now. It would be a shame to wake up in a world not to our liking. Remember, Davala, that this has happened to us before."

"Matteras has nailed Kuriken to a cross," Memmion said. "You want to negotiate? Imagine the loss of dignatas!"

"What do I care about dignatas?" Givaras smiled. "What do any of us? Remember who we are, Memmion."

"Matteras despises humans," Memmion said. "What possesses you to believe he will pay any heed to an acting emissary? He's not even the real thing..."

"Ah yes, about that," Rais said. "My application was made under the patronage of Bahamut. I believe you djinns gathered here around this, um, siege command center are of sufficient auctoritas to ratify my full emissary status."

"Impossible to induct you without a sitting of the Celestial Court," Memmion said.

"There is precedence of a field promotion, in the case of dire need," Rais said.

"Beltrex?" Givaras asked.

"Battlefield promotion?" Beltrex frowned. "He is correct. There have been rare cases of such. We are more than sufficient to enforce such an act, even in Bahamut's absence."

"But he hasn't even fired a shot yet," Memmion objected. "What the devil are we promoting him *for*?"

"Well, I'm offering to walk into the castle. I notice you guys are keeping a fair distance."

"Field promotions normally occur *after* the heroic act."

"There might not be enough of him left to pin a medal to afterward," Maria pointed out.

"Fine, fine, whatever, we'll agree provisionally," Memmion said. He gave Maria a crafty look. "No saying what might happen to him, eh?"

"We will, of course, sign and seal the necessary paperwork before I act on your behalf," Rais said.

"Fine time for petty legalities..." Memmion groused.

Givaras smiled. "Well, you would hardly appoint an emissary who does not understand fine print."

"That's not all," Rais said. "While your ratification is extremely gratifying, I suspect it will not be enough. My dignatas, of course, is pitifully small. As emissaries go, I must rank as the lowest—"

"That's for sure," Memmion said.

"Well, you can hardly expect Matteras to take me seriously."

"That's what I've been saying! Even I do not wish to take you seriously," Memmion said. "We cannot increase your dignatas overnight, however; it's not our fault you've achieved so little."

"Actually, you can. I propose that each of you extend patronage to me. I will be the sponsored emissary of the entire collective here," Rais said.

"Preposterous!" Memmion shouted. "No human has served six masters at the same time!"

"That would make you the preeminent emissary in the world." Mother Davala laughed. "Clever, clever boy. Can it even be done?"

"It is most unusual," Beltrex said. "But I suspect Matteras himself has laid the precedence for this, when he conferred patronage on Dargoman. Bahamut has not formally started proceedings against Dargoman, so technically, even now, he is a man with two masters. The Creationist bloc pushed that through. Matteras can now hardly deny a further multiplication of his own logic."

"Shall I draw up the paperwork then?" Rais asked.

"Oh, rubbish," Memmion said. "Are we to give unlimited dignatas to this untested boy?!"

"Look, you're sending me in to certain death," Rais said. "If I manage to negotiate a settlement, I'll damn well have earned the dignatas."

"Imagine how much Matteras will hate this," Givaras the Broken said with a laugh. "I am inclined to agree. It has been years since I had an emissary."

"Matteras will almost certainly kill him," Mother Davala said. "The auctoritas will return to us."

"All right, all right, why not," Memmion said. "If all of you are so insistent on making this idiot famous."

"Puny-looking man," Mother Davala said. "Let us make bets on how long he will live. I say inside twelve hours."

"He's a good boy, I give him two days," Beltrex said.

"Thank you, Beltrex," Rais said.

"Two days? That's optimistic. He might not even survive the branding," Givaras said.

"The what?" Rais asked.

"Our marks," Givaras said. "Don't you know? You're going to be the first-ever man to carry the marks of six patron djinn. I'm sure it will be an interesting experience." He tossed him a piece of firewood. "Clean that off. You're going to need something to bite down on."

CHAPTER 49

The Six Million Tattoo Man

The branding was not interesting at all, it was just bloody painful. Each of the djinns had their own ritual, complete with exotic-looking stone chops threaded with power, pincers and stamps, intricate needlework, assorted acids, snake venom, and other nasty surprises. Mother Davala gave him peyote and Givaras some rare arctic frog slime, and this combination of strong hallucinogens, plus the tab of acid he kept saved for emergencies, lasted him well through the process.

By the time he gained any kind of lucidity, the worst of the damage was done. His entire torso was now covered in giant, elaborate marks, the djinn trying to outdo one another on his skin. Memmion, starting first, had etched a giant circle on his lower back, intersected by the symbol of ancient Mammon, a cross of stylized lines, and further embellished by his totem bull, an invisible sigil discernible only to djinn.

Beltrex and Elkran took one arm each, moving from shoulder to forearm and trailing lines to his wrists. Beltrex, who had once been called Barkan, the King of Carnelian and the Gold Castle, in the time of kings, carried for his sigil the planet Mercury, etched in blue, and the runes of thunder, and finally the mark of the city itself, long reduced to rubble. Elkran, who wore no honors, used merely the mark of the sword, a thin black blade that curled around Rais's arm.

Mother Davala took his stomach with her three-headed crone, flying snakes for hair, darkness seeping from it like a suppurating wound. Givaras the Broken took pride of place on his chest with the Eye of Horus, his ancient symbol, found etched on the stones of Egypt, on the secret bricks of freemasons everywhere, and the U.S. dollar. Lines of light radiated from it, visible when eyed askance, so that at an angle his chest shone like a star.

For Bahamut, they had left the prime real estate between the shoulder blades, the most favored place for the mark, and Givaras had traced a stylized snake symbol there. It was a dull thing, without runic power, for Bahamut himself would be required to bring it to life.

"You look like a biker," Maria said, when they finally let him go.

"Fucking djinn," Rais said. "I asked for it, I suppose. They could have made the tats smaller."

"Your mom's gonna freak," she said. "Are you seriously planning to walk into that castle?"

"I think I have to," Rais said.

"You know, you've become a lot braver than you used to be," Maria said.

"Don't worry, I'm scared shitless inside," Rais said. "And I've got a big white flag."

"You should take the knife," Maria said. "In case things go bad."

"I don't know how to use it," Rais said. "And anyway, Matteras has already started drowning Bengal. Even if I somehow killed him, we'd be fucked. We actually have to convince him to stop."

"So good luck then." Maria gave him a hug, halfway between friendly and something more, and it was time to go all of a sudden, even though his feet felt a hundred pounds each.

At a signal from Memmion, the guns of the *Sublime Porte* stilled, and silence filled the tundra. The quiet was beautiful. Rais had a last swig of Elkran's single malt, hoisted his flag as high as he could, and started the long walk. His body nicely numbed by drugs and the effects of six djinn brands, it was actually a pleasant trek, the permafrost blindingly white, devoid of human intrusion, much the same as it had been for a hundred thousand years.

As he got close the bands of power surrounding the castle made his hair stand up. The earth was scorched and pitted around the perimeter, despoiled by cannonballs and shrapnel.

Kuriken's home was made of stone, a medieval keep in the Turkic style, the merlons over two man heights in length, the ground in the approach subtly lowered, so that anyone standing at the base of the walls felt even smaller. Despite these impressive fortifications, it was clear that without the djinn force field, the guns of the dreadnought would indeed have reduced the keep to ruble. The real defense of the place was its splendid isolation, the sight lines for hundreds of miles, the runes crowded thick on the ground like a murder of crows, singing dire promises. Rais wondered how Matteras could possibly have taken Kuriken by surprise.

The gate was wood banded with iron, reinforced with a portcullis, both of which stayed resolutely shut as he approached. He could sense rather than see Matteras, studying him from the murder holes, possibly about to douse him in burning oil.

"Lord Matteras!" Rais shouted. "I come to parley, in accordance to the Conventions of War as laid out by the Sublime Emperor Ashoka. Such conventions stating that should a besiegement of a fortified area last beyond two cycles of the sun, a state of war can be said to exist between the parties, and as such all regular wartime conventions should apply." He then stripped to his waist, as advised by Givaras. The sunlight hitting him turned his body into a kaleidoscope.

After a few long moments, the field winked out, the portcullis rose halfway, and a small side door creaked open. Matteras stepped out, looking tired and irritated. Shielding the entire castle, and keeping Kuriken subdued, was no easy task, apparently.

"You again!" he snarled as he recognized Rais. "Am I never to be free of your accursed family?"

"I've come to negotiate," Rais began.

Matteras was staring at his chest, though, mesmerized by the Eye of Horus, the mark of the Broken leaking milky light.

"He's lives then?" the djinn asked quickly. "He got out?"

"Evidently, although I don't know the details."

"It's impossible," Matteras said, mostly to himself. "Impossible."

"He's the one who brought them all here."

Matteras stared at the distant airship. "How many have come?"

"Mother Davala, Beltrex, Elkran, and Memmion," Rais said. "And the Broken."

"And they have each given you their mark," Matteras said.

"I am therefore the Emissary Primus in this world, and I propose an arbitration—"

"You fool!" Matteras snarled. "They haven't sent you to arbitrate! You *are* the message. It is unheard of, for multiple elder djinn to patronize an emissary at the same time. Only an extreme unity of purpose would call for this, *a unity of purpose never before witnessed by our race.* Am I to consider myself that much of a threat?"

"I-I'm supposed to negotiate a cease-fire..." Rais stammered.

"They answer the call of Horus like dogs brought to heel," Matteras said. "Djinns who have not gathered in millennia lay siege to my door. They mark you and send you here. When has Memmion stirred from his sky house? When has the Old Hag Davala answered the call of the djinn? They are all but confirming what I have said exists: the conspiracy of the elders."

"What?"

"Think, *Emissary Primus*," Matteras said. "What are they doing here? Why oppose me with such verve? How have I done anything detrimental to djinnkind?"

"You did nail Kuriken to a cross," Rais said.

"He betrayed me," Matteras said. "Always talking, agreeing, instigating, never quite following through. Delaying, confusing, splitting the conservatives... Why? We are natural allies... his proclivities are well known. He has depopulated entire kingdoms in these northern lands. You call me a mass murderer, but Kuriken is *extinction* for humans. Why is *he* against me? Why is it that every time I want to do something, I am *forbidden by the fucking Lore*?"

"Look, I can understand you're feeling miffed," Rais said. "Why not have a sit-down? What can be the harm? If it fails, we can go back to pounding your castle for the next hundred years."

"I can grab that floating bag of gas Memmion is so proud of and smash it into the ground," Matteras said. "Elder djinn." He spat on the ground. "I piss on all of them."

"Yeah, he said the same thing about your castle," Rais said. "Look, I get the feeling we're all missing information here. Let's try to figure shit out. Fuck arbitration. Can we agree to meet at least? Your terms."

"They must disarm that flying monstrosity and come into the castle unarmed. You will give me Givaras. I will put him, along with Kuriken, in a negative field generator. We will meet in a room that is protected by two-thousand-year-old spells. Anyone twitches, and we are all vaporized. *Then* we talk," Matteras said. He laughed. "They will never agree."

"They don't have to. They've authorized me, even if in bad faith, and I will do my job," Rais said. "What agreements I make are binding on them. To say otherwise is to overthrow everything—the Celestial Courts, the Lore, the very idea of auctoritas."

Matteras shook his head. "You're woefully inadequate, emissary. But there is something relentless about you."

"How about this? We *all* come to the parley: humans, djinns, dogs, cats, our entire camp. You get one hostage. Not Givaras. He leads them, and I have a feeling he can clear up a lot of things for us," Rais said. "We're on your ground, we sit in your room; at the very least, it's a mutually destructive situation."

"You don't understand, emissary, you will learn nothing good from him. Givaras the Broken does not make anything better. Ever." Matteras rubbed his face. "I am tired of this. Fine, bring them. Let us have one last parley with each other."

Kuriken looked gray and withdrawn in the stasis chamber, swapping his cross for the dull iron clasps of the device. It was, ironically, his own invention, a negative generator that created a null space, devoid of the field, a slow death for djinn. Next to him was Elkran, who had drawn the short straw, except that Givaras had held the draw, and it was well known that he cheated. Always. Kuriken's field flickered on and off, a feeble pulse, trying to fight the debilitating effects of his prison. If the concord went on for too long, it was entirely possible that he would expire altogether. Elkran was the shadow of death, their best swordsman, but Givaras had not come here to fight. His sacrifice was symbolic.

Matteras sat alone on a raised chair, a throne in all but name. His face was strained, power kept tightly clenched, his outline smudged beneath the miasma of forces anchored to him, a virulent, reckless air about him. The room was thick with runes, ancient spells promising annihilation, and he held them on a hair trigger. They snapped like wild dogs at his feet, like wolves baying at the moon.

"Welcome to Kuriken's castle," Matteras said, when they sat before him. "Our host is indisposed. Apologies for the tepid welcome."

"He's going to be pissed when he gets out," Memmion said. He had brought his own chair, dragging it in one melon-size hand, trailing a furrow through the dust.

"Fuck him," Matteras said. "And fuck all of you."

"As charming as ever," Givaras said.

"Once again you enjoy my hospitality, Broken," Matteras said.

"I can't say that it has improved much," Givaras said.

"How did you get out?"

"I walked out wearing Risal. You should never have sent her to me."

"I thought you could use the company."

"Did you think that little bit of fire would hold me?"

"It has certainly improved your looks," Matteras said.

"These two will go on forever if we let them," Mother Davala said. "Get this thing started already, emissary."

"Right, ah, Matteras, we would like to propose a de-escalation," Rais said. "Let your hostages go, we declare a truce for twenty years and settle this in the courts. How about it, eh? Oh, and also kindly stop the earthquakes in the bay."

"What the hell for?" Matteras looked at his fellows. "Truce? Here are *my* terms. You so-called elder djinn surrender unconditionally. Givaras goes back into his bottle like a good fucking boy. I will flay this emissary so I can hang his skin on my flagpole. And Bahamut's little ruined city gets flattened. *Then* the rest of you can fuck off and do whatever you want, I've got no fight with you."

"Feisty little djinn, ain't he?" Memmion said admiringly.

"Now, Matteras, be reasonable," Rais said. "You've not got the auctoritas to fight all six of my masters. Your treatment of Kuriken alone will lose you half the conservative party."

"Will it?" Matteras asked. "Check again. I've already taken the Hub. The Great Pyramid of Giza is mine. Hazard is now laying waste to Mohenjo Daro as we speak. Bengal will soon drown. Lhasa is days from falling. And I occupy Kuriken's castle. It is not a question of *my* auctoritas, emissary. I can do whatever the fuck I want. It's a question of where exactly your pathetic group of patrons intend to hide when I allow them to leave here. Because let me assure you, there are none of the old places left."

"Lhasa too?" Memmion asked, aghast.

"The Ghuls have declared for me," Matteras said. "Turns out they're tired of being slaves to the Lore. A sentiment I can sympathize with. I will free them from service. Your precious airships can go hang."

"Beltrex, Beltrex," Givaras said. "How did things get so vulgar?"

"What? Taking Giza? Freeing Ghuls? Matteras, have you gone mad? You are unraveling the Lore, you fool!" Beltrex said.

"The Lore? I'm so fucking sick of the Lore. I started this because I just wanted a few acres of empty space. Every step I took, I hit Seclusion! Laws! Treaties! Ahimsa! The fucking Lore! Everything designed to make us smaller, to rein us in. You sneer at me and call me a conservative? *You* are the conservatives, sniveling old djinn hiding behind nonsensical traditions. I am the divine wind. I am the scourge of God! If you won't give me space, then I'll make my own. I'll scour this fucking earth of man."

"That's not quite true though, is it, Matteras?" Rais asked.

"Shut your mouth, you insignificant shit!" Matteras said.

"He is our ambassador," Givaras said. "And as such, he speaks for us. Do you think I came here empty handed? I would let him continue, if I were you."

"He will not leave this place bearing that title," Matteras said. "And I do not fear you, Broken."

"You fear me more than anything else in this world, boy."

"You say you wanted space, isn't that right?" Rais said, interjecting hastily. "That's the party line. Living space. Go back to the way things were. Make room for those endless vistas you djinn love so much. Except you had some personal stake in it. Something in Bengal was bothering you. How do I know? Bahamut told me."

"What is he prattling on about?" Beltrex asked irritably.

"Hush," Givaras said. "This is interesting."

"Bahamut is a school of fish," Matteras said. "He hasn't spoken to anyone in five hundred years."

"I know, I visited him," Rais said. "I accidentally rammed the pillar of Gangaridai. There was a mark there, a serpent eating its own tail, a rough circle. It looked familiar. I thought it was his sign. Later, at your Assembly, I caught a look at Dargoman's arm. His mark has faded, but it's still visible. I guess those things never really go away. It's close, but not quite the same, is it? Bahamut's mark is more like a horizontal infinity sign. The serpent crosses over itself in a figure eight."

"What of it?" Matteras asked.

"I remember, long ago, seeing my cousin's back. Kaikobad marked him, you know. We all thought it was Bahamut's mark, that he was drunk and desperate, trying to protect him with patronage. But that wasn't it. He marked him with the sign of Gangaridai. Why? Why would he put the mark of the First Empire on his son?"

"What hubris," Matteras said. "Kaikobad was never humble. What relevance is it, this touching story of your damned family?"

"It's your family too, though, isn't it? Indelbed was your nephew."

"Djinn do not have human kin."

"Well, that's not true either, is it?" Rais asked. "I think there was a time when djinn did indeed have human kin. Sometime before the war. Bahamut told me where to look."

"Bahamut seems to have said a lot of things, for a fish," Givaras said.

"Probably lonely down there—no visitors, you know," Beltrex said.

"There are no records left of the Great War," Rais said. "No documents, no history books. Strange. Someone else was interested. Risal. She disappeared too. She was in the murder pit with Givaras. Right?"

"She was, for a brief period," Givaras said. "Rather confused, really, on what she was doing there."

"She must have been," Rais said. "She didn't perhaps appreciate the full implications of her research. I think Kaikobad was the instigator in all of this, once he got involved. She had the evidence, though, a collection of books on the war, including the *Register of Kings*. It was probably the last surviving copy. Destroyed now, of course."

"She also had the *Compendium of Beasts*," Beltrex said.

"I know, I sent it to her," Givaras said. "She asked for it. I must confess, I did not realize why at the time."

"I had Kaikobad's notes, but they were almost gibberish. I had her journal, which gave small hints. I read the *Compendium*, which is what must have inspired her research in the first place," Rais said. "It was like looking at a picture just out of focus."

"You are building castles in the air, Emissary Primus," Matteras said.

"Risal must have found something," Rais continued. "Something about the Great War, which she was researching, except all of her sources and all of her notes were gone. It made me think about my cousin. Kaikobad knew something, and Risal knew something, and my cousin did not know anything, yet you went out of your way to take him—so it must have been something intrinsic about him. Kaikobad marked him with a *royal seal*.

"So maybe he was telling us that Indelbed was from the line of Gangaridai. *Your* line. What are you, Matteras? What blood do you carry in your veins? What did they find out about you? Something from long ago, something from the war, because no one recalls it, no one knows, no one wants to talk about it."

"Except me," Givaras the Broken said.

"Givaras the Broken," Rais said, "fortuitously returned to us. And what, Givaras, can you tell us about the ancestors of Matteras?"

"It is whispered behind his back that he is a bastard from the line of ancient Gangaridai. His ancestors were kings," Givaras said.

"Kings," Rais said. "Anathema to djinns. And I have heard those rumors too, from Golgoras and others. Matteras, the bastard son of Gangaridai, that most reviled royal line."

"So edifying, your concern about my ancestry," Matteras said. "This old canard has been used to beat me for millennia. Matteras, a bastard remnant of the royal line. I do not care."

"But what Kaikobad found was even more alarming, wasn't it?" Rais said gently. "Risal ran some very expensive tests on someone's DNA. As Roger will explain to you in greater depth, mutations carried on the Y chromosome are patrilineal, used to track male lines of descent. I found her musings on it, hidden in her journals, but the tests were so old I couldn't track down the lab that did them. Luckily, Roger could decipher her findings."

"Right, ah, Your Excellencies," Roger said. "The subject appeared to have standard djinn tetraploidy. Mitochondrial DNA did not show anything unusual. The Y haplogroup was part of the hypothetical R2D subclade, the primary characteristic of which is for the subject to produce both haploid and diploid sperm, a most unique mutation. Logically, it is the gene permitting human-djinn interbreeding."

"The Nephilim," Givaras said.

Matteras had grown stark. "The Nephilim are a myth. Djinn and human do not produce viable offspring."

"That is untrue," Rais said. "Risal and Kaikobad tested a sample. I tested Kaikobad, Barabas, and myself. Kaikobad has the R2D subclade, the so-called Nephilim gene. So do I. It runs in our family. Barabas is a tetraploid, but guess what? He also carries the R2D subclade. What's good for the goose is good for the gander. Once a Nephilim male breeds with a pure-blooded djinn, the R2D gene gets into the bloodline, and according to the rules of Y chromosome mutations, *all* future male heirs will carry it. What an advantage, though—in theory, every male offspring would be able to mate with both humans and djinn."

"Half-breed offal," Matteras spat. "Abominations. Misshapen creatures."

"My cousin was perfectly normal, as you know. The question is, who did Risal test? The subject had tetraploid DNA with the R2D subclade. You see, at first I thought it was Indelbed. Kaikobad has the R2D subclade, it would make sense his son having it. His mother was a djinn, so he'd be tetraploid, exactly what Risal found. But why test Indelbed? They already knew he was hybrid. No, it was *you*. They tested *you*. The son of kings. The most powerful djinn in the world. Tell me, Givaras, who was Matteras's great ancestor?"

"It was the last High King of Gangaridai."

"And who exactly was the last king of Gangaridai?"

"The Nephilim Kartiryan, the so-called Master of Time. It was all in the royal book, but the original *Register of Kings* was destroyed after the cataclysm. Republican fervor, you know," Givaras said. "Risal must have found a copy."

"You lie! Traitor! Father of lies! You mean to say some human filth was the High King of the First Empire? What djinn would believe you?" Matteras snapped.

"Me? Oh no, poor boy." Givaras spread his arms toward his fellows. "Memmion. Bahamut. Davala. Beltrex. Elkran. Kuriken. We can all bear witness. We were all there. We all fought the war."

"Some of us more than others," Mother Davala said, glowering at Beltrex.

"You are, as I have known from the start, the trueborn descendant of the Nephilim Kartiryan, High King of Gangaridai, and his queen, the Empress-elect of Lhasa," Givaras said. "Heir to the Throne of Ruin. If the empire stood, you would right now be High King Matteras Kartiryan, the royal union of djinn and man."

"Cheer up, Matteras," Rais said. "Your worst fears are realized. But at least you're not a bastard."

CHAPTER 50

Requiem of the Great War

Rolling shock waves scattered them like chess pieces falling helter-skelter off an upturned board. The room reacted viscerally to Matteras's rage, pressure fronts of expanding spells hitting each other with the reek of cordite, enormous flagstones plowing into the air, turning to dust, killing light spawning in the walls. Kuriken spilled free from his iron maiden and lay prone on the ground at an awkward angle. Something struck Memmion in the chest, hard enough to send him groaning back, turning his deck chair to kindling. In the center of the conflagration, barely visible behind layers of power, Matteras roared his fury like a maddened bull.

It seemed to Rais that they would all die, that the entire structure would be obliterated in a moment, and the spells would run loose, tearing up the ground and sky around them, perhaps not stopping until the whole world burned. He could believe now that these djinns had once wrecked the earth. Through the veil of smoke, he saw Givaras stand up, those peculiar legs braced against the pressure, and the Eye of Horus opened on his forehead, streaming clean white light like a crystal, and there was a momentary cessation of everything.

"Enough! Matteras, stop this tantrum. We have much more to speak of! Do you think I have roused all the elder djinn to ruminate on your bloodline? There are more critical things to do!"

"As ever, you poison all that you touch," Matteras said from behind his screen.

Yet the words brought him back, and Rais watched in astonishment as he somehow pulled everything inside him, his indistinct form swallowing the appalling forces unleashed, lines of power folding like origami into his body. For the first time, Rais appreciated the enormous energies Matteras commanded, why he was the foremost of the djinn. His threats were not idle.

Mother Davala, momentarily upturned, righted herself. "Temper, temper, Matteras," she cackled with bleeding gums. She patted her amphorae. "You don't want to upset the little wolf in here."

"Mock me again, witch," Matteras said. He was still inside a dark nimbus, the air literally humming around him. Something forked out of his hand and struck her square, sending her skittering back. He clasped his hands together and the darkness tightened around him into a ball. His field was an entirely opaque sphere now, luminous black, gravid, all the more frightening for being so tightly controlled.

"Matteras! Stop!" Rais shouted, getting up off his knees. "Please..."

Matteras stared at him. "You've had your fun, emissary, but I think you are done. Perhaps the Nephilim really existed. Perhaps I am tainted with human blood. To separate the truth from the lies of Givaras is beyond even me. If I am to be an outcast, so be it, I accept my fate. I will at least do one last service to djinnkind. These ancient monsters have plagued us for too long." He called to the captain. "Golgoras. We are on differing sides, but with you, at least, I have common ground. Tell the others what these elders have wrought. Say that I killed them for the good of us all. My only regret is that I will not be able to finish Bahamut. The fate of djinnkind I leave to the rest of you."

"Matteras!" the Maker said.

"Enough words, Broken."

The black ball was palpably gaining mass now, keening, buckling the walls of the castle itself. Gravity gave out, bits and pieces started floating up. Something struck the Eye of Horus, and it winked out.

"Matteras!" Rais shouted. "It's not what you think. You're not the only one! Think about it. *Barabas had the Nephilim gene.* Let me test Golgoras. I will bet you anything that he has it too. You're all like this. Don't you see? He did it to all of you. *You're all half-breeds.* Ask him."

The roaring ceased for a second. "Tell me, Givaras, *what have you done?*"

Givaras was dusting himself off, picking up his chair.

"Maker of Broken Things, what have you done?"

"It was war." Givaras shrugged. "We were desperate. The world was destroyed, covered in ice. Do you know how close we were to extinction? How few of us were left?"

"So you widened the gene pool," Rais said.

Givaras nodded. "Our population was too small. Unlike these imbeciles, I at least understood evolution. There was no time for Creationist rubbish.

We would have lasted a few generations at most, if we had kept to the old ways. I gathered what Nephilim remained, and I bred them with djinnkind, and when they had offspring, I killed the defective ones and then bred the healthy ones with Nephilim once again. Over and over. I fucking bred them like brood mares, and I marked the bloodlines."

"The minor hunt!" Rais said. "That's where it came from! It never made sense to me..."

"Yes, that was one of my traditions." Givaras smiled fondly. "There were only a few of us left, after Gangaridai. We had to change everything, to re-make ourselves, to survive. Beltrex wrote the laws and the Lore. His new creed was the sanctity of life. We could not afford to lose a single healthy djinn. Elkran wrote the Code Duello, and we fought to first blood rather than to the death like before. Memmion made the clubs. There would be no more empires, no more kings, ever again. We could not afford the bloodshed. We chose Seclusion and left the business of conquest to humans. Emissary, I have watched your kind spill each other's blood for the past ten thousand years with immense satisfaction."

"What happened to the Nephilim?" Rais asked.

"What do you think?" Givaras said. "The Nephilim became the emissar-ies. We kept the bloodlines tied to us, our ambassadors to the human world. You are the Nephilim, boy, the children of kings."

"Everything is a lie then," Matteras said softly. "You broke us in truth."

"I *saved* you," Givaras said. "Hybrid vigor, Matteras. Do you not see how much stronger you are because of it? There was no other way."

"You bred us like rats," Matteras said. "We are not the chosen people; we are the offal left from some war you lost. Are there no pure-blooded djinn left?"

"Just us few," Givaras said. "The last who answered my call."

"You make me sick. This abomination you have made of us... it's better that we end it all. If we were to die, you should have let us die. But no, Bro-ken, you must always meddle, always cheat. I am sick of it. This is my final judgment. I will yank the iron core out of this earth, Givaras. I swear, I will end *all* life on this planet, beyond even your power to fix," Matteras said. "If you somehow survive, as no doubt you will, you can float in space with the rubble. Do you doubt I can live up to my word?"

"I do not. You have always had that power," Givaras said with something approaching pride. "Don't you see? You are the culmination of twenty thou-sand years of breeding. You are our weapon, our hope for the future. Destroy the world? No, you were made to save it."

"What?"

"The Great War is not over, Matteras. We are fighting it still and have been for the past twenty thousand years."

"With whom?" Matteras asked. "Who is this great enemy? Or have you imagined all of this? For I see no enemy here other than you."

"The enemy is High King Kartiryan and the djinn lords of Gangaridai," Givaras said, "as they have always been. Let me tell you the story of the First Empire of Djinn and Man. Yes, djinn and Nephilim ruled together. There was not such a gulf between our races then. It was their opinion, those proud lords of Gangaridai, the eternal kings, that they had built the perfect city. They wished to preserve it and indeed to preserve their hegemony of the known world. Alas, time moved against them, even the long-lived djinn, for whom centuries were like single nights. Still, they were happy enough with their rule. Then came the Nephilim Kartiryan, a master magician. He could swim in time as a fish swims in water. He saw far into the future, to a time when the empire would decay and their city crumble. This was not to their liking. Kartiryan and the chosen djinn, the High Lords of the First Empire, made a pact to stop time itself. They would have this world remain static, unchanging, untouched by what men call entropy."

"It was so," Memmion said, sitting upright on the floor, panting in huge gasps. "He speaks the truth."

"It was a horror. What they proposed was to rule the world not for a day, or a year, or a millennia, but *forever*, unchanging. This was irreversible. We would have been like flies trapped in amber. We resisted, naturally. To change is to decay, yes, but it is also to evolve. They believed that we had been created perfect. I argued the truth: that we had evolved, just as all other life; that we were changing, even with our longevity. I saw what we might become far into the future, something wondrous, something vast and powerful. They would throw that away for their beggar's alms, their petty kingships. So we fought, the first war of ideology, the Great War, and there was no place on the sidelines. Kemet fought for us, and the scattered folk of Mohenjo Daro, already destroyed by the hubris of kings. The world was sparse then, the djinn spread far and wide in lonely places, yet they came to fight, for or against, and we carried the battle to all the places Nephilim and djinn could reach.

"In the end, in the final battle, only five of us came—"

"Six!" Mother Davala said.

"Six," Givaras said with a bow. "Davala of the Furies, Bahamut, Memmion, Beltrex, Elkran, and I. So few, those who came to the walls of Gangaridai, and we laid siege, and with us were remnants of the Nephilim and their human hosts, so few, so pitiful. Yet the enemy we faced were even more pitiful, weakened by fighting and desertion. Kartiryan was determined to hold and threatened to destroy the world if he could not have it.

"We fought then, in the final battle on the plains of the Eternal City, the greatest warriors left alive, the champions of men and djinn. You look at me mockingly, Matteras, but you must remember that we were then in the full flush of our power, not old and diminished as we are now. Memmion wore gold, and when he fought he faced the sun so that his reflection blinded all those who stood before him. Bahamut was leviathan; his shadow darkened the ocean so that men cried in terror, thinking he had swallowed all light. Elkran was a sliver of flame, so quick you could not see him, his sword longer than the height of a man, and it was the whisper of death, a feather touch that would kill you. Beltrex, gentle Beltrex, fought with a hammer that could crack the earth, that could change the course of entire rivers with one blow. He smashed mountains and made valleys out of hills. And Davala fought with us, not the crone you see today, but the maiden, beautiful, yes, like the North Star, and terrible, our voice of vengeance, driving madness before her."

"You have left out yourself, Maker," Matteras said, "from this roll of honor."

"I was as you see me now. Yet still I fought and stood when those greater than me fell. You measure by power, Matteras, and I by will. We shall see, in the end, which one is stronger.

"Let me finish. In the end, Kuriken saw sense. He was the First Knight, keeper of the gate, their most fearful warrior. He had killed many hundreds of djinn and thousands of Nephilim. His armor was white, like the northern lands he cherished, blessed with ancient spells, so that no weapon could touch him, and in sunlight, his power waxed and he shone like a star. His spear was made of asteroid metal, the head unbreakable, invested with such power that no armor or shield could block it. While he fought, Gangaridai could never fall. You cannot imagine the terror of Kuriken. He would beggar the power of your princes today. Day and night, he called for us to face him in battle, desperate to finish us, and we avoided him. Finally, I answered."

"Let me guess," Rais said. "You cheated."

Givaras nodded. "You begin to understand me, emissary. He came with his arms, his invincible force, and I came with the broken things I had made. I showed him what we were."

"The *Compendium of Beasts*."

"They call me Maker. They do not know how I got that name. It was on that day. The field is what makes us djinn. So I gave the field to other things. I made *djinns*, and I showed him, and he could no longer deny the truth: that we are all lost, wandering on the same path, nothing special, no divinity, no destiny but what we make for ourselves, no nobility other than what we claim, frail things cast adrift, ghosts in truth, awaiting some cosmic turn to wipe us off the board. At first he wept, yet I showed him the comfort in that, for we could make of ourselves as *we* willed, we could fight *for ourselves*, we could cheat our future. Free will comes at a price, but it is still beautiful."

"He threw down his arms, you know," Memmion said. "Though they called him a coward afterward, it was the bravest thing I ever saw. Just cut off his armor and walked away, and no one dared hit him in the back, even though he was naked and vulnerable."

"When he left, Gangaridai fell in spirit. They were lost," Givaras said.

"So you won. The First Empire is long turned to dust, as the songs say, their city in ruins in the bay," Matteras said. "The emissary saw it himself."

"He saw a pillar," Givaras said. "Let us speak plainly. You think that Gangaridai was destroyed. It was not. It was removed from this plane by the enemy. They did not like defeat, so they decided to remove their precious city from this timeline—from time itself—and preserve their miserable lives until a more propitious hour downstream. Their magic cracked the earth, ushering in the age of ice. On the eve of victory, we were scattered far and wide, and for centuries, it seemed as if life itself would not survive. Kartiryan did that, in a ritual with twelve High Lords of the Djinn, the so-called Horologists. By the time we recovered, the ocean had reclaimed even the last ruins of the city. Yet the real Gangaridai lives in the other world, untouched, beyond our sight, waiting. They will return one day and test us once again. If you destroy everything, Matteras, they will win. Time means nothing to them. They will wait and return to a fresh new world to despoil."

"And where is the evidence of this fairy tale?" Matteras asked.

"Why, at the bottom of the sea. They left a gate behind when they sunk the bay, the last road left to Gangaridai, the Charnel Road, made with the bones and flesh of djinn and men," Givaras said. "It was one door, one way back for them. Bahamut barred it with blood. That lock has been weakening over time. Something has been trying to get out. Do you think he enjoys being a fish? He has spent the last ten millennia guarding it. We owe him a debt far greater than all the dignatas in this world."

"Bahamut," Matteras spat. "We will go visit him to determine the truth of this. I will see with my own eyes this dread road."

"We will go," Givaras said. "Your disruption of the earth's mantle has weakened the seals further. Bahamut will need our help. See for yourself what you have wrought."

CHAPTER 51
Return of the Dragon

Boss Kid cycled up to the barricade, pulling a vegetable cart. This was essentially a three-wheeler with a flatbed on the back, loaded up with baskets of fresh produce. He had nothing suspicious, but Abdul recognized him at the check post and stopped him.

"You're the kid from the pump." Shotguns swiveled on him. Juny's men were alert and well trained, all of them ex-military.

"Supply short," Boss Kid said. "We selling vegetables now. Whole cart for the big house. Cheap cheap."

"He's telling the truth, Abdul," one of the guards said, touching everything. He was a fatty.

"Check it all."

They tore apart his stacks, then the baskets, and even checked the underside of his cart.

"What's this?" Abdul was staring at the urn, carefully nestled inside a bunch of cauliflowers.

"Mustard oil," Boss Kid said. "From my village. Best stuff. Make *tehari*."

Fatty rattled the urn and then took a deep sniff. "It's mustard oil, all right. Let him through, Abdul, we can tell the cook to make *tehari*."

"Go with him, drop the load in the kitchen, and walk him back," Abdul said. "Keep an eye on him."

"He's just a kid," Fatty said.

"He's a drug dealer," Abdul said. "Go."

They went around the back to the kitchen entrance. The mad cook from before had been replaced with Juny's own. The little veranda in front of the kitchen door, where all the peeling was done, was much cleaner now. There was a little TV there for the kitchen staff. A couple of women were making ginger and garlic paste with mortars and pestles. Boss Kid unloaded everything in front of them. The cook watched for a while and silently approved the shipment. Boss Kid handed him the bill and sat on his haunches in one corner. He would wait for the money. He set the urn down carefully on the floor beside him. When no one was looking, he unstoppered the mouth and put the mustard-soaked cloth in his pocket. In a soft whisper, the urn started to talk.

Indelbed stepped out without breaking the urn. He had been practicing. He was good at folding space now. He had stuffed over a hundred bodies in there during the past month. The smell of the house hit him hard, brought him down to one knee. He was in the kitchen. Everything was different, everything seemed the same. The mad cook was gone, fired or retired. This new one wore a smart uniform and even a hairnet. One of the sous chefs saw him and screamed, her ginger-flecked hand going to her mouth. She came at him with her kitchen knife, a big, circular scythe-like device used to slice herbs and vegetables.

Indelbed threw a fist of air at her, and she rattled against the door. The cook threw a pot at him and ran from the kitchen, sandals slapping flat-footed against the floor. Indelbed stepped into the center of the room, and the lines of spells shimmered in the walls and across the floor, runes overlaid on one another. They converged thick upon him, snakes of ink suddenly woken up, sniffing him, humming with lethal intent. He stood still and let the script crawl over him, the constructs like little spiders, and they remembered at last who he was and let him go.

It was like walking through soup. Every step was crowded. His senses were overwhelmed by the lines of power crisscrossing everywhere, layers upon layers of protection. He touched the walls as he walked; they were cleaner now, less damp, freshly painted. Whoever lived here was taking care of the place.

"Good kitchen," Boss Kid said, evaluating the appliances with a professional eye. "All new."

"We only had the gas stove and an old fridge," Indelbed said. "Someone rich lives here now."

The cook had been making beef curry. An enormous pot was still simmering on the industrial six-burner stove, a gleaming chrome hood whirring away above. The smell was intoxicating. Boss Kid opened the lid and had a taste.

"It's good."

"We never had this much meat in the kitchen," Indelbed said. "It was mostly rice and dal. On Eid, I remember, everyone would send raw meat, and the mad cook would make a feast. Our freezer never worked well, so she'd cook it all up, and we'd eat it like kings for however many days it lasted."

"Khan Rahman all rich," Boss Kid said with contempt. It was a well-known fact that all Khan Rahmans were loaded.

"Not us," Indelbed said. "But yeah, the others were."

"You had big house," Boss Kid said. "You had cook. You rich."

"I guess, if you put it that way."

"Better than pipe."

They walked up a winding passage, past an abandoned sitting room, on toward the front of the house. This was the corridor to the dining room, the floor worn by thousands of trips by Butloo and the cook carrying food and dishes back and forth, a window with mismatched glass letting in some daylight. It was still grimy, less so than before. Someone had taken a scrubbing brush to the walls and floor, trying to eradicate years of careless footfalls, relocating several tribes of spiders.

There were circular scuff marks all along the walls, from when Indelbed had spent months practicing batting, Butloo slow bowling at him for hours on end with a taped tennis ball. His ambition that year had been to break into the national cricket team. Indelbed traced his fingers along the wall at waist height, remembering the line they had drawn in pencil. Balls hit over the line were considered caught out.

"We broke the window once, playing cricket," Indelbed said. "I thought my father would kill me, but he said he had done the exact same thing when he was a boy. Grandfather had thrashed him, apparently. Most of the time he was drunk, you know, but that time he was great."

"At least you had father," Boss Kid said. "Better than nothing."

They reached the end of the corridor, and he could hear people in the dining room, the cook babbling to someone, the sound of booted feet. Boss Kid crouched behind him, wielding a kitchen knife. Indelbed opened the door and got a shotgun blast in the chest. It was buckshot, twenty-seven round balls per shell, and they hit him at almost point-blank range, dropping him. He scrambled to his feet, and pellets hammered into his back like bits of molten lava. He gasped, trying to crawl back into the corridor, Boss Kid already retreating. It was Fatty from the gate. He didn't look so comical now. He followed Indelbed, continuing to fire, peppering the mosaic with shots, hit and miss, until the barrel was barely two feet from his head.

"It's my house," Indelbed said, turning. "Mine. You have no right!" He grabbed the barrel and pulled, yanking the gun away, and opened his mouth to shout, but what came out was a gout of fire, and the man's face just melted off, crusting black like the edges of barbecued meat.

Indelbed stood up, and the bits of shot fell off his body, his scales rustling back into place, the little dents smoothening out. The buckshot had only bruised him. The body thrashed before him, and the room filled with oily black smoke, the smell of roasting flesh. Boss Kid went over, looting Fatty for weapons. He got the shotgun, which was a shortened double-barrel pump action, a riot gun, but still almost more than his arms could manage. There was a bandolier of cartridges, which he looped twice around his shoulders.

The great table was on fire, slowly starting to sag in the middle. Indelbed noticed that someone had replaced the old chairs with a matching set. No doubt Juny had grand dinners here with actual food. Perhaps she laughed at the Doctor, at how badly he had got things wrong. He felt a surge of hatred for her. What right had she to get rid of his furniture? Indelbed had liked those mismatched chairs.

"You spat fire," Boss Kid said. "Why you no say you do that?"

"What? Oh. It just happened."

Boss Kid was wrapping a napkin around his mouth and nose. "We could have burned this house from the outside," he said. "Now we in it when it falls."

"We have to go upstairs," Indelbed said. "The djinn is up there. I can feel him."

Boss Kid shrugged. "You go first. You bulletproof."

They found the living room deserted, doors open. Everyone had run. It was crowded in here, furnished with desks and chairs like an office, computers, cell phones, and thick files everywhere.

"They running business here," Boss Kid said, impressed. "Big Khan Rahman business."

Indelbed frowned. "Strange place to have an office," he said. "Back in the day, none of the family would ever be caught dead coming here."

Boss Kid was rummaging through the files, looking for cash. "You want to take papers?" he asked.

"What's the point?" Indelbed asked with a cracking laugh. "Neither of us can read." *I can't read anymore, Givaras you bastard. You know how hard it was to get my father to teach me how to read? I'm going to eat your eyes when I find you.*

He looked around the office—all these signs of industry, the whitewash on the walls, something wholesome in the air, as if cleansing light had been streamed into every dark crevice—and felt an odd sense of dislocation, that perhaps he should put down his tools and walk away from this venture, that despite his earnest ten-odd years of longing, the house had grown up in his absence and moved away from previous delinquent childishness. This place felt adult, mature, imbued with an optimistic esprit de corps that had been lacking in their little domestic triangle of master, son, and servant.

He almost left then, almost called off this fight. It was affection for the house itself, regret that he had already set fire to the dining room, causing damage the place could ill afford. Unfortunately, Boss Kid was made of sterner stuff. His laser focus was on the mission, and he had no compunction about setting fires or shooting people. To him, vengeance was a sacred duty; slights had to be answered, cosmic ledgers balanced—this was the code he lived by, and he could not fathom hesitation or ambivalence.

Propelled by Boss Kid, they climbed the stairs side by side, Indelbed leaning on the boy because he still couldn't do stairs properly, couldn't judge depth at all. They got as far as the landing and paused, as Indelbed tried to bolster his faltering courage. He could hear them talking upstairs, the djinn and some woman. Juny? The djinn reeked power, giving off waves of distortion that he could clearly see, and his stomach clenched in atavistic fear.

"Something got past the wards," the woman was saying.

"I can feel him," the djinn said. "It's not any djinn I ever met. It feels like some kind of beast."

"Beasts don't break into houses, Barabas!" the woman said.

Indelbed stood on the steps, hesitating, suddenly a little boy again, unable to face down whatever terrors waited above. Something big came bounding out of the second floor, throwing them back down the stairs with a gust of wind: a great bearded red-eyed beast, black hair flailing, huge across the chest and stomach, literally belching with power, the distortion field flattening everything in his way so that the wooden railings all around him splintered and cracked as if little invisible elves were taking axes to them.

It was the djinn himself, the Ifrit haunting his house. Indelbed recognized his scent on the runes, those lines of magic meant to keep him out, and something like rage at last flared inside him, bringing the delicious, otherworldly chaos of the dragon. He got back to his feet, aches and pains forgotten, adrenaline and dragon hormones rushing around his body like it was an obstacle course. In these moments, he realized he was broken, this murderous coolness that severed the connection between his brain and his conscience a sign of onrushing atrocities; this was deep work Givaras had done on his mind, monstrous urges for monstrous powers.

They came together like two bulls, and Indelbed was tossed back, unprepared for the huge, brutal push of the field. Furniture crumbled all around them. The djinn's field rolled on top of him, trying to paste him on the floor. There was no time to be fancy. It was a simple shoving match with air, their fields ionizing where they overlapped, filling the room with electricity. Boss Kid was brave. He popped up with his gun, shot at the djinn point-blank. It did nothing to him. The Ifrit flung out a hand, and the boy was wrenched into the far wall, making the plaster crack with the impact of his slight frame.

Givaras had been right. Indelbed could barely keep his shield up. His world shrank to a few feet around him, almost opaque, seconds from contracting further into nothing. His field was callow, untested in actual combat. In the haze of overlapping distortion, his altered sight was throwing him off and he kept stumbling on debris. It was unfair. None of his strikes even got off the ground. It was all he could do to draw breath. This nameless djinn was going to pulp him. Givaras had been right. But then, Givaras had taught him to cheat.

Indelbed made one last effort, a supreme push, not to attack, but to escape. For a second he dove under the wrecking ball of the djinn's field, deflecting it up, skidding out underneath, as he had practiced with Givaras for years.

The djinn smiled, reoriented himself. It was only a temporary reprieve. He seemed to be enjoying the contest. He could tell that Indelbed was done. Massive power forked from the djinn's fists in a finishing move, reaching for his throat, his heart, his lungs—all the soft places—a killing blow, but Indelbed laughed, because it wasn't enough; he was dragon inside, his organs weren't in the right places, the old frailties gone, and he needed only time to unstopper the urn and call for his brother. God's Eye was not shy. The goad of so much power was an aphrodisiac for him, a call for gluttony, and he came ravenous to the feast, folding out of the urn like dark origami. God's Eye was enormous now, his reptilian head flaring out, the maw still circular like a rock drill, eyes snapping with hunger, shooting forward like a freight train at the djinn.

The Ifrit stared at it, stunned. No man or djinn had seen a grown earth wyrm in at least ten thousand years. His enormous power contracted into a shield, as he instinctively tried to stop the impact. But rock wyrms ate power, they swarmed it, and God's Eye was something else now, a swarm unto himself. His momentum punched through the bubble, the shield flaying his head, cracking the plates around his neck, but it wasn't enough.

The wyrm drilled into the djinn regardless, those teeth tore into his fat body, they chewed him up, and Indelbed laughed as djinn blood laced into the air and covered him in gore. He could hear nothing, only the blood thumping in his skull and the keening of his brother, as the wyrm twitched and shook in the throes of some kind of ecstasy, his thrashing tail wrecking the place further. Indelbed fell to his knees, exhausted.

"Stop!" a voice shouted, his aunt's voice. "Murderer! How dare you kill Barabas!"

She didn't recognize him. She couldn't tell. He had still cherished a hope that someone would know him, that someone would welcome him back with open arms. She was standing at the top of the staircase. He remembered the day she had sent him away with false promises, pretending to care, standing at the same exact spot, watching him leave with a stranger. Nobody had wanted him, and they had all just thrown him away finally.

Something broke in him. All the hurt of the past twenty years rushed to the tips of his fingers. He felt fire pouring out of his skin, his mouth and eyes and every pore, as if that was all he was made of. It was the dragon taking over, scrambling his brain, stretching his neurons with the humming lust for wreckage. Conscious thought was a distant thing, a thin skin floating atop a volcano. He hit out with a scream, a solar flare of rage directed almost at the house itself. Windows and doors all around him burst, the walls cracked, even God's Eye was flung aside, his heavy body cutting a swath through the remaining furniture.

The stairs collapsed completely, and he saw her tumble, hitting her head on bricks, falling rubble crushing half her skull in. Blood leaked everywhere, and he felt a cold horror trickle over him, staying his hand. The dragon rage winked out. He felt abruptly human again, and at that moment, he would have taken it back, he would have swallowed the hurt, undone everything. He stood over her, afraid to touch her, watching her eyes blink. Her mouth moved, and recognizing him at last, it seemed that she smiled.

God's Eye heard his keening cry and slithered over, encircling him, a rough comfort, two blind brothers mourning the dead. Someone tripped the edge of his field. He jerked his head up, saw Butloo running at him, silver tray in hand, hunched low to the floor. He got up to greet him, to explain, when the shotgun barked behind him, a thunderous blow, and Indelbed could literally see the streaks of buckshot split the air, hitting the old man square in the chest, sending him skittering back. Boss Kid limped up, pumping the gun, his face bloodied and expressionless.

"Stop!" Indelbed shouted. "Stop! Don't shoot!"

"He got a weapon," Boss Kid said.

"It's not a weapon, it's a fucking tray," Indelbed said. He limped over, praying. God's Eye rustled after him, picking up on his distress.

Butloo was flat on his back, the tray clutched across his chest. His face was bloody, but his eyes blinked open when Indelbed approached, and his face twisted in fear.

"Butloo!" Indelbed cried. "It's me! Indelbed." He thrust his face close, not knowing that it was a frightening thing, burned black, riven with scars, eyes crosshatched with fine lines.

"Choto Sahib?" Butloo took a long, disbelieving look.

"You don't look human," Boss Kid said helpfully.

"I broke the window in the corridor when I was seven, playing cricket," Indelbed said. "And you took the blame, except Father never got angry at all. You used to mend my clothes with needle and thread, except the thread was always some weird color, and I'd have the strangest lines all over."

Butloo scrambled to a sitting position. He reached for Indelbed's face. "Choto Sahib, what have they done to you?!"

"Djinn threw me in a hole, and djinn burned me," Indelbed said.

"But we have been looking for you!"

"Impossible," Indelbed said. "Aunty Juny and the Ambassador sold me to that Afghan! Matteras was waiting for us in Mirpur. He put me in prison with a mad djinn!"

"Choto Sahib, you have killed your aunt!" Butloo wailed. "She was fighting the Afghan. She was fighting Matteras! The djinn you killed was on our side!"

"I don't believe you," Indelbed said, a deep pit of anxiety eating into his guts. "You're lying, just like them."

"Choto Sahib, remember the phone she gave you; she paid the bill in advance for twenty years," Butloo said. "She kept your room the same as the day you left, hoping that you would come back. Choto Sahib, she brought your father here!"

"He's alive?" Indelbed grabbed the old man. "Where?"

Butloo dragged himself up, wincing with pain. Boss Kid shrugged in apology and lent him a shoulder.

"He's up there," Butloo said. "You and the snake have destroyed the house. The roof is starting to go."

"Is he still in a coma?"

"He never woke up," Butloo said. "Madame Juny took care of him."

"We should get out," Boss Kid said. The fire from the dining room was spreading this way, smoke and heat adding to the carnage. "Khan Rahman house going to fall down soon."

"Wait here," Indelbed said. "I won't be long."

He launched himself in the air, over the smoldering ruins of the staircase, using his field to push off the ground. His skills were imperfect, and he ricocheted off the wall, but he shrugged off the scrapes and bruises. He burst into the first door, found his father lying on a hospital bed, dressed in a spotless white kurta, looking far healthier than he had a decade ago, almost untouched by time. Indelbed gathered him up, breathed in the clean smell of laundry detergent and disinfectant soap.

After a long moment he lifted him over his shoulder and staggered out, his slight frame barely taking the weight of the Doctor. He somehow made it down again, half falling into God's Eye's coil. The wyrm circled him protectively.

He found Butloo dragging Aunty Juny's corpse out of the wreckage. They laid the two bodies side by side, one dead and the other sleeping, and Indelbed contemplated the awful sequence of events that had brought him back to this place.

"We cannot leave them here, Choto Sahib," Butloo said. He laid a piece of cloth over Juny's head. "You shouldn't have killed her."

"I'm sorry, Butloo," Indelbed said. "I'm... I'm not the same kid anymore. I don't think I'm fully human. I should not have returned. When the fire comes, I can't feel anything, just a roaring in my head like some kind of engine going off. It takes an effort to stop it. We won't leave her here. We will bury her somewhere special."

There were fire engine sirens outside, the yelling of neighbors, police. Someone was shouting into a walkie-talkie just outside the main door.

"We go outside," Boss Kid said, tugging at his sleeve. "You breathe the fire on them. *Fatafat*, all gone. The snake can eat the bodies. No body, no problem." He seemed taken with the wyrm.

"No," Indelbed said. He couldn't take any more burned flesh. "I don't want to do that anymore. I have a better idea. I'm going to take everyone to a safe place."

"No place safe in Wari, after what you done," Boss Kid said with relish.

"This place is not in the city," Indelbed said. "I don't think it's in this world, actually."

It had been a mistake, trying to pick up his old life. He had made everything worse. Monsters could not return home and expect to be welcomed with open arms. Givaras had understood that. Indelbed belonged underground, far away from burning bodies.

He picked up the urn and bought a ticket home.

CHAPTER 52
The Dark World

While Juny was dying and the House of Kaikobad was falling to ruin, the *Sephiroth* was speeding unseen over Bengal, swinging low enough at Rais's request to give them a view of his waterlogged country. The city was flooded, the tops of cars visible as they trailed Vs through the muddy brown water like geese, now and then a brave soul with pants hitched up over his knees jumping across pieces of high ground. Schools, offices, banks, everything was closed, a typical holiday atmosphere reigning for the first few days of any natural disaster. In a week, money would run out, rice supplies in the house would grow scarce, and people would start to suffer. Right now, the rooftops were full of citizens watching the rain.

"I can't reach the house," Maria said. "I can't get your mom."

"Maybe the phone lines are down," Rais said.

"I've got three bars and Internet," Maria said. "Something's happened. Even Butloo isn't answering. We should stop and check."

"We can't," Rais said after a moment. "I don't know how long these guys can stay on point without fighting again."

The dreadnought, coming up behind them, was carrying Givaras, Memmion, and the still weakened Kuriken. Beltrex, Elkran, and Davala were on the *Sephiroth*, ensconced in the bridge with Golgoras, ostensibly to keep him company, in reality ensuring that Matteras did not change his mind and attempt to take the ship. Matteras was in the rear of the airship by mutual consent, in one of the passenger cabins. Neither party seemed eager to interact, and it fell on Rais to carry messages between the two regarding mundane matters such as breakfast and dinner menus.

The weather became nastier. Rain and wind buffeted the airships. The radio had already informed them of mounting casualties, the entire coast wrecked, countless mangrove trees uprooted in the Sundarbans, and the eminent loss of power for large parts of the city. Rais had voiced his concerns to Matteras, but the djinn had just shrugged. He had stopped his devices. As far as he was concerned, this was just bad weather.

Bangladesh was only 147,500 square kilometers. They zipped across it in half a day, even at the dreadnought's ponderous speed. The coastal areas were less pleasant. Many villages had been destroyed, the loss of life minimized only by the fact that this was not the first tango for any of these people; they took the hurricane signals seriously, they knew when to abandon their homes and which storm shelters to go to.

Over the bay, they found a steady patch of air above the clouds, and Rais understood Memmion's plan. The *Sublime Porte* gently lowered altitude until it was hovering directly above the water. After some apparent fiddling around, the entire lower hull clicked open, and an aluminum cigar fell into the water, eventually settling into a half-submerged level. The hatch up top opened, and they could see Memmion standing on deck, waving at them.

"What the hell is that?" Roger asked, eyes bulging.

"It's a full-spec Project 971 Shchuka-B first-gen Russian nuclear sub," Golgoras said with obvious jealousy. "Russians called it the K-284 Akula. It was decommissioned in 2001, supposedly to save costs for the cash-strapped navy. Memmion somehow got his hands on it intact, weapons and all. He rebuilt the hull of the *Sublime Porte* to accommodate the entire sub as the lower deck. It's powered by the OK-650 pressurized water reactor, as well as a steam turbine. Memmion retrofitted it to power the entire airship. It's the only nuclear-powered airship in the RAS fleet."

"That's pretty cool," Rais said. "I don't suppose the *Sephiroth* has a sub attached?"

Golgoras gave him a dark look. "He's got spell work over every inch of the outer shell," he said. "The damn thing weighed over eight thousand tons without ballast. It was a hell of a job getting it airborne. Now it floats like a butterfly. Thing's so spelled up it could probably fly around without the damn balloons."

"What now?" Rais asked.

"We go down there using a rope ladder," Golgoras said.

In his moment of crowning glory, Roger was given the key to the *Sephiroth* and sworn in as acting captain. Golgoras had suffered endless pangs of doubt over this, but the lure of seeing the wondrous gate to Gangaridai had proven too strong even for him. He had tested Roger relentlessly throughout the journey, and finally concluded that he could just about be trusted to fly the *Sephiroth* in a holding pattern above the bay, awaiting their signal.

The climb down was perilous, but Golgoras used his distortion to stabilize them, and eventually they were on the top deck of the Akula superstructure. The submarine was over a hundred feet in length and, once inside, loud enough that conversations had to be done at a half shout.

"Not as fancy as the American subs," Golgoras said, as they walked single file to the conference room. "But more reliable. Nothing breaks down, and everything is easy to fix."

The Akula was a legendary submarine. Once the flagship of Russia's modern nuclear-powered fleet, it had caused shock waves throughout NATO when it first slipped moorage, due to the advanced design and armament. Even now, despite its age, the craft slid through the water like a predatory fish, a sleek, fast weapon enhanced by spell work so that it actually coasted in a small tunnel of distortion, undeniably stealthy.

It did not take them long to reach the ruins of Gangaridai, but the journey was tense, too many high-powered djinns in an enclosed shape, the peculiarities of the Ghul crew adding to the bubbling broth of irritation and disquiet. Their plan was simple: ram the submarine into the ruins, trusting that it could take whatever damage Bahamut's wards could dish out. There was no calling ahead with Bahamut. Without Barabas, they were not certain of their welcome either.

This time around, the colossal squid did not come out. The Akula was possibly too big to tangle with. In fact there was nothing here, the ocean lifeless, eerie and still, as if they were gliding through primordial waters, and inside the sub, their instrumentation started to malfunction in peculiar ways, as if the latent distortion from Matteras's device had subverted the rules of physics, and they could hardly gauge how fast they were going or in which direction.

And then they were stopped cold.

It was instantaneous, frictionless—an arrest so compelling that they were frozen in step inside the sub itself, and even Matteras staggered, dropping to one knee. Eyes blinked open like stars all around the Akula, staring at them in countless number, the weight of their power drilling into the sub. Bahamut was much bigger now. He had co-opted every single living thing in the bay, it seemed like.

"Now we know where all the fish went," Givaras said with some amusement.

"*Intruders!*" Bahamut's voice came in a susurration all around them, the rasping of a hundred thousand gills. "*Die!*"

Pressure alarms began to go off around the Akula as the Marid squeezed. Distortion fields went up in the cabin, throwing up sparks as each of the djinn instinctively shielded up, still moving in slow motion, every step an active fight against Bahamut's stasis field. They all started yelling, unsure whether Bahamut could even hear them inside, as the metal skin of the Akula actually began to groan. Blaring alarms clanged heedlessly throughout the vessel, most worryingly from the reactor chamber, as the OK-650 began to indicate its extreme unhappiness.

"She's going to blow!" Memmion shouted finally. "Turtle up, everyone!"

"What turtle up? What the fuck?" Rais asked.

"The failsafes don't include being squeezed together by a million fucking fish!" Memmion said.

"Bahamut! It's me!" Rais shouted. "Please stop!"

"*Hume? Is that you?*"

"Yes, it's me!"

"*Why are you attacking me?*"

"We aren't attacking, Bahamut. We've come to talk! Remember, I came with Barabas before? You sent us on a mission?"

"You cracked the pillar of Gangaridai," Bahamut said. "I remember."

"Yes, sorry, can you please, please stop squeezing? We have a nuclear reactor in here, and it's minutes away from blowing up."

The pressure lessened somewhat, and there was blessed silence. Rais started to breathe again.

"Where is Barabas, *Hume*? I cannot sense him."

"He's, er, busy," Rais said. "We've been trying to negotiate with Matteras. You know, stopping the earthquake device?"

"The device has been disturbing me," Bahamut said. "I do not like visitors, *Hume*. Why have you brought so many djinn here?"

"Bahamut, it's me," Memmion said. "Your old friend."

"I have no friends."

"Ah... it is I, Memmion. We were allies. Once we fought together, against the old enemy."

"*Memmion,*" Bahamut said. "You have forsaken me. Why have you come to disturb me now? This ship is a weapon. Weapons are forbidden in the ruins. Why have you brought it here?"

"Weapons forbidden except for his," Rais said softly.

"Look, Bahamut, we've got to talk," Memmion said.

"Who have you brought with you?" Bahamut asked. "You are not welcome here. Who is that with you? Is that Givaras the Broken I see? Is he still alive?"

"Yes," Memmion said.

"Too bad. I do not like him."

"And Davala, Kuriken, Elkran, Beltrex, and Golgoras are here," Memmion said. "Oh, and Matteras, of course."

"He has come to gloat?" Bahamut roared. *"Hume,* I will set off the fractal bomb. I knew I should have done it earlier. You have wasted my time. We shall see now whose device is greater."

"No, no, Grand Marid, he has not come to gloat," Rais said. "We have come to parley. He has turned off his device. I have negotiated a truce with him and all these elder djinn. I thought you were all on the same side?"

"We fought a war together once," Bahamut said. "It was probably a mistake. I would not do it again. I think I chose the wrong side."

"Bahamut, stop this nonsense," Givaras said. "We elders have gathered together at last. We have serious business to attend to."

"Your business is normally disastrous for everyone else. So Matteras is here," Bahamut said. "I take it you have learned the truth of the Great War, Matteras? It is a sordid little tale."

"I've learned nothing," Matteras said. "Other than some unlikely fable about the founders of Gangaridai and their precious High King."

"When they left, I sealed the way back. The seal is weakening," Bahamut said. "And your device has accelerated its demise."

"I have halted the device," Matteras said. "I want proof, Bahamut."

"Show him the road, Bahamut," Givaras said. "Let's open it. I think it's time to see what's on the other side."

"Open it? No, that would be foolish, Broken," Bahamut said. "We must renew the seal. We cannot face what is on the other side."

"It has been twenty thousand years, Bahamut," Memmion said. "We are tired. How long must we contend with this? So many of us are gone, and the burden on the ones who remain grows heavier. Let us end it once and for all."

"Time has not passed on the other side," Bahamut said. "They are as strong as ever. Only we have gotten older."

"That's the point, you fucking brainless fish," Mother Davala said. "We've got Matteras now. The pilot ain't weak either. We've got numbers again, and these younger djinn are strong as hell. We've got *modern* armaments. Let's bust that road open and lay siege to the First City one more time."

"Ever bellicose Davala," Bahamut said. "Barkan, do you support this course?"

"It is our war," Beltrex said. "I suppose we have to face that at some point."

"Elkran?"

"I always wanted to fight. I wanted to answer Kuriken the first time. You all held me back, made a coward of me. We should end this, Bahamut."

"It will be us who will be ended," Bahamut said. "I too am tired. If we few true djinn are the only ones left, well, I will defer to public opinion. Let the record show that I advised against this course."

"Don't be so defeatist. Last time we fought with swords and spears," Memmion said with a rumble. "This time we're going to open the gate and ram an eight-thousand-ton nuclear submarine down his throat. Let's see the fucker Kartiryan dodge that."

"Matteras? Do you support this course?" Bahamut asked.

"I care nothing for your so-called war," Matteras said. "So far I've only heard words. If there is some secret city, I will see it. If there is something on the other side, I will kill it. Givaras the Broken could not stand against me, nor could Kuriken. You are all old and feeble, afraid of your own shadows. Let us put this myth to bed."

"Prepare yourselves then," Bahamut said. "And we will attempt to open the Charnel Road."

Later, assembled before the pillar of Gangaridai, they prepared their torpedoes and armed themselves for war, the djinns wielding their old weapons, each one invested with so many spells that it glowed with ripples of distortion. Bahamut stood beside the Akula, his myriad bodies swimming in complicated patterns. Rais could see the seal with his glasses, layers and layers of constructs, impossibly dense, covering the entirety of the ancient monolith.

"You should see the Sphinx," Davala said, unimpressed.

"Before we proceed, have you given thought to what awaits us on the other side?" Bahamut asked.

"If anything twitches, we liquefy it," Givaras said. "Memmion, what human armaments does this craft possess?"

"We are currently armed with twelve nuclear warheads on S-10 Granat ballistic missiles, capable of hitting targets three thousand kilometers away," Memmion said. "In addition to a full complement of conventional torpedoes."

"And what is the efficacy of these twelve warheads?" Givaras asked.

"I believe it is enough to atomize Gangaridai once and for all," Memmion said. "Regardless of Kartiryan's power."

"Got to give it to humans, they've come a long way from bows and arrows," Beltrex said admiringly.

"I don't think the planet would survive twelve nuclear detonations in one place," Rais said.

"What would happen if we fired?" Givaras asked.

"The warheads are two hundred kilotons each," Memmion said. "That would be a combined twenty-four hundred KT if detonated at a single target. The Fat Man bomb, detonated over Nagasaki, was only twenty-one kilotons. It would be hell on earth. The fireballs would be hotter than the sun, far hotter."

"Such an explosion... might destroy *everything*," Givaras said.

"Humans," Matteras spat. "Shameful that you rely on their paltry weapons."

"Matteras, these bombs are hideous. I don't think even djinn could survive the explosions," Memmion said.

"It's ridiculous that we've permitted them to develop such powers," Matteras said. "One more reason to prune them."

"Well, they're not very good at keeping them, eh?" Beltrex said. "Damn impressive, Memmion, walking out with twelve of them like that."

"Thanks," Memmion said. "I've actually got a few more stashed away."

"Let's open the gate, fire the nukes, and shut it again," Davala said. "How hard is it? Let's see the precious Horologists deal with it."

"Satisfied, Bahamut?"

"It is possible that the rules of this universe break down across the gate," Bahamut said. "Consider that your weapons might not work."

"Matteras has the device," Memmion said. "He can go get it. We'll toss that in as well."

"I can move it remotely," Matteras said after a moment of consideration. "I will deploy it as required. Let's get this seal open."

"The seal was made with the blood of djinn, Nephilim, and man," Bahamut said. "We will require the same to break it open."

"It just so happens we have a djinn, a Nephilim, and a man," Givaras said. "Well, a woman, but same thing."

"What do you mean blood?" Maria asked. She was fiddling with her right wrist, where the Invisible Dagger of Five Strikes hovered beyond djinn sight.

"Just a few drops, I'm sure," Givaras said.

"*Actually*, the *whole* amount would be better," Bahamut said.

"Bahamut, come on, I'm your emissary for god's sake," Rais said. "In fact, I'm the only emissary in these parts. Who're you going to send in to negotiate, huh?"

"All right, all right, a few drops then," Bahamut said. "Cut yourselves, the seal will draw in the blood. It will take some time to unravel."

Elkran, predictably, drew the short straw to bleed. By the time the seal unraveled, a full day had passed, and they were well tired of staring at the Escheric tessellations shift and turn. The djinns had dispersed, leaving Rais and Maria to keep watch, their hands throbbing—all except Matteras, who occupied his own part of the bridge and ignored them, staring obsessed at the construct.

When it opened finally, the monolith disappeared entirely, replaced by an eerie, silent black maw, where the rushing water slowed into droplets, misting away completely somewhere deeper inside, a place that seemed to swallow the field around it and give back nothing.

They spent another few hours staring into the gaping hole, sending in probing threads of power, all of them spiraling out as they entered, lines inexplicably lost in the midst of fishing a calm lake.

"Nothing's coming out," Givaras said finally. "We should go in. Have a look around."

"What?! No!" Maria protested. "Why, Givaras? Let's just lock it back up!"

"Come on, human, Bahamut has so kindly opened the way. It would be rude not to cross. It's not every day you'll get a chance to walk into a different universe." Givaras smiled, his cracked face infused with a kind of unholy glee, and Rais could understand why they hated and feared him. It wasn't evil he embodied, so much as a reckless disregard for anything permanent. This was not the nemesis of man or djinn, but rather the natural wrecker of safety. Curiosity ruled him. With an open door in front of him, no power on earth could have stopped him from crossing. It took only a few more hours of his cajoling before the other djinns gave in.

They flew the Akula in, trusting in the submarine's spell work to keep them mobile. Bahamut waited outside, rebuilding the seal. If things went south, he would at least be able to lock the door.

It was frictionless inside, lightless. The Akula floated easily, its propellers moving now against waves of the field, shifting in alien patterns. There was, indeed, no time here, no directions either. None of their gauges worked, and the clocks ticked without purpose, measuring nothing. They positioned the submarine so that its tail end was anchored in the real world, a means of quick exit in case things went sour. Also, no one quite trusted Bahamut.

"There's actually a road down there," Golgoras said, his eye telescoping out. "Paved and everything."

"An invitation," Givaras said, "from the High King. Let us walk to Gangaridai, Memmion." He turned to Matteras. "Are you convinced yet?"

"Of what?" Matteras asked. "I see only darkness."

They centered the Akula over the road and drew lots. Givaras held the straws again, and it was the pilot's turn to stay back, which he did with ill-concealed grace. No one ever played a game of chance against the Broken and won. Excitement gripped them now, a fevered anticipation, as it became clear that they would actually be setting foot on alien soil, on a road that existed beyond the surface of the known universe. Even Kuriken limped out of his cabin, swathed in old blankets, leaning heavily on Davala, a long staff in his hands, the aristocrat and the crone making an odd tableau. There was a strained truce between him and Matteras; they simply ignored each other.

They climbed down a short ladder, single file, the air acrid but breathable; a strange undulating wind buffeted them in waves, making the rope sway, yet Rais was not afraid of falling, for the pull of the ground seemed much weaker, as if gravity was only a halfhearted thing here, a mere suggestion. Indeed Matteras disdained the plodding descent, leaping down instead, his distortion field as efficacious as ever, and after that, several others followed, leaving the injured Kuriken to hobble down last.

"This place is not real," Givaras said, as his feet touched the ground. "It's a construct, a piece of mimicry. These forms are artificial."

"A lot of power expended on it then," Davala said. "Incredible amounts, to make every speck of dirt."

It was pitch-black, but Givaras raised the Eye of Horus above his head, and there was electric-blue illumination for everyone. The road snaked out in front of them, and some distance away, crystal and airy, were the walls and towers of the fabled city, the pristine version stolen from earth by the Nephilim Kartiryan.

"Once again we lay siege to this damn city," Memmion said with satisfaction.

"Incredible," Beltrex said. "What a beauty. I regret that we destroyed such a jewel."

"It was inevitable," Givaras said. "What Kartiryan wanted was anathema to life itself." He turned to Matteras. "Do you believe us now?"

Matteras was stunned silent, his face unguarded, chasing emotions of wonder and fear. This was the First City, the root of their history and culture, the very heart of djinndom, the cause of the only war djinnkind had ever fought. She sat like a precious gem, almost sparkling even at this great distance, and it was impossible to disregard her majesty.

"Why did you rebel, Givaras?" Matteras asked. "Was it just to break it open? Are you in truth the incarnation of your name?"

"Kartiryan wanted to reverse entropy. He could not imagine a better world, so he wanted to ossify us, like insects pinned in a display," Givaras said. "He wanted to play god, to change the fundamental balance of our universe, not just for our world, but for everything that *existed*. What hubris. What false pride, to think that he could just legislate away suffering and want and conflict by changing the nature of reality. We would cease to be. There would be nothing after, no evolution for us, no change, no *hope*. Memmion understood that in his gut. He was the first to rebel."

"Millions of years of boredom," Memmion rumbled. "That's what that pissant promised us."

"Guys," Rais said, "why is the city dark? Where are all the fountains and lights and fireworks? Where are the flying carpets?"

"More importantly, where are the sentinels?" Givaras asked. "Would the High King leave his precious city unguarded?"

"I guess we walk the road and find out," Rais said.

"I will wait on the observation deck," Golgoras said. "The submarine sensors do not work. If anything hostile comes up this road, I will have to manually signal the Ghuls to open fire. Good luck. If you cannot return within a day, signal with three green flashes of light. If no signal comes I will assume you are dead and leave. Memmion, if you die, I'm gonna take the dreadnought."

"That's just greedy." Memmion looked disgusted. "It'll take more than a dark road to kill me."

They walked the road in a clump, Memmion in the lead, trailing his broadsword along the ground, the tip gouging a furrow, a pair of RPG launchers strapped around his back for good measure, followed closely by Givaras, who lit the way. Matteras brought up the rear, his field a solid brick wall protecting them. The road was springy, inconsistent with the natural firmness of paving stones, one more confusing detail adding to the sensory overload.

"Something ahead," Memmion said, stopping. "Arm yourselves."

Seven djinn dialed up their distortion fields, sparking the air with interference. They busted out weapons, a mix of the old and new: Beltrex pulling shotguns in each hand; Elkran with his long, sweeping katana, the edge invisible, only a diamond molecule thick; Davala with an oversize revolver and, peculiarly, an urn that reeked of the sea. She whispered into it, cosseted it like an old lover. Kuriken straightened at last and threw off his blankets. He wore white enamel armor beneath, dull, stained, a deep crack across the chest plate. His staff was tipped with a black spearhead, old and pitted, and he could hardly hold it straight. Even his field guttered on and off like a candle, giving him scant protection. Nonetheless, he limped to the front, claiming the role of champion, and the others parted for him, Memmion moving slightly to his left, to protect his off hand. It was a strangely touching gesture, an odd faith in the efficacy of the warrior, as if time robbed no one and it was unfathomable to them that Kuriken could fail.

Givaras merely smiled and raised the light higher.

They approached the sentinel with caution. It was a looming figure armed with scimitars, hulking forward, great helmet adorned with antlers—a warrior as large as Memmion, although possibly not quite as fat.

"He's not moving," Rais said, as they got closer. "Like not even trembling or anything."

"Shield's not up either," Givaras said. "Is he even alive? Kuriken, just poke him a bit with your spear, will you?"

Kuriken gave him a disgusted look. The two parties faced off for a second, before he at last held his spear out gingerly and prodded the guardian.

"Stone," Kuriken said. "He's a damn statue. This place is a joke."

"Just as well," Givaras said. "Wouldn't want you fighting a duel for the next three days."

"It's Thoth!" said Memmion, who had wandered up for a closer look. "Look, Kuriken!"

Kuriken also had a closer look, peering up under the great helmeted head. "Yes, it is. Master of the Hounds. Loyal till the end."

"I don't get it," Memmion said. "Did they make a statue of him? Is this some kind of homage?"

"Hmm, I think it is *actually* Thoth," Givaras said. "I'm getting a faint whiff of sentience underneath all of this stone. I think he's been petrified."

Maria, meanwhile, had walked slightly past the statue and was staring down the road, her wrist cocked, her face suddenly slack with fear. "Guys, look down."

"What?" Memmion asked.

"Bodies," Maria said. "Bodies everywhere."

Givaras swung out his light and they stared in shock. The road was wide, and the bodies were stacked all across, women and children, men and djinn, families hunched together, mothers covering little ones, misers clutching jewels, a Ghul carrying wine—all jumbled together, piled up where they had fallen, no decay in this place, just the scything wounds, limbs scattered, eyes open, pools of black blood ankle-deep. These people were not stone.

"What the fuck?" Rais stared down the road. The light was enough to see: the dead lined the road all the way to the city walls, on and on, dunes of them, in numbers that beggared belief.

"The people of Gangaridai," Givaras said after a long time. "They're all dead."

"So your old enemies are finally vanquished," Matteras said. "Are you satisfied at last? Do you rejoice?"

"No," Givaras said. "I feel... disturbed."

"Murdered," Kuriken said. "Not by our hand. Whose then?"

"They're all facing us," Rais said. "Their backs are to the city. They were running away. Look at them. They're carrying bundles, food, drink. They were trying to escape the city."

"He's right," Memmion said. "Running for the gate, looks like. They wanted out."

"Kartiryan," Givaras said. "They must have been fleeing the Horologists."

"There is another possibility," Matteras said. "This realm might have its own denizens, creatures not pleased with the intrusion of the city."

"Look at the wounds," Kuriken said. "This is not tooth and claw. These are edged weapons, very large ones. This is how one would butcher with a giant's cleaver."

"The city is dark, and all the people fled at some point and were cut down," Davala said. "Kartiryan would die before despoiling his precious city or his people, so I suppose Matteras could be right. Horus, do you sense any life behind the walls?"

"I cannot be sure. The field here is confusing," Givaras said. "There is something irregular in the city. Let us investigate."

"I would not mind walking those walls again," Memmion said.

"These bodies look fresh," Davala said.

"There is no time here, or at least it doesn't work the same way," Givaras said. "This could have happened twenty thousand years ago or yesterday. The bodies will not decay. Kartiryan was afraid of entropy. Where we are... we must investigate the nature of this realm. We are somewhere deeper in the universe than we have been before."

"We're going back," Matteras said. "This is foolish. There are what, a hundred thousand bodies here?"

"More," Kuriken said quietly. "Double that number lived in the First City."

"Something wiped out that number of djinn and Nephilim? Something took this city, which was supposed to be impregnable?" Matteras asked. "Where are we? If something harmful lives here, it knows about the gate. There's a fucking road pointing to it."

"So?" Memmion asked.

"Don't you see? They know where *we fucking live*," Matteras said. "Bahamut said something was weakening the seal from this side. What if it wasn't Kartiryan? What if it is, instead, whatever the fucking thing is that *took his fucking head*? What if they want to come through into our side? We've got to go back and prepare."

"He's right," Maria said. "You're only seven djinn, and Kuriken can barely walk. Beltrex looks like a hundred years old—no offense, Beltrex— and Memmion could have a heart attack any minute if he starts swinging that sword. You're wearing someone else's legs, Givaras, for god's sake. Are you seriously thinking you can fight off whatever army depopulated the entire city?"

"Matteras's theory is not tested," Givaras said. "I do not believe that Kartiryan would be killed off so easily by some mystery enemy whom we have never heard of. It is too convenient. I wish to check the city."

"If he's dead, we need to find his body," Memmion said. "That fucker doesn't die easy. Givaras is right."

"None of you die easy," Matteras said softly. "That's the problem."

"That is the First City!" Givaras said. "Somehow, the Horologists *removed it* from our world and brought it here. Those spells are still there. How can you not want to investigate?!"

"The city is only a ruin to me," Matteras replied, and shrugged.

"It is everything to us," Kuriken said. "Everything we are comes from that."

"Let's be practical, guys," Maria said. "There are two miles of dead bodies between us and the walls. Do you really want to slog through that? Then what? What if the walls are barred, or defended. You couldn't take the city with entire armies, Givaras. Why don't we go back and get the sub?"

"That would be prudent," Matteras said. "We are too exposed here."

"All right, all right," Memmion said. "We'll get the Akula. And then we'll blast down those damn walls with my torpedoes. Agreed?"

They reversed course and walked back, Matteras in the lead, this time much more cautious, and Memmion literally walking backward with his RPGs in hand. The sheer scale of the dead weighed on them. It was not to be a happy homecoming. They argued the whole way, Matteras and Maria to leave, Givaras and Memmion to remain, the rest strung out in the middle.

Golgoras saw them and flung down the rope ladder, whereupon Matteras turned around and struck them with a concussive blast that rolled them over, something so powerful that it actually caused the road to buckle and reverberate like an elastic band.

Rais watched in stunned bemusement as Matteras leaped into the air, one arm around Maria, carrying her like a sack of meat. He landed on the upper deck, colliding with Golgoras, all three of them sent sprawling by the impact. The pilot got up first, his field contracted into a shimmering blue sphere, tusks bared. Rais saw him lunge at Matteras. The two djinn clashed, a full-throttle shoving match, resulting in a stalemate where the pilot proved he was almost as strong as Matteras.

Maria popped up, flicked her wrist in the motion Rais had seen her practice countless times. But it was Golgoras she hit, deliberately, in the back. Golgoras went stiff and then fell to his knees, his spherical shield shredded, dissipating into blue wisps. Five rents appeared on his back, welling dark blood.

"The ship is mine!" Matteras shouted down, holding the pilot's head in a vise grip.

Almost in response to his statement, the Akula repositioned itself slightly, and the front torpedo tubes opened, signaling a willingness to fire.

"What the fuck?" Memmion roared, clutching his RPG launchers with helpless rage.

"Your Ghuls have broken contract," Matteras said. "As I stated earlier, we will be going back. Without the rest of you, I'm afraid. Feel free to continue exploring this realm..."

"Maria!" Rais shouted. "What are you doing?"

"She has quite sensibly realized that the door must be shut permanently," Matteras said.

"I'm sorry, Rais," she said. "We can't take a chance. They'd never resist coming here again and again..."

"And Golgoras?" Givaras asked.

"A necessary sacrifice," Matteras said. "Don't look shocked. How do you think Bahamut sealed the gate in the first place?"

"Maria!" Rais shouted again.

"She chose me, emissary," Matteras said. "I always win."

The Akula backed out of the rent and hovered in front of the gaping maw, weapons trained into it. Matteras sat in a bubble on the upper deck, spell work flying from his hands, accreting around Golgoras's spread-eagled body, floating in the center of the gate, leaking blood from wounds physical and psychic, at the literal halfway point between two realities. Matteras knit the seal back together, incorporating his own talent into Bahamut's ancient design, using the remnants of the old magic, tying them into Golgoras's living body.

For a while, the giant school of fish watched over his shoulder in silence. When he was at last done, Bahamut spoke.

"What has transpired, Matteras?"

"Dead, the entire road is a mausoleum," Matteras said. He was stuck fast in stasis, this time so strongly that it was an effort to turn his head, to speak. "Did you know, I wonder, when you called it the Bone Road? The city is there, but I doubt anyone still lives. Two hundred thousand dead, by Kuriken's estimate. Something else rules that realm, something not too pleased with the intrusion."

"And where is my emissary? Givaras? The rest of the elder djinn?"

"We had a difference of opinion," Matteras said. "They chose to stay there."

"I trust this choice was entirely voluntary?"

"You may have the sworn affidavit of the human witness," Matteras said. "She was their companion. She will testify to everything. Her word will suffice for any court."

"Ah, you have brought a witness then," Bahamut said. "Very wise."

"Bahamut, whatever monster lives in that place, whatever dread army wiped out the citizenry of Gangaridai, it is not friendly," Matteras said. "That thing knows about the gate, it will want to come here. Let Givaras fight it off. Let them all kill each other, so much the better for us."

"And Golgoras? I notice that he is still alive inside the gate. I suppose he also volunteered to be thus interred."

"That was born of necessity," Matteras said. "The seal you built was too weak. You only used blood. I'm using an entire living djinn. It is much stronger now. He attacked me, Bahamut. I never touched him. The human Maria stabbed him with that pernicious weapon, the Invisible Dagger of Five Strikes. You will find those wounds on him even now. The weapon, I believe, was a gift to Kaikobad from you. Ironic, then, the base use it has come to... Still, he lives. I have put him in a coma. He does not suffer. I daresay he is much more useful like this than flying around in a balloon all day."

"Hmm, yes, you are good at inducing comas. I believe I will question this Hume," Bahamut said. "You will give her to me, Matteras."

"I regret I cannot," Matteras said. "She is my newest emissary. A battlefield promotion. In light of her sterling service, defending me from the crazed pilot."

"I see," Bahamut said. "You appear to have a surfeit of emissaries, while I have none. This is the second one you have cost me, Matteras."

"It is not my fault you are careless."

"Careless, yes," Bahamut said. "I have secured your device, Matteras, while you were in the other realm. It is most ingenious. I trust you will not be requiring it any further. Nor will you make another, I suppose?"

"Of course, keep it as a gift," Matteras said. "It is paramount that we protect this gate and ensure nothing crosses over. That's all that matters now. I believe we are agreed on that point."

"We are."

"In that case, I will desist from the depopulation of Bengal."

"I like this submarine. The Akula, you call it? I will keep it, I think," Bahamut said. "I have neglected the surface world for far too long. It is time I walked the earth once again."

"Certainly," Matteras said. "And am I supposed to swim out from the bay?"

"I will escort you to the surface. You and your emissary may take the lifeboat. Be sure to return it after you are done," Bahamut said.

"You *will* keep an eye on the gate, won't you?"

"As I have for the past twenty thousand years."

"And we keep this a secret between us?"

"For now, yes," Bahamut said. "Unless you wish for this to become a tourist destination."

"And the... truths revealed by Givaras?" Matteras asked.

"You are djinn," Bahamut said. "Does it matter if he put a few strands of Nephilim into all of you? Is your power any less? You cannot be of this world, Matteras, and disdain all of it at the same time. You must accept that we are all part of it together."

"Were it to become common knowledge, it would end the Creationist Party," Matteras said.

"Then I suggest you calm Hazard and his ilk down and allow them to retreat to their more natural state of muttering under rocks," Bahamut said. "I have no interest in the Creationists, as long as they do not attempt to infect the rest of the... body politic. They are too noisy, this new breed of djinn you have gathered around you. Seclusion was agreed on for a reason, Matteras. As you know now, we have greater problems than Hume real estate."

"Problems? That is an understatement," Matteras said. "We must prepare for the day something strange comes out of that gate. It *will not* be friendly."

"I agree," Bahamut said. "Good work on the seal. I have tried many designs over the years. Your use of Golgoras as a power source was ingenious, if unfortunate."

"For him," Matteras said. He grimaced. "It will not hold forever. No seal does."

"Especially if Givaras is on the other side picking at it," Bahamut said. "Hopefully there is enough else to occupy him."

"That was the idea," Matteras said.

"He was always like that," Bahamut said. "Give him a puzzle and he will spend a hundred years trying to take it apart. I do not agree with your methods, Matteras, but perhaps the world *is* safer without all of them."

"Then we are done here. I am ready to get out of this godforsaken bay, Bahamut. Take us up."

"With pleasure," Bahamut said. "Oh, and Matteras? Since you have a new emissary, I wonder if you would return my old one."

"Dargoman?"

"I would... remind him that he once swore an oath to me."

Matteras shrugged. "Have him, by all means. As you say, I have already found a replacement."

They were camped around Thoth, watching the gate seal slowly around the inert Golgoras.

"Beautiful spell work," Givaras said. "I always said that boy was a prodigy."

"Your boy has fucking stranded us here!" Memmion said. "And stolen my ship!"

"Never mind," Givaras said. "The city is before us. We get Gangaridai. They can have the world. He's given us the opportunity to explore this realm at our leisure, on our terms. I think that is a grave error on his part."

"And this unknown killer of djinn?" Kuriken asked.

Givaras looked around. "We few brought Gangaridai to her knees. Can you not feel your old potency returning? We are in a place that is made of pure energy, I suspect. We are more powerful here than we ever were before. We are not townsmen, to be slaughtered while we flee. We will hunt this killer, Kuriken. And we will find Kartiryan and wring some answers from that sorcerer."

They were silent for a moment as they flexed their distortion, searching for this potency.

"I can't believe Maria betrayed us," Rais said finally, voicing what was really eating at him.

"There are people, Rais, who embrace the unknown," Givaras said. "Other people lock the door. She opted for security. She is not as adventurous as you, I think. Cheer up. You are the only emissary in this realm. Imagine the auctoritas you have accrued."

An amorphous cloud was forming below Thoth's head, a concentration of energy that had so far escaped their notice.

"That's not quite true," the cloud said. "I'm the emissary Kaikobad. I've been waiting for you."

"Abdul! Abdul! Come here, you moron!"

GU Sikkim was hobbling over the ruins of the old house, feeling elated despite the twinge in his hip and the bruised toe he had suffered when the roof had collapsed. He was free! The fat traitor Pappo had run away; he had seen him hightailing it out of the burning building. Abdul, shocked by this calamity, was once again responding to his commands. The world was right again!

"Did Madame Juny get away outside, Abdul?" he asked.

"No, sir, she was inside when the... the giant worm attacked," Abdul said.

"Right, the giant worm," GU Sikkim said with awful sarcasm, even though he had seen the worm with his own eyes, seen it devour the djinn Barabas. Good riddance to all of them! Still, no one wanted stories of giant worms being bandied about a Khan Rahman residence.

He searched the living room where the worm had fought; everything was charred and wrecked. He could make out bloodstains here and there, the abandoned silver tray of that ridiculous butler, an emptied shotgun, but no bodies—not worm, nor human, nor djinn. But then he found the safe, which was still intact, filled with all the land deeds and the other papers of the trust, the checkbooks for the accounts, the memorandums, and the detailed ledgers meticulously updated by Juny, and his heart raced as he stuffed everything into a bag. This was enough to take back power, it was *everything*. Juny had actually managed to increase their net worth!

"We're leaving, Abdul!" GU Sikkim said. The police and the firemen would come in soon and start looting the place. "Let's go! Carry this bag, you oaf."

On the way out his foot brushed against something clammy. He looked down and found an ancient, cracked urn, stoppered loosely, giving off a whiff of the sea. It looked valuable in an antique kind of way, no doubt one of Juny's fancy pieces. He'd gift it to his wife! She was always saying he had crass taste. He stooped down, grabbed it, and walked out of the wreckage of Kaikobad's house.

GLOSSARY OF ABSOLUTELY 100 PERCENT FACTUAL THINGS METICULOUSLY RESEARCHED BY THE AUTHOR DURING HIS LUNCH BREAK

Types of Djinn

Marid: Big, powerful djinn shrouded in mystery. These djinn are also typically older and have gone strange. Not sure if they are a separate race or just a strange subset of Ifrits. There are not too many Marids walking around.

Ifrit: Most numerous djinn race. Known to be particularly bombastic and troublemaking. Creators of the first civilization. The bulk of djinndom is composed of Ifrit.

Ghuls: Inferior race of djinn typically organized in hunter-gatherer clans. Rumored to have no control over their distortion fields, although this is probably just racism. Tend to keep to themselves and do menial labor. Physically very strong and coordinated, thus in high demand as workers.

There might be other races of djinns. So far we have not seen any, and the djinn aren't talking about it.

Nephilim: Giant humans of biblical fame. Most probably these were human-djinn hybrids with powers of their own (i.e., limited abilities to affect the field) and known as shamans, magicians, sorcerers. Curiously, in the First Empire, Nephilim were accorded same rights and respect as djinn and, in fact, were indistinguishable from them in social and legal terms.

Djinns Relevant to this Story

Matteras: Psychotic djinn of stupendous power. Rumored to be a bastard son of the royal line of Gangaridai. Currently enjoying towering auctoritas as the leader of the fractured conservative faction.

Golgoras: Pilot and captain of the *Sephiroth*, a legendary airship (named after the character from *Final Fantasy*). Also a high-standing member of the Royal Aeronautics Society, which is said to be the oldest djinn society in existence. This claim is disputed by all the other djinn societies, of course. They say he's a pirate, but that's just calumny.

Barabas: Patron Ifrit of the Khan Rahman clan. He in turn is a client of Bahamut, the legendary Marid. Considered to be somewhat of a dumbass.

Bahamut: The Marid of the Sea. A legendary, ancient djinn who seldom leaves the oceans. Does not interfere directly in djinn politics but enjoys a hefty dignatas and many clients. Rumored to be stark raving mad.

Givaras: Also known as Ghorus, Horus, the Broken, the Maker, the devil, and a variety of other names. An infamous djinn who is almost universally hated. Every bad thing can be attributed to him in some way. An infamous cheater. Like even in board games.

Hazard: Leader of the Creationist faction of the conservative party and rabidly antihuman. A famous duelist. Jackal headed. Not known for having a sense of humor.

Beltrix: Also known as Beltrex, Barkan, the Blue King, the Lord of Thunder. An old, kindly-seeming djinn with a penchant for wine making.

Elkran: Barkan's cousin. A silent, mysterious djinn with a black blade and a reputation for swordplay.

Kuriken: King of Siberia. An ancient but very stylish djinn aristocrat who hates humans and leads a faction of the conservatives.

Memmion: A giant Marid of great power and bulk. The founding member of the Royal Aeronautics Society and patron djinn of Golgoras. Somewhat of a glutton by all accounts. Has grown pretty fat in fact. Not sure he'd fit in an airship anymore. Lives in the Hub, which is a hidden aerial base for the RAS.

Mother Davala: A djinn from Baghdad. Also referred to as the Erinyes, or the Angry Ones, the Furies. Mother Davala is strongly associated with the Crone.

Mesonychoteuthis hamiltoni: Colossal squid, estimated at fourteen meters long. This squid is probably the largest of the squid species. It has the largest recorded eye in the animal kingdom at twenty-seven centimeters. It is almost certainly an example of abyssal gigantism, which is the phenomena of deep-sea creatures having greater mass and size than their shallower-water relatives. A squid reference: www.tonmo.com/community/pages/giantsquidfactsheet/.

Djinn Concepts

Societies: Organized clubs/parties/voluntary associations. The extent of djinn political organization. Societies tend to perform multiple functions on an ad hoc basis, from providing entertainment to tackling real-world problems.

The Celestial Court: The highest djinn court.

Djinn Lore: The full sum of djinn culture, tradition, expectation, and history. A sort of guideline for good and proper action in all circumstances. The Lore overlaps with the complex djinn legal system and in some cases might even supersede it. There have been occasions when djinns acting according to Lore have contravened serious laws and have been "let off." On the other hand, repudiation of the Lore is unheard of and considered an act of madness, a total rejection of essential djinndom.

Dignatas: Ancient djinn concept that measures a character's worth, entitlement, public credibility, ability to command followers, charisma, prestige, sex appeal, sheer handsomeness, wit, intellectual might, willpower, and cussedness, among other things. It serves as a sort of bankable account, in that it allows one to command goods and services. A similar watered-down concept was found among the Romans of the republican era. Djinn are not materialistic in the traditional human sense, as their powers and long life imbue them with a self-worth attuned to more than the simple accrual of possessions.

Auctoritas: The ability of a particular djinn to influence djinndom as a whole, to bend situations and actions of others to his will. It works on multiple levels, from being a simple favor bank among individuals to commanding policies that affect the entire planet. Auctoritas is a result of dignatas, but the correlation is not 100 percent, djinns being whimsical creatures. There have been many cases where an individual of low personal dignatas might suggest some audacious plan that higher-level djinn might agree to. In this situation, the low-level djinn might be said to have exercised auctoritas higher than his predicted level.

The Field: A prevalent field of energy, a naturally existing phenomena that the djinn can manipulate.

Distortion Field: The area around a djinn that he can distort. Sort of the zone of control in which he can affect reality.

Seclusion: An ancient postwar precept that reflects the decision of djinn to seclude themselves from humanity, in an attempt to build up their numbers and protect their culture. Part of the logic was to avoid further earth-shattering conflicts by pursuing a path of isolation. It was widely theorized that human hubris and Nephilim ambitions led to the Great War, thereby absolving the djinn from actions that destroyed the first civilization and by all accounts resulted in an ice age and mass extinction. In modern-day practice, this translates to hiding in plain sight, something the younger djinn chafe against from time to time.

Djinn Clubs

Royal Aeronautics Society: One of the oldest chartered clubs. Almost all airship captains are members. The RAS is headquarted at the floating town called the Hub.

Numerists: Political party/club whose members believe that humans are breeding much too quickly for djinn welfare, yet are not militant enough to do anything about it. Not to be confused with the Rabid Numerists, a fringe group obsessed with physically writing out the largest number possible. So far this has been identified as the De Graff number, which is a 1 followed by one million pages of zeroes.

Creationists: Archconservative djinn faction that denies evolution and strongly maintains that djinns were created superior to all other life-forms, as evidenced by their powers and long life. A stalwart subset of the conservative movement.

Secret Archaeological Conservation Society: Group strongly in favor of preserving ancient sites of great and mostly obscure significance, the selection and importance of which is only known to itself.

Angling Enthusiasts: One of the most powerful clubs in djinndom. Almost all waterborne vessel captains are members. Djinns in general are great amateur fishermen. The oldest standing member is Bahamut, although he has, for many years, refused to attend meetings, so his exact position is in flux. Also, some have argued that since Bahamut is, in fact, a school of fish, the deliciously piquant situation might arise where Angling Enthusiasts are in a position to bag him. This and other similar concerns continue to amuse the djinn as they while away the ennui of centuries. The group's main event every year is the Whale-Bashing Run in the Pacific Ocean.

Ageist Society of Young Djinn: ASYD is one of the pioneers of the neo-club scene among younger djinn, forming a counterculture to the traditional club-oriented hierarchy of djinn. The neo-clubs are deliberately without charters, rules of membership, or even any stated purpose. ASYD itself was formed as a protest against the stifling rules and regulations imposed by elder djinn upon society at large, in the form of the Lore and the laws.

Cabal for Zoological Variety: A very old club founded by Givaras the Broken before his fall from grace. Its overt function is to protect favored animals and plants from extinction, although many of the members in fact are more interested in creating new kinds of animals and plants, sometimes with disastrous results. While not as powerful as before, Zoological Variety still boasts an impressive membership and is home to many of the scientific-minded djinns.

Geography

Bengal: Historically wealthy region in the Indian subcontinent, located at the deltaic confluence of multiple Himalayan rivers. An ancient trading hub and population center, the fame, industry, and wealth of which enticed the British to first come to India, where they proved to be the sort of houseguest who just wouldn't to leave. Currently suffering a hangover from the colonial era: Bengal was split in two by the British and remains divided to this day. West Bengal is a state in India, and East Bengal is the country of Bangladesh. Combined, there are 250 million plus Bengalis in the world, which, anyone will agree, is a damn high number.

Dhaka: Capital city of Bangladesh and one of the most densely populated places on earth. Dhaka has between sixteen and twenty million people, and the urban sprawl is expanding, so at some point it might just straddle the entire delta.

Gulshan, Baridhara, Banani: Suburbs of Dhaka that are somewhat nicer than other suburbs. Known as the tristate colloquially, this is where most embassies are, as well as a larger concentration of restaurants, hotels, clubs, etc.

Wari: An older suburb of Dhaka that was once posh, now not so much.

Sylhet: District of Bangladesh that is somewhat hilly and known for tea gardens. Sylhetis also speak some incomprehensible dialect, and anyone venturing out there would do well to take a reliable translator.

Chittagong: Main port city of Bangladesh and inferior to Dhaka in every way, despite what the Chittagonians may claim. The question is, if Chittagong were so great, why the devil don't Chittagonians stay there instead of all flocking to Dhaka?

Other districts: Not really important.

Gangaridai: Ancient heart of the first civilization and the jewel in the crown of the djinn empire that was at the core of the Great War.

Kehmet: Egypt, one of the old bastions of djinn civilization. Ruled previously by Horus, also known as Ghorus, Givaras, the Broken.

Lhasa: One of the centers of djinn civilization. Several important Ghul clans resided in the Tibetan plateau, and Lhasa was always considered a Ghul city, even though it was ruled by the Ifrit Empress-elect of Lhasa, who was later married to the High King of Gangaridai in an alliance of the two cities.

Mohenjo Daro: Harappan city, one of the oldest in the world, the ruins of which still continue to amaze us with new findings. It was a primarily Nephilim city, destroyed prior to the Great War. Rumor has it Memmion destroyed it and blamed Gangaridai, thereby precipitating the civil war and causing many Nephilim to join the rebels against the High King.

Foods of Interest

Tehari: A delicious combination of rice, lamb, and green chilies flavored with mustard oil.

Biriyani: Rice, lamb, and potatoes cooked together in sealed pot, typically over a wood fire, and further flavored with dried plums. Possibly the best food ever made. The best version is definitely found in Bengal. People of Hyderabad seem to think they make a good biriyani. Unbiased studies have shown the Bengali kachi is infinitely better. Anyone wishing to dispute this is invited to come find out.

Ghono Dal: Lentils cooked to a thick slurry, this particular version with coconut oil.

Appendix A

"The Charnel Road" (Djinn Nursery Rhyme)

Long ago I walked the black road
Dark and frightening,
The charnel road of endless winding,
In heavy wind and bone dust grinding.

What fresh hell approaches here?
What putrid breath that lurks so near?
Upon a bend I hear a sound,
Panting, snorting, stinking fear,
The deathless baying of a deathless hound.

My lungs are acid slowly floundering,
And in the dark I slip and stumble,
The valves within my chest are pounding,
On the road my courage crumbles.

Breathless curses rend the air and
The rasping flair of tempered steel.
Hooves are sparking in pursuit,
Some heartless foe is hunting me.

We battle upon the forlorn road,
Gray and dark and hopeless still,
Through leafless trees and blighted ruins,
In lifeless lakes and rootless hills.

Decades later, the days are brighter,
I sit at peace beside the sea.
The sole survivor of the day, I
recall that dread stranger upon
the road bent on killing me.

A luckless fellow and his dog,
I think perhaps that fateful day,
He'd been a traveler just like me,
A lonely djinn who'd lost his way.

Appendix B

Excerpt from the *Register of Kings*
By His Excellency, the Grand Ifrit Mohandas, the Most Efficacious, Lord of the Frozen Waters and the Lands Therein, Holder of One Hundred Patents

In writing this preface, I must humbly include that my own excellence and stature are such that the reader might wonder at this peculiar whim, in listing and enumerating the reigns of the petty kings of Gangaridai, an interest which, I admit, stems from my love of the macabre.

While there was once widespread interest in the doom that befell Gangaridai, the so-called Grand Empire, the First City of Djinn— claims no doubt conflated beyond all reason—it is no longer the fashion to be curious about that epoch, seeing as all the principal characters have fallen out of vogue.

Gangaridai itself seems to have endured a catastrophe due largely to war and mismanagement, for which her kings must be blamed, insofar as they were a singularly stupid lot. A more talentless race of royals can hardly be found. In fact, such was their infamy that in their fall they tarnished the entire occupation of kingship, so that thereafter most premier djinns of the time abandoned that form altogether for the present fashion of republicanism. Had I been consulted in this matter, the Great War would have been over before winter, and everyone would have been home and merry, and the world would have enjoyed its springtime, instead of the prevailing Ice Age, which promises to carry on for quite some depressing time.

Megrim I the Ill-Bred

Nothing surpasses the absolute lack of culture and refinement shown by this Ifrit, the so-called builder of Gangaridai, who chose the riverine land of current Bengal as the site of his residence, having found nowhere else on the continent a place as swampy, unpleasant, or mosquito infested. For the next two centuries, such a great builder was Megrim that he denuded this godforsaken land of all its jungle, replacing it with a blighting eyesore of a sprawl hardly rivaled anywhere in the world until recent times. Had I been consulted by Megrim the Ill-Bred, I would have created a magical capital of soaring towers and pleasure domes. Megrim, instead, created a giant slum and peopled it with djinn, Nephilim, and an assortment of apes.

Eltham the Miser

Having first endured the coarseness of Megrim, the poor denizens of blighted Gangaridai were forced to put up with Eltham the Miser, a nephew of Megrim's, elected king following an accident that caused the Ill-Bred one to be torn apart by griffins. Eltham the Miser started off his reign in good form by taxing everyone into poverty, driving all trade away from the city through punishing port charges, and literally sinking the far-flung maritime power of the empire by using his navy to pirate the very ships coming to do commerce in his hideous city.

What he did with his obscene wealth is unknown, but it is rumored that he converted everything into gold and hoarded it in a reverse basement pyramid, which he constructed using a race of Neanderthal cousins who were afterward put to death, thereby adding specicide to his list of personal faults.

Once having bankrupted a thriving economy, becoming reviled by djinn and man alike, and suffering from plummeting dignatas, Eltham then went on a ruinous expansionary drive, conquering hapless farmers and fishermen with excessive pomp, claiming a lot of useless land and celebrating fatuous triumphs, until the whole of Gangaridai became a bloated, pus-ridden empire full of half-bred peasants.

Megrim II the Short

So called because his reign was quite short. He abdicated within a paltry hundred years, terming the empire too difficult to manage, and retired to a life of leisure and frolic, thereby gaining significant dignatas for his farsightedness. His actual height, as far as I can determine, was average.

Almas the Terrible

The so-called First Reign of Terror, giving rise to the nascent republicanism movement, although if you ask me, Almas was a perfectly decent ruler who brought some much-needed reform to the decadent empire of the delta. Almas was noted for two great acts. The first was the massacre of the bay dolphins, who were allegedly showing signs of sapience. The second was the ill-fated massacre at Mohenjo Daro, which destroyed a large number of Nephilim as well as thirty-two djinns and an almost countless number of regular human vermin. This did not sit well with either djinn or Nephilim, all of whom were of course interconnected through familial lines. Ultimately, the war to remove Almas was mostly conducted in salons and drawing rooms and assemblies. Nonetheless, the political divisions between royalists and republicans were sharply drawn, and the seeds of the catastrophic Great War were sown. Almas abdicated from power three hundred years after his ascension, on a very sad day for all djinn I am sure. Mohenjo Daro was not rebuilt until after the Great War, when a largely human empire were resurrected with the same name.

Regency Years

An unspecific number of years passed when enough volunteers could not be found to rule the absurd First Empire of Djinn, leading to the formation of the Regency, which was variously filled by humans and djinns of different stripes.

Notable regents were:

1) Subdas the Bore (Nephilim), who reigned for thirty-five years, presiding over a period of unsurpassed and excruciating boredom, during which many notable djinn went into hibernation.

2) Trifan Storm Caller (Nephilim), who professed to be able to call lightning down on people. It is probable that he was either a sorcerer, or had a djinn hiding behind him, using the field to create a lightning effect. Trifan was very popular with the peasants, and his reign was almost fifty-five years, during which lightning struck a large number of people.

3) Engineer Sukoma (Nephilim), who built a lot of roads. This allowed one lot of horrible peasants to meet up with another lot of horrible peasants. Pretty soon they were moving around everywhere. It is my opinion that road building is a terrible mistake. Bridges are even

worse, allowing the unwashed horde to actually cross perfectly good natural barriers intended by God to pen them up. Peasants should stay in one place. Their job is to farm. How are they supposed to farm if they're out wandering around all day? Engineer Sukoma's reign was even longer and more unfathomably dull than his predecessors, stretching to eighty-eight years. He lived to 120.

Aside from building a lot of unnecessary stuff, Sukoma also apparently codified a lot of laws, created a common measurement scale, standardized seagoing vessels, and reestablished the maritime lanes by eradicating pirates. Pirates in the bay and the ancient submerged isles to the east were a colorful and enterprising lot. Their harassment by Sukoma was a tragedy that resulted in many deaths, destruction of their hidden island forts, and a general loss to the world of a unique and dashing people.

Return of the Kings

The line of kings was returned with the Nephilim line. The descendant of the last regent wedded the daughter of the Emperor of Lhasa and was crowned the King of Gangaridai. They reigned for fifty-five years of alleged terror, until the Great War ended their rule and, indeed, the entire world. During this time the republicans came to the fore, and the subsequent conflict got entirely out of hand, with the final withdrawal of the great city by the High Lords of Gangaridai, the sundering of the world, and the onset of the great Ice Age. Those of us left behind are faced with extinction, and many of us pure-bred djinn are forced to contemplate a permanent dilution of bloodlines and a loss, entirely, of djinndom. It is the fall of the Kingdom of Fire, a final end of the chosen people.

It is my hope that those who crossed to the other side, both Nephilim and djinn, are able to preserve our race better than we, the inheritors of the earth, have. The traitors Horus the Light Bringer, known as Givaras the Maker; the Marid Bahamut of the Deep; the Lord Memmion of Gold Mountain and the Eagle's Crest; and the others who have contributed to this war... well, I hope you reap what you have sowed in a much-diminished world. I hope you enjoy the years of darkness and cold ahead of you, I wish you all the centuries of boredom and pain you deserve. Horus, I name you Givaras the Broken, breaker of all things good, and I curse you that you may never find peace, that all things you touch turn to ash.

I retire now to go to sleep. Do not wake me up until the return of Gangaridai.

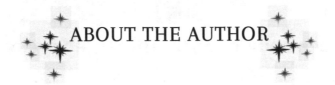

ABOUT THE AUTHOR

Saad Z. Hossain is a Bangladeshi author writing in English. His 2015 war satire, *Escape from Baghdad!*, was published in the US by the Unnamed Press, as well as in Bangladesh, India and France. *Djinn City* is his second novel.

@unnamedpress

facebook.com/theunnamedpress

unnamedpress.tumblr.com

www.unnamedpress.com

@unnamedpress